Z.E.R.O

Zombie Elimination and Rescue Operatives

Jessica Ungeheuer

Published by: Jessica Ungeheuer

Book Cover by Jessica Ungeheuer

Edited by Edward Crocker

1st edition 2024

To my parents, Robert and Daisy, for supporting me every time I had a new creative endeavor. To my husband, Danilo, thank you for supporting me and having faith in me, not letting me give up my dream.

Please see Content warnings in the back of the book.

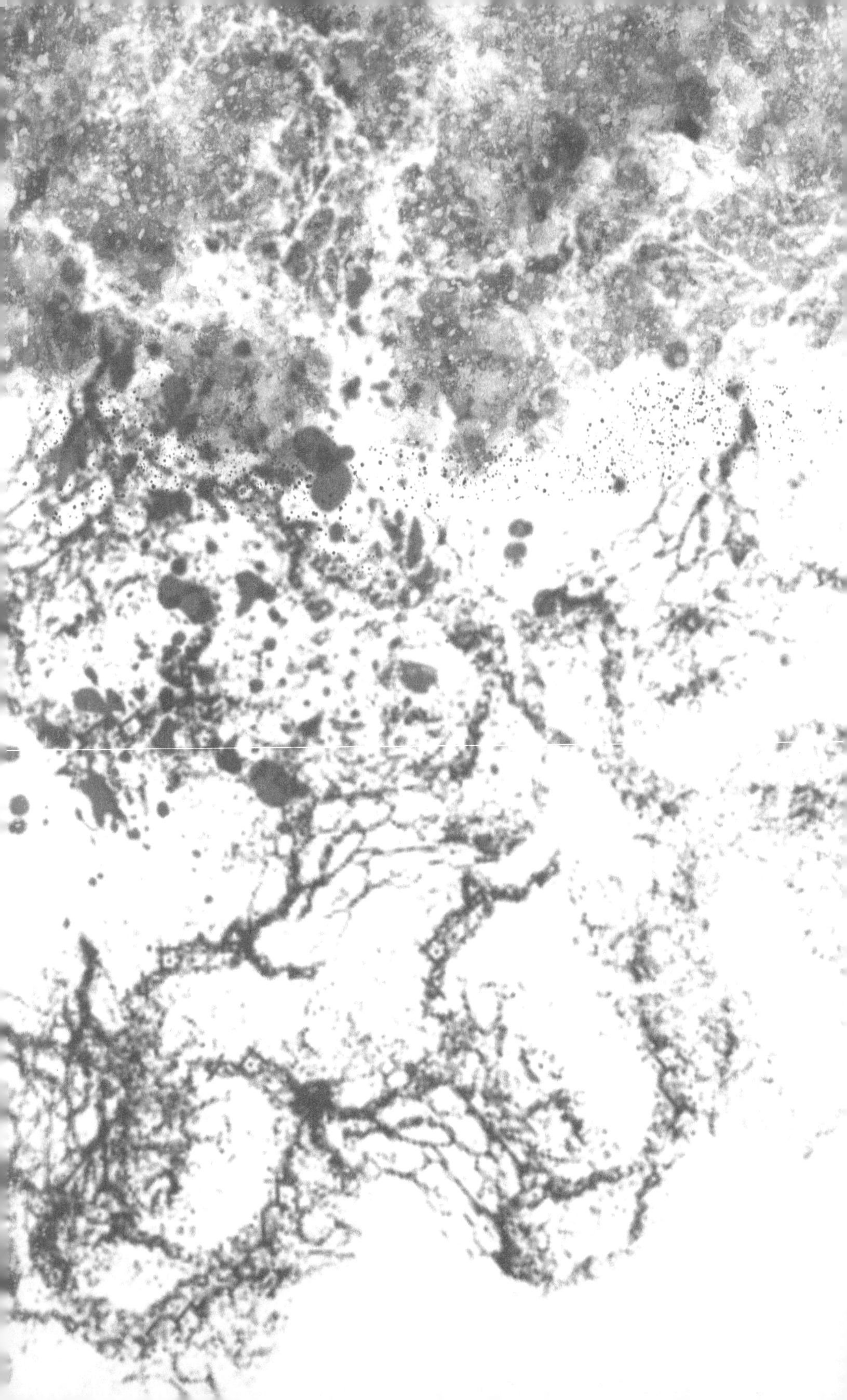

CHAPTER 1

She hurried through the damp grass. This was the third time in the past week they'd had to come out to this particular cemetery to garden some *daisies*. It was another hot and humid summer evening on the Gulf Coast of Florida. Phoenix couldn't wait for the scalding hot shower that awaited her back at the base when she was done with this irritating errand. Her first objective: to remove the haunting smell of death from her body.

The cemetery around her was a bit smaller in scale than what she usually dealt with. Unlike some of the larger gravesites in the area, this one was not well lit. There was a single street lamp to illuminate the grounds. The older headstones, with more elaborate angel statues, seemed more like demons resting on a stone perch as deep shadows cast across their surfaces. A fog began to roll in as the heat of the asphalt paths sizzled from the recent rain.

"How much farther?" Phoenix made sure her irritation was heard by her partner through her communicator.

"*You're almost there. Just a couple more yards. What's the rush? It's a nice night.*" Sentinel's Texan drawl radiated through her ear.

"You could have come out instead of lounging in the parking lot if you enjoyed the weather so much." She blew a stray strand of her dark brown hair out of her face and wiped her sweaty palms on her pants again before readjusting her grip on her pistol. This was one problem of being half Puerto Rican and half German—thick hair that was almost unmanageable in humidity.

"*But you have Wi-Fi in here. Gives me a better signal so we can get done faster. Gotta make sure nothing is gonna sneak up on ya.*"

"Your feet better not be up on my dashboard when I get back Sentinel, or you'll be washing my whole truck with your toothbrush." There was a slight rustling of fabric in her communicator as Sentinel adjusted himself. She cracked a smile and examined the area around her for movement. "I don't understand why we have to do this. You could have sent Bravo Team."

"You know the Commander. It's too important. He doesn't trust them NOT to screw it up. We rely on these sensors too much."

"Well if we don't start letting them go out on regular assignments, we are going to have a workers' strike...or worse, a rebellion." There was a brief silence between them as they contemplated their worst unit arranging a mutiny. Sentinel chuckled.

"Hold up, Phoenix, I think you're there." She stopped and looked at the rows of head-stones around her. *"I'm forwarding the active GPS to your map."*

Phoenix pulled out her phone, examining a small red dot which pulsed on the screen, with a similar green dot signifying her position. She holstered her handgun, with the silencer still attached, and used her fingers to zoom in. The cemetery was separated into a grid formation, each area designated by a letter and number. The dot pulsed around area F4, about three spaces north of her position. She walked slowly, her eyes shifting between the flashing dot on her screen and the surrounding landscape. There was no wind, and an eerie quiet. She had to be aware of any sound that stood out. A rustling of a bush; a cracking twig in the grass. Vigilance kept you alive.

She searched the ground. As she neared, she pulled out her large maglite from her belt. A small glint of reflected light on metal stood out from the surrounding darkness, indicating what she was looking for.

Thank god you were easy to find. I didn't want to be crawling in the dirt the rest of the night.

"Found it." She kneeled down and picked up one of their broken sensor rods. The rods were custom-made by her organization to be unnoticeable to the passer by. They were slim sticks of metal, about two inches in height and one centimeter in width, packed full of telemetry technology that recorded a constant stream of seismic data. Each nodule was connected on a network chain by thin hard wires easily hidden in grass. She held the exposed wires up to her light of the broken unit. The ends were unfrayed, clearly cut with a sharp object—no animal did this. "The wire's cut."

"Well it could have been a civilian who saw it, and didn't know what it was. Happens sometimes. You find the lead?"

"Yeah." She grabbed the lead cord that tied into the rest of their network. The fog from the stone paths was beginning to roll in closer. She hesitated a moment to listen again to her surroundings. What was that? A bush? She looked around at the nearby sprouts, staying completely still. She felt a slight temperature drop in the air as goosebumps raised on her skin. A small breeze was most likely the cause. Jennifer sighed and brushed back her loose bangs again. "I'm getting this done and then we are calling it early." She reached into her side pack for her tools and the replacement sensor, and got to work.

"Hot date?" If she was sitting next to him, she would have slapped him.

"Yeah I think I'm done with you men for a while." She laughed at the thought of meeting any guy she would be interested in. It wasn't going to happen again. Not with this job. Her mind wandered and pain filled her chest as memories flooded back. She shook her head. Working was the only way she could function. It didn't give her time to think about it. She wasn't going to make the same mistake again. If she had an urge to feel connected to someone, she would meet up with her ex, Demon, for a casual hook up.

"We ain't all bad. I've NEVER left a lady unsatisfied." She tried to focus on finishing this last task as Sentinel prattled on. *"I can promise you a good evening, take you out to a nice restaurant...fireplace nightcap after—"*

"It ain't happening." She grunted as she pressed the sensor back into the sandy ground beneath the grass to the left of the headstone. Florida was nothing but swamps, sand, and gators. Luckily for her, she didn't come across the latter tonight. "Check it."

"It's singing with the others. All good!"

Phoenix dusted her hands off while she looked at the space around her—then she saw it. An untrained eye might have missed it, but there was another hole in the ground centered in front of the headstone, very small, about five millimeters in width. She glanced at the headstones on either side of her. There were similar holes in front of all of them. If it was only around a couple of the headstones, she wouldn't have thought much of it, but the fact that it was in front of all of them sent her warning signals off.

"Sentinel...is there a new landscaping process I'm not aware of? All these graves have deep holes in front of them...and the ground feels extra moist." She removed a stick she had jammed into one of the holes, and sniffed it. It smelt of the Earth, but there was something else there she couldn't make out. A bitter, chemical smell. Maybe it was just bug killer.

"Well it did rain this afternoon, and we did just re-sod a lot of those. I'll look it up, it's probably just—Shit! Phoenix, look out!"

She didn't hear the creature approach from behind. Before she could get back to her feet, cold dead skin slammed up against her body, knocking her to the ground. The smell was putrid, like a bowl of fruit left out to rot on a hot summer day. She grabbed her large flashlight and bashed the creature on the side of the head, getting it to release its grip on her before it came down for a bite. Its skin was pale and dirty, but the scars of the sun were still visible. There was little decay on the pallid skin of the face except for its foul rotted teeth. She shoved it off of her and got to her feet. It was strong. Must have been turned recently. She needed to take it out quickly rather than risk a struggle. She pulled her sidearm out in one swift movement, releasing the safety as she aimed for its head. Two quick pulls of the trigger; the body collapsed with a heavy thud in front of her. She brushed her bangs from her face, heart still pounding in her ears, as she knelt down to inspect the body.

A homeless man, judging from his sun-scarred skin and tattered oversized clothes. Based on his state of decay, he was probably infected by the small horde in the area two days ago. The body remained inanimate as she pulled a beacon from her side pack, stabbing it into the creature's chest for the clean-up team to easily locate.

"Target was neutralized and the area seems to be clear of any other hostiles. Send in Bravo to clean up."

"Roger...Phoenix, you okay?"

"Yeah..." She holstered her gun again, taking in a deep breath, "We need more people out here."

"The Commander said—"

"I know what he said! That doesn't change the fact there's a growing number of these things. We need new recruits, outside of the bloodlines."

"Remember what happened to the last civilian we recruited for field work..."

"Yeah I remember..." Phoenix swallowed back the lump in her throat. "We still need to try. Their numbers go up, while ours go down. Let's call it a night. I got somewhere to be."

"Alright, Phoenix. I'll discuss tomorrow's gardenin' with you when you get here."

"Roger."

She looked at the body that had attacked her again. She was right. They needed more soldiers. Even if it was just one more set of boots on the ground. The D-Day event was drawing near. They weren't ready. Hopefully this "game" she was going to would have some good prospects.

***

"Hey! We're going to keep the party going tonight with DJ DirtyKnuckles up here in Ybor City. Come out and join us for some drinks and good times! This is 93.9xfl Chris speaking and I have Hallie here with me giving out tickets for our Summer Concert series."

"That's right guys, we are gonna be up at the Ritz all night! As a reminder from Tampa PD, please be careful if you're coming out. There's been increased reporting of people going missing in the area. We love you guys, we don't want anything to happen to you."

"Yeah, be safe guys! Alright let's get back to—"

Jeff turned off the radio and gazed at the large group of players gathering at the gate of the cemetery just beyond the small parking lot. It was one of their biggest groups yet for their zombie-themed paintball match. He could see why Adam didn't want him to miss it. Jeff and Adam had started this game in college with another kid whose family maintained the land. It was old. Most of the headstones were faded and crumbling. The ground was uneven from years of settling in the sand-filled land. Past the old iron gates there was no light; only a single lamppost in the middle of the parking lot illuminated the area. This cemetery didn't receive new residents, and the few families that did visit were slowly fading out of existence. As long as they cleaned up everything, and weren't too disrespectful, they were allowed to use the area.

His phone began vibrating in the cup holder next to him. Sure enough, it was Adam calling him, again. Jeff didn't want to come out tonight. Ever since his break up with Kylie, it'd been hard to get out of his apartment. *Their* apartment. Jeff sighed.

"Hey, I'm in the parking lot. Be there soon."

"Good! You see how many people we got? It's gonna be awesome!"

"Yeah..."

"Get your sad ass out of the car an' hurry the fuck up! I got someone I want you to meet." There was a small beep that cut off Adam's mischievous laughter.

"Stupid ass..." Jeff smiled. Adam had been Jeff's best friend for years. When they were ten, Adam's father had let them watch the original black and white *Night of the Living*

Dead. Of course, Adam hadn't slept well for a week, but that fear had developed into a fanatic passion in the genre for both of them.

Jeff stepped out of his car, stretching his arms up over his head and then bringing his fingers into his short brown hair. He scratched his scalp briefly before he twisted and cracked his neck. His crystal blue eyes felt dry, despite the humidity around him. He rubbed his face; he was going to need to shave soon as his skin felt rough from the small stubble that was beginning to show. For the middle of July, it was surprisingly cooler weather this evening. Most nights in the summer were a hot humid swamp, but not tonight. Jeff's boots smacked against the wet pavement as he walked to the back of the car. A thick cloud of fog rolled in, raising the goosebumps on his arm. Jeff felt the pressure change in the air as he watched a creeping white cloud fill the cemetery before him. It definitely added an extra element of unease to their event tonight.

He opened his trunk and pulled out his paintball gear. As he began to fill the hopper on his gun, a large silver truck pulled up beside him. A woman with long, dark brown hair hopped out, talking rapidly on her phone while she struggled to remove her jacket.

"Make sure B-team runs prints on the subject...yeah...it sounded interesting...I'll play nice with the other kids." The woman's brown eyes caught Jeff gaping at her. People skills were not his strong suit and it had been six years since he had tried to openly speak with a woman that wasn't his ex. "I gotta get going. Be on standby."

The woman put her phone in her back pocket and wrapped her jacket around her waist. Her eyes caught his again. He couldn't help but stare at her. If he had to guess from her features, she was part Hispanic. She had a curvy figure, plump lips, and an olive-toned complexion. Frankly, she was hot. Her eyes were almond shaped, and wide, but there was a coldness to them as she caught him gazing at her dumbfounded. Embarrassed, Jeff began to grab the rest of his gear out of his trunk.

"Um, excuse me?" The woman's voice was much closer. Jeff shot up, banging his head on the top of his trunk.

"Ow! Uh, yes? Hi! Sorry..." He rubbed the back of his throbbing head as the woman giggled.

"You okay? That sounded like it hurt."

"Yeah, I'll be fine. So...uh...how can I help you?"

"A, um, student invited me here. This is the zombie game thing right?" She crossed her arms and shifted uncomfortably. When she turned her head left toward the group of people, Jeff spotted the top of what was a rather large tattoo. It started at the nape of her neck and disappeared under her shirt. A head of a bird. A peacock maybe?

"Yeah. New player?" Jeff closed his trunk as she nodded. "It's paintball, you have a gun?"

The woman walked to the back of her truck and opened the back hatch. She slid some heavy bags out of the way, pulling a smaller one toward her. She took out a slim paintball gun, with no custom adornments of stickers or decals. The casing looked sleek and new, like she had just purchased it for the evening's event. She reached into the bag again, pulling out a container full of bright green ammo. Good thing Adam wasn't on the hunter team tonight, or there would be a problem. Every player had their own paint color to distinguish the winners, and that shade of green was Adam's favorite.

"Okay cool. I'm Jeff by the way." He began to reach out his hand, but stopped, shoving it awkwardly in the pockets of his tactical pants. She didn't seem to notice his failed gesture.

"Jennifer."

"All the players are gathering over there. I can go over the rules with you if you want." Jeff turned slowly toward the group at the gate, hoping she would follow. Jennifer smiled warmly at him, but it didn't match her gaze. A lump formed in his throat. Jeff couldn't figure this woman out, but he felt compelled to try as she followed him. He glanced in her truck as they passed by, noticing a small zombie keychain dangling from her rear-view mirror. Something you would find at an anime convention. The style was like a kawaii chibi, ugly yet cute at the same time.

"So there are two teams, hunters and zombies," Jeff said as they stepped through the crowd of zombies and hunters, the view of the cemetery opening up to them. "Players on the zombie team help with set up, hiding the surprise elements for the hunters."

The pale gray stones were haphazardly spread throughout the yard in different states of erosion before them. The deep green leaves of the surrounding foliage was a stark contrast to the carved rocks. Life and death in one place. The rolling fog creeped up on the crowd, and all these elements of the environment would work as good cover for the zombie team tonight. In the rear section of the property was a small hill filled with a variety of large headstones with gothic fixtures and smaller name plates transfixed to small stones on the ground.

"Okay," continued Jeff as they walked, "we've got long range targets that pop up from pressure plates if you kneel in front of certain headstones. You gotta shoot them in the head before you can move off the plate. Everyone is going to have a different paint color, so at the end we can tally up who got the most kills. The person with the most zombie kills wins on the hunter team. If the hunters are wiped out by the zombies, we lose. Oh! If someone has already hit the target, you just move on. No double tapping. Ah! One more thing, if one of our zombies nab you, you get a bright red ribbon tied to your arm and you join the infected team."

Jeff grinned brightly as he finished summarizing the rules. It had been a while since he had smiled with no effort. He studied Jennifer as she searched the faces around her.

Might have been too enthusiastic there... What are you thinking? She is waaaaay out of your league anyway. Just help her and go find Adam.

"Sounds simple enough." Jennifer smiled again when she caught Jeff staring at her. Jeff opened his mouth to speak, but didn't get a chance to respond. A heavy mass jumped on him from behind. His years of martial arts training kicked in as a survival response. He grabbed whatever it was, and flipped it over him, slamming it hard into the ground in front of them. The zombie-dressed figure moaned as he hit the hard dirt. The group of players around them began to laugh loudly.

"SHIT MAN!" Adam's muffled voice came from behind the rubber zombie mask.

"Adam?"

"Who else would be stupid enough to try and get the drop on you?" Adam chuckled as he groaned, gingerly picking himself up. Jeff, embarrassed, glanced back at Jennifer, who was stifling a laugh. Adam wasn't a small guy. He had a big build, and lately an ever-growing beer gut.

"I told you not to do that..." Jeff felt his ears burning bright red. Whenever he blushed he never got flushed cheeks like normal people—no, his ears became red as cherries. Adam ripped off his mask, revealing his sweating bright crimson face glowing through his espresso-toned skin. He looked surprised as he glanced back between Jennifer and Jeff. A big smile spread across his face.

"You two met already! Great!"

Jennifer raised a confused brow at Adam. Of course...Adam was already trying to set him up with someone new. It had only been two months since Jeff had found Kylie cheating on him—specifically her nude, sweat-covered body, entangled around the equally naked and more muscular trainer she had hired as a personal coach. The both of them ambivalent to Jeff entering the bedroom as they pleasured each other on *his* bed...he wasn't ready for something new yet.

"Adam—" Before Jeff could finish, Adam wrapped his arm around him, pushing Jeff back toward Jennifer.

"This is my buddy Jeff Knight. As you can tell, he's better at martial arts than I am." Adam chuckled and addressed Jeff next. "This is Jennifer Mayer, my self defense instructor. She runs a dojo off Fowler called 'Z Dojo.' I wanted to get you to go to her classes, but you never had time."

"You teach martial arts?" Jeff asked.

Jennifer nodded back with a new air of pride. "So you're the fighter friend that he doesn't shut up about. What styles did you study?"

"Uh. Tae Kwon Do mostly. A little Karate." Jeff's heart pounded furiously in his chest. Why was he so nervous?

"This guy is being too modest." Adam gave a hard slap to Jeff's back, "My buddy here is PRACTICALLY a black belt."

Adam's grin spread wide in his cheshire cat smile. Jennifer looked skeptically back at Jeff. His ears felt like they were going nuclear.

"Practically?" Jennifer asked as she scrutinized him.

"Yeah, I guess you could say I have all the training for a black belt, but I dropped out before completing the belt ceremony."

"Why?" Jennifer's eyes had a fire behind them that made him even more nervous.

"Just got bored with it, I guess." He darted his eyes away from her burning gaze.

A small smile curled on her pink lips. Jeff felt like prey in her eyes as she continued to evaluate him.

"Interesting...the style I teach is more of a tight close quarters combat. You should come check it out. Just one thing." She took a step forward toward him. Close enough that he caught a whiff of a rose scented perfume, "I'm not a fan of quitters."

Jeff swallowed at the lump forming in his throat. She was intimidating as hell, but there was something else there. Something behind her hard facade. Her eyes were fixed on his, like she was awaiting an answer.

"Yeah." Jeff's voice cracked hard as he struggled to regain the base in his vocal chords. "I'll try to swing by sometime."

"Awesome! You're gonna like it!" Adam cheered. He leaned over into Jeff as another player began talking to Jennifer, introducing themselves, recognizing she was a new player to the games. Only Jeff could hear him now. "It's a weird style, makes me think like it was designed for handling drunks mostly. Just imagine if zombies were real though dude. Her style would have you deal with them like nobody's business!"

God Adam...then again, that's kind of cool...but hey! Don't let him change the subject Jeff!

"We are having a talk later..." Jeff whispered back. Adam's face twisted into his signature stupid smile Jeff knew too well meant trouble, and pulled away before Jeff could protest.

"Alright people!" Adam announced, addressing the group. "Time for the zombies to all hide! If all you hunters would kindly walk into the old gravekeeper's home over there so you can't see where we are!" Adam then turned to Jeff and Jennifer. "You guys can team up tonight. Good luck!"

Adam let out one of his annoying cackles, walking off before Jeff could say anything. Jeff swallowed hard as he gestured Jennifer toward the old house.

"Shall we?"

She nodded, walking ahead as her ponytail flicked in his face. Jeff took a deep breath. This night could go in two directions.

Once inside, Jeff crossed his arms tightly around him in the crowded room, shifting his weight every few seconds as he stood close to Jennifer, who was gazing at the other group of players. They were in what used to be a living room when the gravekeeper's family lived on the grounds. They had left behind some old shelves and tables that some players rested on while they waited for the game to begin. The decorative wallpaper was peeled, cracked, and hanging from water damage and humidity. He was sure there was a small tuft of mold on the stuffed dear head that still rested above the fireplace in the room, gazing blanky at the crowd of people around it. The wood creaked in the floorboards as different people moved around the room, and thick dust was kicked up in the air, beginning to make his eyes water. They always gave the zombie team five minutes to hide. He glanced at his watch for the tenth time as the seconds slowly passed. He couldn't help staring awkwardly back at Jennifer whenever their eyes met. He didn't know what to talk about. Martial arts again maybe? It'd been so long since he'd actually done anything in it, there wouldn't be much for him to say.

His phone vibrated in his pocket. When he managed to juggle it out, the name displayed across the screen caused a hollowness in his gut. He swallowed, trying to moisten his tightened throat while he answered.

"Uh Kylie, what's up?"

"What's up? What's up? Really, Jeff? Where the hell are you? Weren't you supposed to be here to take my copy of the key?"

"Sorry, I forgot you were coming tonight. Adam reminded me of the game, and I couldn't leave him hanging."

"Adam, always Adam!" Kylie raised her voice, and Jennifer looked up at Jeff, concerned for a moment before breaking eye contact with him again. *"When are you going to grow the fuck up? You can't spend your whole life playing zombie larping or whatever you do."*

"I thought you liked—"

"Like any real adult actually likes that shit. You know why I cheated on you? Because you have no spine. When things are tough, you walk away. Like you walked away when you caught me and Lucas. You walk out, and then it takes two months before I see you again? Really?" Kylie sighed.

"Kylie..." Jeff pictured Kylie's body wrapped around another man, in *their* bed, and the familiar presence of hollowness surrounded him again. He tried to moisten his dry mouth. A soft hand on his arm startled him back to his surroundings. Before Jeff could react, Jennifer took his phone from him.

"Kylie Seitz?"

"Who the hell is this?"

"A friend of Jeff's." Jennifer winked at him. "You would think someone that graduated Magna Cum Laude with a degree in communications from a university like USF would know how to communicate better."

"Who? How do you—"

"My firm is international and works with a variety of large corporations around the world. I put in one word, and your career will be over." The sweetness in Jennifer's voice was gone, and replaced with a viper's venom. Goosebumps formed on Jeff's arms as Jennifer continued. Who was this chick?

"You're bluffing!" Jeff could barely hear Kylie's muffled voice from the receiver. Jennifer glanced down at her phone in her hand, and smiled.

"I'll be sure to tell Calvin how you treat potential clients." Jennifer waited, the other end became silent. "That's what I thought. My advice. Leave him alone. Get your crap, and leave the key somewhere out of sight, so he will know where it is. You've been together for six years. You'll figure it out. Have a good night Miss Seitz."

Jennifer hung up the phone and handed it back to Jeff. His heart was racing, not from anxiety, but excitement. Jennifer smiled warmly at him. Not the fake smile she bore earlier.

"How...how did you know all that about her?" He studied Jennifer. Her confident grin faded as he asked her and her eyes wandered, like she was searching for something.

She held up her phone. "I saw her name pop up on your caller ID. Just did a quick Facebook search. She posts a lot, and her profile isn't private. Wasn't that hard." Jennifer smiled as she hastily forced her phone in her back pocket under her jacket.

"Yeah, I guess that makes sense."

"Are you going to be okay?" Jennifer placed her hand softly on Jeff's arm.

"Uh, yeah." Jeff cleared his dry throat. "Bad breakup. You think you know a girl until you find her doing some naked yoga with her personal trainer in your bedroom."

Jeff chuckled awkwardly, but the memory was still a fresh stab wound in his chest. It made his palms sweat and his head hurt every time he was reminded of it.

"That's rough."

"Yeah."

"Well don't let her dampen your evening. We are going to have some fun tonight." Jennifer smiled and pointed to Jeff's watch that he didn't notice was buzzing. "Time's up Captain."

"Thanks."

Jennifer nodded and removed her soft hand from his arm. Jeff silenced the alarm on his smart watch and took a moment for a deep breath before he held his fingers to his mouth. He whistled loudly; immediately, all conversations in the room stopped and everyone turned to hear what the group leader had to tell them. He caught a glimpse of Jennifer's face as she smiled briefly when he took charge of the players. Every time he saw her smile, it sent butterflies through him...maybe he was starting to like her smile too much...

"Alright people, looks like we're ready to start. Remember to keep low and stay on your toes. If you get marked by a zombie, you're no longer a hunter. You can't cheat yourself out of it...I'm looking at you David!" Jeff pointed his fingers at his eyes and back at the acne-covered face of a young man by the fireplace, who shrugged his shoulders back at him. Their audience laughed at the exchange. "Let's go kill some zombies!"

The group raised their paintball guns in the air with Jeff and cheered while they donned their protective goggles. The hunters began to make their way out of the house and through the cemetery. People that were friends tended to work in units together. Some really got into it, creating unit uniforms, logos, and badges. Jeff and Adam used to be like that, but it became more difficult as the group became larger. To keep things organized and fair, they split up, one on each team. Tonight he would be working with Jennifer. They maintained the same pace as they methodically scanned each row of headstones they approached. She checked the dark shadows for any hidden zombie players with precision. She was a natural at this.

Jeff let her take the lead. As she knelt behind a headstone on the next row, there was a soft click, followed by a small whoosh of pressurized air. A zombie target popped up a couple of rows ahead of them. With no hesitation, Jennifer fired one shot, hitting the cutout figure in the middle of the head. She stepped off and began moving again. She stopped at another stone a few meters forward that looked like someone had hastily thrown some leaves in front of it. There was another click and a board shot up behind a bush to her left. A smile curled up on her lips. Jeff caught a twinkle in her eye as she pulled the trigger.

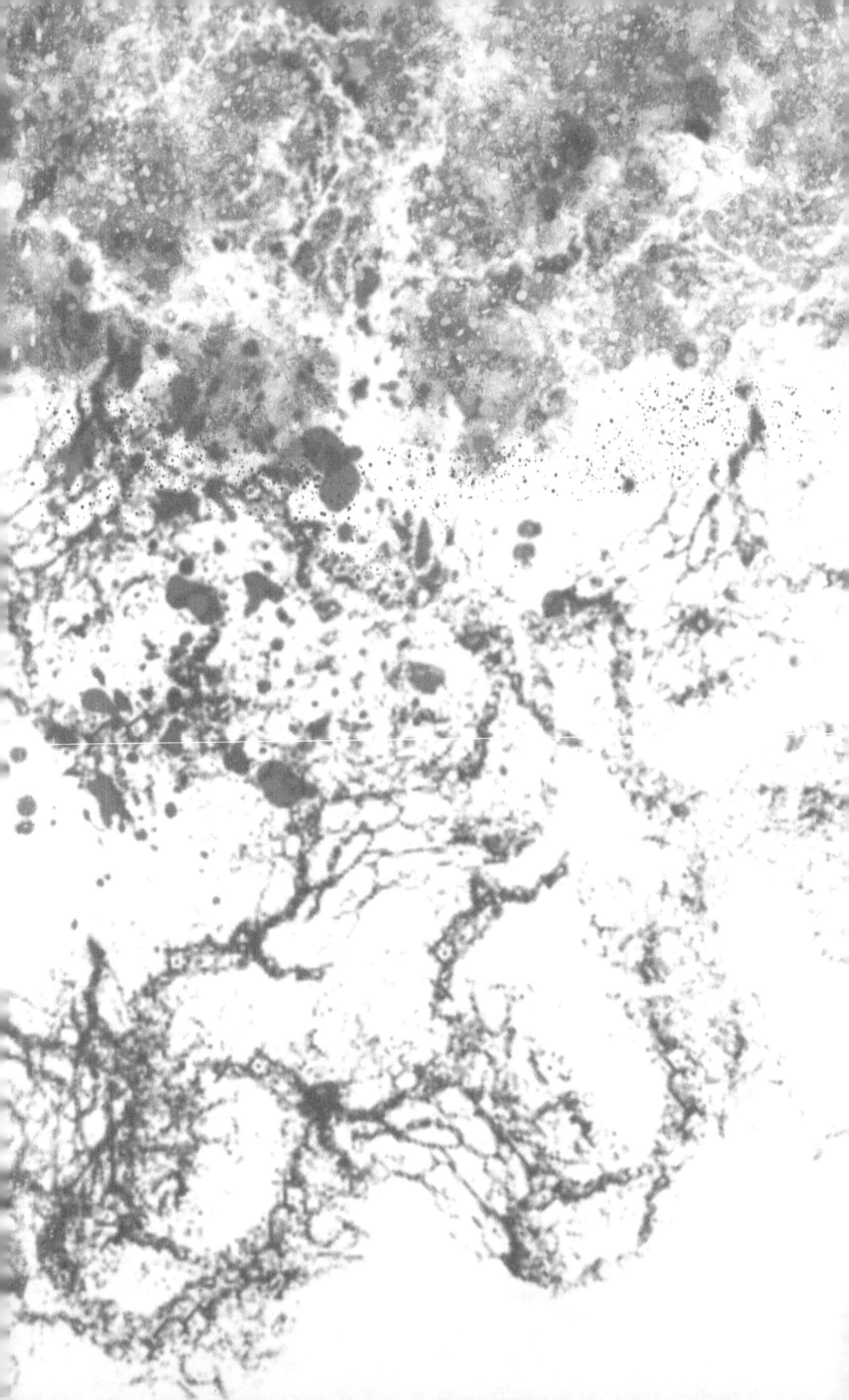

CHAPTER 2

Jennifer didn't expect this to be so enjoyable. She was glad she had let her curiosity get the better of her. She needed new recruits, and this might not be a bad place to look for them. She turned to see how Jeff was faring. When he had flipped Adam over him on a reflex, she knew he had latent potential. This game could give her a chance to assess his more tactical abilities.

She observed how he moved with almost the same precision as she did through the grounds. He would hesitate momentarily to see where the zombie painted boards were going to spring up, but managed to blast his targets—albeit with several shots of ammo. He would be the one to beat for the night's festivities. She picked up her pace, moving uphill faster, as she tried to leave Jeff behind. She wanted to get under his skin, see how he dealt with pressure.

Just as she had observed earlier, his ears began to turn red. She wasn't sure if it was from embarrassment or frustration, but it was a tell that she would take advantage of.

Jennifer cursed as her tennis shoes slipped on the wet grass. She wished she had at least kept on her boots from earlier tonight. They would have gripped the ground better. Regardless, she pushed deeper into the cemetery toward the larger bushes and trees. She noticed her first zombie player. Considering these were just *kids* acting out what they had seen on TV, they were going to be no harder to her than the wooden boards she already shot. Since Jeff had informed her they had to react to her shots, she would take advantage of that feature for accurate headshots. They may be wearing protective masks, but she didn't want to hit them in the eye. It was paint, but it still hurt on impact.

She caught one in her peripheral vision to her right. It moved quietly, but its little theatrical moans gave it away.

Bad move...

Jennifer clipped them on the ball of their knee, causing the player to trip forward. When they tried to get up, she plugged them twice in the head. She checked behind, observing how Jeff dealt with his approaching horde. His aim was not as skilled as hers. He targeted their heads only, narrowly missing getting grabbed by other players. If he slowed them down by hitting the knees first, it would be easier for him. She decided to press forward toward the rusty spiked wrought-iron black fence at the edge of the property. The end of the line. She picked up her speed.

Let's see if you can really keep up with me.

She snickered quietly while dashing across the wet grass. The fog had steadily grown thicker as the night moved on—maybe that's why she didn't see it. A small foot sized headstone laid in the groundline rushed toward her, connecting to her forehead with a hard smack. Her ears rang and head throbbed. A rookie mistake. Once again, she cursed that she wasn't wearing her combat boots. Pulling herself up, the world spun violently and the picture around her became dark. Muted. She rolled onto her back to see *It* coming for her.

A man was yelling her name, but the piercing tone in her ears wouldn't let his words through. The cemetery had fallen away, replaced by the familiar woods of her childhood. Dressed in black tactical gear, and waving an assault rifle, the man kept shouting at her to move. She scrambled backwards while debris from the forest floor scratched her legs. Her favorite pink shorts, ruined by moss and dirt. Jennifer frantically looked around for her little sister, who she was just playing with moments before.

Then she saw *It*. Pungent pus leaked from where half its face had been clawed away while the remaining flesh melted off. Maggots crawled between the crevice that should've been its cheek. Its neck cracked loudly, as clouded eyes turned attention on her—and lunged!

Jennifer shut her eyes, waiting for the inevitable end, but no pain came. Cold liquid splattered across her face. Opening her lids slowly, she saw dark brown blood on her clothes. The monster was gone. The man who'd yelled her name towered over her, his smoking rifle at his side. He reached his hand out.

"Are you okay?" Jeff asked, concerned. His hand outstretched toward her.

Jennifer looked around her. She was back in the cemetery. The hit to her head had brought up visions from the past she wanted to forget. She knocked Jeff's hand away, opting to get up on her own. As she dusted off her jeans, she felt the blood trickle down her face. She avoided eye contact with Jeff's worried gaze.

"Yeah, I'm fine. Just tripped."

"Are you sure, that looks pretty bad..." He reached into one of the pockets of his pants and pulled out a small ziplock bag of gauze pads.

"I said I'm fine! I just cut myself on that. I'll clean it up when I get home." Jennifer didn't mean to be rude, but she hated that she'd fallen in the first place. She was trained to be observant.

"Just take it, I don't want to be liable if you bleed out." He forced the gauze into her hand.

She placed it against her head, actually thankful for the cloth, and applied pressure to stop the bleeding. She looked in the direction of the zombie player that had approached her when she'd fallen. They were writhing on the ground in some pain, clawing their mask off. Adam's sweaty red face was glaring up at Jeff.

"Ow! What the fuck man?! Did you really have to hit me in the face FIVE times?" Adam rubbed his red forehead, "Shit..."

"Sorry about that Adam. But you're the last one. Just felt like emptying out my extra ammo." Jeff shrugged. "Hey, if Jen didn't trip on that pressure plate, I would have used it up on the target board."

Adam stared angrily at Jeff. In silent rage, he picked up his mask and marched down the hill toward the front gate. Jeff jogged to catch up with him.

"Oh come on! It wasn't like I knew it was you under there!" Jeff yelled after him.

The daze from her head injury started to wear off. Jennifer was more focused. She knelt down to look for the pressure plate he had mentioned. There was nothing there but grass and bulged sand in the ground from a possible animal burrowing underneath. She paused at the sight of a deep five millimeter width-hole in front of the headstone. She gazed at the headstone suspiciously as she bent down and wiped her blood off. She lingered, taking one more look at the ground before walking back to meet the others.

***

Jeff wrestled playfully with Adam in the driveway just beyond the front entrance gate, holding his friend's head in a headlock. They could be angry with one another, but all would be forgiven pretty quick. The longest time they ever went without talking to one another was about a month in middle school, when they had a dispute over a girl they both called dibs on.

The remaining groups of players marched down the hill, carrying the targets with them for scoring. The group gathered near the only light next to the cemetery office building and laid the boards down so the paint side was visible for everyone to see. A majority of the boards had only two colors showing, Jeff's bright blue and Jennifer's neon green paint. The crowd began to chat away excitedly about the game. Adam checked his watch and scowled. It must be late. Jeff checked his own watch, it was midnight. Adam turned to the group, clapping his hands together to get everyone's attention.

"Damn, it looks like Jeff and Jen hit all the boards! Alright people let's make this quick. Raise your hand if you were shot by my boy Jeff." Of the twenty people dressed like zombies, only six raised their hands, including Adam. "Whoo! Awesome. Alright, now who got shot by Jen?"

About six more zombies raised their hands, covered in Jennifer's green paint. A small "ooh" that could be heard from the group, impressed by the newbie. Adam turned to Jeff and gave him a pat on the back. He felt his ears burning from embarrassment. They tied. She almost beat him, which was pretty impressive for a newbie. If she hadn't tripped at the end, she would have. He turned to Jennifer, who was unfocused on the events around her. Lost in her own thoughts, biting her lip. When she finally realized everyone was looking at her, she shrugged and smiled. It seemed off. The look in her eyes didn't match the sparkle of her grin, like when he had first met her.

Adam rallied the group's attention again.

"Alright, that's it for tonight. Thanks for coming. Remember to take all your stuff so we don't get in trouble here and to check the message board for sign up for next month to see what team you're playing on. See y'all next month!"

The group quickly dispersed. Jeff picked up his bag and started to walk toward the parking lot beyond the entrance gate to catch up with Jennifer. He was stopped abruptly by Adam, who jumped in front of his path.

"What the heck man?"

"Hey! You know the rules. If I set up, you tear down. You gotta collect all your pressure plates. Think of it as payback for shooting me in the face five times. Besides, I wake up to make my commute to work in five hours. Yay for being management."

Jeff sighed. Adam had a good point. Jeff had more free time by only working part time since he'd lost his second job. He glanced at the parking lot. Jennifer was climbing into the front of her truck.

"Fine, I'll see ya around."

"Yep. Shouldn't be too much to clean up. Later brother."

They bumped fists before parting ways. Jeff jogged over to Jennifer, who was surprisingly waiting for him. He was glad that she hadn't just driven off. He had another chance to talk to her.

"So, what did ya think?" he asked as he reached her open window. He struggled to keep his shaking nerves from showing as they spoke. Not like when he used to speak with Kylie. His heart raced when he looked at her deep almond-brown eyes. He didn't want to mess this up...whatever this was.

"It was interesting." She leaned out her window, an amused expression spreading over her soft olive-toned face.

"Yeah, it started with just me, Adam, and a couple of guys from college. Kinda grew from there. We keep adding stuff, trying to make it more fun."

Jennifer giggled at the word, *"fun."* He didn't quite see what was amusing about it. Yeah, it was a bit of a dorky game. Maybe this was a bit too geeky for her. He smiled back, nervously.

"Yeah, we're a couple of nerds I guess...but...yeah..." He trailed off.

There was an awkward silence as he shifted his weight uncomfortably. He was having a hard time coming up with something to say. He found himself drawn again to her bright brown eyes. Small flicks of amber glowed back as the lights hit them. Jennifer glanced at her watch and frowned.

"Well, I gotta get going. I have a class in the morning. Are you going to come?"

"Oh sure!" He hated how loud he sounded when he said it. "I mean, yeah of course. Uh, what time, and uh...what's the address?"

She laughed as if he had said something funny again. A sweet inflection in his ears.

"Give me your phone. I'll put in my number." Jennifer held her hand out as Jeff anxiously searched the fifty pockets on his pants for his phone. He knew he shouldn't be this excited to get her phone number. It was just for her class tomorrow. He placed it in her hand. Her skin was rough, despite looking delicate and soft. "Here. Send me a text later, and I'll send you the address."

"Yeah!"

She turned on the engine of her truck, which roared in the silent night. "Well, I guess I'll see you..."

"Yeah, I'll be there."

"Alright, have a good night. I hope you don't have too much work to clean up."

"Nah, I just gotta make sure there's no random paint on the headstones. Don't want to be TOO disrespectful to the dead." Jeff mimed making the sign of the cross over himself and mocked a prayer.

Jennifer tried to stifle a chortle. He liked making her laugh. She lingered a moment longer before waving goodbye.

Jeff felt good for the first time in what felt like a long time. He walked over to his car and opened his trunk. He threw in his paintball gear and headed back up to the cemetery to get started on cleaning. He hoped to get some sleep tonight, though he wasn't sure if he could sleep. He had Jennifer's number. He wanted to talk to her more. Should he text her now? He hadn't been this nervous to speak with a girl since he'd first hit puberty. He pulled out his phone and began to write a message.

> Hey, this is Jeff. I had fun tonight. What's the address for your class?

He lingered for a moment before he finally hit send. Even if she just left...it would just be for an address anyway. Jeff sighed as he grabbed the crate out of the trunk full of the cleaning supplies.

"Let's get this shit finished..."

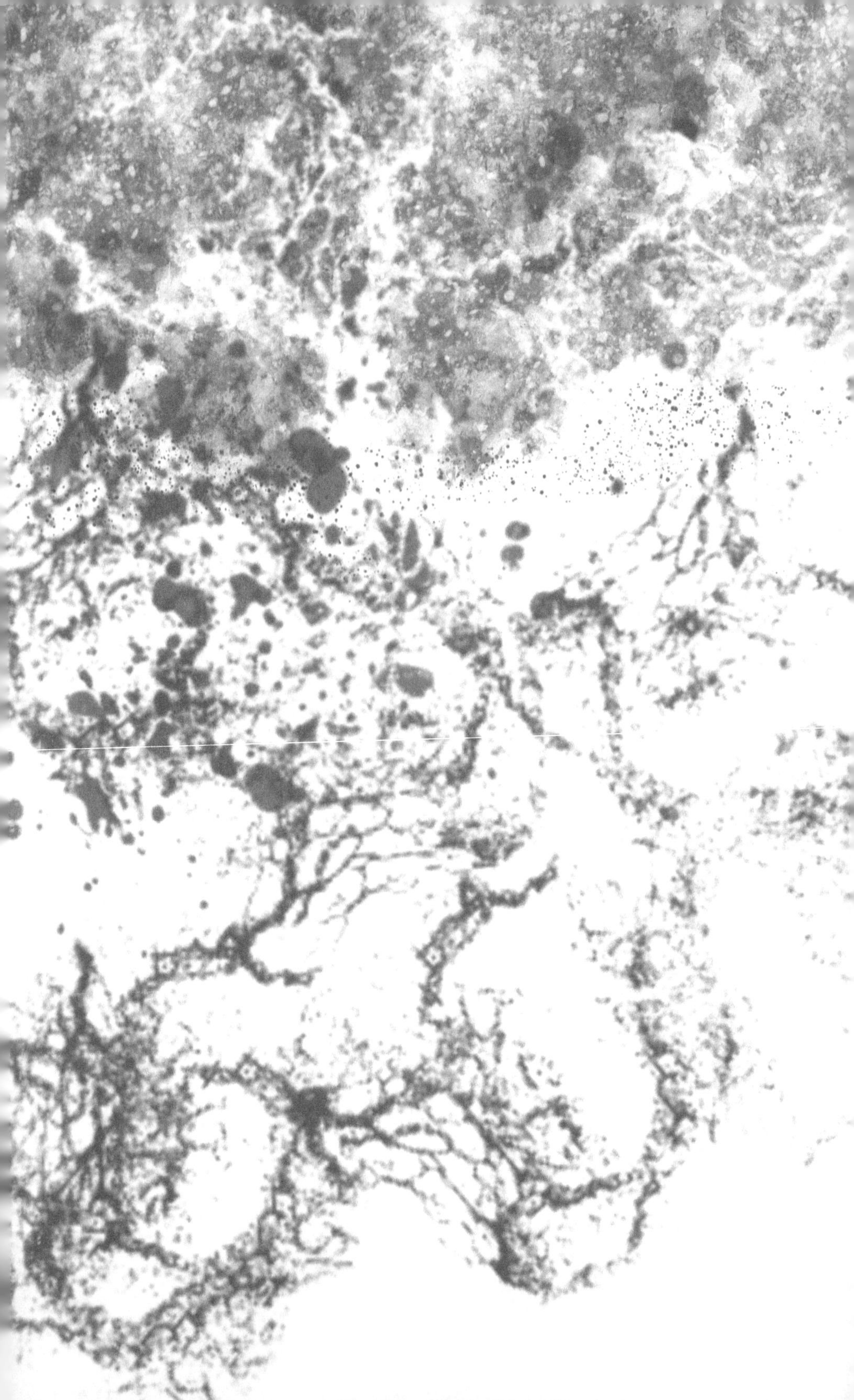

CHAPTER 3

Jennifer drove down the dark streets of downtown Temple Terrace. There was still quite a bit of traffic out despite the hour—one of the drawbacks of living in a big city like Tampa. It was a college town, so you could bet even on a Thursday night, the streets were still active. It made her night time crusades a little more difficult, but having lived down here for most of her life, she was used to it.

She turned on the A/C as the humidity was starting to get to her. It was still eighty degrees outside, but the warm air stuck to her skin like a hot wet blanket. She bit her lip as she drove, a nasty habit of hers when she was in deep thought. She tried to remember what had happened when she'd tripped. It bothered her that Jeff had mentioned her stumbling over a plate, when she clearly had not seen one there in the grass. There was the hole again too. Just like in the cemetery when she fixed the sensor earlier that night.

You're overthinking it Jen. You probably just slipped on the grass because you're wearing these crappy shoes.

She could have sworn her foot had caught on something. Something cold and hard. Maybe it was another small inlaid headstone she hadn't seen from the fog and low lights?

Jennifer slowed her truck at the red light, tapping her fingers on the wheel. She peered over at the dash, noticing the time. The remaining field teams should be finishing up soon. She could start reviewing the reports of their findings. No one believed her claims that the number of undead they were dealing with had been higher than usual. To prove her hypothesis, she had started logging the number of undead encounters a month ago. Hammer, their Commander, was supposed to be back from his meeting with the

Northern divisions tomorrow. If he didn't lose his temper like usual with them and come back early that is. She would compile the last of her data tonight and present it to him. He couldn't dismiss her theory if he could see the numbers.

She pulled out her phone. There were six missed calls from Sentinel.

The light changed on the street and she juggled her phone as she tried to reach her voicemails. Yes, bad driving behavior. Something she vowed to work on... Her phone vibrated. It was Sentinel again. She answered it, starting to worry by the amount of times he'd tried to reach her already.

"This is Phoenix."

"*Shit! Finally!*" His Texan voice rang loud through her ear and she had to pull it away. "*I thought you said you were gonna be quick?*"

"Sorry, it took longer than I thought. You got the reports from tonight?"

"*Nah. Not yet. You gonna tell me why you been actually wanting the reports every night yet?*"

"Maybe. Depends what they say. What's the problem? Don't like going behind Hammer's back after he gave me that 'talk down' about obsessing?" Sentinel was actually older than her. She liked to pick on him because he had been a straight arrow about the rules since she'd met him five years ago.

"*Haha, very funny. Listen, I've been gettin' seismic readings from the ground posts we have in the cemetery you were tonight. There is definite ground movement goin' on there. I wasn't sure at first because of the amount of people you were with, but it's been gettin' worse in the last half hour.*" Sentinel's voice started to register a tone of urgency.

She slowed her truck as she approached another red light. There were no other cars around her. Jennifer's mind wandered to the twenty strangers she'd played the game with tonight. Her hands went cold as she gripped the steering wheel. She remembered her fall, the feeling of something cold latching onto her foot, causing her to trip, and the upended ground near the headstone. The pieces began to fall into place.

"Are you sure?"

"*Yeah I am. You know as well as me that it takes a good while for those things to dig themselves out of the ground. We haven't gardened that location in a long time.*" Sentinel's tone became more serious as he continued. "*Are there any civilians there? I'm organizin' a team now for clean up.*"

At the mention of "civilians" a knot formed in her stomach. Jeff was still out there. Alone.

"Yeah there is. I'll meet the team there. What's your ETA?"

"It's on the other side of town, so even takin' the highway, it will be about forty minutes from here. Secure the civilians and the area. We'll get there as soon as we can."

"Roger."

Jennifer threw her phone in the seat next to her. She focused on one thing: getting back to the cemetery before Jeff could get hurt. When the light turned green she did an immediate, not quite legal, U-turn. She sped off into the night weaving through the other cars. She was only fifteen minutes away. She pressed the gas pedal down harder.

***

Jeff walked uphill toward the back gate, the area only partially lit by the small moonlight escaping the clouds overhead. Aside from the sound of sirens in the distance, the area was eerily quiet. He was almost done collecting all the plates and wiping down the headstones of any noticeable stray paint. He kneeled by what should be the last one, placing the crate he kept the plates in beside him. His mind wandered through the night's events. Jennifer was really cool. She was caring despite her slight cold exterior. She had managed to pull him out of the cesspool of anxiety that just seeing Kylie's name on his caller ID had brought up. She barely knew him, but had helped him right away. Aside from all that...she was extremely attractive. Jeff's mind kept remembering her soft pink lips, her curvy physique, the way her dark brown hair made the slight amber in her dark brown eyes glow. One thing he knew for sure, he wanted to see her again.

If she would even be interested in hanging with a loser like me...

Jeff sighed and went back to work. There was a noise of rustling leaves in the bushes behind him. Probably a small breeze caused by the coastal air. They were inland from the gulf coast, but that didn't stop the windy weather. Especially during hurricane season in the summer. Jeff continued to scrub away the paint on the headstone in front of him, paying no mind to the warm breeze.

The leaves rustled again. The sound of heavy footsteps on the ground behind him. Jeff shot up, squinting as he looked around in the darkness. The solitude of the cemetery was fading, replaced by a feeling of dread. Now that everyone was gone, the increasing fog reminded him more of the horror movie he'd watched with Adam yesterday.

"Hello? Anyone there?" Jeff called out, squeezing the dirty rag in his hands.

There was no response. He stood perfectly still as he tried to listen for any movement. There was nothing but the sound of cicadas chirping back at him. His heartbeat sped up as his natural survival instincts set in. Something was off. His instincts were telling every nerve in his body to leave. Jeff picked up his crate and headed back to his car. His stride got quicker, until he got to the dimly lit parking lot. Tension left his body as he stood under the low light of the nearby street lamp. The fact he didn't see anyone the whole way back brushed off his sense of fear.

You're getting in your own head...stop that. It was probably a stray dog or cat.

When he got to his car he dropped the crate in his trunk. Using the illumination of the trunk's light he started to sift through its contents, counting everything to make sure he didn't miss any items.

"That's weird. I could have sworn Jen tripped on one of these...did I go back to where she fell? Maybe I was in the wrong space?" Jeff riffled through the piles of pressure plates again. "They're all here though."

He looked back at the cemetery leering behind him. These plates were expensive and he didn't want to leave any behind if there was another one still out there. Maybe Adam bought a new one and forgot to tell him. He decided it would be better if he took another look, especially toward the back where Jennifer had tripped. He reached in the crate and pulled out his flashlight. He gazed at the looming graves before him as he closed his trunk and walked back into the cemetery.

As he approached the back outer fence, he heard the rustling of leaves again. He stopped, standing as still as he could to hear better. Someone had to be playing a trick on him.

"Alright, who's there?" Jeff yelled into the dark where the sound had come from.

Again, no answer.

He continued to walk through the graves, faster than before. He just wanted to finish here, lock the gate, and go home. He searched around him with the flashlight, ready to blind whomever might be stalking him in the fog. He heard the brush move again behind him. Jeff torqued his body, ready to confront his tormentor. Something cold grabbed his boot. Not able to get his balance centered fast enough, he fell over. His flashlight lay at his side, barely casting light in the direction of his leg. Jeff squinted to see what was entangling his leg. It was a weird looking tree root, shaped almost like a claw.

He reached over to untangle the root, and recoiled back. He grabbed his flashlight.

Why is it so cold and slimy?

He cast his light, following the root into the shadows. It was not attached to a tree like he expected, but to an arm! Jeff shone the beam in the direction of the arm, revealing the torso of a man. The man's face was disfigured from years of rot, covered in sand and grime. Maggots crawled out of its orifices. When the breeze flew in, he could smell rotten decayed meat. The creature let out a gurgling moan as it pulled Jeff's foot toward its chomping maw.

With no time to process, Jeff kicked it in the head several times with his free leg with as much force as he could until its grip let up on his foot. He clambered backwards into a nearby tombstone, breathing heavily.

"Shit! What the hell!?"

The corpse began to pull itself out of the earth and clawed in his direction. Its eyes were pale and blind, but he could feel its hungry gaze on him. Jeff's body was numb, his heart beat in his ears, and his brain told him to move, but he couldn't.

"What the?" Jeff watched as the creature struggled to crawl forward. He slapped his face in disbelief, trying to wake up back to reality. Maybe he'd tripped on a branch and hit his head? The creature's putrid smell continued to fill his nostrils as its broken body wormed its way toward him.

This isn't a fucking dream or video game. That is a fucking ZOMBIE! You have to get up, you have to move!

He managed to use the headstone he was leaning on to pull himself to his feet, but couldn't take his eyes off the corpse clawing out of the ground. He willed his feet to move. He had to get to the parking lot. He had to get to his car and get the hell out of here.

But what about the people in the homes nearby?

Jeff felt the gate keys in his pocket. He could lock the gates and call 911. They probably wouldn't believe him, but he had to try. He ran down the hill as quickly as his numb legs would take him. He turned to see if his undead attacker had followed. Before he could turn his head back forward, his foot caught something and he fell again.

He looked over: another rotting, dead hand was grasped around his ankle. He took his metal flashlight and used it as a baton to beat the cold flesh off of him. He scrambled to his feet again. The putrid smell of earth and rot was stronger in the hot summer air. He looked around, counting at least ten more bodies clawing out of the ground. Additional silhouettes in the dark shambled in his direction. The moans grew louder as they all neared.

"Fuck...what the fuck? This shit can't be real!"

He smacked himself in the face again hoping to regain his focus as he bolted to the parking lot gate. As the lights of the parking lot grew closer, a set of bright headlights headed toward him. He dove out of the way of the oncoming vehicle. When he rolled over he squinted to see who it was that had almost ran him over through the bright lights.

A female silhouette jumped out of the vehicle, wielding a handgun that appeared to be also equipped with a silencer.

"Knight, get behind me!"

"Jen?"

Jennifer rushed over to him and threw him behind her, acting as a barrier between him and the monsters. She held up her gun, taking aim at the corpses. She clipped the closest one in the head first. The gunshot was a small whisper due to the suppression of the silencer. The body dropped to the ground with a hard thud. She pushed Jeff toward her truck, while she continued to shoot off nine more rounds into some of the other walking corpses. She had the same precision he'd seen from her earlier tonight. After her tenth round, her gun clicked empty.

"Shit. Out of ammo," Jennifer muttered.

"What do you mean you're out of ammo? What the hell are we supposed to do?!"

Jennifer dropped her handgun to the ground. She pulled back her hair and tied it into a tight bun, and ripped off her jacket from around her waist, throwing it to the ground next to the gun.

"We need to crack their necks and sever the connection of their brains to their nervous systems." Jennifer's voice remained calm as she spoke.

"What?"

"There's a community around here, we can't let them out. Close the gate. Watch what I do. Follow my lead. There's only twelve of them, we can do this."

He felt like he wanted to throw up. The smell of the approaching dead bodies was nauseating. He could hear Jennifer talking to him, but he couldn't grasp the words she was saying.

"Jeff, you need to focus! Don't let them scratch or bite you, and shut the damn gate!" Jennifer's eyes glared at him with a fire he hadn't seen in her during the game. They were angry and stern, and they made his heart race.

He took a deep breath and ran as he fumbled the gate keys out of his pocket. Despite the hot weather, his fingers felt cold and numb. He slammed the gate closed, inches away from the back of Jennifer's truck. There was a loud clunk as the old locks turned over. Jeff's heart sank. He was sealing himself in his grave.

He spun around. Jennifer was already in a group of monsters, using the headlights of her truck to illuminate the ground in front of her. She methodically drew one away from the group, grappled it by disabling its arms, knocked it to the ground, and cracked its neck in a sickening snap. Her movements were quick and fluid. Jennifer walked back toward her truck, awaiting her next target. Jeff stepped warily toward her. His heart was a loud drum in his ears. His eyes raced back and forth between the horde and Jennifer. She drew another creature away from the pack. Just as quickly and fluid as before she pulled it in and cracked its neck. He wasn't sure what martial arts style she was using as the movements reminded him of the grappling of Jiu Jitsu, but also Aikido.

How could they stop all these monsters with their bare hands? But Jennifer was doing it. Jeff glanced at the approaching horde. She would be close to being surrounded if he didn't do something soon. Standing here like an idiot wasn't going to help them survive. He couldn't rationalize this. There was nothing rational about what was occurring tonight.

Jennifer worked fast to cut down the number of zombies that approached them. However, as fluid and quick as she was, the process was slow. The numbers were growing around her. One of the zombies shambled into the small safe space dividing Jennifer from him. The corpse resembled an old grandmother. It wore a dusty-looking navy blue dress suit, with a matching navy blue small hat haphazardly pinned to what little hair remained on its head. The creature could grab Jennifer from behind. As talented as Jennifer was, she didn't seem aware of it. Or was she planning for him to grab it away from her?

With no time to think, Jeff launched forward toward the animated corpse. He reached out, grabbing it around the collar, copying the same movements that Jennifer had done to disable the reach of the zombie's arms. Its skin felt like soft dirty rubber against his hands. The smell was a mixture of earth, with meat left out in the sun too long. Not like when someone was making jerky, just hot and rotten. The monster struggled against him, its arms still reaching for Jennifer. The teeth snapped furiously. Jeff was surprised at how easy it was for him to twist its neck until he heard the snap. The grandmother zombie's arms collapsed, and the clacking of teeth ceased. The undead body became an inanimate corpse again in his arms. He let it fall to the ground.

Feeling more confident, he put his back to Jennifer. He would protect her from this side while she did what she had to on her own. They worked in tandem and the remaining zombie horde was reduced in minutes. It surprised him how effective the way her defensive style was. Adam was right, it was perfect for stopping zombies!

Jeff heard a low moan behind him. He turned to attack the remaining creature, but froze. It was just a girl. Probably not that much younger than him. She had blonde hair that appeared almost white in the light from Jennifer's truck, wearing only a set of shorts and tank top. Her skin was deathly pale with a slight bluish tint in her lips that could have been a result of the moonlight. Her eyes were not clouded over as the other corpses were. Just a light blue. She still looked...alive. The girl stood for a moment, and a small labored breath came from her chest. She tilted her head as she gazed back at Jeff, her neck cracking as her head moved. Before Jeff could utter anything, she ran at him. She was fast, not staggering like the others had been. Jeff hesitated.

Is she really a zombie? Maybe she got hurt and just came here looking for help? Besides—

The others looked DEAD. Their skin was decayed. Their eyes had clouded over. Their flesh smelled of death. Jeff couldn't sense any of that from her.

Jennifer moved quickly and noiselessly behind the girl and wrapped her arm around the girl's neck in a choke hold. The young woman desperately reached for him against Jennifer's hold. She screamed louder as she struggled to be free. As Jennifer wrestled against the girl's strength, she reached back behind her, pulling a combat knife out. The girl finally managed to lunge forward out of Jennifer's grasp, and as she reached toward Jeff, Jennifer brought the knife down into the front of her temple. The blood splattered out of the wound onto him as he remained frozen in shock.

She killed her...

"Did she scratch you? Did any of her blood get in your eyes or mouth?"

Jennifer pulled her knife from the head of the girl and wiped it on the ground. She ripped the bottom of her shirt as she walked over to Jeff and hastily wiped the blood off his exposed skin. He was still frozen, numb to her touch. She scrubbed his face, prickling his cheek, breaking through the numbness. He began to stutter as he struggled to form words.

"What the hell? You...you just killed that girl!" He pulled away from her, for the first time terrified of her, "Get away from me!"

He ran back to the gate and tried to turn the lock open again. It was frozen in place. Infuriated, he kicked the gate several times, but it wouldn't budge.

"Knight, calm down. She was already dead." Jennifer's voice was soft and soothing, "You can't get out. Remember? You locked it."

He turned around. His eyes were drawn to the knife by her feet, smeared with the blood of the innocent girl. Jennifer followed his gaze. She kicked it away from her. Jeff's body remained tense, so she held her hands up in a surrendering gesture. Her eyes had lost the urgency they had before, replaced with regret the longer he looked at her in fear. He still wasn't sure if this show of concern and disappointment was a guise to make him feel comfortable.

"Jeff, I'm not going to hurt you. I'm actually a little surprised you did so well." She walked over to the body of the girl and hoisted it up, dragging it under the light of her truck. She rolled it over onto its back, so the wound from the knife's penetration was clearly visible in the light.

"Come here, I wanna show you something." She beckoned Jeff over, pointing to the wound.

He walked slowly to her and knelt down near the body. He made sure to keep his distance from her. She leaned in closed and he recoiled away. Jennifer looked disappointed, but continued.

"You see here?" She pointed again to the wound, "She was already dead. The wound isn't bleeding. Her blood, for the most part, is coagulated. If I had to guess from this, and how cold she feels, she must have been dead for about a day."

"If she was dead for that long, how come she didn't look like the rest of these things?"

"Have you actually seen a dead body before?" Jennifer frowned.

"Uh...not since my Great Aunt Lorelai died..."

Jennifer sighed and began to check the limbs on the body. She started around the neck, moving her hair, looking for something. He grimaced with how nonchalant she was with touching a dead person. Finally, she held up the girl's forearm, pointing to a bloody gauze wrapped around it. She peeled back the medical tape, revealing a festering wound with a chunk of flesh gnawed out of it. Jeff gagged at the sight of it. Maggots wiggled around the open flesh.

"She's pretty fresh. Must have been bitten about a day or two ago. She was drawn here probably because this was the closest horde...they migrate together..." Jeff watched as the gears in Jennifer's brain worked. "This isn't good."

She got up and wiped her hands on the back of her jeans as she walked over to her truck. He watched as her tiny form clambered to reach something inside. She popped back out with her phone and immediately dialed out.

"Hey, this is Phoenix. Sentinel, where are you? Mhmmm..." Jennifer gave a reassuring smile to Jeff but it did nothing to ease him, "There was a civilian present and he is secure. There were a large number of them, we got lucky...about twenty-two...yeah I know."

He watched as she paced back and forth. She wasn't phased at all by the traumatic, gory events of the last few minutes..

Phoenix? Sentinel?

"Yeah, it bothered me too. Another fresh one...I gotta talk to Terrence...my truck is locked inside the gate. Mind bringing it back for me? Alright, meet up later." Jennifer hung up the phone. She picked up her gun and jacket from the ground.

She screwed off the silencer to her weapon, tossing it in her truck. She struggled to reach something inside again. When she clambered back out, she had a ragged towel in her hand. She walked to the knife and folded it in the towel. Jennifer glanced at him as she carefully handled the bloody weapon. He gazed back blankly, still numb. What would happen to him now? It was clear that she was part of something. Maybe the military?

Jennifer tossed the knife in the truck and turned off the engine. She slid the gun in the curve of her spine, tying her jacket over it. When she was done, she slammed the door shut and turned toward Jeff as she pulled her hair down again. Jeff knew her secret.

"Are you a soldier or something?" he finally managed to utter through his dry mouth.

"Something like that...more like a mercenary for the paranormal," she responded, her cheeks flushed a slightly rosier pink as she tucked a loose hair behind her ear. "Come on, the clean up crew is on its way."

She climbed onto the bed of her truck and jumped toward the gate. She grabbed the top where the ugly loops were fixed into the metal and lifted herself over with ease. She nodded for Jeff to do the same.

Unlike her, all the adrenaline had left his body now that the threat was gone. He felt shaky and weak. He clambered onto her truck and jumped with what little energy he had left. He haphazardly grabbed the fence, his fingers almost slipping off the cold rusted metal.

"Easy now," she coached him from below.

Jeff pulled himself up and slid down the other side. As he was close to the bottom, he felt Jennifer's hand on his lower back as she helped him balance. She smiled that comforting smile again at him when his feet finally touched the ground. Maybe he could trust her. He would figure out what was going on first at least.

The two of them walked toward his car, which sat alone in the dimly lit lot. If he had just left when he'd first collected everything, he would never have found out that zombies were real, or what kind of person Jennifer really was.

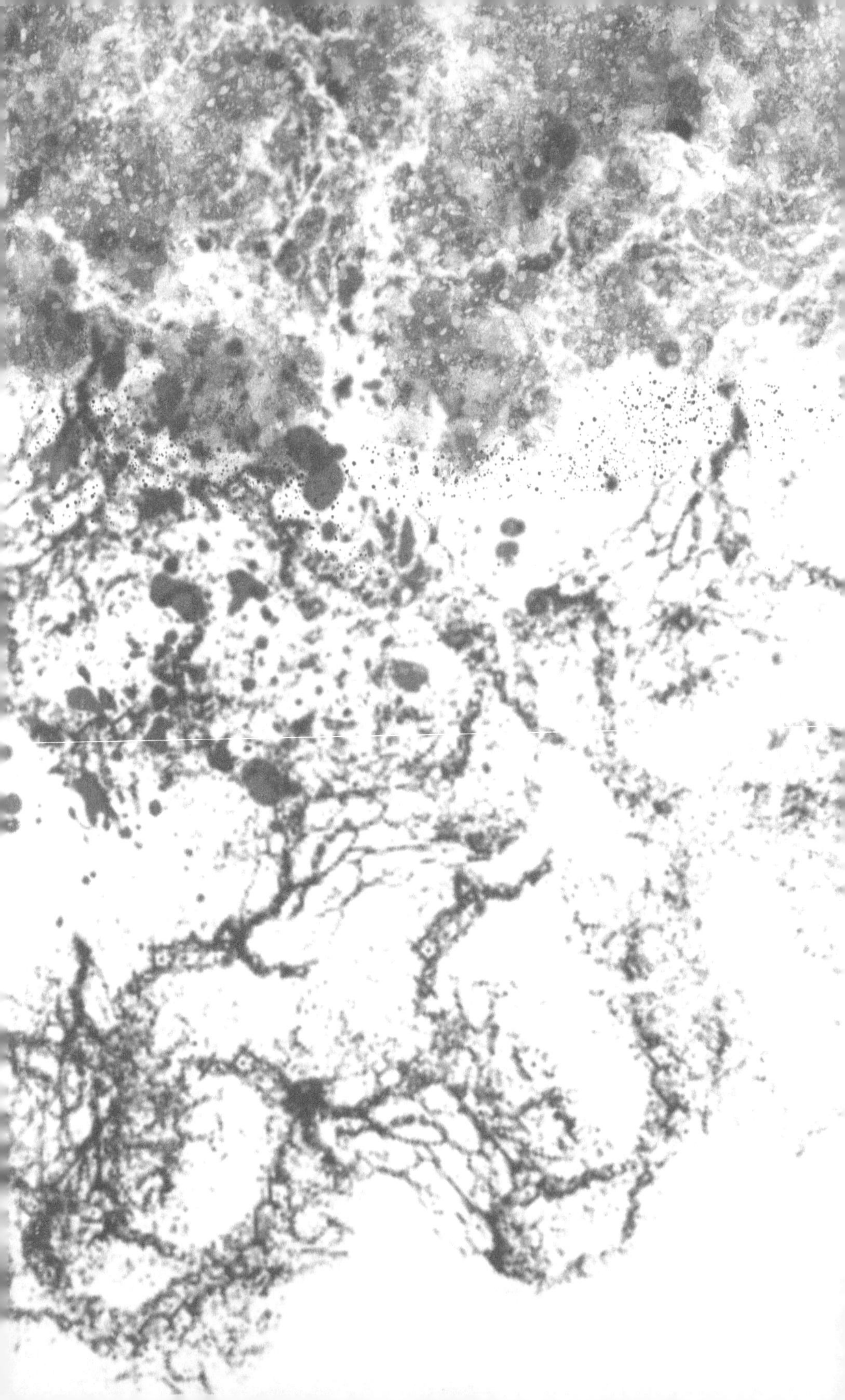

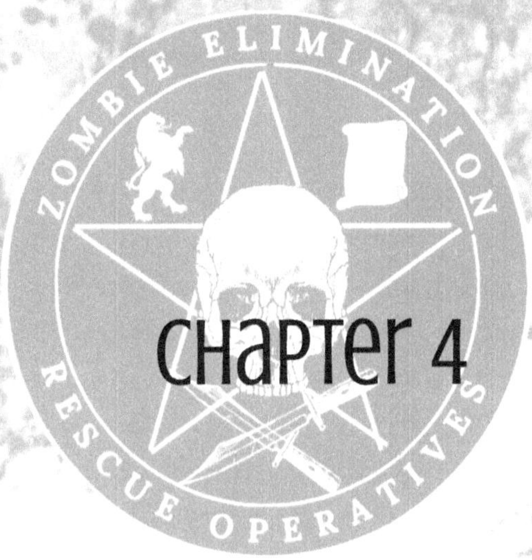

CHAPTER 4

Jennifer observed Jeff's pale clammy skin. She had seen this look on many of her new recruits. She hoped he would recover back to the man she met earlier tonight. Kind of dorky, yet confident in his own way. Jeff fiddled through his pockets looking for his keys. His adrenaline must be crashing. She marched in front of him and held her hand out. He looked up, startled.

"Give me your keys. I'm driving. You're still in shock, and who knows when you're gonna puke. I don't wanna die now because you passed out at the wheel."

Jeff's crystal blue eyes gazed back at her, devoid of emotion and thought. He dropped the keys in her hand without protest. She opened the door and adjusted the seat for her small height so she could reach the pedals. She wasn't exactly short. She was five feet and three inches, which the last time she checked was considered pretty average for a woman. Everyone around her were just giants.

When she turned the car on, the clock on the dashboard lit up, flashing 1:57 A.M. There wouldn't be many people left at the base at this hour. Most of the field teams would be done for tonight, already headed home. It was the best time for her to bring him in. He needed answers and she wanted to give them to him.

She drove them around for about an hour, giving him time to decompress before she bombarded him with new information. Jeff stayed silent, his forehead pressed on the window; his gaze blank and unfocused. His skin still looked clammy and pale. His hands were shaking whenever she glanced over at him. She finally pulled into the parking lot of an old dive bar that was also fashioned as a dine in restaurant. At least that's what it was meant to look like from the outside to the *normal* populace. A large neon sign blasted the name, *"The Silver Bullet Pub."*

She turned off the engine and stepped out of the car. Jeff stepped out quietly, following her toward the bar. The parking lot was still full for the hour. There were probably some locals around getting a slice of pizza with a beer—one of the only foods they served here. Their drinks were cheap and so it attracted a lot of the local college scene. Jennifer glanced back to make sure Jeff was still following her. As she turned her attention forward, the door to the bar swung open, and she almost collided with a woman on her way out.

"Oh! I'm so sorry! I didn't see you there!" Jennifer apologized as she stepped back from the door. She looked at the woman, who didn't seem surprised at all by her fumble. She had the look of a high fashion model. Not someone she would have expected to grace their establishment. She had short raven black hair, reminiscent of the style of Trinity from the *Matrix* films, as well as a tall slender frame that was only complimented by the curves of her body. Her clothes also screamed high influence. Jennifer recognized the Michelle Smith Milly dress, black with pink fabric, that showed beneath the skirt as the woman shifted her weight. The dress alone cost about four hundred dollars second hand. Jennifer loved the style, but she refused to pay more than a hundred dollars for any clothes meant for everyday wear.

Jennifer glanced at the expensive handbag dangling from the woman's arm, and that's when she saw it...a black dog...in the bag. It wasn't that Jennifer didn't like dogs, but she knew there was a time and place for them. A bar that served food was not one, unless it was a service animal. If she let one person bring a dog in without good reason, then others would follow and they could get a health code violation warranting unwanted attention.

"That's alright, I should have been paying more attention before I opened the door." The woman wiped her bangs away from her face as she smiled at Jennifer.

"I hate to be rude ma'am, but there are no dogs allowed in the establishment." Jennifer crossed her arms and nodded toward the woman's purse. She looked shocked by Jennifer's statement.

"How could you reject this cutie?" the woman said as she raised her purse and made a bunch of baby noises to the dog. It took Jennifer every fiber of her being to not physically roll her eyes at the woman. The woman stopped doting on the small animal and looked back at Jennifer with a coy smile. "Well I was on my way out anyway. Your boyfriend there looks like he already had enough for the evening. Maybe you two might want to call it a night as well?"

She nodded toward Jeff, who was still waiting behind Jennifer. His skin color seemed worse than before. The puke part of his revelation was coming soon. Jennifer felt her cheeks burn up red as she realized what the woman implied.

"He's uh...not my boyfriend...just a friend that I'm helping."

"Whatever you say dear." The woman winked her light amber gold-brown eye at her, and pushed past them. Jennifer glanced back briefly at the woman, annoyed, as she walked off. She turned to Jeff, who didn't seem aware of the recent exchange.

"Come on." She led the two of them inside the bar.

The interior was designed to be part bar, part dine-in restaurant that had not been updated since the nineties. She weaved through the collection of hightops and booths made of old dark hardwood as she walked to the wooden bar in the center.

As she approached the bar, she saw a large burly man nursing a draft of beer. He was dressed in business attire, but any passerby could see he was not an executive. His light brown hair was unkempt and his face had a dark five o'clock shadow. His jacket, a cheap looking blazer, sat on the seat next to him with a clip-on tie thrown on top. He had his dress shirt unbuttoned at the collar and his sleeves rolled up. He didn't seem to notice they had entered the bar, his attention transfixed by the small worn knight chess piece in his hand. She waved to Jeff to sit at the nearby table behind him and then took a seat at the bar next to her disheveled commander, Hammer.

Yep, pretty sure he's lost his temper again...

"Terrence, how did I know I would find you here already?"

Hammer looked over at Jennifer and let out a big exhausted sigh, hastily stuffing the small chess piece back into his pocket. Jennifer remembered it from when they were children. It was around his mother's funeral that he'd started carrying it. Maybe some form of comfort when he was frustrated, though she didn't remember Aunt Lydia ever playing chess with him.

"Probably because you know as well as I the conference was garbage. Everyone thinks they are better than us when it comes to training rookies for the hunt. Bunch of goddamn pussies acting like they know shit."

"That good huh?" She placed her hand under her chin amused.

Hammer took a long swig from his beer and scruffed up the hair on his head some more. He looked over at her with a new fire in his eyes. She sat up straight, ready to give her full attention for one of his signature rants.

"It's damn kids and bureaucrats Jen! They're fucking around, thinking they're all gonna be big-time movie badasses that don't know cocks from cobras about killing anything. They wouldn't shut up long enough to let anyone get a word in. I got pissed, flipped them all off, and walked out. I know my old man wasn't too happy with me, but fuck that shit." He slammed his fist on the counter, taking another drink of his beer. "I booked an earlier flight back. The fact they weren't in the obituaries by the time I got in my seat was nothing short of miraculous..."

Jeff wiggled uncomfortably in his seat, causing it to screech against the hard floor. Hammer noticed him for the first time. Jennifer stifled a giggle as Jeff attempted to scan the room to avoid eye contact with him. She understood how her friend could come off as a little scary, but it still amused her when people were scared of him. She grew up with Hammer, so to her, he didn't give off a threatening aura.

"So who's the kid?"

"My new recruit." Jennifer said it proudly to show she wasn't joking to him. "He's actually the reason I was hoping to talk to you."

"Jen, I told you we don't need another recruit. We have more than enough people working this outfit. We'll be ready for the next Day of the Dead."

"There are more people living here than there were twenty years ago. You just said it... we have more recruits that have no real application training. We have to recruit outside of the families now." Jennifer tried to keep her temper in check. "There were twenty-two tonight Terrence! That's more than we've had for a long time. We have to stay organized. I want him on *our* team. This guy handled himself pretty well." She pursed her lips to keep herself from saying anything else that might dissuade him.

Hammer took another look at Jeff, sizing him up again. Jeff was nervously tapping his leg on the ground while his fingers played with the napkin-wrapped silverware at the table. Hammer frowned.

"Yeah, he looks fucking exceptional."

"Terrance! Trust me. He already has martial arts training, and even though it was only a paintball gun, he was pretty good. He had this game that I actually think we can use to maybe train some of the crappy recruits—"

"Paintball...Jesus fucking Christ..." Hammer flagged down the bartender. "Alright, take him to the back. Let him meet everyone. Make sure you're careful around George. He's been acting up lately. I hate to admit it when you're right." He grabbed the new pitcher of beer that the bartender dropped off, refilling his pint glass, "Hey Tina, can I have a couple of shots here?"

"Comin' right up Honey." Their resident bartender, Tina, was an older woman in her fifties. You couldn't tell by looking at her. She was platinum blonde, with slightly bronzed skin from her constant days out on the beach, but it didn't tarnish her youthful looking features. She was more than a bartender for them though. She was the adoptive mother of the various teams that passed through the bar on their daily errands and one of the best goddamn hunters they'd ever had.

Hammer slid her a twenty dollar bill that she slipped into her apron. She walked down the bar and pulled up two shot glasses, filling them with tequila. Jennifer was not in the mood for shots.

"Yes! I mean...not about being right, but thank you!" She gave Hammer a hug, who, given how rigid his body felt in her arms, was clearly not comfortable receiving it.

Tina came back and placed the two shots in front of them.

"Give these two to him. He looks like he's going to piss his pants." Hammer spun on the stool and raised his glass to Jeff, "Here's to you kid. May the rest of your life never be boring...'cause it might be short!" Hammer let out one of his more sinister cackles and turned back toward the bar. Jennifer tried to hold in her laughter as Jeff's face was a mixture of confusion and panic. Hammer turned back to Jennifer. "Hey Jen, tell someone, I don't care who, to give George a fucking shower! He stinks like high hell..."

Jennifer rolled her eyes at him as she hopped off the bar stool. She grabbed the tequila shots and carried them over to the table with Jeff, placing both in front of him. He looked anxious.

His innocence is kind of cute...

***

Jeff had no idea where he was and who the big guy was that Jennifer had spoken with. She was very comfortable around him, but there was something scary about the man. Maybe it was his gruff exterior, or the wild look he had in his eye when he glared at Jeff. He definitely had a mouth on him too.

Jeff tried to listen to them, but it was hard to make out, except for the loud outbursts.

Recruits? Day of the Dead?

The toast was really strange too. Who toasts like that? Jeff watched as Jennifer gave the big guy a hug. She hopped down from the high barstool and came over with two shot glasses. Is it poison? Is this how they were going to get rid of him for knowing too much? The thought that his life would end here, in a dive bar, really sucked. He knew he hadn't done much with his short life, but he'd hoped that he would have done at least one memorable thing before leaving this Earth. Maybe they were the reason for all the missing people in the area lately. Jeff glanced around the room. He could try flipping the table at Jennifer and running out the way they came in before they could grab him.

Jennifer gave him the same eye roll she'd just given to the man at the bar when she saw Jeff was wary of the shots.

"If I wanted to kill you, you would have been dead a long time ago. Drink 'em, they'll calm your nerves."

He nodded. She already had plenty of opportunities to kill him. She could have kicked him out on the highway into the other traffic. Or just finished him at the cemetery. Besides, he'd watched the bartender pour the same tequila for another customer. His paranoia was getting the best of him. Jeff grasped the first cold glass in his hand, kicking it back quickly down his throat. The smooth liquid burned as it made its way down, but he didn't mind. It was the first real sensation he'd felt in his body since everything had started tonight. He grabbed the second glass more eagerly. With the second one, he felt the warmth returning to his whole body. He felt better. Surprisingly, a little more normal.

"Alright, come on. Follow me." She beckoned him to stand and follow her as she led them around the bar to the kitchen in back. It was a small space, full of metal counter tops, a set of pizza ovens, and an unused grill and fryer set. The crew line was limited to a chef, sous chef, and dishwasher. The two chefs worked by the two tier pizza oven. One was in the process of tossing new dough, while the other sprinkled cheese on a new pie. Each stopped what they were doing as they saw Jennifer and Jeff enter. The dishwasher held his hand in the soapy water of the sink, but his forearm was tense, like he was gripping something beneath the surface. Jennifer shook her head at them and they went back to their duties like nothing had just occurred.

Jennifer brought them to a walk-in perishable storage room. She held the door open and gestured for him to walk in. Jeff reluctantly stepped into the cold space as she closed the door behind them. She walked to the back wall to a fuse box. He didn't see what she touched as the shelf in front of him moved away, revealing another door behind it.

Jennifer opened up the electrical box, moving the fuse panel out of the way somehow and revealing what looked like a card reader.

She pulled a green and black card out of her back pocket, swiping it through the mechanism. The light on it changed from red to green. He heard a small click as the lock released. She closed the panel back up and smiled at him. He was amazed, yet remained cautious.

She stepped forward and opened the door, revealing a set of stairs that led into a sub-basement. She walked down ahead of him. The door shut behind them as they began their descent. He heard the shelf sliding itself back into place too. There was no going back now. As they stepped further down the stairwell, motion lights flickered on, illuminating their way. The steps were hard concrete. Each footstep echoed against the solid walls.

When they reached the bottom, there was a very heavy, and large, metal security door. The lock next to the door looked more sophisticated compared to the one upstairs. Jennifer approached it and leaned forward. A light radiated out, flashing into her eye several times. This time the lock release was a series of heavy clunks as large metal moved in the walls around them. The door popped open an inch, releasing a small breeze of air accompanied with a suction sound as an airlock was released. Jennifer pulled the heavy door open wider and urged him to step inside first again.

Jeff walked into a brightly lit hallway, squinting his eyes at the fluorescents. It was a short hallway that lead to a well-lit wide, round room. He walked into it and noted the two halls jutting off on either side. He looked down at a large insignia painted onto the floor and spun around as he tried to make it all out. There was a sigil of a lion, a scroll, a knife, and a skull. Surrounding it were the words *"Zombie Elimination and Rescue Operatives."* Jeff glanced up and examined the rest of the room. The walls were a bright white, the floor a dark slate gray. The top of the atrium was designed with a stained glass aesthetic. His fear began to fade as curious excitement rose instead. This wasn't a small operation. Who were these people? He turned back to Jennifer who stood with her hands on her hips, smiling at him. He couldn't help but smile back.

"Welcome to Z.E.R.O, the Zombie Elimination and Rescue Operatives." Jennifer gestured for him to follow her down the hall to their right. "You will be the first recruit in a few years to join the elite Alpha Team that isn't a bloodline descendant of a previous member." She looked back at him. Jeff wasn't sure if she was eager for a question, but he was too busy soaking everything in.

"Terr—" Jennifer cleared her throat. "Hammer, the man at the bar, is our base commander, and I will be your leader on that team. We handle the big jobs. You know, renegade vampires, werewolves, demons, other monsters, most importantly what this establishment was founded on, the undead."

Jennifer looked back at Jeff like she was expecting some sort of reaction from him. Jeff hadn't really heard half the stuff she'd said because his mind was rushing with a million thoughts as he tried to process everything.

They reached an elevator and stepped inside. Jennifer selected a button to a floor labeled B3. The ride was short, opening to a hall that looked identical to the one they'd just left. She led them through a maze of similar-looking corridors. She finally stopped at a door and opened it.

"There are two more members in our team," Jennifer mentioned as they walked inside.

He stepped into what looked like a locker room. The room was large and circular in shape. Large metal cabinets lined the walls and the center. There were benches positioned just a couple feet away from them. Propaganda posters were posted on the walls of soldiers in black uniforms with slogans declaring *"Only you can stop the spread of disease."* The same insignia that he saw upstairs was on other posters with other similar messages. Jeff's eyes circled the room and stopped on the two soldiers standing at the door at the other end.

One was a white male, about the same height as Jeff at six foot one. The way he stood, and judging by his haircut, Jeff figured he might be ex-military; marine maybe. They had dirty blonde hair, with a short-cut beard that followed his chin line. He was excitedly chatting away with his compatriot who was a taller, *very* muscular African man who didn't seem much older than his partner. In fact, everyone so far seemed to be young, in their early thirties. The man's face was framed with a well-kept beard that circled his mouth, with edge work following his jaw line that faded, going up to what would have been sideburns, but his head was clean shaven and bald. Both looked like models out of a men's magazine. Jeff begrudgingly realized he really had no game with Jennifer tonight if these are the "normal" guys she sees on a daily basis.

"Hey, Sentinel, you two clean up the bodies already?" Jennifer crossed her arms as she questioned them.

"Yes ma'am," replied the blonde one, "we delegated Bravo Team to clean up." Sentinel had a heavy southern country drawl to his speech.

So that's Sentinel, from the phone earlier...

The taller, still unnamed soldier walked over to a locker with a name plate reading *"Demon"* and began unloading his gear. He seemed uninterested in giving Jennifer a briefing.

"We took a pic of the fresh one and it's currently making its rounds to our contacts at the hospitals and urgent care clinics. We'll find out who she was and where she was treated. Hopefully figure out where she was bit too." Sentinel finally noticed Jeff standing behind her, "Who's he?"

She stepped behind Jeff, placing her hands on his shoulders. "Our new team member. Demon, Sentinel, this is Jeffery Knight. He's the civilian that helped me with that mob."

Demon stuck his head out from behind his locker door to silently observe him. Jeff felt uncomfortable being in Demon's gaze. He couldn't quite pin down why. It was almost like when he went to the zoo as a child and the lion in the exhibit had peered at him intently through the glass. Demon nodded at Jeff in a "hello" gesture but disappeared back behind the locker to remove his vest and holster.

Jeff looked around the room nervously as Jennifer began discussing work matters with Sentinel. He noticed there were four weapon lockers in the room on the far wall, each with a different label: demons, zombies, werewolves, vampires, and miscellaneous. He stared at the cases as Jennifer continued to talk with her comrades.

Werewolves...vampires...

"Wait...rewind a minute...Did you say vampires and werewolves before?"

Demon closed his locker, joining the group. He was rid of all his armament and wore only a black T-shirt with matching black military tactical pants and boots.

"There are more things out there than you are aware of." Demon's voice was deep and booming.

"Our group started many years ago," explained Jennifer, "just dealing with zombies. While facing them, we met other things...like vampires...like Demon here." Jennifer flipped her hand over like she was introducing him again.

Jeff couldn't keep his mouth from hanging open as he stared at Demon in surprise. That probably explained the feeling he had a moment ago. Demon flashed a toothy smile at Jeff and popped out a set of two very sharp fangs over his canines. His eyes shifted quickly from dark brown to a bright yellow. Jeff jumped back, scooting closer to Jennifer. Demon chuckled as his eyes returned to normal. Then he quickly returned to his locker, acting like he'd forgotten something to get out of the conversation and Jennifer's chastising gaze.

"Yes, we work with vamps, but Demon is *cool*." She gave Demon another look that he better behave himself. "He's been working with our families for years."

Finding out that vampires, werewolves, and demons were actually *real* was an amazing yet also horrifying concept. This revelation was going to keep him up for many nights.

"ANYWAYS," Jennifer spoke up again. "Yeah, we met the vamps because killing zombies was becoming a problem as they spread fast from merely biting, scratching, or bleeding into their victims. The vamps didn't like the fact their food supply was dwindling, so they agreed to work with us. We have about one vamp in every state unit. Only the best of the best get a vamp on the team." She chirped, a small laugh escaping her lips.

Demon closed his locker again and returned to the group carrying an old book. Jeff attempted in vain to read the title. It had an old, dusty, red faded cover. The title looked like it was once written in a gold foil, but now gone and illegible from age. The pages were yellowed and the spine had creases from constant readings.

"Old, dried, dead blood just doesn't taste right. A little poisonous, like spoiled food. Besides, working with Z.E.R.O still allows me to tear into some flesh." Demon smiled again, without his extra fangs this time. He placed his hand on Jeff's shoulder. It felt cold. "Well, I'll be seeing you around kid. It's almost daylight, and I like my sleep."

"Yeah, you don't want to burn up or anything." Jeff smiled nervously.

"Actually, that's just a rumor we pass around so humans, like you, feel safe." Demon laughed darkly again, and Jeff's body shivered, "We don't burn, just get severely physically weakened. Practically mortal, like you."

Demon patted him on the shoulder and headed out the door, waving behind him as he walked out. Everyone could hear his laughter out in the hallway. Jeff was still frozen in his spot. If vampires didn't die from sunlight, what else that he knew about monster legends was actually wrong?

"You get used to it." Sentinel tilted his head and shrugged.

"Yeah, I bet..." Jeff gulped back the nausea still sitting in his stomach.

"Well, finishing introductions." Jennifer walked over to Sentinel. "Sentinel's real name here is Richard Matthews. Rick for short. He's our strategist. Pretty damn good too, hence the code name."

"But Sentinel means guardian right?" Jeff was confused about how a strategist is a shield.

"I am one. I make sure the team has all the information they need to get in and out of a situation. If I don't do my homework, somethin' could go wrong, and in our business it means ya'll get killed." Sentinel grimaced briefly but then smiled. "Even if I'm not actively with you in the field, I'm still runnin' reconnaissance for you."

"Oh."

Sentinel leaned into Jennifer, but Jeff could still hear what he was saying. "Hammer approved him?"

"Yes." Jennifer crossed her arms tightly and glared back at Sentinel who jumped back, waving his hands in surrender.

"Alright then! Well this has been fun. I gotta go report our findings for records." Sentinel began to stroll out, but stopped and turned to Jennifer, "He met George yet?"

Jennifer grinned, shaking her head. Sentinel began to laugh. He clapped Jeff on the back on his way out. Jeff looked at Jennifer, still utterly confused by everything that was going on.

What is the joke? That guy upstairs, Hammer, he mentioned George too...

"George?"

"I'll show you," Jennifer said as they turned to leave the same way as everyone else.

He followed her back to the elevator, where she selected floor B2. They stepped out and she led them down another set of hallways. Jeff noted the plaque on the wall that read, "*Research Laboratories*" as they walked by the next turn.

There were many doors and windows along this hall, all illuminated by bright harsh fluorescent blue lights. It made Jeff feel like he was walking through the sterile halls of a hospital. He peeked inside each as they passed. There were rooms with microscopes, beakers, and other lab testing equipment. He found what he expected to be the medical bay as it contained hospital beds and various other medical equipment. At the end of the hall stood a single soldier guarding a door, holding an assault rifle. The soldier saluted as they approached, turning to unlock the door as they stopped before him. A smell of putrid rotting fruits smacked Jeff in the face. He started to cough from the smell, and tried with every fiber of his being not to release the contents of his stomach.

They stepped into the room; it was freezing. Jennifer directed him with a firm voice to stay very close to the wall. The room was pitch black and he couldn't see a thing. The nauseous smell radiated through his nostrils. He tried taking shorter breaths through his mouth so as not to smell it. She stood next to him while she hit a switch on the wall and the lights flickered on. Jeff barely had time for his eyes to readjust when a badly decayed body launched at him. He flattened himself against the wall and closed his eyes.

So this is how they'll kill me! All that recruitment talk was for me to let my guard down! Shit!

He heard the snarl, inches from his face. The smell was stronger and more unbearable, but he wasn't feeling any of the physical pain of his flesh being severed from his body that he expected. He peeked open his eyes slowly. The ghoul was a couple feet from him. He looked straight at *It*. The clothes were the same he had seen on Demon and Sentinel moments before, except these were torn, covered in dry blood and dirt. More importantly, he noticed the zombie was chained to the far wall. Unable to reach him.

"Why the hell do you have one of those in here?" Jeff turned to Jennifer, who was amused by his reaction.

"Bad, George! We don't greet people like that!" Jennifer scolded the creature, before she turned to Jeff. "Sorry, he's usually better behaved. We keep him for studying. Kind of became our strange pet. I know it's messed up, but we do learn a lot from him." She wiped a tear from her eye as she looked at the zombie.

"Study? What kind of studying?"

"We're trying to see if we can find a cure. We've confirmed their bite is like poison. You can die just a few hours after being bit. Some people can go days. So we're still not sure about that. After you die, you always come back as one of them though."

"Oh, you mean like Romero zombies." Jeff was thinking of every *Living Dead* film he had watched with Adam.

"Where do you think Romero got the idea for his zombies? Though we did ask him to add some flair of possible origins for the virus." Jennifer placed her hands on her hips matter of factly. "It seems like every fifteen to twenty years, something goes off in the universe, and the dead all rise in greater numbers. Leading up to what we call, "*The Day of the Dead*" or "*D-Day*" for short. We get more and more of what happened tonight."

"So this has happened before?" Jeff couldn't even fathom another night like he'd experienced earlier.

"Yeah, when I was six there was a big event. Though not a D-day, but I've been training every day of my life since then for the real one." Jennifer's eyes began to water, a whirlpool of anguish and sadness. She brushed away the tears along with the thoughts that pained her. He felt compelled to say something to her, but he didn't know what.

Jennifer did an about face before he could ask her anything. She led them back down the hall to the elevator. She pressed the button for the ground floor of the facility, and the two waited in silence as the elevator descended. When the doors opened, they walked back toward the entrance. A million thoughts clouded Jeff's head at once. When they approached the emblem of Z.E.R.O on the floor, she slowed her pace. She lingered for a moment, before looking back into his eyes. A new fire in them.

"I need to know. Will you be willing to join our group?"

"Does it look like I have a choice?"

Part of him thought it would be really cool to join this underground mercenary group against the undead and other creatures from the history of horror. But the other part of him was scared; terrified. He had almost died tonight. Was he really ready to lay his life down for strangers he just met? But this would be an opportunity to actually help people. Even if they never knew he was.

He shifted his weight. His response was not what Jennifer was hoping for. She frowned briefly, and the fire burned in her eyes brighter. She placed her hand softly on his arm. Her intense gaze made his heart race, and her touch gave him goosebumps.

"You will always have a choice, Knight. After what you showed me tonight, I think you're a natural fit for this...we need your help. The main branch doesn't know where the major outbreak will occur, so they have been keeping us pretty thin." She released his arm and paced up and down, her words coming quick, "It's not like we can go public with all this. We're a private organization with a deep history in the country's government. I mean because of that the pay is good..."

Jennifer continued her uplifting speech for a while. When it was finally over, she spun back quickly into Jeff's face and waved her finger at him. "Long story short, we need you Knight. What's it gonna be?"

What was it gonna be? Jeff had never really committed to anything before tonight. Not martial arts, not work, not fighting for Kylie. Now this woman he'd just met was asking him to risk his life. For who? The world? For her? Jennifer continued to gaze intently at him, waiting for a response. He had to say something...and he still wanted to know more...about Z.E.R.O, and about her.

"This is just a lot to process...wait." He remembered back to the middle of her rant. He wasn't doing this for her—it was an opportunity. Maybe a chance to do something with his life. "You get paid to do this?"

Her already large almond shaped eyes expanded further from his surprise question. Out of everything that she said, it seemed that was not the question she expected.

"Yeah...about 25,000 dollars a month."

"Damn! Sign me up!"

Doing something good, and making a living? Maybe this won't be so bad?

***

Jennifer leaned on the open door to the bar as she watched Jeff drive away. He'd taken everything better than she'd thought he would. She sighed, walking back into the smell of stale pizza, taking a seat at the counter. Tina came over with a rum and coke, placing it on the coaster in front of her.

"New boy seems cute," Tina mused in her sweet North Carolina accent.

"Huh?" Jennifer felt her cheeks flare up, and averted eye contact with Tina, "I guess."

Why am I blushing!?

"You okay Sugar?" Tina smiled wide. Jennifer knew what she was thinking. There was nothing going on between her and Jeff. She needed to change the subject.

"Yeah, I'm fine. Have Christopher start on Knight's security details." Tina nodded, grabbing the phone behind the bar to relay the order.

Jennifer glanced at her watch. It was almost 3:30 A.M. She let out a deep breath and played with the straw in her drink. She glanced at the locals still in the bar. It was late and she was too tired to drive. She would have to stay the night here. She sat and drank while she reminisced of the evening's events. She'd had fun today, even with the zombie intrusion in the end. Her mind wandered to when Adam had introduced her to Knight. The first thing she'd noticed on him were his crystal blue eyes. They reminded her of someone her heart had tried desperately to forget.

Conor...

She absently placed her hand on her stomach. The tears started to well up. She caught her reflection in the bartop's waxed surface and wiped her face furiously.

She guzzled down the rest of her drink. She was always a lightweight when it came to drinking, especially Tina's overly heavy mixtures, but the alcohol would help her shut off her brain and get some sleep. Her face felt flushed as she went back down into the base and took the elevator to the third basement level where they had their bunks. She walked down the long hallway of free and open bedrooms until she saw one with a light. Only one other person would still be up at this hour.

She bit her lip as she approached the door. She lifted her hand to knock but hesitated. Finally, she took a breath, knocking softly.

"Come in." Demon's voice vibrated through the crack of the door. She pushed it open. Demon was lying on the bed. His well sculpted body was fully visible, only sporting his boxers.

"Mind if I join you? I'm too tired to drive home." Jennifer crossed her arms tightly around her. She couldn't place it, but she had a nervous knot forming in her stomach. Being near Demon felt awkward tonight. She couldn't tell if it was just awkward anticipation. It had been a while since she'd last come to him like this.

"Of course." Demon closed his book as he got up. He placed it on his desk, before walking back to the bed, sliding in toward the wall.

Jennifer kicked off her sneakers, putting them next to the desk. She unbuttoned her jeans, and slid them off, folding them once, letting them hang on the chair nearby. She noted the dirt and grime on them. She should probably wear her sweats from her locker tomorrow when she headed out. She removed her shirt and folded it, placing it on top of her pants. She climbed into the small twin bed with Demon and got settled as he reached to turn off the light. He scooted forward, wrapping his body behind hers. He reached his muscular arm around her small waist and she shivered from the coolness of his skin. Due to his vampire nature, he never radiated heat like a normal person. Jennifer tried to make herself more comfortable. She was annoyed with herself for feeling so weird. This was Demon; they'd spent a hundred nights together.

Demon began to kiss her neck. His lips were cold like the rest of him, but his kisses were soft and welcoming. His hand slid down her thigh. Instead of the usual excitement she felt from his touch, she felt withdrawn. She tried to brush off the feeling and pressed her lips into his while he caressed her body tenderly. Again, it felt wrong; a small voice in the back of her head screamed at her to stop. They weren't "*officially*" together anymore, but when they needed it, they would meet up like this. However, tonight, it wasn't what she needed. At least not from him.

She let go of Demon, and pulled away from his embrace. He raised a questioning brow at her, surprised by her sudden change of mood.

"I'm sorry...not tonight." Jennifer kissed him on the forehead and rolled away from him.

"Alright. If that's what you want." Demon wrapped his arms around her. He held her until she fell asleep.

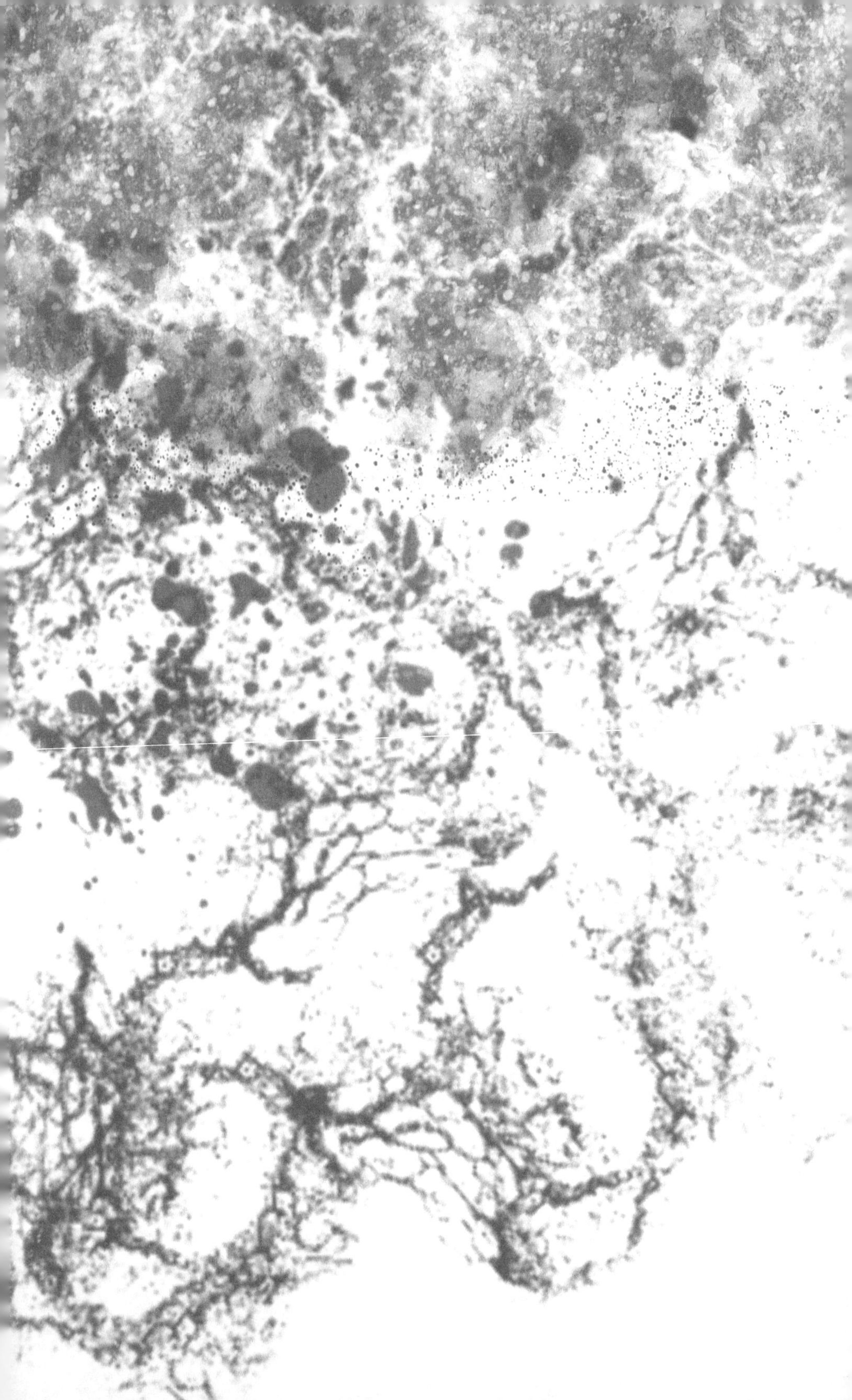

Jeff shot up in bed, his body covered in sweat. The images of his dream; no, distorted memories of last night flashed before his eyes. He had showered when he'd made it home, but he could still smell the putrid smell of death. He took in a shaky breath as the room swam back into focus.

Last night? What? Was that real? Did that really happen?

Jeff wiped the grogginess from his eyes. What time was it? His digital clock flashed on his bed stand. Noon. He sniffed his sweaty armpit. Another shower was definitely needed.

When he was done, he checked his phone. Two missed calls. One from Adam, the other from Jennifer. Suddenly his phone vibrated as a text came in.

> Hey, I know you had a lot of revelations last night, but where are you? You said you would be swinging by my dojo today to begin your training. Get back to me.

He forgot he had agreed to call her when he got up. He really didn't plan on sleeping so late. He was lucky that he had no work for the next couple of days because Jennifer wanted him in one of her beginner classes so she could start teaching him the basic movements of her fighting style.

Jeff ran to his room and threw on some gym clothes. He decided to wear his flip-flops, because if he was doing martial arts, it was the least amount of work to become barefoot. He grabbed his gym bag, shoving in an extra set of clothes with a clean towel. Jeff's stomach growled loudly as he zipped shut the bag. He could probably stop by a Starbucks on the way in to grab a quick egg sandwich and coffee. As he was just out the door, another text came in.

> Meet me at the Silver Bullet for orientation and training when you feel like gracing me with your presence.

The fact their secret base was under a bar was crazy. Jeff tried to remember how to get there. He had used his phone to get home last night, so he didn't remember the way. If the bar had been a legitimate business, he could have searched his maps app for the location.

Sure enough, there it was. His fingers hovered over the text field as he struggled to think of what to say back to Jennifer. Sorry I'm late? Overslept with nightmares? Probably not a good idea. He settled for, *on my way*, as he ran out of his apartment.

When Jeff arrived at the bar, there were barely fewer cars in the parking lot than the night before.

He grabbed his bag and walked inside. Now that he had more of his senses working, he could smell old pizza and stale peanuts in the atmosphere of the dark room. There were some customers eating lunch over a beer at the bar. A few others were spread around the room, nursing half empty pints. He didn't know what he should say or do. Should he get a table and wait for Jennifer, or should he just ask the bartender? He pondered how many people worked in the bar and actually knew the nightmarish experiments and maze-like corridors directly beneath them.

Are you stupid? Of course they do. They're probably the elite first guard to the base you idiot!

Jeff walked up to the bar, tightly clutching the strap of his bag across his chest. The pretty southern belle bartender from the night before was gone. Instead, there was a large, burly, biker-looking man cleaning the bar top. He was balding, but the white hair he did have left was pulled into a short ponytail. He looked up at Jeff questioningly as he approached, twitching his large gray mustache that blended into his long white beard.

"Can I help you kid?" His voice was as gruff as his features.

"Um, yeah. I'm waiting for a friend. I mean...um...manager? Uh, Jennifer...Jennifer Mayer?"

The man let out an acknowledging grunt and dived behind the bar to dig something out. He pulled out a black leather bill holder that had seen better days and slid it over to Jeff.

"Your card that you left here last night. Must be our new *dishwasher*. The name's Ralph. Jen said you can head in back. Don't lose this again kid." Ralph winked at him and walked down the bar to handle the new customers that had walked in.

Dishwasher?

Jeff opened up the binder; inside lay a lime green and black card similar to the one Jennifer had used yesterday. The card was blank except for the large numeral "0" printed on the front. He took it out of the binder and walked around the bar to the back. There were more staff. They looked at him suspiciously. Nervously, Jeff flashed the card up and pointed to the walk-in pantry that Jennifer took him to last night. The crew turned away as they continued to work in the kitchen.

Inside the pantry, Jeff walked to the back shelf.

How did she get this to move last night?

He remembered Jennifer stood by the fuse box. His hands slid around it, searching until a small button hidden from view brushed his fingers. A small click. The shelf moved away, but the hidden door was still locked. Jeff sighed, and opened the door of the panel, only to be greeted by the normal array of switches. The card reader...where? Jeff shut the panel and began his search again, starting at the button. A fine line break in the metal of the box was off. He tugged on it, revealing the card reader. Jeff swiped the card from his pocket, and the light flashed from red to green. He hoisted his bag, and stepped through to the stairwell. Goosebumps rose on his arms as he walked down the cool passage without Jennifer, each step echoing back loudly in his ears. A solitary steel door stood firmly at the bottom, built into the unmovable cavern walls.

Great, how am I supposed to get in here? I don't have a retinal scan...

Jeff examined the door to see if he could get lucky and find an alternative lock, or maybe even a buzzer system to notify the occupants he had arrived. He checked the box Jennifer had used to scan her eye last night—nothing. After about five minutes, a male voice, which sounded very familiar, boomed through a hidden sound system.

"You could have just knocked you know. We would have seen you there sooner." The disembodied male voice chuckled into the chasm.

Jeff looked up to see a camera above the door pointed down at him.

"Sorry, I've only been here once before."

"No problem. Do me a favor and hold up that card Ralph gave you upstairs toward the camera so I can confirm your identity."

Jeff did as instructed. The tiny mechanisms of the machine adjusted its aperture as it focused on the card. There was a soft click as a blue light flicked on under the camera. The front of the card illuminated, revealing Jeff's name and driver's license photo.

"Whoa..."

"Alright, come on in Mr. Knight. Come down the hall to the left to the security wing so we can finish setting up your credentials."

The heavy locks clanked open on the steel door again, followed by the same air lock as it released. Jeff pulled on the heavy door and walked into the main corridor. The base was much busier than last night. There were a mix of people scurrying hurriedly along the halls, different groups in different attire. Some wore business clothes and lab coats, carrying various documents in their hands or tablets. Others were dressed in military tactical garb, each set a different color: royal blue, forest green, or black.

He headed down the hall as instructed until he saw a sign that read *"Security,"* with an arrow that directed him further down the corridor. He followed the path until he approached a door labeled, *"Security Office."* He knocked on the door softly, and a man with red hair and freckled skin, sporting a tactical uniform in royal blue, answered the door.

Is everyone in this place young?

"Good, you made it!" Jeff recognized the voice from the camera. "My name's Christopher Thompson, but you can call me Chris. This is my partner Hallie Walker."

A small blonde behind him leaned back in her chair and waved.

"Wait...Chris and Hallie...are you two?"

"93.9xfl radio personalities?" Chris grinned wide.

"Yep!" Hallie chirped in happily. "That over there is Gary, but you probably know him as DJ DirtyKnuckles."

Jeff turned, seeing a third person that he'd missed before, a middle-aged balding man with coke bottle glasses. He waved briefly, a vacant expression on his face. He turned back to his computer with his headphones back on.

"We use a stand-in at events. I imagine a lot of our audience would be as surprised as you are. Besides, he's really shy. But he does some damn good mixes," Chris chuckled.

"Uh yeah..." Jeff gazed nervously back at Hallie and Chris' happy faces. "Um, is there a reason that you guys are on the radio every night?"

"Well, we actually were DJs before we got recruited," Chris answered proudly.

"Remember the *club fire* in Ybor from three years ago?" Hallie asked as she walked over to the nearby printer and picked up some documents.

"Yeah..." Jeff vaguely remembered hearing a report of one of the clubs burning. The whole block was supposedly shut down as they tried to contain the flames.

"It wasn't a fire," Hallie stated as she handed the papers over to Chris. "It was zombies. Someone got bit before going in the club. Z.E.R.O came and cleaned up...Chris and I were the only survivors."

"So we got recruited, and offered to use our medium to help with spreading disinformation when needed, and provide warnings, like the PD announcement last night to try to deter people from going out." Chris put the papers in a folder and then stuck them in a bin near the door.

"You said recruited...is this place run by the government?"

Hallie laughs, "Not exactly...I mean, the organization is as old as this country—"

"But we don't really answer to what you know as the government..." Chris finished her sentence. "You'll learn all about it. So, anyway...nice to meet you." Chris stretched out his hand to Jeff to shake.

"Uh, same..." Jeff shook his hand hesitantly, still struggling to process the idea that a secret military existed beneath the government. "My name's—"

"Jeffrey Knight. We know who you are. Alright, I heard the Lieutenant Commander gave you a tour last night, so that will save time." Chris stepped back, letting Jeff into the small room, "This here is our security hub. We monitor the base and outside. We pretty much run the facility cameras all day and are the first line of defense."

"Lieutenant Commander?" Jeff couldn't make out who that was. He had met Demon and Sentinel the previous night, but Jennifer was the only one who had shown him around.

"Jennifer, or Phoenix, as you will be calling her when in the field, *sir*." Hallie responded.

"Oh...Oh!"

She's Lieutenant Commander?!

"Yeah, and she asked us to get your clearance taken care of pronto. So we need to get that done." Chris led Jeff out of the office a couple doors further down the hall. "You must have made quite an impression. No one has ever made it into Alpha Team right off the street before. Well, not for a while anyway." Chris opened the door to a small office with an eye exam device sitting on a desk, with a pretty ordinary industrial stackable chair on one side of it, a weathered office chair on wheels on the other. The cheap seat looked uncomfortable, made of hard plastic bolted to a metal frame.

"Really?"

"Yeah, Hallie and I were civilians until a few years ago, you know, doing radio. We got put onto Charlie team. Can't say I can complain. I'd rather be sitting with computers all day than hunting out there. We are still able to do what we love too. Besides, only family blood lines usually make it on the hunter teams."

Jeff got an uneasy feeling in his stomach. Maybe Charlie team would have been a better choice for him than Alpha. Chris pointed for him to sit at one end of the eye device sitting on the desk between them and instructed him to lean his head in.

"Alright, we're gonna make an image capture of your retina so you can access the base. Now it won't work in our level four securities. That's only for commanding officers, but you will have access to what you need while training."

"I heard Bravo Team mentioned last night. What do they do?"

"They are the people that want to be Alpha and are only allowed on the field under strict supervision. They aren't skilled or level headed enough to really handle what Alpha does. They're not really my type of people. A lot of loose cannons, children of former generals wanting special treatment. They mostly get restricted to clean-up work by Alpha."

"Oh."

Chris typed in a few things in the computer connected to the device. A blue LED came on. He positioned himself in the eyelets on the other side.

"Alright, I'm gonna take an image. Try not to blink, I'm gonna get very close with this thing. Try to focus on the blue light."

Jeff hated eye exams. The light came slowly toward his eye, blinding his vision with royal blue hues. As his long lashes brushed near the light, he struggled not to blink in response.

"And done!" Chris jumped back and entered some more data into the PC. "Alright, so you should be able to get in now."

Chris rolled back in his chair and opened a drawer in the nearby desk with a key he had on his neck. He pulled out an earpiece and a small key on a chain.

"What's that for?"

"This is your access to the hunting weapons lockers. It's a master key, all Alpha team members have unmonitored access. Keep it on your person at all times." He handed it over to Jeff and held up the earpiece. "And this is your communication with the base and your team when out in the field. Please don't lose this, it's very expensive."

Jeff nodded, placing the earpiece in his pocket and the chain around his neck. His mind flashed back to Jennifer. Now that he thought about it, she also had a chain around her neck with a key.

"So now what?"

"That's it, you're done. The Lieutenant Commander wants you to meet her in the training room. It's just past the lockers. You know the way?"

"Yeah, vaguely."

Chris patted Jeff on the back and led him back to the main elevator.

"Just take it down to floor B3 and follow the signs. Looking forward to working with you *sir*."

"Why do you and Hallie keep calling me sir?"

"Because technically you out-rank us."

"How? I just got here." Jeff felt even more uncomfortable. How did he outrank someone who had already been with the organization for three years?

"Well, you're on Alpha Team. They're the highest position you can get in the base. Remember what I said. Everyone wants to be on Alpha." Chris laughed. "I prefer Charlie. I'm not fit to hunt monsters. We're technically the lowest rank, even though we handle most of the base's security. So as long as you are on Alpha, you are higher up than me. Now you better hurry to your training, *sir*."

Chris waved good bye, leaving Jeff alone in the corridor. He was barely in the door and already had people that answered to him. He wasn't used to being higher up on the totem pole. He walked down the hall, following Chris' directions.

Jeff stepped into the crowded elevator. There were only three levels to this base, which was not surprising because this was Florida. There was nothing but sand everywhere, so buildings didn't have basements. It was usually too unstable with the shifting environment to build below ground. This base must have taken a lot of work to be reinforced enough to keep from collapsing.

When the elevator stopped on floor B2, most of the business attired and lab coat-wearing people stepped off. What kind of experiments did they perform here? The heavy airlock door suddenly made sense in line with every viral outbreak movie he'd seen—do whatever it takes to keep the pathogens from reaching the public.

When he reached the bottom floor, he tried to retrace his steps down the hallways back to the locker room. He peeked into some of the rooms on his walk through.

Eventually he found what seemed to be a records room. There were a few computers on a series of desks with an adjoining room full of boxes. Further down, he found an empty room, except for one chair sitting in the center. It looked like a make-shift interrogation room. Jeff heard the small pop of gunshots in the distance. He followed the sound to a shooting range with three or four soldiers practicing. Jeff took a minute to get his bearings. He must have made a wrong turn. He began to head back the way he came when Demon popped out from around the corner. His dark skin appeared gray and ashy compared to hours earlier.

"Are you okay?" Jeff jogged over to him.

"Oh, hello." Demon raised an eyebrow over his dark sunglasses upon recognizing Jeff, "Yeah I'm fine. Like I said last night, daytime makes me weak. It's like being exhausted to the point of nausea. You would think after a few hundred years I would be used to it by now."

"A few hundred years? How old are you?"

"Don't you know it's rude to ask someone their age?" Demon smiled at Jeff, but it was labored as Demon progressively looked more ill.

"What are you doing up then?"

"Had some research to get done." He pointed to the files in his hands. "What are you doing here so early?"

"Jen told me I would start training today, but it seems like I can't find my way back to the locker room."

"Ah, follow me, I'll take you there." Demon turned and walked back down the hall toward the shooting range again.

"Thanks." Jeff walked silently behind him clutching his bag strap.

"Is there something you wanted to ask me?" Demon kept looking forward as he spoke.

"Oh. Well um, why do they call you Demon? Seems everyone has a call sign related to what they do here."

"Let's just say that I have a past I'm not too proud of. I am far enough from human that Demon is more appropriate."

Jeff opened his mouth to ask a follow up but no words came. He continued to walk in silence behind Demon.

What kind of history could he have that was so bad he got the moniker of Demon?

"You don't have to be scared of me. I have been watching over this team for four generations. This is my family now and you are my new brother." Demon came to a halt. Jeff couldn't read Demon's expression through his sunglasses.

"I'm sorry. This is all still just a lot to process. You barely know me and everyone has been so nice."

"Be wary of some of the people that you speak to here. We may all be on the side of humanity, but different people have different ideas of what that means." Demon's eyes had a slight yellow glow as they peered over his sunglasses. "And we've arrived. Sentinel and I got your locker set up already. You'll get your call sign printed on it once we have an idea of who you're gonna be."

Demon opened the door to the locker room. Jeff walked through the row of lockers, until he found one labeled "J. Knight." Demon waved goodbye at the door. Jeff turned back to his locker. Inside were some more sweats with the organization logo, body armor, and a uniform similar to the one Demon and Sentinel had worn the previous night. On the sleeve of the shirt was the Z.E.R.O Insignia with a small moniker of Alpha team stitched below it. He put the earpiece he was given in the pocket of his tactical vest and slid his gym bag in the locker. He took off his flip flops, and tossed them in the bottom. Maybe he could get some stretching done before Jennifer arrived.

He shut his locker and walked into the training room at the other end. The floor was covered in gray mats and there was an array of weapons on the wall. He walked over, observing the collection of training staves, blades, knives, and swords. He picked up one of the small knives, which had a hole large enough for a finger at the end of the hilt, and held it in his hand. The hilt was wrapped in leather, which added more weight and balance to the double-edged blade. Jeff examined the lining, and noted a small silver edging. He slipped his finger through the hole on the end, and started spinning the small knife in his hands. He hadn't held one of these in years: a kunai. He started running through routines, and flipping it back and forth between his hands. He didn't hear the door open behind him.

"So you are all set with security?" Jennifer's voice startled him. The knife was already in the air and on its way down. He was going to miss it. Jennifer's hand caught the knife right in front of his face, about an inch from his button-shaped nose. Jennifer had a twinkle in her dark eyes as she smiled coyly upon seeing the look of bewilderment spread across him.

"Um...thanks. Heh..." Jeff scratched the back of his head nervously as Jennifer replaced the knife with the collection. "Yeah, it was no problem."

"Good, because starting today, you will train with me in my dojo for an hour while I teach my other classes, then we'll come here and I will teach you to defend yourself from creatures other than zombies. You are also going to study past D-Day events and other supernatural cases we have covered." Jeff began to protest, but Jennifer held up her finger. "And finally you will be doing firearm training and coming with me on field gardening expeditions."

"And I'm doing this all today?"

"Everyday that we can. You aren't getting paid until we take you out of our probationary period, and you need to keep up appearances with your normal life while we create your cover and transition. We'll work around your schedule the best we can."

Jeff sighed internally. This was not going to be as fun as he'd hoped...

***

Jennifer found herself home, but it felt wrong. Her brain rationalized this was her condo, but at the same time it was like her memories were trying to show her a different place. One that she left five years ago. She heard the humming of a man in her upstairs bedroom. She pulled herself up from the chair and let out a labored breath. She felt...heavy?

She looked down at her white thin nightgown and her round swollen stomach. She smiled as she felt the familiar kicks beneath her skin. She rubbed her hands over it. A joy she hadn't experienced for many days filled her heart as she walked toward the humming sound at the top of the stairs. She pushed open the door. There was a man standing there, with his back toward her. A figure that she longed for. He continued to hum while he cradled something in his arms.

Jennifer's gown felt wet and warm. She looked down to see her pregnant stomach was gone, replaced with blood and pain. Her hands were red with blood.

"Did we wake you love?" The thick Irish accent rushed to her ears. A voice forgotten. "Are you done resting?"

The man placed whatever was in his arms in the bassinet in front of him and turned toward Jennifer. She held her breath. She had not thought of him in so long. Her heart raced. She longed to see his smooth, chiseled jawline, his dark brows that contrasted with his light green eyes. His soft pink lips, that had met hers so many times.

If only her dreams could reward her more than her life. The man turned toward her. His perfect face was slashed and scared. His green eyes were clouded. She wanted to reach for him.

"Jenny...I'm sorry."

"Conor!" Jennifer shot up in bed. Her heart beat furiously in her chest. She felt like she had fallen from the sky and crashed back into her body. She looked over at Demon who had rolled over in his sleep, barely making a sound.

Jennifer glanced at the time on her watch. It was still early Saturday morning. She had only slept for four hours.

"Shit..." She looked down at her shaking hands, no longer covered in blood. She felt her flat stomach, as the tears began to well in her eyes. Jennifer shook her head, breathing in a deep breath. "Just a dream..."

She slid out of bed and dressed as quietly as she could. She watched as Demon grumbled softly again as he moved to fill the whole bed space. She grabbed a piece of paper off the desk, writing a quick apology note as she gave him one last look before finally sneaking out the door.

She figured she would go back to her place and shower rather than use the one here at the base. Maybe grab a bagel for breakfast while she was out too. She still taught classes every weekend. Her more advanced students were in the morning and her intermediate classes after that. She liked training civilians on how to defend themselves from monsters, even if they didn't know what she was training them for. Like her father, she felt that the more that people knew, the safer they would be. Jennifer was lucky Hammer and her uncle were able to vouch for her when the board of High Commanders had objected.

It didn't take her long to shower and change. When she waited in line at the bagel shop, she looked at the time and her messages. Nothing from Jeff yet. She wasn't sure if he would really be coming back. He still seemed to be in a bit of a daze when he'd left. She knew where he lived already, as she had run a background check on him. She contemplated if she should stop by, just to make sure he'd made it home alright.

Yeah and look like a crazy stalker... Real smart thinkin' there Jennifer...

She pulled up her contact list. Maybe she should just call him. She contemplated if she should really be the one to train him. If she trained him, she was sure she could get him in the field within the next three months, rather than leave him to the training class they did with Bravo recruits. She wanted to make sure he learned everything right the first time. Jennifer bit her lip and pressed call.

She swallowed back the dryness in her mouth as the phone rang in her ear. She couldn't tell if she was actually worried about him, or if it was something else causing her anxiety. She had been off since she'd woken up today. It rang a few more times before she heard his voicemail pick up.

"Hey, you reached Jeff, sorry I can't get to the phone right now. Just leave a message. I'll get back to you."

She would try again later. She grabbed her bagel and headed off to her class. She had some aggravation she needed to get out. Sparring with her students would help.

Her class was pretty uneventful. It was the end of summer vacation. A lot of her younger students hadn't return yet from their getaways. Her older pupils were college students finishing summer classes, or working new schedules in their part-time jobs. Florida was a transitory state that had seasons revolving around two age groups. The young families in the summer and the older "Snow Birds" in the winter. Jennifer didn't care for the latter.

In between her morning classes she went to her office and checked her phone. There were no new calls or messages from Jeff. She was a little annoyed by his lack of communication. He *had* agreed to join her organization. You would think he would have tried to contact her to find out when training started. Jennifer tossed her phone on her desk, and picked up a pencil nearby. She started to work on her schedule for the next few weeks.

She tapped her pencil on her desk at the same rate her foot hit the floor. The analog clock ticked annoyingly in the corner of the room. Jennifer dropped the pencil and stared at the black screen of her phone.

Just text him...

She picked up her phone, typing a quick message to him. She gazed intently as the loading circle next to the message rotated, until she received the confirmation it was sent. There was a soft knock at her door and Jennifer dropped her phone on her desk.

"Come in." Jennifer looked up, curious to which of her students it was. In came one of her intermediate level students, Abby. She was ten years old. Her father was one of

Jennifer's more advanced pupils and she had started training Abby when she was six. Jennifer didn't teach many children. Kids made her nervous. The few young students she had were the exception. Ideally, she would like to have more if she could get over her awkwardness talking to them.

"Hello, Master Mayer...are we still having class today?" She shyly asked as she played with her fingers. Jennifer noted the time on the clock. Class should have started about ten minutes ago.

"How many people are here?" Jennifer asked her as she got up to check through the blinds.

"Just me, Billy, and Devon." The girl peeked out the same crack in the blinds. Jennifer saw her two other students that had shown up. Billy was a kid a little younger than this girl, who definitely had a lot of energy to get out everyday. It was probably why his mother so willingly signed him up for this strange class. Devon, on the other hand, was a freshman in college, trying to find something to fill his time with while he waited for the new college semesters to begin.

"I don't think so. I wanted to run drills with you guys today. I needed more of you. We'll have to reschedule...I'm sorry Abby." Jennifer sighed and turned toward her protege. "Do you need a ride home?"

"No, Billy's mom can take me."

"Okay. Can you do me a favor and tell them?"

"Sure!" Abby smiled and Jennifer gave her a high five.

Abby stepped out of the office and Jennifer watched as she informed the other two students that class was canceled. She saw the look of disappointment on the youngest and the *"whatever"* shoulder shrug of the older student. She waited for them to leave before stepping out and killing the lights on her dojo. She locked the door as she went back to her office. Today wasn't going to be a complete waste of time. She was a good teacher, she knew she was. She was going to train Jeff. She walked back to her phone. Looks like Jeff had seen her first message, but hadn't replied.

Is he trying to ghost me?

She sent him a second text. He read it right away. She sat down biting her lip again as she bounced her right leg up and down from her toes. The writing *dots* shot up on her phone, signifying him replying. It buzzed on the screen, but then stopped. After another minute the dots appeared again for a few more seconds. Finally a new message arrived.

"Okay. See you there."

She caught herself smiling to the point it hurt her cheeks. She hadn't trained a recruit in a while. Her anxiousness before was probably jitters. She organized the paperwork in her office and headed out to the base. The drive took her a little longer than she was hoping, but she wasn't concerned. The sun was bright in the blue sky, and there were no clouds so the weather was actually pleasant. She left instructions for the staff about getting him oriented.

The parking lot had the usual amount of cars for the daytime. When Jennifer arrived she noted the Charlie Team members who sat as plain clothes civilians in the bar in case any maleficent intruders mixed among their "normal" local patrons. All faces that entered the bar were scanned and processed through the Z.E.R.O and government systems. If there was a flag, it was sent within seconds to one of the Charlie officers in the bar to take action. Ralph nodded to Jennifer when she came in.

"New kid came by. Sent him downstairs to Chris," Ralph gruffed as he went back to making his rounds around their dining area.

"Thanks, Ralph." Jennifer headed back into the pantry.

She walked straight for the training room, building a training syllabus around Jeff's needs. He was a blank slate as far as she was concerned. Firearms Training? His paintball skills left much to be desired. Fight training? Not bad. Maybe she could start teaching him some lycan techniques. Werewolves could be challenging, so the sooner he learned that the—

Jennifer turned the last corner and bumped into a cold hard mass. She began to fall backwards, but was stopped by an arm around her waist. She looked up to see what she had run into, only to see Demon smiling down at her.

"You don't change. When you're lost in thought, you don't watch where you're going." Demon chuckled as he helped her balance on her feet again.

"Sorry." Jennifer adjusted her bag on her shoulder. "Was trying to figure out my training schedule for our new recruit."

"You mean Knight? So you are training him." Demon's tone was flat. She couldn't tell what he was implying by that statement. He was probably mad about last night.

"Yes I am. Why? Is that a problem?" She crossed her arms. He seemed taken aback by her reaction, but his body relaxed and he was less defensive as he answered.

"No...uh, I was just surprised." He picked up his sunglasses that had fallen on the floor. "You haven't trained anyone for a while. It's usually given to Bravo."

He was right. She hadn't been involved in training any new recruits for about three and a half years now. She had trained the recruits when she'd first transferred into the base five years ago, but had handed it off to the Bravo Team commander after a few months. Maybe that was part of the problem with the Bravo Team soldiers and their lack of discipline in the field.

"I want him on our team as soon as possible." She uncrossed her arms. "That's all it is." She looked up into his eyes again. She could tell he hadn't eaten yet today; his skin was ashy, and his eyes had a faint yellow glow. He only used sunglasses when it was dark or if he was hungry because the dark lenses hid his predatory eyes when they began to shine. "About last night."

"Don't worry about it." Demon put his sunglasses on, making his face harder for her to read. "We're not together. Just friends with benefits." He smiled coyly at her. She used to fall so easily for that smile.

"Yeah…" She shifted her weight, adjusting her bag on her shoulder again.

"Well I'm going to get something to eat, and head back to sleep before I puke. If you need anything, let me know." Demon began to head toward the break room, where he kept his blood bags.

"Demon, wait!" She jogged up to him. "I never got to ask. The *Tenebre Orbis*, did they agree to a meeting?"

"No." Demon's body became rigid again, "I told the local coven leaders in the council meeting about our higher numbers of undead, but *Orcus* has their ear. The council will not bring it to the *Tenebre Orbis* unless we have more proof we are in a D-Day event. Of course, Orcus was very pleased with himself when they took his suggestion to wait."

"Dammit. I'm sorry I made you go to that meeting." Jennifer bit her lip. Demon was fully excommunicated from his coven about seventy-five years ago due to false accusations and internal politics. Sending him to plead for help from the *Tenebre Orbis,* the high vampire council, was risky but she was sure they would need more help. She had to think of another way to get more aid.

"Well, on the bright side, they extended my banishment another fifty years. Seems like you are stuck with me." Demon smiled and kissed Jennifer on the forehead. "Your recruit is waiting for you." He lingered for a moment, gazing at her, before he walked on.

What's done is done. He's right. We're not together anymore, and that was my decision. What I'm doing with him is cruel. Maybe we shouldn't visit each other anymore…

She sighed and continued to the training room. The space was empty. Not a soul could be seen despite the current level of occupation the base had today. She walked over to her locker and noticed Jeff's name on the one across from hers. The door was shut but a strap from a gym bag dangled on the outside. She put her bag away and tied her hair back into a high ponytail. She really should just cut it, but she had never liked how she looked with shorter hair.

She walked toward the training room and peeked in the windows. Jeff was in there, playing with a kunai, a short black dagger laced with silver, to be a more effective monster killer. His hair was curling and seemed a little damp. He must have rushed over after she'd texted him earlier. She smiled and opened the door to the training room.

"So you are all set with security?"

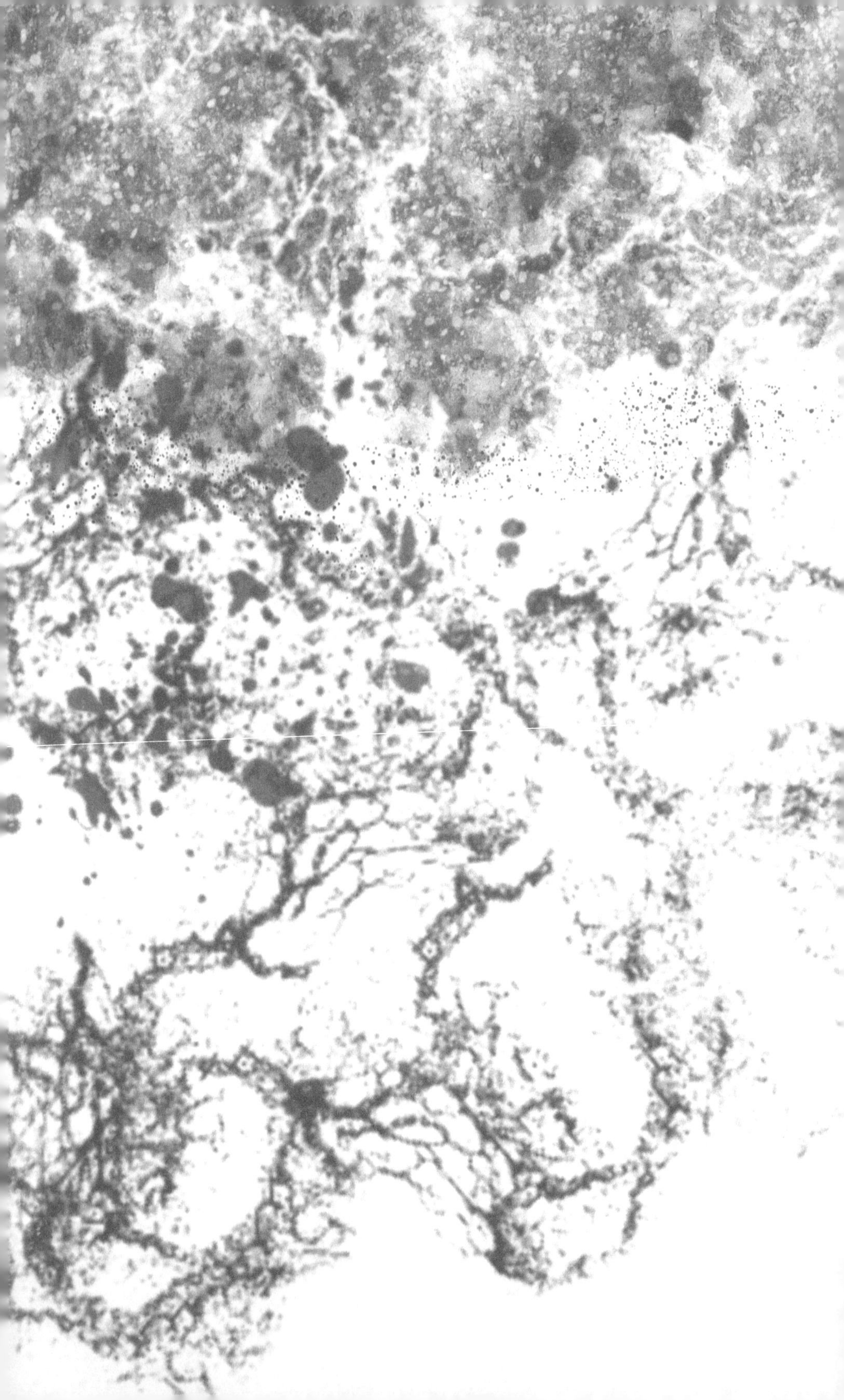

CHapTer 6

The next few weeks went by quickly. The training Jennifer put Jeff through was brutal, especially when she trained him in the different combat styles for various creatures. She started with lycans combat, which encouraged using distance to avoid their fangs. Jennifer had him train with pole arms made of a long wood that felt light in his hands, but heavy every time she smacked him with it. Despite how much faster he would get each day, Jennifer always managed to knock him on his ass.

"Get up." Jennifer stood over him, barely breaking a sweat. "You're never going to be able to handle a pack of werewolves if you leave yourself open like that all the time."

Jeff wiped the sweat off his brow, "Don't suppose we can just give them a bone or throw a stick?" He laughed, but Jennifer showed no amusement.

She banged her rod onto the ground. "Again."

On occasional evenings, Jennifer would take him for "field training" in the local cemeteries. She always took him to the small, older plots, where the headstones had seen better days. Their stone etchings had faded from years of salt water air and hurricane force winds. Only a few seemed modern and well maintained. Jennifer walked up to a headstone and kneeled down next to it. She pointed to what appeared to be scratches in the shape of a cross at the back of the stone, near the grass line, hidden from the view.

"You see this?"

"Yeah, what is that?"

"It means that this guy isn't gettin' back up. We go through the cemeteries making sure that all the residents have been taken care of, and when we're done, we mark the graves. It keeps the numbers down so we can handle a crisis event. We call it *'gardening.'*" Jennifer laughed at her term for disposing of reanimating corpses. "We don't know what causes some to rise and others to not, so we just do this to them all to make sure."

Usually after martial arts training, she had him research the paranormal. Which wasn't as exciting as you'd expect.

Jennifer sat him down at one of the small rows of computers in the records room. There was a projector system in the center of the office space. Along the walls of the adjoining room were rows of shelves with boxes piled on top of them and a set of filing cabinets crowded together.

"Homework. You need to know how to handle any supernatural thing you come across." Jennifer pulled up some files on the computer for him.

"How much is there?"

"Well, we document every encounter we've had with any creature. This computer currently stores everything starting from 1960. The room over there has everything else we haven't scanned in yet. Considering we were founded around the same time as America...you can guess how much there is. Have fun." She roughed up his hair, a wide smile on her face as she walked out.

Jeff leaned back in his chair and blew out a deep breath. He sat for a moment, silent, as he scanned the empty room before he closed his eyes. Jennifer's rose perfume lingered in the air. He fixed his hair and smiled.

"Alright, let's get started." Jeff cracked his neck, pulling up closer to the screen to begin reading.

The supernatural incidents were monotone as regular police reports. Jeff's eyes glazed over as the words blurred together on the screen.

The firing range was one of the highlights of training. Jeff used to go shooting occasionally with Adam when they had the extra cash to rent a gun at the range, but this was something else entirely.

Jennifer taught him to concentrate his shots around the head, contrary to how most people are taught to target the larger center mass. More specifically, she wanted him to target the front temporal region above the eyes. Jeff was used to shooting off .22s as they were usually pretty cheap, but Z.E.R.O used 9mms. They weren't that much larger, but the change in size had a stronger effect on the recoil when he fired. His hands would move with every shot, making firing consecutive shots in the small cluster Jennifer wanted difficult.

Jeff focused his aim on the head of the silhouette target. He fired nine shots in a row, feeling the singe of the bullet cases as they popped out of the gun and hit his arm. When the gun clicked empty, Jennifer moved to his side, and hit the button that recalled the target back to them. Jeff cringed as the sheet came closer into view. Four of his shots had met their designated target; the rest were in the white space bordering the silhouette.

"Seriously, Knight? If you encounter a horde you need to take out as many as you can with one magazine before they get too close. With this crap shooting you would be lucky to hit one moving target." Jennifer tore down the sheet and put up a new one. "Again."

"Again?" Jeff looked at her exasperated. "We've been at this for hours!"

"Again." She said it coldly, sending the goosebumps up his neck. She flicked the switch and sent the target down the line. Days like this infuriated him. She was relentless.

The daytime hours were just as grueling. To keep up appearances, Jeff retained his old part-time job at the mall as a retail clothes assistant. If there was a Hell on Earth, it was retail. Angry customers returning products received as gifts from friends or family. The constant question of stock that doesn't exist in back rooms. The adult tantrums when things don't go in the customer's favor.

Maybe a zombie apocalypse wouldn't be so bad, if it meant out of this hell.

Jeff often found himself drifting off at work. Daydreaming about sleep, ironically. Before this new life, he would work for six to eight hours, maybe hit the gym for an hour after, and then go home to watch re-runs of *Chuck* and play through *Resident Evil 4* for the hundredth time. Now, he was lucky if he got three hours of sleep. His PlayStation was acting more like a giant paper weight, and his muscles were so sore, he could barely move. His growing six pack was definitely a plus, however, he was exhausted and didn't know how much longer he could keep this up.

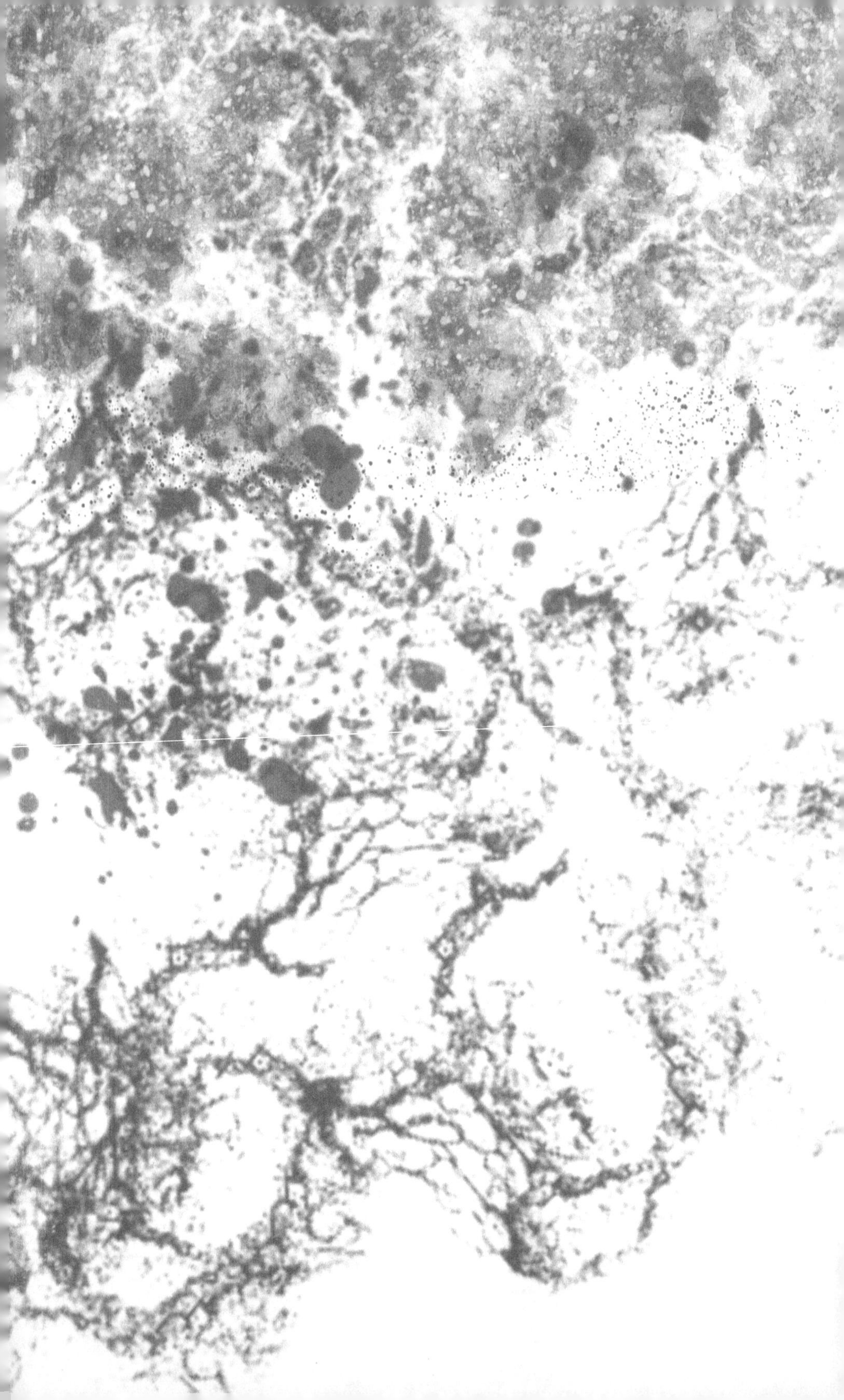

CHapTer 7

Weeks flashed by in an endless loop of repeating events. Get his ass handed to him in the morning by Jennifer, suffer through his work schedule, followed by late excursions into the various cemeteries in the area, and reading old paranormal encounter reports when they didn't go out.

The most difficult part of leading a double life was not being able to tell his best friend Adam anything. He had to lie to Adam, explaining he got a second job working night security through Jennifer's company. The disappointment in Adam's face every time he turned him down was getting harder to deal with. Jeff never liked liars, and here he was turning into a master one.

On the other hand, he was spending more time with Jennifer. She didn't say much about herself in their time together, but she didn't need to. If she shared anything personal with him, he valued it.

After training, she usually had some sort of takeout food waiting for them. It was these quiet moments between their meals when he got to know her more. She had no unhealthy greasy paper bags with her today though.

"Hey, I didn't bring anything to eat tonight. You want to go out? Take a quick break? You've been working really hard." Jennifer wiped the back of her neck with a towel as they put up the equipment. Her form-fitting gym clothes were covered in sweat. She picked up the long black swords they had been sparring with and placed them on the rack on the side of the room. The room was big enough to hold at least twenty people normally, but since it was only Jeff and Jennifer, they had a lot of space to run around and move around each other while they trained.

"Uh sure. Where do you want to go?" Jeff looked at the time, it was already after midnight. There wouldn't be much open. He lifted his shirt and wiped the moisture he felt dripping down his face. He was going to need to buy some more gym clothes. The few he had were wearing out with the constant regime.

"There's a twenty-four hour burger joint near here. They serve milkshakes too." She smiled and walked into the locker room. He followed her.

"Sure...uh, you wanna shower first?" Their shower room had multiple stalls, but Jeff had never had a co-ed room before. He didn't know the protocol. Usually Jennifer would hang back in the training room while he showered. He walked over to his locker and pulled his clothes from his bag.

"It's a Co-ed." she laughed. "If you're not comfortable with it, I can wait." She grabbed her toiletries out of her locker, setting them on the bench.

"Uh, no that's okay. I'll take the last stall." Jeff walked hastily into the showers. He moved fast through the door, slamming it shut behind him.

He stripped quickly, rushing into the stall before it reached its ideal temperature. They had no curtains for the stalls and the dividers weren't high. Jeff was six foot one. His head was just above the small divider, and he caught a glimpse of Jennifer as she entered. Only a towel around her body. She put her supplies in the caddy that hung over the shower, paying no attention to Jeff. He turned away and threw shampoo on his head. When he heard her water turn on, he snuck a glance back over. Her back was turned to him, and for the first time, he could see her tattoo in its entirety.

An image of a Phoenix ran down her right side. The head was on her neck, and it flowed down her shoulders, where the wings spread in mid lift for flight on her back. The body of the bird followed the contours of her body, the tail feathers wrapped up right at her waist and upper thigh. It was a highly detailed tattoo, monochromatic, only in shades of dark brown and black. Jennifer began to turn her body in his direction, and he looked away hastily, throwing more soap on his face. He scrubbed hard as his ears burned. His heart pounded hard in his chest. He felt guilty for peeking, and didn't want to come across as a creep.

They were friends now, and that was more than enough for Jeff. Sure, she was beautiful. And kind. And beautiful. But...she was his boss, and there was no way she saw him as anything more than a subordinate. He must've set the temperature too high, as his entire body turned a vibrant red. Jeff rinsed off quickly and grabbed his towel, hastily wrapping it around his waist.

"I'll meet you at the restaurant and grab a table." He stood with his back turned to her stall as he waited for a response.

"Oh okay...you know where it is?"

"Yeah, the one off Fletcher right?"

"Yep. I mean, I'm almost done; if you wanted to wait, we could ride together." Jeff heard the water splash against her body as she rinsed. His blood was pumping. He needed to cool off. Fast.

"That's okay. It's Friday night, they're probably going to be busy at this hour. I'll just head over. See you there." He tried to speed walk out before his curiosity made him do or say something he'd regret.

He dressed in his street clothes, his hair still dripping wet. He took a last glance at the door to the showers. The image of Jennifer's naked body filled his head again.

Think of something else you idiot...

He rushed to the restaurant to put some distance between Jennifer and his libido. As he thought, the place was packed for a Friday night. He waited in line for the hostess to arrive and seat him. She was a short old woman; her face was aged with time and her expression showed she had no craps left to give.

"How many?" Her voice was raspy like a heavy smoker.

"Uh, two?"

"Mhmmm..." The woman gazed at him suspiciously as she glanced at the available dining area. "I got a booth, that okay?"

"Yeah, booth will be fine." The woman pulled out two menus and continued to look unamused. She marched off to the dining area, stopping at a booth near the back. She tossed the menus on the table.

"Your server will be with you shortly." She groaned and went back to the front.

Jeff sat down and fiddled with the silverware on the table until he felt his phone vibrate in his pocket. There was a text message from Jennifer.

> Sorry, I'm coming now. Hammer grabbed me for something real quick. Can you get me a sweet tea and a mushroom Swiss burger with a cookies and cream milkshake?

He looked in amazement at the screen. Then again, they do burn a lot of carbs; he was peckish himself. Jeff replied and waited anxiously for her to arrive. This wasn't a date. It was just dinner with a colleague. He tapped his foot anxiously, until his server finally walked over. Like most of the employees in the area, it was a college student, but he looked like a kid. Jeff couldn't believe it had already been ten years since he'd graduated.

"Hi, my name is Nick. What can I get ya?"

Jeff gave him Jennifer's order, and added a cheeseburger meal and coke for himself.

"Hungry?" Nick asked sarcastically.

"Been a long day." Jeff tried to laugh it off, but knew his ears were still bright red.

The server walked off and Jeff glanced down at his watch. Jennifer said she was on her way and he needed to do something about his nerves. He looked around the restaurant. There were a lot of college students and a few late night workers looking for a meal. The hostess sat a father and son a couple of tables down. The kid looked tired as hell.

I feel ya kid.

Jeff's mind wandered back to when he was younger. His father used to take him out late like this, but it wasn't because they spent days having fun at the theme parks.

Jeff's eyes began to burn. He was surprised when he wiped away a warm tear. Staring at the kid with his dad had stirred up memories he hadn't thought of for a while. He looked away from the happy family, sniffling as he wiped his nose. He had to think of something else while he waited. He pulled out his phone again, and reviewed his game apps. They were all zombie survival related, of course. He chuckled and loaded one up.

Jennifer finally showed up about twenty minutes later, right as the server began placing the food on the table.

"Sorry about that. Thanks for ordering." Jennifer slid in the booth across from him.

"No problem, you made it just in time." He grabbed the ketchup dispenser and splattered it all over the inside of his bun. He swirled some more over his handful of fries.

He handed the ketchup over to Jennifer. She swirled a little onto her burger, and then placed it back on the counter. She started popping the plain fries in her mouth. He picked up his burger and took a large bite. He couldn't take his eyes off of her. She popped another fry into her mouth, but stopped when she noticed him staring at her. Her cheeks blushed slightly.

"Can I help you, Knight?"

"Oh, nothing." He popped one of his ketchup loaded fries into his mouth. "You eat your fries plain?"

"Yeah, they already have salt. They don't need anything else." Jennifer popped another fry in her mouth and looked over at Jeff's ketchup-soaked plate and laughed. "My sister used to put ketchup on everything, even scrambled eggs, and worse, my mother's *pasteles*."

"That does not sound appetizing." He chuckled, he couldn't imagine eating ketchup-covered scrambled eggs, and he had no idea what a *pa-steh-lays* was, but he was sure from her statement that it didn't go with ketchup.

"It wasn't." She picked up a knife and skillfully cut her burger in half, easily tearing through the thick flesh.

"You have a sister? Is she part of Z.E.R.O too?" Jeff took another bite of his burger. He regretted asking immediately as she dropped the knife loudly on her plate. The happy sparkle in her eyes vanished.

"HAD a sister. Victoria. We were about a year and a half apart. Which meant that we used to fight all the time." She smiled, but it wasn't happy. It was sad and longing. "That was a long time ago..."

They ate the rest of their meal in silence. Jeff had officially killed the good mood in the air. Like a cloud of darkness was hanging over her. He tried to change the subject.

"So, where are you from originally? You don't sound like you're from down here."

"I was born in New York, but lived in North Carolina most of my childhood. I was there for about six years." Jennifer bit her lip. "I want to be honest with you, but we still don't know each other that well—"

"No, that's alright. You don't have to te—" Jeff stopped when Jennifer held up her finger, motioning him to let her finish again.

"How about this? Seems like I'm always the one sharing. You share something about you, and I'll share something about me." Jennifer smiled warmly at him. It seemed fair.

"Sure. What do you want to know?"

"Well I told you about my sister...you got any siblings?"

"No, Adam is the closest thing I got to a brother. My parents...well uh..." Jeff looked into Jennifer's deep brown eyes. She was right; if he wanted to learn more about her, it was only fair he told her more about himself. "They divorced when I was ten. My dad was...well, he liked to drink. He uh...made life difficult for my mom and me until she was finally able to take us away from it."

He tried to gauge her reaction. Most people looked at him with pity when he spoke about his parents and childhood. She didn't, it was different. Like she understood, and he didn't have to explain more.

Jennifer fixed him with an intense gaze. "I uh, know how hard this job can be...do you think that will be a problem for you?" Her question caught him off guard. There was nothing condescending in her tone either. "It's just...what I'm saying is, we won't judge if it is."

"No...I never want to be like him." Jeff clenched his hands on the table. He had his father's anger, but he had kept that in check over the years with his martial arts, fueling that energy into something more productive. Jennifer took a quick sip of her soda. She either didn't see his reaction to that question, or had just chosen to ignore it.

"Fair is fair. I'll tell you a bit more about me...I lost my family when I was little. My parents...and my...little sister. Terry's...um...Hammer's family was close to mine, and took me in. Raised me." She paused, her eyes wandering, not focused on anything in front of them. "I try not to live in the past, and just aim to make a better future." She poked the top of her remaining burger with her finger, her eyes still void of emotion. Maybe speaking of his parents wasn't such a good idea.

"I'll do whatever I can to help you make that future." Jeff wanted to fix the evening. He struggled to find what to say next. "I've only been with Z.E.R.O for a few weeks, but you guys are really doing something amazing...I guess what I'm trying to say is, thank you for letting me be a part of it."

He gazed into Jennifer's eyes as her face turned red. She stared down at the table and Jeff followed her vision. He didn't realize he had grabbed her hand in his effort to comfort her. Her small fingers were crossed between his. Yet she didn't move them away. They lingered in his hand. With timing as bad as Adam, the server came over with Jennifer's milkshake and she ripped her fingers away. Jeff's ears continued to burn, and she blushed a bright red hue as well. Jennifer grabbed the two spoons placed on the napkin between them.

"How about you help me devour this milkshake first, and then we can concentrate on the rest of the world." She smiled warmly, handing over one of the spoons.

"Yes Ma'am." He stuck the spoon into the thick milkshake and scooped out a large chunk. Jennifer laughed at the face he made from the shock of the cold cream when he shoved it in his mouth.

When they finished eating, he walked Jennifer to her truck. It was still humid out, being only August. They had several more hot days and nights ahead of them.

***

"I actually don't feel like going back to the base right now," Jennifer laughed, rubbing her full belly. She had eaten too much and felt a little nauseous. She approached her truck, opening the door. When she turned back toward Jeff, he was gazing at the dim night sky.

"Wasn't there supposed to be a meteor shower tonight?"

Jennifer sidled up next to him and gazed up. The stars were barely visible, and the moon was bright. "I thought I read that somewhere, but we won't see anything because of all the lights."

Jeff continued to gaze up, finally turning toward her with a large grin across his face.

"I know somewhere we can go. Just follow me."

"Um, okay?" Jennifer jumped in her truck as Jeff dashed over to his small white car. He turned on the engine quickly, driving over to her. He flashed his lights at her, and drove to the end of the parking lot. "What are you up to Knight?"

Jennifer's heart skipped in joyful anticipation. She had no idea where Jeff was taking her, but she wasn't worried. She felt a sense of calm when she was with him. Her nerves relaxed, and the rigid caution she was so used to was gone. They drove through back roads for about twenty minutes, until Jeff pulled up to the closed city park. She watched as he searched the ground for a large rock, and then began beating the padlock off the park gate.

"What are you doing!?" Jennifer leaned out the window.

"Getting us in. What does it look like?"

"It's closed, we're not supposed to be here." Jennifer caught herself smiling. If they got caught, nothing would happen to them. They had many assets in the police and sheriff's department. The thought of breaking the rules was still exhilarating.

"Not like we haven't trespassed anywhere else." Jeff shrugged, and hit the lock a few more times. It finally gave with a thud into the sand. "Come on!"

Jeff jumped back into his car, driving into the parking lot. If it wasn't for their headlights, it would've been completely pitch black. She pulled up next to him as he hopped out. As she was placing her truck in park, he jumped in her vehicle.

"Knight?" Jennifer looked at him, confused.

"We're gonna drive a little farther in." His eyes had dark circles under them, but there was an air of excitement in them as well. "There's a perfect spot just a little further in. Trust me, you're gonna like this."

Jennifer backed up, and followed Jeff's directions to an opening in the trees of the park. Rolling to a stop in the middle. Jeff smiled, grabbing the woven blanket she had in her seat for when she took a nap, and jumped out. Jennifer turned off the car, and followed him curiously. He had lowered the hatch, and climbed onto the back of the truck, laying down her blanket. He reached his hand down to her. She took it hesitantly. He pulled her up, then instructed her to sit down on the blanket.

"What are we—"

"Look up." Jeff nodded to the sky that she hadn't noticed before. The dark indigo blue of the night was illuminated with thousands of stars. The moon was bright, casting all the light they needed around them. A small twinkle dashed across their view and disappeared.

"It's beautiful...I haven't stargazed like this since Terry and I were teens."

"My dad used to take me here." Jeff smiled, but there was a weight in his eyes. "Before there were problems..."

Jeff flopped back, and folded his arms under his head. Jennifer lay down next to him, staring at the show of dashing lights above them. They lay next to each other in a contented silence. She could feel the heat emanating from his body. Outside of training, this was the closest they'd ever been. She glanced over at him as he looked upward, and felt her heart skip.

Don't be stupid Jen.

"I've been at this stuff a couple months now," Jeff said suddenly, "and it's still crazy to me. Demons are real. So does that mean that gods are real too?" Jeff turned to her as he asked, and caught her gaze. She noticed, even in the dark light, his ears began to blush.

"They were...at some point. Actually the werewolves have a whole belief system around an Ancient Greek goddess."

"They do?"

"Yeah." Jennifer rolled over so she could talk to him better, "Hecate. She's known as the Goddess of Witches, but she is also the creator of the first lycan."

"Wait, you're saying lycans were made by a Greek goddess?"

Jennifer nodded, "Yeah. The story goes that when the city of Troy fell, Queen Hekabe threw herself into the sea. Hecate took pity on her, and transformed her into the first lycan, who still stays loyal by her side. You can see it in her iconography, she's depicted with a black dog."

"Wow..." Jeff's crystal blue eyes had a haze on them that made her feel excited yet nervous. "You are a hidden nerd aren't you?"

"What?" Jennifer shoved Jeff playfully and lay on her back. "I'm well informed."

"Nothing wrong with being a nerd." She didn't have to look at him to know he was smiling. A breeze flew between them. Jennifer shivered. "Come here."

He grabbed her, holding her tightly in his warm arms. Her heart beat furiously in her ears.

"Thanks."

"We can go if you want." Jeff's ears were bright red.

"No, we can stay. Meteor showers are rare." Jennifer smiled and gazed back up at the sky.

They didn't talk much after that. Quietly enjoying the light show above them. Jennifer felt a heavy weight on her chest lift as she lay close to him. A sense of calm. Of...

Home...

Her lids began to grow heavy as she heard Jeff's own breaths begin to soften, and his heartbeat slowed under her hand. She blinked as another star streaked by, and then again, until she drifted off to sleep.

"Jenny..."

"Conor?"

"It's time to wake up."

"What?"

"Jen, wake up!"

Jennifer opened her eyes to see Jeff looking down at her anxiously, a small smile spreading across his quivering lips. The light around them was a golden orange as the sun was peeking on the horizon.

The sun?!

"Oh my god, what time is it?" Jennifer shot up and looked at her watch. It was 6 A.M. "We should get going."

She hastily scooted out of the back of her truck bed. Jeff, as usual, nervously gathered himself and followed her back into her car.

"Sorry," he mumbled as they got in.

"No, I had fun. I'll take you back to your car, and see you tonight, okay?"

Jeff smiled sheepishly.

"Of course!"

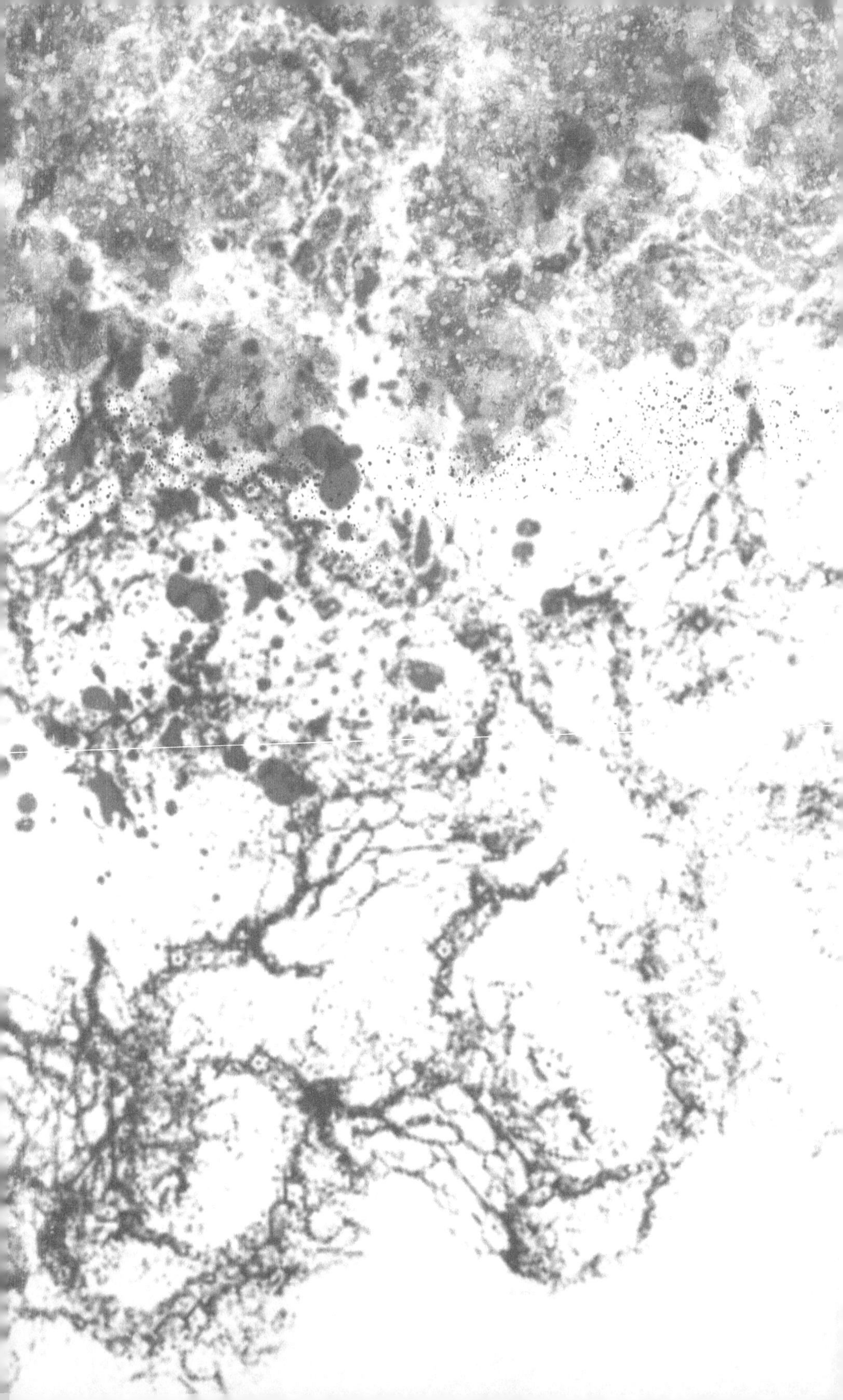

CHAPTER 8

After two months, Jeff improved with everything. His first accomplishment was when he defeated Jennifer in a sparring match. He finally saw an opening, completely managing to disarm her. He knocked her to the ground, like she had done to him a thousand times before. He watched as Jennifer lay on the floor in complete shock, and stifled a laugh. When Jeff reached his hand out to help her up, she accepted it, while cracking a smile of approval back at him.

He even got better at *gardening*. It usually consisted of him digging up the graves, planting a long nail in the corpse's decaying head, and covering it up with new sod. At first, it took him all night to just get one grave done. Now he was able to complete a whole section, with more speed and vigor than he had before.

Jennifer usually patrolled while Jeff worked on the graves. One night, she came around as he laid down the last bit of sod by the gravestone.

"And done!" He got up and patted the dirt off his hands.

"Wow, you've managed to finish this area in three hours. Good job. Make sure to mark the graves—"

"Already did." Jeff beamed as he picked up his shovel and headed out of the cemetery. He was going to bed early tonight.

After another week, all he had to do was finish up on his studies for the proper disposal of supernatural creatures. He read up on werewolves, ghosts, demons, wendigos, banshees, and vampires. He looked at the clock and saw it was still early in the night. He closed down the last file, and sat back in his chair to relax. Jennifer would check on him in half an hour. He figured he finally deserved a little "*me*" time now that he had finished everything.

He opened the web browser and found the total defense game he played every once and a while. He enjoyed playing it when he had time to kill because it involved a little strategy. As a player, you set up towers that produced different minions; some soldiers, archers, or grenaders. You positioned the towers along the given path of the map, and then waited as the enemies troops walked the winding roads to your base. The goal was to destroy all the enemy soldiers before they could take down your home base. The computer was laggy, and slow, but the game was basic so it didn't tax the system. He was well into it when Jennifer came in with two cups of coffee. She slammed his cup down on the table beside him when she noticed the screen.

"Okay, you're wasting time. You need to be up to speed on proper disposal and you're here just playin—"

Jeff held up his hand; it was his turn to speak. He had almost passed Adam's high score.

"You kill ghosts by burning the bones, they hate rock salt and iron. Werewolves hate silver, but you gotta get them in the heart or the head, and they are easier to kill in their human form, considering when they're in beast mode they get more agile and a shit load bigger. Demons hate the Holy Trio of holy water, holy relics, and the name of God in Latin, '*Cristo.*' Zombies need to have the brain cut off from the rest of their body, which can be done in a variety of ways which include but are not limited to..." Jeff sped off his responses and didn't break his eye contact with the screen.

"Okay, I get it. You finished reading everything." Jennifer relaxed in the chair next to him. She took a sip of her coffee as she gazed at the screen. "You know I can have you reprimanded for using the computer for games."

"Noted." He smiled while he continued to play. She continued to sit next to him, pointing out weaknesses in his defenses as he finally beat Adam's record. It was a good night.

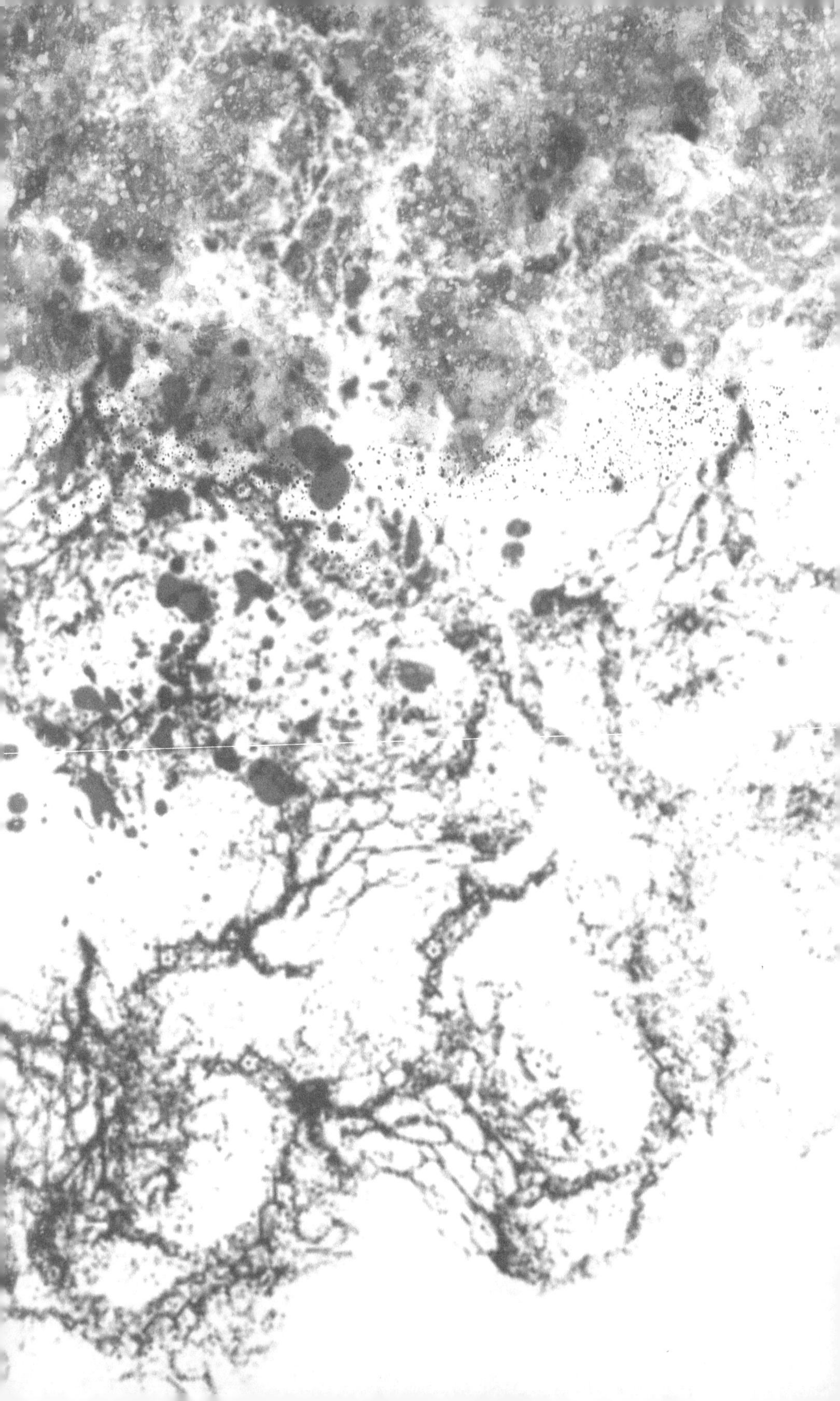

CHAPTER 9

September came quickly, changing the season to fall; however, the heat and humidity shifted little from the summer. Florida lately only had two seasons. Hot, and swamp ass hot.

But global warming isn't real right?

Jeff chuckled as he walked into the cool air conditioning of Jennifer's dojo. The decor was a mixture of Western and Eastern cultures. There were tatami mats across the floors, and a similar assortment of weapons to the ones he used in the base's training room. The walls, however, were covered with thick grey gym mats. It helped contain the echo in the room. Out of habit, he walked straight to Jennifer's office. He tapped lightly on the door, noting the unusual lack of lights radiating from her office.

"Come in." Her voice was soft and weary.

"Hey, how's it going?" He shut the door behind him so they could talk.

"Hey. Just the same old crap." She rubbed her eyes and looked up at him with a faded smile. Dark circles enveloped her bright brown eyes.

"Anything I can do to help?" Jeff glanced down at the open file on her desk. There was a picture of the blonde girl from the first night they met. "You found her?"

Jennifer looked confused at first and then glanced back at her files. She nodded, rubbing her temples. "Yeah. Like we thought, a runaway. Got in touch with her parents. She's from Nebraska."

"That's a long way from here."

"Yep, asked them why she might have come here. They didn't know." Jennifer pulled out a picture from the autopsy Z.E.R.O had performed. It was a close-up photo of a tattoo. "Apparently this was something she had done after leaving home. So we're looking into it."

Jennifer handed Jeff the photo. The tattoo looked strangely familiar, but he couldn't process his own tired thoughts on where he might have seen it before. It was definitely not a normal tattoo for a girl like that. It appeared more like a logo. An eye rested in a sun, like in depictions of Ra, the ancient Egyptian god of the sun. There were some stick figures of people below it in a position of prayer, or begging for deliverance to the eye. The whole piece was outlined in a triangle.

"Weird..."

"Very." Jennifer grabbed the photo back from Jeff and placed it back in the folder. She glanced up at the calendar on the wall as she tucked the file away back into her bag, and turned back to Jeff. "Why don't you take the night off?"

"Really?"

"Yeah. You worked hard for these last three months and I think you deserve it. Besides, I think Adam misses you." She got up and pulled apart some of the blinds on the window to her office. Adam was sitting alone against the wall with his gym bag. He had his phone out, but he wasn't paying much attention to it.

"I've been so busy I haven't been able to hang out with him."

"Yeah, I figured. The double life is hard. Let's go. Our audience awaits. You bested me in training, but I'll be damned if I let you beat me in my house." She laughed as she opened the door.

Jeff cackled. "Today your tyranny will be over!" The first time she'd brought him to her class, she'd challenged him to a duel. Within a minute, he was on the ground. However, today would be different. He was still riding the high of his previous win.

Adam jumped up from his position when he heard Jeff approach. He looked back and forth between the two of them, and gave Jeff a nod of approval when Jennifer walked by. Jeff pretended like he hadn't noticed, taking a spot next to Adam as Jennifer called the class to order.

"Hey you wanna go get a couple beers after this?"

Adam's eyes looked like they were going to start the water works before the question was completely out of Jeff's mouth.

"Sure, I don't have anything planned."

"Cool."

***

Jennifer finished her demonstrations with the class, and caught Jeff talking excitedly with Adam. Normally she would say something, but she felt guilty for stealing Jeff away for so long. He had accomplished a lot in the short time Hammer gave her to train him. He would be going on his first field mission soon with the rest of the team now that she had cleared him for active duty. She wanted him to have one more day of a normal life. There was no telling what could happen when they got a call. Alpha Team didn't handle easy missions.

And now for your last test with me.

She wanted to see if he could defeat her again. The first time might have been a lucky occurrence. She needed to know he was really ready to be on his own. She had to stop protecting him.

She faced her pupils, who sat in two rows before her. "Alright, so this will be the last class for the novice group. You all will be graduating to my more advanced classes after this, granted you pass the trials I set up." The class began to murmur at her news with excitement. "So of course first, I would like to use my guinea pig, Knight. Come on up."

Jeff stood up, cocky as ever. As assured as he was of himself, she perceived that he was going to take this match a little more seriously than their first bout.

"Okay, what do I have to do to pass?"

"For you? Pin me, just once."

Jeff's cheeks and ears flared up red as they tended to do when she teased him. It was still easy to throw him off.

"Alright, and I meant it. Your reign over me is over." He chuckled, his face awash with nervous energy.

"Begin." She smiled back.

She observed his movements as he stepped around her. She needed to read which way he was going to go. She never liked to be offensive when sparring with her students. The fighting style developed by her family was meant to be defensive, using the strength and movements of the attacker against them; similar to Jiu Jitsu or Judo. If her students could understand that, then they would pass her test.

Jeff stopped pacing, and waited in front of her. Jennifer froze; this was not what she was expecting.

"Aren't you going to come at me?" She eyed him curiously. He didn't change his position.

"Ladies first. I learned the hard way." He gestured for her to come at him, using a *come here* motion with his fingers.

I guess he did learn. Alright, let's see how much.

Now that he had passed her initial test, she advanced toward him. He stepped away from all her reaches and grabs. He was a lot quicker now that she had been drilling him relentlessly for three months. The class became silent, watching in awe as the two of them dodged and weaved around each other. Seeing he had improved, she wanted to see if she could throw him off by incorporating some other fighting styles. Jeff kept up with her, until she saw him lose his footing.

Victory is mine again!

Jennifer quickly closed the distance between them. She was going to land a blow on his face to knock him to the ground. A smile spread across his features as she stepped in.

He tricked me?

She felt his arms reach around her in seconds, and they moved her in the direction that he needed. In a blink she was on the ground and he was on top of her, pinning her down under his weight. His breathing was heavy, but she could see the twinkle of excitement in his eyes.

They stayed entangled from their bout. Exhausted, gazing at each other. She couldn't help but notice how contagious his smile was, as her own lips parted into one. She wouldn't mind staying here for a moment longer.

"Yeah Jeff! That's my boy!" Adam screamed as he jumped up. The rest of the class began to clap and cheer along with Adam.

Jeff blushed a deep red as his crystal blue eyes gazed intensely at her. Jennifer's cheeks felt warmer as she became more nervous in his arms. As the students surrounded them, he hastily let go of her, rising to his feet. He held out his hand and helped her up, while nervously scratching the back of his head. Another tell she noted of his that showed he was uncomfortable. She extended her hand to him for a congratulatory handshake that he accepted.

"Congrats, you ended my reign." Her heart beat furiously and she struggled to catch her breath.

"I told you I would." Jeff laughed weakly as he breathed heavily. Adam jumped on top of him and rough-housed with him, removing Jeff's hand from her grasp.

"Well, that got me tired." Jennifer chuckled as she turned to her other students, "Alright, split up into pairs. Everyone who wins the match I'll move up this week. So do your best!" She waved the crowd of students into groups, and grabbed her water bottle, guzzling down the cool refreshment. "Jeff, help me monitor the groups since you passed."

Why is it so hot in here today?

Adam paired off with another student, and Jeff walked to the other side of the room. She caught herself watching Jeff's body as he went back and forth between the students. She felt goosebumps again and butterflies in her chest and stomach as her heart continued to race. This wasn't because of her recent cardio...she had to keep her distance from him. She didn't want to be hurt again. Jennifer bit her lip as she glanced at Jeff one more time, before turning her attention to the other students.

***

After class, Jeff and Adam met at their favorite sports bar. Now that his adrenaline had dissipated, he was exhausted. He slid into a booth while Adam went to the bar to order their drinks. Jeff leaned back, closing his eyes. The murmur of the bar faded away from his ears as he drifted off.

He thought of Jennifer and how she seemed more stressed than usual today. The image of the blonde undead girl and her tattoo flashed into his mind. Where had he seen that before? Jeff tried to think of old documentaries he had watched on Ancient Egypt and of the god Ra, given the *Eye of Ra* in the design. Nothing came up. Fuck it.

Jeff decided to reflect instead on his match with her. She only relaxed around him when they trained. Most of the time she was stoic and hard to read. He smiled at how surprised she'd been when he'd flipped her over and pinned her to the ground. The olive skin of her cheeks had had a rosy glow.

Wait…was she blushing? Or was she just turning red from our match?

He frowned. Did they have a moment—

There was a large explosive sound as something slammed in front of him. Jeff jumped in his chair, only to see that Adam had banged his beer pint on the table.

"Shit man! What the hell? You scared the crap out of me." He glared at Adam, who smiled his usual dumb grin when he thought he was being funny. Adam shrugged, taking his seat across from him.

"You fell asleep, you were fair game." Adam laughed. After he was settled, he looked concerned at him. "You okay Jeff? You've seemed really distracted lately."

"Yeah I'm fine. Just this new job has me working awful hours."

He rubbed the sleepy seeds that crusted his dry eyelids, and sat up straight at the table. He grabbed the wheat ale Adam had placed in front of him, taking a long slow drink. He was glad Adam hadn't gone with his usual dark beer. They were always too bitter.

"Well, if you quit your day job, you'd have no problem," Adam said matter of factly. If he only knew the truth.

"Can't. Still in my probationary period," Jeff sighed.

"Seriously? How long does that last? You've been working there for about three months now."

"Yeah I know. But I stay on probation until Jen, and our boss, agree I'm good to stay on permanently." He tried to keep his beer from spilling as Adam's hand slammed onto the table. Adam was already smiling from ear to ear with his Joker-esque grin and now he could barely suppress the laughter bursting from his lips.

"Wait! You've been getting your ass kicked everyday by her in class, and now you're her work bitch too! I thought you were just coworkers, but this is just too great!" Adam cackled so loud that the patrons in the booth behind him turned over, looking for the commotion. Jeff glared back at him as he squeezed his hands around his glass.

"It's not like that. It just so happened she was high enough in her firm that she had pull to get me in fast. It's going to be a good paying job. You'll be begging me to bring you in after you see how much money I'm making."

"Sure." Adam wiped tears from his eyes as his laughter died down. "I'll believe it when I see it."

The bar was pretty empty, with only a few other patrons drinking and watching the Bucs vs Giants game on the televisions. After some quiet self reflection, Adam looked up at Jeff, and put his half empty glass down.

"You know you're doing it again."

"Doing what?"

What did I do this time?

"You always change your interests when you're into a chick."

"No I don't." Jeff scoffed as he finished his pint.

Adam gave him a look, *"Really? Are you that Stupid?"* Jeff opened his mouth to protest, but Adam spoke first. He held up one finger as he made his first point.

"High school, Jenna. She was a Honey Dancer for the school color guard. You joined the football team to get her attention. It worked, but after you two broke up, you quit the team." Jeff gawked at Adam and crossed his arms in defiance. Adam held up a second finger.

"Senior year, Tracy. She smoked cigarettes and some other things." Adam chuckled, "You started, and got me in on it. Not that I can really complain, but almost getting arrested didn't help that relationship. I mean, she was justifiably crazy."

Jeff nodded in agreement with this one. That was from his black period that he tried not to remember. It took him forever to kick the habit of smoking. He quit cold turkey. Adam, on the other hand, still vaped. The two of them still smoked the occasional blunt together when they could get their hands on some. Much easier now that it was legal.

"And then there was Kylie. Now *that one* was special. She controlled every aspect of your life, and you let her. You even let her throw you out of YOUR apartment for a month, when she was the one cheating with that—"

"Alright, I get where you're going with this. First, I got her out of my apartment, and second, I swear, this time is different." He looked Adam dead in the eye. Adam put up his hands in surrender and leaned back into his seat.

"Mhmm..." said Adam thoughtfully. "You're lucky I like this girl. She might be good for you." Adam took a swig of his beer and waited for Jeff to respond. Jeff avoided Adam's gaze and stared at the scratches on the table. "You should tap that," Adam muttered, just loud enough. Jeff glanced up at him, completely embarrassed at the implication. "Unless you already have."

Adam grinned like an idiot again, and then laughed like a hyena. Jeff picked up the napkins on the table and threw a handful at him. His phone vibrated in his pocket; a text message from Jennifer greeted him.

> I'm soooo Sorry! Commander Hammer is calling us all in for a gardening expedition. I need you to get here ASAP.

"I gotta go. Jen needs me to come in tonight."

"Sure she does. Gotta go take care of a little booty call," Adam chortled.

"You're a douche." Jeff got up to leave, digging in his pocket for his wallet.

"But I'm a lovable douche."

"Yeah, whatever. I'll see you later." Jeff threw his money on the table and punched Adam in the arm as he walked out.

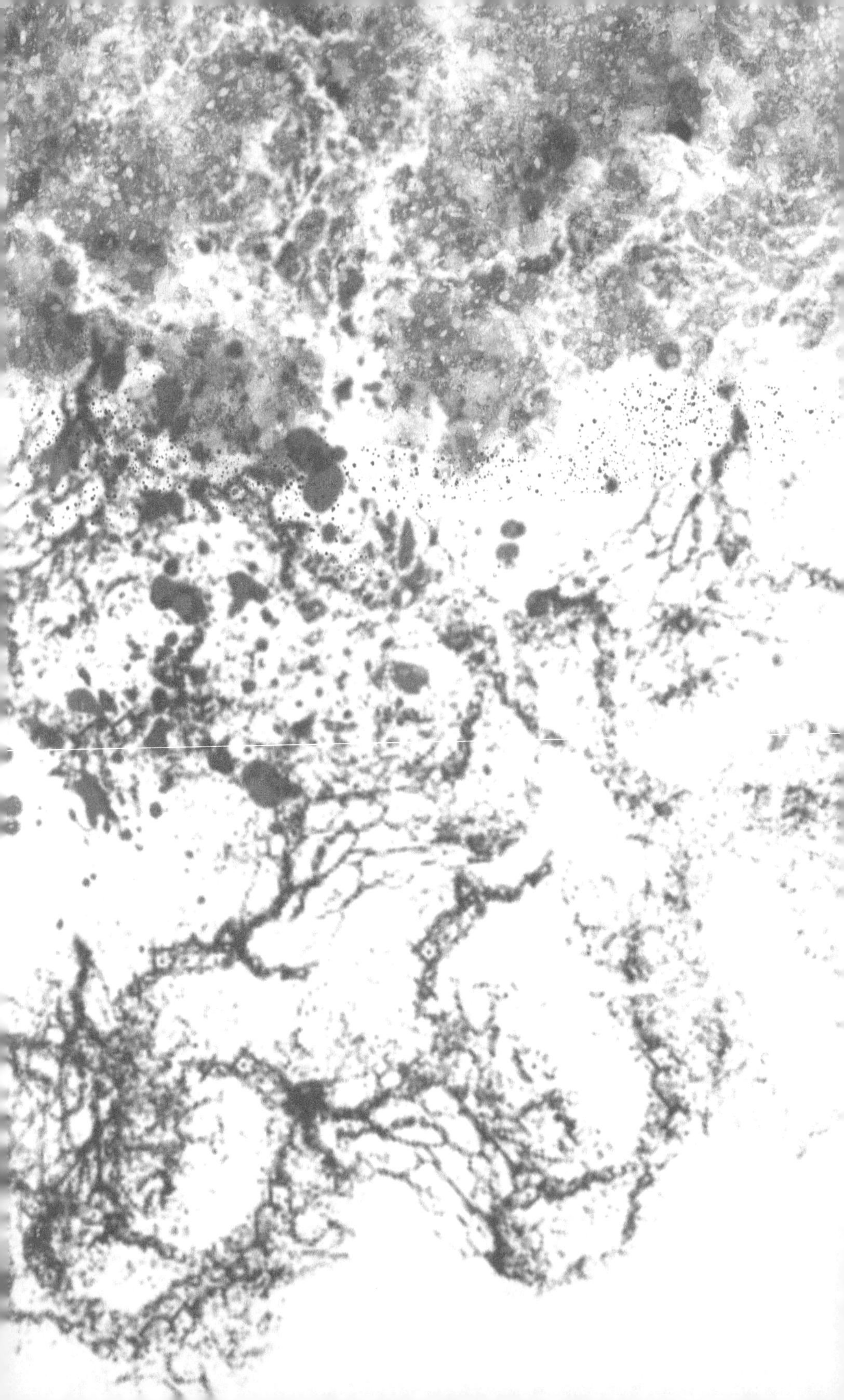

CHAPTER 10

Jeff walked into the locker room to find Jennifer was already in her combat gear—black t-shirt with the Z.E.R.O. emblem sewn into each shoulder, tactical pants, combat boots, and to finish it off an armor vest with a shoulder holster to house a blade and belt with side pouches for extra ammunition. She was straddled over one of the benches, pressing bullets into a magazine. There were two large duffle bags on the ground next to her containing a couple of AR-15s, a shotgun, and some M1911 handguns. There was no one else in the room with them. He thought that the rest of the team would have been there gearing up, too.

"That's a lot of gear," he commented as he walked to his locker. He took out his vest and hung it on the locker door. He began checking the pockets for all his accessories like he had done every night so far.

"That's because we have a big gardening tonight." Jennifer stopped what she was doing and looked up at him apologetically. "Sorry about cutting into your night off."

"Nah, it's alright. It wasn't that big a deal." He tried to sound as nonchalant as he could. He was actually kind of glad. Adam was making him uncomfortable with all the talk about her. He pulled out his uniform and placed it on the bench beside him. "So what's so special about this gardening?"

"Well, Rick called me and said that it's at the Myrtle Hill Memorial Park."

"That's right off of MLK isn't it? That one's huge!"

"Yeah, and according to the report, there has been a lot of activity going on in the area. Hence the big guns. Remember how bad it was your first night? That one was small." She finished loading the magazine in her hands, and placed it on the floor next to the others she had already filled. She tossed the empty ammo box in the trash and picked up one of the large duffle bags from the floor. "Hey, help me get this stuff in the bags and then I'll leave for you to get changed. I know you're not comfortable with me here while you do that." She began to fill the bags, a slight grin on her face.

It's not that I'm uncomfortable. I just—

"It's not a problem. You can stay if you have things to do. I never had a co-ed locker room before. Didn't know if YOU were comfortable with me changing here." Jeff's ears were on fire again; he hated this happened to him. Jennifer laughed.

"OH please! I change in front of the guys all the time. It's no big deal. You seemed okay showering in the same room a couple of weeks ago." Jennifer smiled coyly. "Besides, one of these days, if we are unlucky enough, we'll see each other's insides. Formalities are out the door."

He laughed nervously. That was a bit morbid, but she had a point. He walked over and picked up the other bag, filling it with the rest of the items, and zipped it up.

"So the rest of Alpha is going to be there?" Jeff looked around the rest of the empty locker room. "How come they aren't doing all this?"

"Yeah, they'll be there. They're already out on other assignments tonight and will meet us there. Today's when we get to see how you work with the rest of us. I guess you can call it graduation."

"Does this mean I have to do a test or something?" Jeff took off his shirt and tossed it in his locker. As he reached for his uniform, he glanced in the mirror on his locker door at Jennifer behind him. He thought he noticed her blush briefly upon catching his gaze, as she quickly turned her attention back to her current task. She unfolded a cart they kept between the wall and lockers and rolled it over to the pile of bags.

Was Adam right? Am I doing all this for her?

"Well, it's pretty simple. Live, and don't get anyone else killed." She grunted while she piled the heavy bags onto the cart.

"Great..."

"It won't be that bad. You will have the whole team there with you. We're a family here." She smiled and began to roll the cart she'd filled with the bags out the door.

"I feel so safe with an alcoholic, a vampire who I can't tell if they want to eat me or not, and a 'guardian' that I haven't seen since I came here." Jeff kicked off his shoes and placed them in the locker. Jennifer stopped midway through the door and turned back to him.

"Oh come on, Terrence and Demon aren't that bad! And Rick has been busy, he's like a phantom that lives here. You'll learn to love them."

"Yeah, if they don't kill me first," he muttered under his breath. He started unbuckling his belt, and Jennifer hurried out the door.

"I'll meet you at the truck!" She yelled from the hall. He finished changing, throwing his boots on quickly. He grabbed his tactical vest and slammed his locker shut as he dashed out. He would finish gearing up on the way over.

***

Jennifer looked over at Jeff, who had managed to fall asleep. They were only on the road for about fifteen minutes and he was out. It's funny how innocent people looked when they slept. Even the scariest individual in their group, Demon, looked so peaceful when he was dreaming.

Jennifer had been surprised when she'd got the call from Hammer earlier, ordering her to rally the troops. Hammer had been back and forth between working with the team and his duties as head of the division. She had been delegating the gardening to Demon and Sentinel for the last two months, as well as the investigation of the attack three months ago. She'd probably separated everyone out too thin. This cemetery they were heading to was supposed to get checked once a month due to its size and location. Maybe she'd focused too much on Jeff.

She pulled into the cemetery, noting the other two cars of her team members, a black Hummer, and a black 1971 Chevrolet Chevelle. She pulled up behind them. Jeff was still snoring into her window. She punched him in the arm, laughing as he shot up startled and awake.

"You know, Knight, you should have grabbed some coffee before you left the base."

"Wait, you guys have coffee there? I thought you were always ordering out when you brought it," he asked while yawning.

Jennifer looked at him confused, "We work under a bar..."

"Yeah I know, I'm just teasing," he chuckled as he rubbed his eyes. "A cup of coffee would be worth its weight in gold right now."

"Come on. Don't quit on me now. You'll be fine." She hopped out of the truck and placed her earpiece in her ear. There was a soft buzzing noise, followed by the murmur of her teammates' voices. She smiled coyly as Jeff sluggishly jumped out of the truck and followed her into the cemetery.

"You know, I remember when I first got introduced to the team after training. I couldn't sleep straight for a couple of weeks."

"Really?"

"Yeah, once the shock value goes down you'll have no problem with adrenaline spikes." She turned to see if he was relaxed.

Jeff grimaced, "And how long do you think that's going to take?"

"Well, you know that will differ between people. For example, we had this one guy we tried to break in. He didn't sleep for eight weeks. Poor bastard." She glanced over at Jeff again as they walked; the color was fading from his face again. She listened carefully to their surroundings for anything that sounded out of place. This was a large area, but it was crowded with family plots that included grand mausoleums and very ornate giant headstones. Many places for re-animated corpses to lurk. Per Sentinel's report, they should still have time before there was any *real* activity.

"Jesus...how the hell did he function without going into a coma?"

Jennifer laughed at his question.

"Well, the brain does this funny thing of shutting down other functions when it gets the chance, so the body can recuperate. Call it involuntary micro naps." Jennifer checked to see that he was still following. "Anyway, this guy was suffering from them bad for a week. Each nap getting progressively longer. You couldn't wake him up."

"So what happened to him? Did he ever get over it?"

"Nope, he went MIA." Jennifer stopped walking.

"So he went batshit crazy...awesome."

As Jeff looked at the cemetery in front of them, Jennifer saw in his face that he was worried that would be his worst fate. She grabbed his arm, and turned him back to her, so that she knew he understood what she was about to tell him.

"Z.E.R.O operatives don't die Knight. They just go missing in action." The hard truth. Z.E.R.O does not exist, so when they die, they just disappear. "He got devoured by a horde of zombies. He was asleep on his feet. Never even felt them tearing out his insides." She watched as his face processed the horror of what she'd told him. She spun back around and began to walk again, holding her smile in so he wouldn't see.

They approached the remaining team members. Jeff seemed lost in thought, still contemplating her story. She hoped she hadn't scared him too badly, but the payoff would be worth it, for her at least. Demon was using one of the headstones as a small chair—no respect for whomever was buried there. He looked up and waved at them when they approached.

"Hey, Jeff. How you doing? You seem tired." Demon had a slight chuckle in his voice. Jeff didn't notice it.

"Yeah man, you look like you haven't slept in a week! Don't space out like that last guy, ya hear?" Sentinel walked over to join their small group, his sandy blonde hair highlighted by the moonlight above them.

"Poor guy...he never saw it coming." Demon spoke with a weight to his words. Jeff's eyes were wide, his skin pale, and Jennifer was sure that Demon could hear Jeff's anxious heart beat in his chest as he stared at all of them. She exchanged glances with Sentinel and Demon, confirming silently that Jeff had had enough. They burst out laughing.

"Oh my god! I can't believe ya bought that bogus story!" Sentinel leaned on Demon for support as his laugh bellowed out louder.

"You should have seen the look on your face." Demon wiped blood-red tears of laughter from his eyes. Jennifer remembered the first time she saw Demon cry blood—it was five years ago when he'd come to aid her...when Conor...she brushed off the thought. The Z.E.R.O archives said it had something to do with the regenerative nature of their blood and the mutation of the tear ducts. A vampire with pink eye wouldn't be a good hunter.

Jeff looked over at Jennifer, completely clueless as to how they were all cued in on this horrible joke. She simply pointed at her ear where she had installed her communicator. Jeff's ears turned bright red again.

"Fuck you guys!" His facial expressions were contorting through disbelief, anger, and embarrassment.

"Come on, Knight. You gotta have pretty thick skin for this," Jennifer smiled, as he continued to glare back at everyone.

"Relax. If we didn't think you couldn't handle the joke, we never would have done it." Demon put his hand on Jeff's shoulder, like a parent giving a talk down to a child.

"Yeah, you gotta learn to laugh at these moments, if you want your head to stay together for this job." Sentinel chuckled. Jeff seemed to be calming down as his color returned. Hammer approached from the path behind them. Everyone immediately stood in line at attention.

"Good evening everyone." Hammer addressed the group with a degree of brevity. "I'd like to take this opportunity to have a moment of silence for our dearly departed Chet, missing in action who, as some of you may remember, was devoured a year ago today by zombies, while suffering from micro naps..."

Everyone chuckled except for Jeff. He was clearly uncomfortable being the odd one out. She wasn't usually one for hazing, but knew this would have been better than anything that Hammer might have planned for him. Her brother could be cruel with his humor.

"Alright alright!" Hammer called for order again, still laughing himself. "As all of you know, I'm a bit skeptical about bringing anyone from the outside into our crew, but Jen can vouch for him, and personally assures me that he can handle anything we throw at him. So let's all make sure to invite Jeff to sing Kum-bi-ya around the campfire in our happy little circle-jerk."

Why can't you be serious for five minutes Terrence...

"Jeff, I'm assuming you've been introduced to everyone." Hammer turned his attention to Jeff, who stood very rigid. She had never seen him so nervous before.

"Sir yes Sir!" he hollered back like he was in a marine boot camp. Hammer hated formalities.

"Oh, Christ." Hammer roughed up his already scruffy light brown hair and spit on the ground, "Unless I'm your spiritual adviser or sleeping with yer momma, you can call me Hammer or Commander Hammer if you must be formal. That sir shit's gotta go."

"Uh yes si—" Hammer glared at him as the words left his lips, "I mean, yes Hammer!"

"If you couldn't tell, we're a pretty informal unit. As long as everyone involved pulls their weight and watches each other's backs, we're all happy pandas." Hammer patted Jeff, as if saying "*good talk*" and returned his attention to the rest of the group.

"Okay people, this is going to be a routine gardening expedition. Sector we haven't hit in a while. There are some buggers here that don't want to stay in the ground. Oughta' do just fine to break in the new guy. Apparently, he likes to shoot paintball guns at cardboard cutouts of zombs."

The group chuckled quietly. Jennifer glanced over at Jeff, who was shifting his weight awkwardly. She elbowed Sentinel in the rib to cut it out. He looked at her surprised, and she mouthed to him, "*Enough.*" Sentinel frowned and passed the message on to Demon. She watched as Demon leaned back at little to get her in his line of sight. He raised an eyebrow at her, and she gave him an icy stare back. He stopped laughing immediately and stood back straight. Hammer continued to lecture on like he hadn't noticed the exchange.

"We're using live ammo tonight, so Jeff, try not to shoot us in the face as it might take the sunshine out of our evening. Everyone, for pete's sake, call your shots! This place isn't the best lit, so staying out of the line of fire is critical." Everyone nodded, but unenthusiastically. This was not new information for them. Hammer was making a show because of Jeff, and it was starting to annoy her too. "Alright people, let's get ourselves locked, cocked, and ready to rock. Let's reconvene over there at the mausoleum gates in about twenty minutes."

The group dispersed to their separate vehicles to get their gear together. Jennifer walked with Jeff back to her truck.

"Hey, I'm sorry about that. We may have taken it a little too far…" She walked quietly by his side as she waited for a response.

Jeff shrugged. "Nah it's alright. The group I get, but what's up with Hammer? It's not like it's really my first day anymore. He was really laying in to me." He peeked over his shoulder, making sure no one else was listening.

"Don't mind him. He's just busting your balls a little because you're our ranking 'F-N-G'…" Jennifer trailed off at the end when she realized what she was about to say.

Oh stupid Jennifer. This is not going to make things better with him and the group. This is why we don't talk with the rookies…

"You're what?"

"It's our acronym for '*Fucking New Guy*'" she muttered quickly. "Hammer comes off like a hard ass, but once you get to know him, he's a teddy bear, I swear."

"Great…can't wait." Jeff picked up his pace. When they approached her truck he quietly fumed as he walked to the back. He opened the bed hatch hastily, pulling out one of the duffle bags and sliding it within her reach—all the while refusing to make eye contact—then silently retrieved his own gear.

Jennifer had seen him scared and nervous, but never really angry. Except when she'd got him to talk about his father. She tried to think of what to say as she stood next to him. This was partially her fault.

He pulled out four magazines for their M1911s and placed them on the door hatch and hurriedly grabbed the hunting knife out of its sheath, sliding it into the sheath on his vest. Jennifer handed him his handgun, and he loaded it with one of the four magazines.

He slid another into the empty space on his vest. After holstering his gun, he handed the remaining magazines to her roughly, then dug through the bag, and pulled out their two large Maglites. She liked that they were heavy so they worked well as clubs if ammo became sparse.

Jennifer rattled her brain for how to end this anxious silence. He'd said he wasn't mad at her, but the hazing was her idea. She took a deep breath to start her apology, when she heard him chuckle.

"To think, I'm here now because Adam pressured me into coming to the paintball game. I never would have imagined this turn of events."

"Why did Adam have to pressure you to come? Was it your ex?"

"Uh—" He seemed like he was trying to figure out what to say as his eyes looked at everything except her. "Yeah. You remember that phone call."

"Yeah. She was a real bitch." Jennifer could see that he was still glum, "Sorry. Though, being part of a secret organization with government ties has its perks. I wasn't lying when I told her I could ruin her life."

She smiled at him playfully as she elbowed his ribs, so he could see she wasn't serious. He let out a small sigh, and returned the smile back.

"Thanks. I needed that." He pulled the communicator out of his vest, and popped it in his ear.

"Well, if you ever want to talk about it, you can confide in me." Jennifer reached out, and touched his arm gently.

"Thanks." Jeff smiled. He lingered a moment before removing his arm from her touch and tossed the duffle bags back in the trunk. The remaining items made a loud clunk as the metal in the bags collided with the bed of the truck.

She heard the static in her ear as her earpiece began receiving a signal again.

"*ETA, Phoenix? Remember, rollout in five,*" Hammer's voice bellowed.

"Copy. We're on our way. Just having a little chat." She gave a reassuring smile to Jeff—she wasn't gonna let them bother him anymore. They began their walk back.

"*Does the baby need you to hold his hand when he pulls the trigger too?*" Jeff's jaw dropped as he gaped at Jennifer. She wasn't surprised by his reaction to Hammer. Despite his misgivings, Hammer was actually a good leader. If you could get past his bullshit.

"Hey! Go easy, Terrence! This isn't a closed channel and he already thinks you don't like him." She was getting annoyed by her adoptive brother's behavior.

"Maybe he's smarter than I thought." Hammer chuckled, *"If he's got an issue, get him a tissue. Now get your asses back here. One minute late to rollout and I'll make a burnt cookie outta the rookie. Over and out."*

The static died in their ear pieces.

"Yeah, *real* nice guy." Jeff marched forward angrily to their destination.

The rest of the walk back was in silence. Jennifer was livid with Hammer and if he didn't let up on Jeff, tonight would be his last day as Commander, because he would be leaving this cemetery in a body bag. She followed Jeff as he walked off to the side of the mausoleum and waited with him. He was tense, his muscles flexed and tight as he crossed his arms, tapping his foot anxiously. Jennifer scanned the area around them. There were more multi-family mausoleums to the west—large structures with shelves for multiple bodies, covered by stone name plates. To the east were more individual burial sites. Tactically, it was more open, and better to operate in. Jeff would do better if she could go with him that way. The moonlight grew brighter as she looked up; thick clouds slowly swam across the sky. It wasn't a bad looking night. She checked her watch—for all the rushing Hammer did, he still hadn't come back yet. When Jeff noticed Hammer's approach, he walked off to where Demon sat instead.

"You remember a party favor for our stray dog?" Hammer asked her while he flicked his cigar ash to the ground. Jennifer made sure he could see her scowl as she pulled a silencer and laser sight attachment out of her side pack. "Sure he doesn't need training wheels?"

"Be nice."

"Where's the fun in that?"

This is going to be a long night...

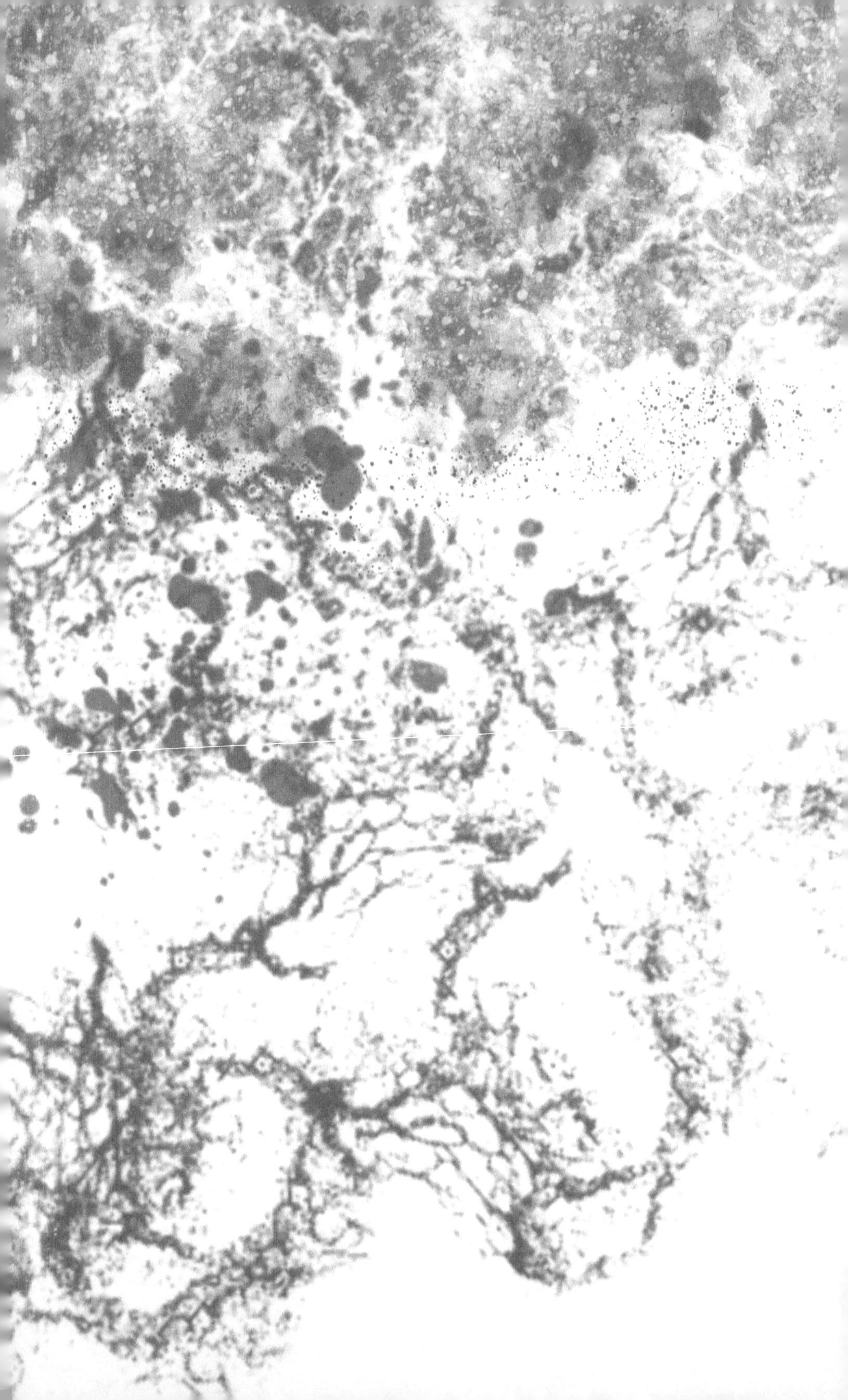

Chapter 11

When Jeff noticed Hammer approaching, he decided to step away before he did something that he would regret. He knew they were busting his balls, but he still didn't appreciate it. Their laughter at him still rang in his ears. He was initially mad at Jennifer for starting it in the first place, but this unit was her family. He'd learned enough about her to realize this must have been her idea for how to break the ice. It's not that he hadn't met everyone before, but this was the first time he would actually be working with them. He decided to speak with Demon first, since they had already spoken more than once.

"So is he always so charming?"

Demon looked up at Jeff, confused by his question, but then he noticed Jennifer arguing with Hammer in the background.

"You get used to him."

"Sorry. Just a bit nervous today. First time I'm shooting live targets with real bullets."

"Yeah, Jen mentioned that to me. First time killing anything?"

"Well, not really, because the day I met Jen we killed a bunch of these things. First time shooting *them*."

"Well, it's the same principle as your game when you shoot one." Demon's yellow eyes flashed mischievously at him. "Except instead of paint you are dealing with blood. Paint is a lot easier to clean up than blood, trust me."

Jeff laughed nervously. Hearing Demon talk about blood was uncomfortable, as it had a different function for him. Jeff looked around briefly at his teammates. Everyone was equipped with a gun except for Demon.

"Hey, don't you have a weapon?" He scanned Demon to see if he'd missed it on his first observation. With a devilish grin, Demon reached over his shoulder, unsheathing an obsidian katana blade. The metal of the blade sang when it brushed against the sheath. Demon held it out to Jeff.

"This is the only weapon I need."

"Wow! This is beautiful!"

"Indeed. This weapon was made by the master swordsman Koga Ushido in Japan in the year 1801. The blade, as you can see, is reinforced obsidian. Cuts three times cleaner than steel, and will never go dull. It was blessed by Shinto priests a short time after that and has an inlay of silver. This makes it my all-purpose killing machine for vampires, werewolves, zombies, demons, and humans." Demon beamed with pride over his weapon.

"Amazing! But...how do you know all that history is really true?"

"Because I was there." Demon said it like it was nothing special, but to Jeff that was the most amazing aspect of the story.

How old is he?

Jeff stared at Demon in amazement, failing to realize Hammer had walked over. His commander waved a laser sight and silencer in his face.

"Ever used these before?" Hammer pointed to the silencer first.

Jeff nodded and pulled out his handgun. Jennifer had him doing firearm practice the past couple of weeks with the silencer and sight to get used to the extra weight on the gun.

Hammer made him nervous and he realized too late he'd made a mistake as he held the gun. The barrel pointed slightly in Hammer's direction.

"Kindly do not point loaded weapons in my direction," Hammer growled.

"Right sorry!" Jeff hastily pointed his gun to the ground.

"Fresh meat. Tell me what you know about line-of-fire."

"Line-of-fire? That's uh—" Jeff began to stutter as he had a hard time focusing his own thoughts in his growing rage toward the Commander.

"It's the straight line between your barrel and your target through which Mr. Hollow-point moves like a bat outta Hell," Hammer answered for him. Jeff felt his blood boil. Doesn't matter what Jennifer said, this guy was an asshole. "Try not to get in the line of fire, or put any of us in there, as someone will DIE from an acute case of lead poisoning."

I really want to punch your lights out you pompous ass head.

"Right. Okay," Jeff muttered, barely audible.

"Say 'copy.'"

"Okay...er, copy." He was done with Hammer and hoped this would not be the whole night. Clearly Hammer was not done with *him* yet, as he opened his mouth to lecture Jeff some more.

"You obviously play paintball and like to shoot your load off. You know all about the parts of a gun right? Phoenix did go over this with you?"

"Are you serious? Yeah...I mean COPY." Jeff said it loud and as annoyed as possible. Hammer either didn't care or didn't realize it because he kept going. He took his handgun out of its holster and pointed it at a nearby tree.

"Trigger discipline. Keep your trigger finger along the side of the receiver, until you've aimed, and are ready to shoot. So don't put your finger on the trigger until?" Hammer looked at him for an answer.

"I'm ready to kill something." Jeff answered, unenthused.

"My god, there just may be hope for you yet!" Hammer beamed, putting his gun back in his holster. He slapped the silencer and laser sight attachment into Jeff's hands.

Jeff attached the items to his gun with Demon's help to line up the laser sight. When they were finished, he placed it back in his holster, surprised it still fit. Then again, he thought they were pretty big for the guns they were using. Now he knew why.

"Okay everyone!" Hammer boomed. "Demon and Phoenix, you guys take the west side, follow the fence line, and meet us back here. Sentinel, you, me, and the Fresh Meat are taking the east." Hammer gave out his orders. Jeff felt sick. He was going to be stuck with Hammer for a majority of the night. He looked at Jennifer for assistance and she gave him a quick look of sympathy, before nodding to show she'd accepted his orders.

***

I am going to kill him...

Jennifer fumed as Hammer barked off orders. She would have liked it better if Hammer and Sentinel had gone off on their own, and left her with Jeff and Demon. The two of them together would not be a fair combo to Jeff. She let the others pass by before she went to confront Hammer on his behavior.

"Will you take it easy on him, Terrence?" Jennifer clenched her fists.

"Jesus, Jen! Lighten up. Just breaking in the F-N-G." Hammer grinned wide at her; as usual, he did not get the message.

Jennifer pursed her lips. "You're making him nervous. If he gets nervous, he's gonna make a mistake. I don't want anything going wrong tonight. You put me in charge of this team, remember?"

"Relax, Mom. With me and Sentinel as his chaperones, we'll have him home on time..." Hammer pulled his flask out of his vest and took a swig. She couldn't take her adoptive brother's behavior anymore and slugged him as hard as she could in the arm. He glared at her while he juggled to keep hold of his flask.

"I'm serious!"

"It'll be fine." Hammer said it with a calmness to his voice that surprised her, "Can I go play with the new kid now? Or do you want to scowl at me some more?"

She flashed Hammer another icy glare. She loved him, but as with any older sibling, he got on her nerves from time to time. It usually didn't bother her when Hammer was rough with a new recruit, but this time it really did.

Her last candidate for Alpha had been George. With Hammer taking a more administrative role in the base, they'd needed a new member to replace him on the team. Jennifer had originally met George when investigating a wendigo attack in New Mexico. Impressed by his performance, she'd recruited him to Bravo Team. He had performed reasonably well in the short months he'd worked with them, and Jennifer felt he would be a good pick for Alpha. Unfortunately, he hadn't been as ready as she'd hoped. That's why she wanted to take individual time to train Jeff. She wanted to make sure he was really ready. She hoped Jeff would be okay tonight.

Jennifer jogged to catch up with Demon. She knew he was waiting for her. They walked together in silence until they reached the western section of the yard. The graves and mausoleums were tightly packed in this area as the clients were expanding, but the groundskeepers were running out of land to bury them in. There was barely a foot of space between each large stone structure. Who knows how many bodies were behind each web-covered wrought-iron gate. The family plots had large stones marking several members of a family, their bodies most likely stacked on top of each other to retain the small plot area they were assigned to. She preferred them to the mausoleums, because most didn't make it to the surface. She felt a cold chill as a breeze passed through them. Demon drew his sword and Jennifer equipped her pistol.

"Sword versus guns, Phoenix? Lowest body count buys the first round?"

"Deal." She grinned with the excitement of competition. She liked working with Demon. They got along, and there were no issues as long as they stayed professional...to a point. She hadn't worked with him for a while, now that she thought about it. She hadn't really spoken to him either. If he felt awkward about their team-up tonight, he didn't show it.

She stepped forward and searched the ground in front of her for any fresh *daisies*. There was a sickening crunch behind her and she cursed under her breath. She turned around to see a zombie's head peeking out of the ground a few inches from Demon, his sword plunged into its skull.

"I guess I'm up by one then." Demon laughed.

"You're an asshole..." Jennifer turned back around, determined to get the next one. He'd probably heard it and that's why he'd made the bet to begin with. She scanned the field in front of her and noticed the same five millimeter holes she had seen in several of the other cemeteries with activity lately. She bit her lip. She needed to discuss this with Hammer when they were done tonight. It was becoming more than a coincidence.

The ground pulsed near a family plot. She walked over as a couple pulled themselves from the ground. They didn't look human anymore. Their skin was almost completely gone, only dry, brown pieces of sinew barely connected to the exposed yellow bones. The clothes they were buried in were torn and tattered. Jennifer always wondered how the very decayed zombies could even see or hear. The first one that peaked its head out of the ground cracked its neck in her and Demon's direction as if it had heard their conversation. She popped a shot in each and turned to Demon to see his face.

"Fine, Karmic Retribution," Demon sighed.

"Two for one special, just as I like them." She flashed a smile and moved ahead.

***

Jeff kept his distance from Hammer. The less he had to talk with that guy the better. He examined the ground in front of him for any signs of movement as Jennifer had taught him. Look for changes in the ground structure. Upended sand or grass, a shifted head stone... If he could show them he knew what he was doing, then maybe the Commander would back off.

He glanced behind him to see what Hammer and Sentinel were doing. They walked casually side by side, wielding their flashlights in their hands, unfocused on their surroundings. They were enjoying a normal conversation. Like walking through a graveyard in the middle of the night looking for zombies was not important.

"So this gun can fire rounds that are .45, .50, or even a 12-gauge buckshot!" Sentinel pulled his tablet out of his side bag and was showing what Jeff could only assume was the masterful weapon to Hammer.

"No shit. And this is a revolver?"

"Standard six-shooter set up."

These two aren't even trying to take this seriously. They're just fan-girling over a gun.

The surrounding trees rustled as the wind blew through them. Jeff waited, his hands clutching his gun tightly. Maybe he was being too alert? He tried to clear his head as memories of his first experience with the undead distracted his senses. The trees rustled again.

"Guys, I think I heard something!" He called back to Hammer and Sentinel, just in case it was a real threat, and not his nerves again.

Hammer took a brief look at the surrounding area. "It's only an outdoor graveyard in Florida...what could it possibly be?" Hammer waved his arms at the space around them.

Jeff spat on the ground as he advanced again. He could feel the heat of his anger rising in his veins. He squeezed his gun tight.

"Will you please quit holding that gun like you're about to kick in an apartment door?" Sentinel yelled. "You're making me nervous."

I thought we were out here to kill monsters, not chit chat. How am I supposed to defend myself if something pops up?

Jeff gaped back at them. Were they being serious? Or was this just another stupid hazing ritual? This is why he'd never joined a fraternity in college. Adam had gone through it and it was horrible. Among some very unpleasant things, Adam had to wear one outfit for a week without cleaning it. That was a week Jeff's nostrils never got back.

He angrily holstered his weapon, pulling out his large Maglite from his tactical belt instead. At least he could see better if something tried to jump out at him. Sentinel and Hammer went back to their stupid conversation as Jeff pressed on. The sooner they cleared this area, the sooner he would meet back up with Jennifer and go home.

***

Jennifer followed Demon out of the mausoleum, smiling ear to ear. It was a family entombment, with some fresh members that had decided to put up a fight. She cleared more of the undead than him. Vampire or not, the area was too small for him to swing around his long sword efficiently, causing him to hit the walls and shelves of the small space. Due to the stipulation of their bet, he had to use his sword and not his knives. In this instance a gun was more effective.

"You stole my kill," Demon frowned as he walked out behind her and shut the heavy door again.

"You were taking too long." She stuck her tongue out at him.

"You are not beating me tonight," he chuckled.

"We'll see." Jennifer sat down on the small step leading up to the mausoleum door. They had been at this for half an hour. It was a good chance to take a quick break. "So what do you think about Knight?"

"The new kid?" He sat down next to her. "Is 'Knight' going to be his call sign by the way?"

"Up to him. He can change it if he wants. It's his last name, but I thought it kind of fits. You didn't answer my question though." She frowned at him as he pulled a small rag out of his side pack to wipe the slime and body fluids off his blade.

"He seems like he has a good heart." Jennifer looked at Demon questionably, "I'm not talking about the beating one. Though I could tell he's nervous."

"Yeah, well, Terrence isn't helping at all." She ejected the magazine from her gun and loaded a new one. They needed to mark the mausoleum as complete, so she pulled out her knife and began scratching the gardening complete symbol into the steps.

"You are the only one who's really worked with him. So it really only matters what you think."

"I think he has a future with us. Though that's not set in stone. I have a hard time keeping him focused. If I can't, he's gonna get killed."

"Well he is definitely focused, just not at the task at hand." Demon smiled down at her. His eyes were the piercing yellow of his vampire form, due to the dark light, but they were offset by the softness in his gaze, as the corners of his eyes crinkled slightly along the edges. The only part of him that showed some sort of age. The old Jennifer would have been swooned over by that gaze.

"What do you mean? What is he more focused on?" Jennifer dug the tip of her blade harder into the stone step.

"On you of course."

He laughed as Jennifer dropped her knife. She hastily picked it up and shoved it in its sheath as she turned to him. Her cheeks were already burning as she gazed back at his amused face. She tried to hide it under the icy stare she had before to get him back in line.

"Oh give me a break!"

"You're telling me that you never noticed how he looks at you sometimes?"

"I...well..." Jennifer racked her brain trying to think of something to say, anything but what Demon was implying "I bailed his ass out when we met and I think he's just looking at me as a friendly face. Or a role model maybe? I'm sure once Terrence lightens up, he'll be looking to him—"

Demon's lips curled as he tried to hide his smile, but the quick whiff of air that escaped his nostrils confirmed he wasn't buying this excuse. Jennifer's face was definitely on fire.

Why am I so embarrassed and defensive that Jeff might like me? He's just another recruit. But...every time I look at him...I see you...I know he's not you, but you're so similar, it hurts...

"He likes you...a lot. His heart starts racing every time you look in his direction. It's kind of annoying to hear," Demon mused, throwing the rag he was using into a biohazard-labeled bag. He rose to his feet and grabbed Jennifer by her hands, pulling her up before she could escape back to the hunt. "You need to be honest with how you feel too." Demon's eyes pierced into her soul. She couldn't face his gaze. She released herself from his grasp, trying to put some distance between them. She knew he wasn't letting her out of this conversation now that it had turned more personal, but she couldn't talk to him when he looked at her like that. Especially about feelings for another man.

"What makes you think I like him?" Jennifer crossed her arms, pressing her fingers into her skin.

"You're standing up to the Commander for one. Always defending the kid."

"Only because he's taking this '*break in the F-N-G*' crap too far. Besides, you and Sentinel have gotten into it with him before too!" She felt a lump fill in her throat.

"True." Demon walked over to her. He grabbed her shoulders and turned her toward him again. She reluctantly looked up into his eyes. A pit formed in her chest. "Even when we were together, Jen, you never defended me like that with him."

He wasn't wrong, but it was probably more that she didn't think he needed protection. He always felt he had to protect her. She had known Demon since she was six. As she'd grown up, they'd become closer, and their friendship had blossomed into something more.

Being with Demon wasn't all bad, but there were things he could never give her. She wanted a partner she could grow old with. She wanted to be a mother. At least, that's what she thought she wanted. She'd only experienced a glimpse of that life. The hole in her chest widened, and her breath became tight as she let herself think about it.

"I told you when you were in Europe, and liked that boy Conor, vampires mate for life. But if you want to move on I will be respectful to your wishes. It's a shame, because I did like our little trysts." Demon held Jennifer's face in his hands and smiled down at her. Her eyes burned, as warm tears streamed down her face. His touch was always cold, but there was a warmth to it when he held her. She let him draw her in close, and he kissed her forehead sweetly, before pulling her into a full hugging embrace. "I know you were hurt, and lost a lot five years ago, but if you really want the life you dreamed of, you have to open yourself up again."

"Thank you, *Ayo*." He had told her his real name years ago. She leaned into his chest, accepting what he was telling her, letting his real name fall gently off her tongue as the pain she kept locked up released for the first time.

"You're welcome, my, Fire." He squeezed his arms tightly around her.

***

Jeff looked at his watch again. It had been an hour since they'd started their patrol. There were no zombies and nothing lurked in the shadows. He was disappointed, sure, but that was probably for the better. It meant the area was safe. He heard two soft whistles of a silencer behind him. He turned around to see Sentinel with his gun drawn. The smoke was still hovering over the end of the barrel. There were two dark mounds a few feet away from him.

"Finally! I was beginnin' to worry Demon and Phoenix might be gettin' all the action tonight," Sentinel exclaimed as he holstered his weapon.

"There's enough to go around. Always is." Hammer had his flask out again. Jeff guessed it was filled with whiskey, based off the smell that came off his breath when he spoke.

"Yeah, but you and I both know that Phoenix wouldn't let us hear the end of it if they had all the work." Sentinel walked over within speaking distance of Jeff. If they were going to work together, now might be a good time to get to know them better.

"Hey, so how do you guys all know each other anyway?"

"Our families have been in this organization since it was officially organized," Sentinel explained. "I knew of Z.E.R.O, but not every nightmare that existed until my return from my tour about five years ago. I'm sure Phoenix told you she learned about everything much earlier?" Jeff nodded. He never tried to pry, because it seemed like a hard subject for her.

"Why only keep it in the families? Why didn't you guys recruit more people on the outside, like me?"

"You took this all pretty well, but even I wasn't too sure that first night I met you. It would cause major panic if everyone knew. We keep it in the blood line, it's our families' burdens to bear." A dark shadow fell over Sentinel's eyes. "We fight the wars the rest of the world doesn't know, or *want* to know about."

Jeff had stumbled into this world, and had made the choice to be here. He'd had a normal life up until three months ago. Everyone else here had lived with the knowledge that monsters exist their whole lives. They didn't get a choice in what they wanted to do with their lives. This was the only option they had. He glanced back at Hammer, a few meters behind them, taking another swig from his flask. He remembered his conversation with Jennifer in the diner. When she asked if he used alcohol to cope with stress. She was probably thinking about Hammer when she asked him.

"Phoenix called Hammer 'Terrence'—how come she calls him by his first name? I noticed with everyone else she uses last names only or call signs." Jennifer had briefly mentioned it to him before, but Jeff thought this could be a way to get to know the other team members and Jennifer a little better.

"Uh." Sentinel's mouth hung open as he nervously glanced around him, looking for a way out of this questioning. To his relief, Hammer came up from behind and pushed Jeff's head forward, leading him back to the task at hand.

"Forget it, kid. You have to earn the right to ask those kinds of questions." There was a fury behind Hammer's eyes. Jennifer had told him that after she became an orphan, Hammer's family had raised her.

"Why don't you scout ahead again. It looks pretty dead over here anyway." Sentinel pushed himself between them.

"Uh, yeah. Okay." Jeff walked ahead again and reached what looked to be the edge of the property. Martin Luther King Boulevard sat quietly on the other side of the fence line. He checked behind him. Hammer and Sentinel were still where he left them, chatting among themselves.

"I've seen more action playing paintball with Adam." Jeff kicked the dirt with his boot. This evening had been nothing but ridicule and disappointment.

I wonder what Jen and Demon are—

A blur of motion passed his vision as something lunged out of the bushes to the left of him. Jeff tripped backwards onto the ground and scurried away from the shadow. He looked closely at what had grabbed at him, glimpsing the face of a young man salivating, skin a pale white. There was blood on their shirt and mouth. This was a zombie! It was wearing a Kappa Delta shirt, a local fraternity at the nearby university.

It rose from where it fell after its unsuccessful attack, and spotted him again. It immediately rushed for him. Jeff tried to get himself off the ground, but struggled at the strength of this frat-boy zombie as it landed on top of him.

"Shit!" He pushed it off, barely getting to his feet. Jeff backed off from the zombie a couple of meters as he strategized a plan of attack. The frat-boy recovered quickly from the kick, turning its attention to Jeff, again. Without hesitation, Jeff turned and bolted back toward Hammer and Sentinel for aid. The zombie also ran full speed as it gave chase. He didn't know they could be so fast.

"Hey look!" Sentinel pointed in Jeff's direction, "New kid got one!"

"Help me!" Jeff screamed, while he tried to inhale more air into his burning lungs.

"You're going to be just fine pal," Hammer waved to him, like a parent telling a child to walk off a small fall.

Realizing he wasn't getting any assistance, Jeff spun around, and in one movement pulled his gun out of his holster. He fired eight shots into the zombie's face, and it collapsed at his feet. Jeff bent over, leaning on his knees for support, while he tried to gulp in some fresh air. His heart was racing and he felt every pulse of it pounding in his ears.

"Dude! Kid just turned his head into a hamburger!" Sentinel yelled out, laughing. Jeff attempted to laugh along while he tried to catch some air. "Shit! Knight, look out!"

He felt a heavy force ram into him, knocking him onto the hard ground. He hadn't been sacked that hard since he'd played football. Whatever had hit him had continued to roll over with him. He moved to see what it was, even though his mind knew. It was dressed in a matching t-shirt as the other one. He looked human still. The eyes hadn't lost the color yet in the pupils. Its skin was intact and just pallid. It looked normal except for the splatter of blood on its cheek and the gaping hole of a bite that had ripped out half its neck. The zombie clawed for his face, and Jeff managed to grab its hands before it could do any damage. He shifted his weight as he tried to kick it off of him. He finally managed to wedge one boot on its chest. He used all his might to kick it away.

He looked at the ground around him for his sidearm. It was knocked a few feet away. Jeff tried to calculate if there would be time for him to scramble for it, before his attacker came at him again. The new zombie was already on its feet, and his gun wasn't going to be a viable option. Jeff desperately looked for something to hit it with before it reached him in the little time he had. He noticed his heavy Maglite was still close enough. Just as the zombie was within arm's reach, Jeff grabbed the light and swung it up like a club, hitting the creature in the head. It rolled down again into the hard sand and sod. Unfortunately it was not far enough for Jeff to be able to get up. The zombie quickly recovered, and was after him again, leaping on top of him.

Jeff used his light as a bite guard. He tried to focus on the monster, despite the warm, already noxious breath that filled the air around him. He twisted his head as Jennifer and Demon approached the group. A look of sheer terror was on Jennifer's face. Hammer motioned to Demon to restrain her.

"Let me go! He's gonna die!" Jennifer screamed.

"Just wait." Hammer's tone was calm.

"Fuck you!" Jennifer screamed again, and Jeff could hear her struggle against Demon's grasp. As much as he wanted to see what they were doing, he had to focus on his attacker. The saliva was beginning to gather around the light, and Jeff struggled to keep its fingers from reaching his skin, pushing the creature away with his feet pressing against it.

"Jen, will you just fucking wait!" Hammer yelled this time as the struggling continued.

Jeff felt his heart drum louder in his ears. He was sick of this, of the whole night. Why the hell wasn't Hammer letting her help him? How could he trust this team? All the rage built up inside him; his head hurt as his veins pulsed. He was going to die if he didn't do something now!

Jeff howled, what he would later recount as a warrior's scream. Using all his strength, he pushed the zombie off of him, and rolled to be on top of it. He began to bash its head repeatedly with his flashlight, screaming with every hit. The soft face of the monster caved in and crumbled to the weight of the pressure, applied by his flashlight baton. He wasn't as phased by the sound of the meat squelching with each blow as he thought he would be. He continued to relentlessly pound the creature, until he was sure it had stopped moving. Jeff dropped the bent and broken tool to his side. He looked up toward the team, exhausted. Jennifer's expression slowly changed from fear and anguish, to relief. Demon released her, and she smiled proudly back at Jeff. Hammer walked over to him, and held out his hand. Jeff accepted it, feeling dizzy as he stood. The rage and adrenaline had left his body.

"Hardcore!" Sentinel cheered, breaking the silence.

"You don't do anything half-assed do you?" Demon chuckled as he examined the bodies.

Hammer put his hand on Jeff's shoulder. "Congratulations Knight. You just made your bones. Welcome to the family."

The group applauded him. Jennifer walked over, and pulled a wet towelette out of her side pack. She offered it to him to clean up.

"Happy Graduation." She smiled up at him. Jeff could have sworn he noticed a different sparkle in her eyes tonight, despite her eyes being red and puffy. It was either allergies, or she had cried recently. They stood awkwardly for a moment. Demon elbowed her in the back as he walked by, causing Jennifer to blush in the dark moon light.

"So uh…" He didn't know what to say. His eyes wandered as he tried not to stare at her. He noted Sentinel walking off from the group behind her, holding a finger to his ear as he spoke to someone through his communicator.

"Um, can we talk? Alone…later?" Jennifer sounded nervous as she spoke.

"Uh, yeah…sure."

She smiled wide, and walked briskly over to Demon. Jeff wiped down his arms and face with the small wet towel. He opened up his side pack and grabbed the small biohazard bag they were all equipped with for situations like this, and tossed in the used wipe. He pulled out more wet wipes from his own pack, and cleaned himself some more. Luckily, he didn't get that much on him. He checked to make sure he didn't have any scratches either, as that would be a death sentence.

"Shit…are ya sure? Alright, show us responding." Sentinel's panicked voice broke through the cheerful chatter.

"What's up?" Hammer wiped his hands on his pants as he got up from examining Jeff's kills.

"You're not going to believe this. You see those two?" Sentinel pointed to the fraternity zombies. "They came from a party near here that's gone very wrong."

"What? Why are we just now hearing about it?" Jennifer closed her fists, digging her fingers into her palms.

"Nobody noticed it until security was called to tell the party to settle down. When they arrived there was a slaughterhouse. One of the guards got grabbed too..."

"We could have Bravo Team meet us there." Demon looked toward Hammer, checking for approval.

"Nah, they wouldn't be able to handle it. We don't know how many are infected." Hammer rubbed his chin. Plan formed, he turned to Sentinel. "Call whoever we got over there, have them quarantine the area and evacuate if necessary. Have Bravo come here to clean up, and tag these two."

Sentinel nodded and marched away from the team to relay the message to dispatch. Jeff looked at the two bodies of the zombies he had just killed. There were more of them like this. He was barely able to handle just two. He felt a shiver run across him at the idea of handling multiple, fast, and insanely strong undead creatures in the close future. He walked over to his gun, picking it up. He watched as Hammer stuck a small device with a blinking light into one of the bodies.

"It's a GPS for Bravo, to know where the most toxic bodies are located," Jennifer said, answering his silent questioning gaze.

"Oh..." There were so many gadgets that he was yet to become acquainted with.

"Let's get going." Jennifer jogged back to the entrance.

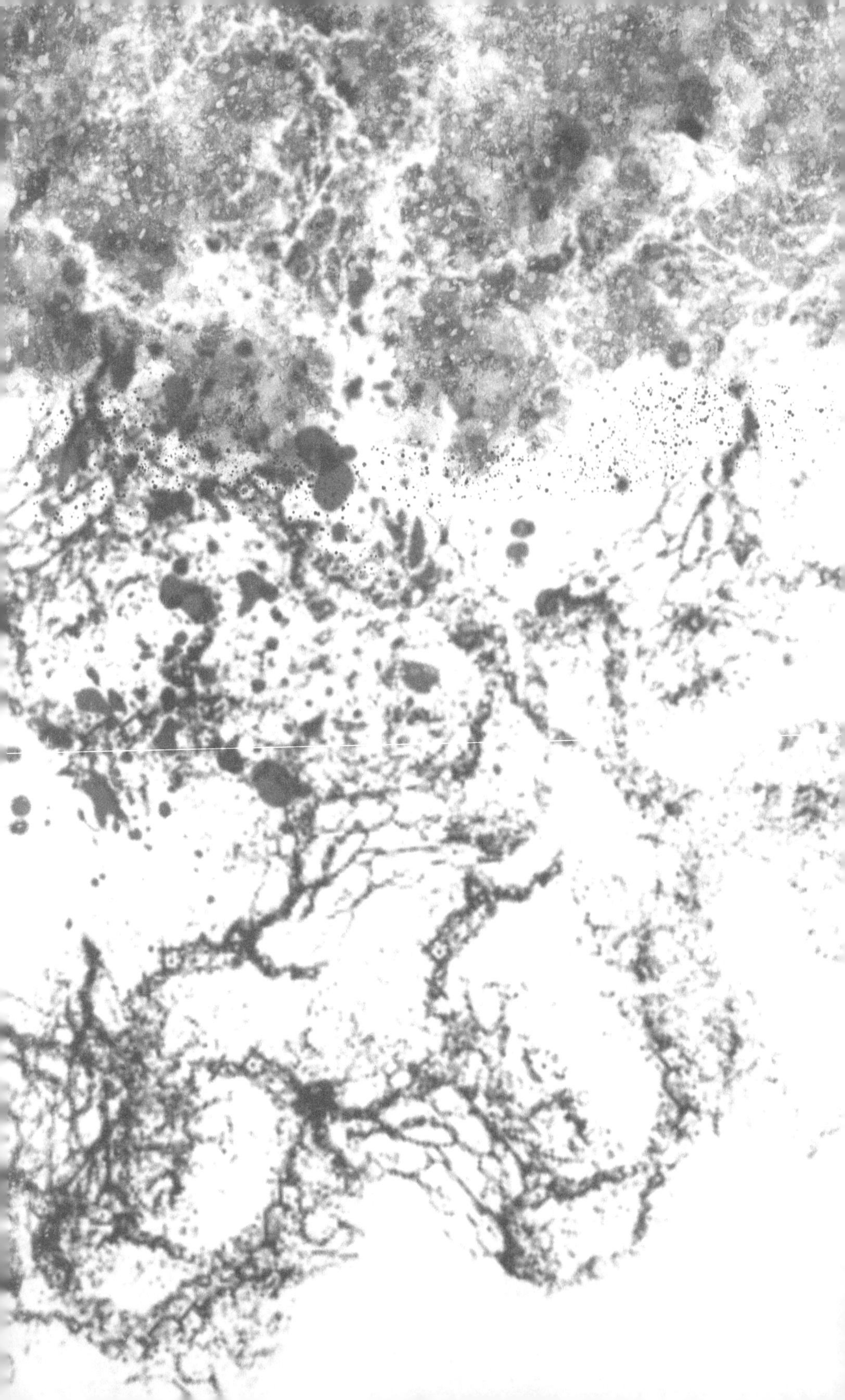

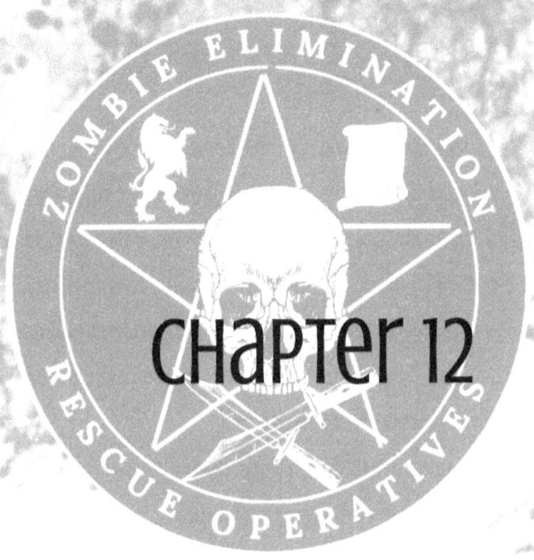

CHapTer 12

The roads were clear of heavy traffic as it was almost close to midnight. Jennifer took the rear position of their car convoy as they traveled. Sentinel and Demon were in the lead, and Hammer right behind them. They weaved around the few cars on the road when necessary, but always formed their line back after passing. Sentinel informed them the apartment complex was twenty minutes away from their last location. It worried her how far the two zombies Jeff had slain must have walked before reaching their location. How many more people might be infected? Plus, the timeline didn't make sense. If they were infected at the party, and died on the way back through this area, it was an insanely fast amplification period. Unless they were driving... She made a mental note to get Bravo Team to search for a vehicle near the cemetery and canvas the surrounding areas for other possible victims. They couldn't risk a mass spread of infection. Jennifer was startled when Jeff spoke up beside her, breaking her concentration.

"Hey, you okay? What's wrong?"

"Something isn't right. There are too many zombies out here recently. We're not close enough to a normal D-Day event for this many."

"*Off the top of my head, with our usual undead numbers, I agree.*" Sentinel's voice came buzzing through their communicators.

"*So what is everyone saying? That we are already in a D-Day scenario without realizing it? That doesn't seem possible.*" Demon was next to speak.

"I don't see any other conclusions. What other explanation could there possibly be?" Jennifer gripped her steering wheel tighter.

"Well, every other D-Day event has occurred concurrently across the globe," Sentinel responded.

"No covens have reported fighting off any of the hordes that occur with the usual event either. You remember what I told you when I got back from my last meeting?" Demon was right. He had just pleaded with the local covens a few months ago. If it was an event, they would have been contacted by their reps in the vampire community. Jennifer pressed harder on the gas. She was annoyed that no one seemed to be processing what she was trying to get at. Her mind wandered again to the small five millimeter holes she'd been finding at every active site they'd been to recently.

"I know," she replied, trying to hide her frustration, "Look, what if, hypothetically, the zombies were evolving this whole time? I'm not talking major advances, but a simple trial-and-error system that showed someone the weaknesses in our defense patterns?" This idea was a big shot in the dark, and not entirely what she meant to say. Hearing Hammer's dejected sigh as the first response enforced how unpopular it was.

"Phoenix, you know full well the maggot eaters can't employ any kind of higher level thinking beyond hunt-kill-feed. Whatever has them up and walking around, whatever bug, virus, or Biblical plague it is, it doesn't evolve. It just turns whatever it touches to shit."

There was a quiet after Hammer spoke. Everyone knew once you turned, you lose any relevance of thought you once had. She bit her lip as she pumped the gas pedal again.

Think think think…the damn holes have to be connected…but what group or creatures would want to create zombies? No one has been able to replicate the virus yet to come up with a transmission method like that. All Bio Weapons are created by bite, or blood. That can't reanimate a corpse. But still…

"Okay then. What if they were getting some help?"

"From who?" Sentinel questioned.

"I don't know from who! But again, hypothetically, what if there were some group out there that wants to help the zombies take over? I mean, Demon, aren't there vampires who think they should lord over us, like farmers with cattle?"

"Yes, an immature trait. Usually only exists in non-bloodline vampires. Humans who lusted for power in their previous lives." Demon's response had a bit of a growl to it. It's people like that, like Orcus, which had led him to being banished from his coven.

"And we all know werewolves and demons wouldn't be doing anything, because they need humans just as much as the vamps do." She was hoping that someone else would pick up what she was getting at, and maybe explain it better. When she was frustrated, it was hard for her to formulate her thoughts coherently.

"So you think there's a group of humans that's somehow helping zombies populate?" Jeff broke the silence. Finally someone was getting it. There was a reason why she liked him.

"I can't be sure but there has to be something going on here. Think about it. Terrorist groups have experimented with all kinds of biological agents in the past. It was only a matter of time before they discovered a way to use a virus that turns people into the undead, or reanimate corpses that haven't fully decayed..."

"*Alright,*" said Hammer, "*so you're saying that some terrorist extremist asshole discovered there was a virus that is reanimating these fuckers, and figured out how to weaponize it? Why would they be injecting their undead cocktail into a few random graveyards in Florida? What about this place we're going to?*" He made a few good points.

"I'm saying that maybe this is the first step toward something bigger. Maybe they're using random locations as a control group. They could just be testing their virus, and aren't even aware that we exist yet. That being said, if these locations are random, they aren't too far apart, so their lab must be nearby and—"

"*Sorry to cut you off, Phoenix, but we're here.*" Sentinel spoke up, and she could see Hammer's blinker indicate they would be turning right. They would have to finish this conversation after they cleared the current situation. She pulled the truck up next to Hammer's Hummer, and placed it in park. Before opening the door, she turned to Jeff.

"Hey, when we're around civilians, we use our code names. I'm gonna call you Rook because we don't have one for you yet, okay?" Jeff nodded that he understood. They hopped out of her truck, and walked to the back, pulling the AR-15s out of the duffle bags. Jennifer screwed suppressors onto each, and handed Jeff extra ammo. They walked with the others, now more heavily equipped, to the door leading into the interior apartments.

She looked up at the building before them, and was thankful it was a modern design. It was only two floors. The stairwell could be seen through the glass wall exterior that made the front facade of the building. It appeared to go up to a small landing and split into two adjacent hallways of the second floor. The first floor exterior facade that winged the lobby featured regular stucco walls. The second floor was more interesting in design. Apartments only lined one side of the hall, and the exterior wall facing the parking lot was nothing but glass, same as the lobby. Jennifer noted the lights were off, however, on the left wing. The number of people or zombies up there was unknown. The design of the building would make it easy to quarantine as she could make out a set of doors at the top of each landing, leading into the halls. They shouldn't have to worry about too many stragglers getting by.

"Sentinel, where are we headed?" Hammer racked back his gun.

"It's through here, second floor." Sentinel responded. "Our contact is waiting by the apartment in question for us."

That's good, bet it's the dark hallway. Hopefully everyone downstairs is alright…downward walking is difficult for zombies, no matter how fresh they are.

Sentinel held his tablet up to the door lock, and it beeped, allowing them entry. They headed into the building, the cool air conditioning sent a chill down Jennifer's spine after being outside for so long. They crept as quietly as they could with their heavy boots. A woman peeked her head out of a ground floor apartment door. Jennifer stopped, and held her finger to her lips. She pulled out a Tampa City police badge they kept on them for civilians, and motioned the woman to head back inside. She was obviously nervous and confused by the military look of them, and closed the door hastily.

We're going to need civilian control over here. This is such a mess!

The stairwell was narrow, and they had to walk in pairs. Hammer went first, followed by Sentinel and Demon. Jennifer formed the rear with Jeff. Their boots made the metal stairs ring as they climbed. There was a large window that displayed the back courtyard where the stairwell split to a landing. Sentinel signaled to move up the left hall. The dark one. When they neared the top, they slowed their pace.

"Hey, Phoenix, let me ask you something," Jeff whispered. "You really think there's a group out there trying to weaponize zombies?"

"It's a theory." She knew they weren't supposed to talk, but he was her rookie.

"Yeah, but we're their food. Why would there be a group of cattle trying to help the slaughterhouse?"

"Maybe someone believes that we, as humans, have done a thorough job of fucking up the planet, and deserve to die as a species. I don't care why they are doing it, I just want to stop them." They reached the top of the stairwell and Hammer reeled around, glaring harshly at her.

"I can't believe I have to tell you, Phoenix, no chit-chat."

She nodded, and gave Jeff a *"stop asking me questions" glare.* Hammer opened the door to the hall of apartments, and crept in. A single flashlight turned on down the hall. Jennifer could barely make out a security guard at the far end. When he noticed the group, he approached them hastily.

Jeff glanced at Jennifer questioningly. She could tell from his nod toward the guard that he wanted to know if that guy had anything to do with their organization, probably because of how calm he looked when they arrived. She sighed, and moved as close to Jeff's ear as she could so she could whisper.

"Informant. Civilians that keep us tapped into what's going on outside our little group, but have no way, or wish, of being tactical like the rest of us. Not even good for Bravo or Charlie teams." Hammer whipped around again. He looked directly at Jennifer with a look a parent gives when reprimanding their child a second time. They nodded their heads, and she heard a small chuckle escape Sentinel and Demon.

"Glad you guys showed up! You missed the party though." The security guard shook Hammer's hand. He was an older black man, probably in his late forties; heavy set and short in height, barely 5'6", with a bald fade cut. His forehead was slicked with anxious sweat.

"Story of my life. What's the shit-tuation?" Hammer asked.

"Got called out to this place, and it was a fucking bloodbath! My buddy didn't make it out..." The guard had a blank look in his eyes Jennifer was all too familiar with. "Due to the openness of the building, I had the power cut to the hall so no civilians could see anything they shouldn't."

"Alright. Take the rest of the night off, and we'll take it from here."

"Take the night off? I'm quitting. Working at the damn burger joint was safer than this shit!" The guard hurried out of the hall, muttering under his breath, "How do I always find this crap?"

Hammer signaled the group to prepare for a breach. They gathered around. Light from inside the apartment glowed out of the peephole of the door. Demon and Sentinel lined up against the wall behind Hammer. Jennifer and Jeff took the wall on the opposite side. She knew Hammer was going to bust the door in his normal, boisterous fashion. They never had to carry a battering ram. Hammer took a step back and smashed the door in with his foot, the loud bang echoing down the corridor.

"Very neatly done sir." Demon commented.

"Blow me. I have five shells full of silver in the car. You want them in your ass?" Hammer answered and proceeded to enter the apartment.

"Subtle." Demon chuckled as he followed behind him.

***

They fanned out by the door as they entered. Jeff held his rifle ready, scanning the room for any sign of movement. The place was trashed, but how much was from the attack, and how much was the party was hard to judge. There were various empty bottles and red Solo cups strewn across countertops and tables, stains on the sitting furniture from foodstuffs, and cigarette buds, with an assortment of clothes over it all. If it weren't for the pool of blood leading from the door to the back bedroom, it would have looked like a regular kegger.

"What a mess." Jennifer was the first to speak after it was determined the room was clear.

"Charming," Demon grimaced as he examined the blood pool.

"This place looks like hell," Sentinel stated as he slowly walked around the room, assessing what had happened.

"I think I crashed here once. Should be a cigarette burn under the left cushion." Hammer walked over to the couch and lifted the cushion with his gun. He chuckled.

"So there was a random outbreak at a frat party? Where is everyone if this place has been locked up?" There were no bodies or remnants of bodies anywhere. Jeff scanned the room again.

"That's what we're here tryin' to investigate." Sentinel answered with a puzzled expression as he looked over the mess again, "It is very strange there is nothin'...somethin's not right'."

"As far as I'm concerned, we are not here to investigate. We're here to destroy any and all flesh-munchers," Hammer gruffed while he checked the kitchen area.

"Spoken like a true Sherlock Holmes," Demon muttered sarcastically.

"Go fuck yourself, you chupacabra," Hammer responded, as he glared angrily back at Demon. Jeff couldn't read if they were playing with each other or serious in their disdain for one another. He glanced at Jennifer, who only rolled her eyes at the two of them. Hammer and Demon laughed boisterously. Jeff still didn't understand their dark humor.

Jennifer cautiously followed the large trail of blood toward the back of the apartment. She slowly rolled her feet with each step to reduce noise, investigating every piece of furniture she walked by for hidden crawlers.

There could still be a threat in the area, and these guys are joking like nothing is going on. How are they the best? Seems like Jennifer pulls all the weight around here.

She stopped a few feet from the back bedroom door, furrowing her brow like she often did when she was concentrating. Carefully, she leaned slightly forward toward the back door. There were smears of blood on the frame and a smeared handprint on its face. The stains appeared like someone had struggled not to be pulled in at one point, and someone else had slammed the door shut.

"Hey guys, I think Phoenix found something." Jeff turned to the rest of the group and nodded in her direction. All conversations stopped. A tense silence lingered. Jennifer pointed to her ear, signaling them to all listen as she backed away from the bedroom door.

The only audible noises in the air were their breathing and the hard floorboards creaking under Jennifer's steps as she rejoined the team. A sound of wood creaking started from the back room. Jeff swallowed back into his empty mouth as sweat beaded down his brow. It was hard to hear at first, but when he focused, he could make out the signature sound of air passing through the vocals of the undead. The hairs on his neck rose. Gradually more moans joined the chorus, turning it into a haunting choir. The door to the back bedroom bounced as large thuds began to beat against it. A steady rhythm at first that only increased in fervor as the moans grew louder. Jeff took the safety off his rifle.

Jennifer pulled herself back in line with her team as they raised their firearms, and Demon pulled out his sword. There was a loud pop. A head burst through the wood of the door. No one fired. The hole around the head grew larger as hands ripped at the open space.

Jeff had already experienced the raw strength of these monsters; it was inhuman. The zombies had full use of their muscles, which were not yet decayed. They had no pain inhibitors to tell them to stop straining themselves. They pushed themselves over their limits for one thing, to feed.

The zombies continued to tear at the door as if it were made of paper. Within seconds of the head appearing, bodies pushed through from the widened gap and hit the floor with hard thuds. Jeff turned nervously to his comrades. How close were they letting the monsters get before opening fire?

Three zombies made it through the gaping hole. More peeled their way in through the opening, clambering on top of the bodies in front of them. They continued to force their way through until the wood of the door finally buckled and collapsed onto the zombies that had already made some distance. A group of about twenty people—God, they still looked alive—marched through the opening, tripping on the fallen door and the bodies of their brethren that struggled to get to their feet. Despite their desperate efforts to escape the room, they were unaware of Alpha Team's presence. Jeff took in a short quick breath as he tried to calm his raging nerves. One zombie in front of the pack turned toward the team. Its blank eyes gazed at them. Jeff adjusted his grip on his rifle, and the undead fiend's mouth opened wide, releasing a piercing scream.

"Drop 'em," Hammer said calmly.

The team opened fire on the zombie horde. Despite their gun silencers, the gun fire was still loud enough to alert the zombies that hadn't made it through the door yet. The horde rushed the doorway. Each zombie pushed frantically against the body in front of them.

Despite the actual speed of the event as it unfolded, objects and motion slowed down in Jeff's vision as he focused. He released a breath every time he pulled the trigger. The faces of the people these monsters used to be were plaguing his vision and mind as they fell before him. They were normal; no decay, no rot. Just blood. Just a few hours ago, they had been someone's son, daughter, sister, or brother...their bodies made hard thuds that rang in his ears as they hit the ground. Just as quick as their attack was initiated, it was over. Demon wiped his blade with a rag and threw it on the pile of dead that lay before them.

"Hell of a party!" Hammer said as he released the magazine on his rifle and replaced it with another. Sentinel and Jennifer advanced toward the backroom, inspecting the bodies before stepping over them. Jeff released the magazine on his rifle, and reloaded, just in case.

There was a small creak of a door hinge. On a normal day it would have been inconsequential, but tonight the sound was amplified. Sentinel and Jennifer were closest to the door and had their guns up in seconds. A white strip of toilet paper waved through the crack of the doorframe.

"Don't shoot! I'm a human!" A man's scared voice could be heard, muffled through the door.

"Come out slowly and have your hands up where we can see them," Jennifer commanded. The door creaked open to reveal a middle-aged, balding man. He was in a food service delivery uniform, a bright red polo shirt with a small white logo on the upper shoulder of a fast-food bag with wings. He held his hands up, still clutching the torn toilet paper like a flag of surrender. One of his hands was stained with blood. He was probably the one that had shut the door of the bedroom. He looked in awe at the fallen bodies in front of him. Jennifer raised her gun higher, so it was in line with his vision.

"I said I wasn't one of them! Can you get that thing out of my face, sweetheart?" The man sweated profusely, dabbing his forehead with the tissue.

"Have you been bitten, scratched, ingested any blood accidentally, *sweetheart*?" Jennifer shoved her barrel on the man's forehead.

"No! None of that!" The man's eyes were wild and he continued to sweat despite the cool temperature in the apartment. He was either hiding something, or maybe it was because of Jennifer holding a gun to his face.

Sentinel walked back to Demon. "How'd he manage to stay alive with all those things in there?" Demon shrugged, but from his facial expression, Jeff could tell he was also skeptical of the man.

"What's your name?" Demon asked with a growl in his voice.

"Uh...Chaz."

"How did you manage to survive this long?"

"I...I...I locked them in the bedroom when they grabbed that guard, and then locked myself in the bathroom. I've been trying to stay quiet and to not attract them. I only came out now because of all the commotion I heard. Goddamn it stinks!" Chaz's eyes shifted nervously. Jeff still couldn't tell if Chaz was lying or just terrified.

"Are there any other survivors in the apartment?" Hammer questioned as he walked over.

"Uh, no...just me," Chaz answered, his eyes darting frantically around the room. Hammer analyzed Chaz, his eyes narrowed as he studied him for any sign of changing, and abruptly turned to Demon and Jennifer with new orders.

"Demon, Phoenix, clear the rest of the apartment. Check for survivors, and make sure all these things are really dead."

"Yes sir," Jennifer acknowledged and lowered her gun finally from Chaz's face.

"On it." Demon walked into the back bedroom, and Jennifer followed.

"I said I was the only survivor!" Chaz yelled at Hammer. Hammer reeled around, looming his enraged face over Chaz who turned away quickly, terrified.

"Then having my people clear the apartment won't be an issue. Will it, Buttercup?" Hammer's words filtered through his gritted teeth.

"Uh...no...sorry," Chaz muttered almost inaudibly. Hammer slammed his fist on the wall near the survivor, causing him to flinch again. A cruel smile spread on Hammer's face as he turned and walked out of the apartment. Sentinel followed Hammer outside.

Jeff, having not been given any new orders, thought it would be best if he followed as well. Chaz wasn't going anywhere, and he would be an idiot if he tried to do something to Jennifer or Demon. Jeff took one more look at the bodies in front of him. Their eyes open, gaping back at him with the same blank stare they had when they were moving. They were already dead, but it didn't change the fact they still looked human. He gave them their final death. Jeff forced himself to swallow a deep shaky breath, and stepped outside to join the others.

Outside, Hammer had pulled a cigar out of his vest, and was puffing on it vehemently, while he paced in the hall. The lights were back on.

"Why is it always the assholes that survive?" Even though the question was rhetorical, Sentinel and Jeff shrugged. "I want you guys to check with all the neighboring apartments. One hall over, one floor down. Make sure that no one came into contact with anyone at this shitter. Clean-up's gonna be pissed at this horse mess. I don't want any more bodies tonight. Capiche?"

"Got it." Sentinel responded and headed off to his next task, but something wasn't sitting right with Jeff.

"A word with you, Hammer?"

"Knight, what you got?" Hammer asked while taking another puff of his cigar, thick smoke clouds wafting in Jeff's face.

"Something about that guy's story doesn't add up. He locked himself in the bathroom for hours before we got here? We saw those bastards turn the door into sawdust in a matter of seconds. If he was really hiding in the bathroom, they'd have busted in and ripped him apart by now."

"You're right. We'll finish up here, and interrogate him back at HQ. Clean up takes priority unfortunately. Don't worry, I'll make sure he doesn't go anywhere." Hammer took one last big puff, and tossed the used cigar to the ground. Plumes of smoke exited his nostrils as he stomped out the embers with his boot. He grabbed a set of black handcuffs from his belt, and marched back into the apartment. "Hey Chaz! Got you some new bracelets!"

Jeff met up with Sentinel on the landing. He gazed out the large back window to the back courtyard. The moon light bled into the space, casting a pale blue hue. He took a moment to clear his head as he peered out at the night sky. He had never joined the military after high school, because the thought of taking someone else's life scared him. What he was killing wasn't human anymore, but it didn't change the fact their faces were. He followed the skyline down, as he leaned his head against the cool glass. He glanced at the courtyard, and noticed a tree that seemed to line up with the window of the apartment the death kegger occurred in. The window was open...maybe some more of those monsters got out than they wanted. They could have fallen out the window, considering how determined they were breaking through a door.

"Hey man, you good?" Sentinel was holding the door open to the other set of second floor apartments.

"Yeah sorry. Just needed a minute."

"Alrigh'. I'm not one to pry, but if y'all need anyone to vent to, we're all family here. Ain't always gotta be Jen. I mean she's fine as hell, but just sayin'." Sentinel came down the stairs, and placed his hand on Jeff's shoulder. Jeff let out a chuckle. "Alright! Just gotta speak to a few more apartments on that end, and this floor will be done."

"Well let's get this finished." Jeff jogged up the steps to the adjacent second floor hall, with Sentinel catching up behind him. "Did anyone ever tell you, you kinda sound like Matthew McConaughey with all those 'Alrights'?"

"The ladies do all the time." Sentinel gave a suave smile and reached for the door.

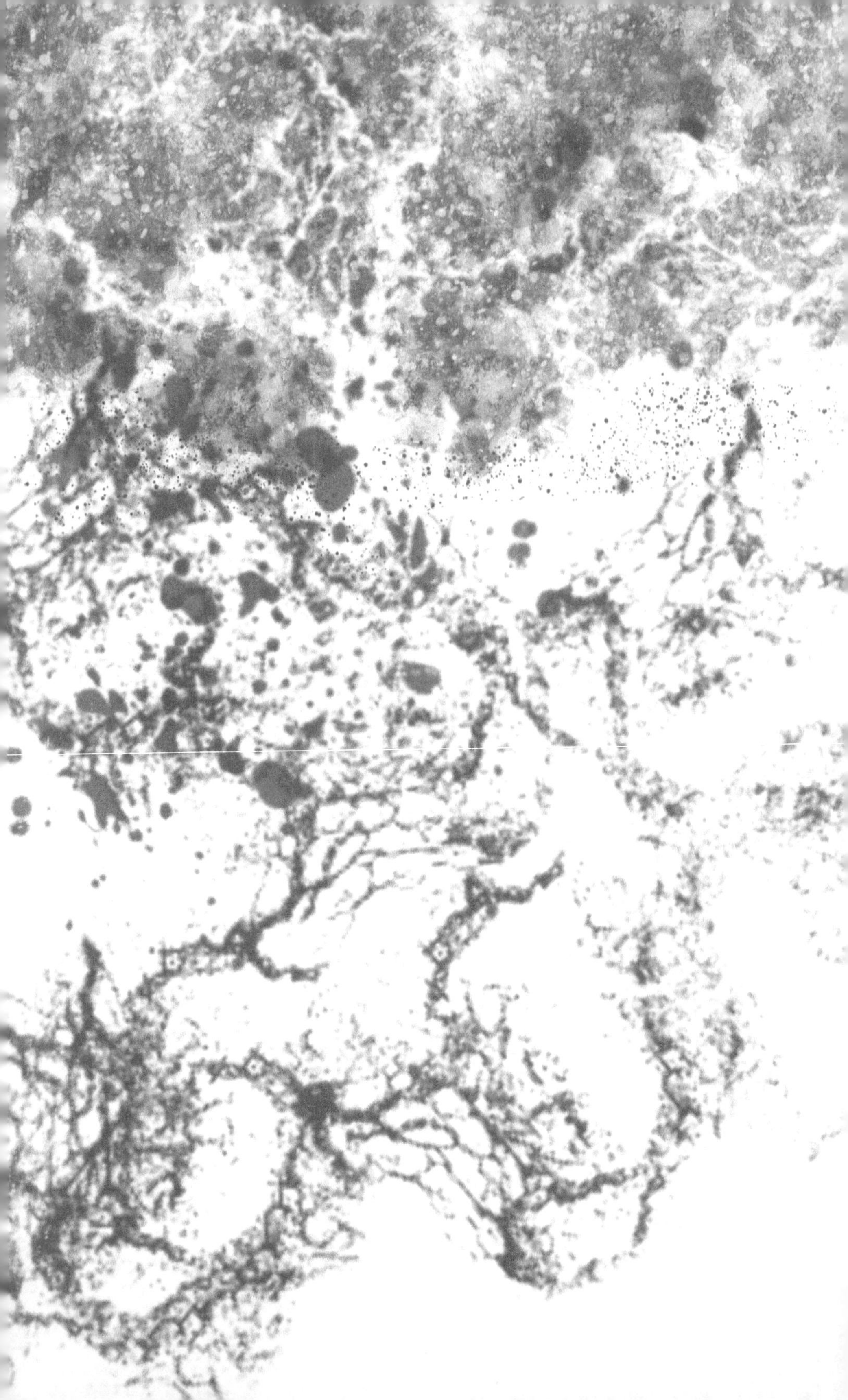

Interviewing the neighbors took an hour to complete. It seemed everybody was accounted for that attended the party. They were lucky. Jeff was exhausted, but knew the night was far from over. They left as Bravo Team pulled in with the clean-up vans. Hammer had taken custody of Chaz, blind folded and gagged. He drove him back to the base in his vehicle. When they arrived, Jennifer wanted to "escort" their suspect inside, through the back of the bar. She was still annoyed for being called "*sweetheart*" back at the apartment.

Amazingly, even with the blindfold, they were able to walk Chaz down all the stairs into their facility, although Jennifer didn't use as much care as normal to ensure he didn't tumble down on his ass. Chaz yelled up a muffled storm of expletives on the elevator ride to the second level. They removed his gag when they stepped out of the elevator.

"What the hell!? I told you guys what happened at the apartment. Where are you takin' me?" Chaz began to struggle the further they walked.

"Well there's just a small problem with your story," Jennifer spoke softly into his ear.

"What's that?"

"Frankly...it's bullshit." She pushed him further down the hall as she grinned from ear to ear.

"So what is this, the whole '*good cop, bad cop routine*?' Eat shit! I've seen this a hundred times before on TV! I got rights!"

"Brother, you've never seen anything like this routine before." Hammer gave Chaz a push, leading him around the next corner.

"Sir!" Jennifer stopped abruptly, saluting a tall man that stood in their path.

He was older than anyone Jeff had met yet at this organization, probably in his late sixties. Jeff glanced back and forth between Hammer and the mysterious stranger. Hammer balled his fists by his side and his body became rigid.

The man's hair was already silvered. Jeff noticed his facial features were very similar to Hammer's, just older and more hardened with time. They had the same blue eyes and jawline. This man was fit for his age, clean cut and well shaven. The opposite of their commander. Every aspect of this stranger's expensive black suit was particular and chosen specifically, down to the crisp, pewter gray pocket chief. He wore a small pin of the Z.E.R.O emblem on his lapel.

"Dad? What are you doing here?" Hammer crossed his arms, his look of displeasure remaining. The man walked over to Hammer, with his arms open wide in a welcoming gesture.

"Can't a father drop by to check on his son?" He laughed and turned to Jennifer. "At ease. No need to get so formal with me Jenny. I mean, I practically raised you as my daughter."

"Yes, Uncle Tobias. Bad habit I guess." Jennifer sheepishly brought her hand down.

Who is this guy?

"As much as I could hope those were your intentions, I have to call bullshit on that." Hammer continued to eye his father suspiciously, but he laughed it off again.

"I should have guessed. Nothing gets past my son. But believe it or not, I did come to see you. I'm here at the Council's request. We weren't too happy with your behavior at the last meeting, and now you are failing to respond to our inquiries."

"Well maybe if you had real soldiers to train, I would have stuck around longer." Hammer continued his unrelenting staring contest with his father. The uneasy tension in the air spread to the rest of the group as Sentinel and Demon exchanged uncomfortable glances with Jennifer.

"True. Now is there somewhere we can talk privately?"

"Yeah, in my office. Let me take care of this first and I'll meet you there." Hammer grabbed Chaz, and began to push him down the hall again. His father looked questioningly at Chaz and turned to Jennifer.

"I hope this isn't your new recruit."

"No, just a suspect." Jennifer turned and pointed toward Jeff. "Knight is our new team member."

The man nodded, and walked over to Jeff. He held his hand out. Jeff pulled off his glove; he was still dirty, and covered in sweat and grime from the night. He wiped his hand on his pants before shaking the man's hand.

"I see they got you working hard. Enjoying yourself?" the man asked, while holding a firm grip.

"Uh, Yes sir," Jeff responded. He knew this guy was important to this organization, based on his teammates' reactions. Even Demon, who was three times this guy's age, seemed intimidated.

"I apologize for my ill-mannered children for not introducing me. The name is Tobias Hammer, member of the High Council, head of the Eastern District of the United States. Pleased to meet you."

There was something about Tobias' smile that was offsetting. A false warmth? Something underneath it put Jeff on edge. He couldn't tell if it was just intimidation because of Tobias' position, or something more.

"Nice to meet you sir. My name is Jeff...er...Jeffery Knight. It's an honor to meet you." Jeff shook off the uneasy feeling as nerves. One of the leaders of this organization was standing in front of him, shaking his hand. He didn't want to embarrass himself.

"Nice to meet you, Knight. You seem eager, that's good. We need more people like you. I look forward to watching your future." Tobias winked and released Jeff's hand. He waved to the rest of the group as he walked off toward the elevators.

"Now where were we?" Hammer said as he brought everyone's attention back to Chaz, "Oh yes, please step into the interrogation room."

Hammer opened the door to a room adjacent to them and Jennifer pushed Chaz in. There was no furniture in the room, just one metal pipe running along the back wall. The fluorescents bounced harshly off the white linoleum tiled floor. There was nothing identifiable in the room to show their location. Not that he would have seen anything due to the fact they were underground. Jennifer kicked Chaz behind the knees, causing them to buckle as he fell forward.

"Goddammit! What the fuck?!" Chaz exclaimed as his face hit the cold hard floor of the room. She unbound one hand from the handcuffs and connected the cuff to the pipe in the room, restricting his movement. She removed the blindfold from Chaz's head. His eyes were blood-shot as he looked around the room frantically. Chaz took his free hand and scratched himself insistently on his neck. Jeff pushed it off as nerves. He would be anxious too if he was brought to an unknown location by a bunch of gun wielding strangers, under a gag and blindfolded.

"Wait here cupcake. I gotta go get the *bad cop*." Hammer laughed as he left the room.

"What the fuck is this? Fuck all of you! I have rights!" Chaz's skin turned deep red from anger, and he continued to aggressively scratch his neck.

"Those rights of yours don't work here, because we don't exist in the eyes of the world." Jennifer stood in front of Chaz, smiling coldly at him. It sent shivers down Jeff's spine how dark she was being. "If you promise to cooperate, we might just let you go on with what's left of your boring life."

She whipped around and walked toward the door. Jeff caught her wink at him to follow. Sentinel and Demon came as well. She locked the door using the keypad on the side and leaned against the wall, satisfied as they heard Chaz's screams in the room.

"Well, I guess we'll just let him stew for a bit before we start with the real questions." Sentinel said as he slid down the opposite wall to the floor.

"He shouldn't have called me sweetheart." Jennifer laughed and everyone joined her.

"What the hell was High Commander Hammer doing here?" Sentinel asked, directing the question at Jennifer.

"I have no clue. I wonder if it has to do with all the zombie encounters I've been reporting."

"Not likely. In all the years I've worked with this organization, they have never sent a member of the High Council to just '*check up*' on things." Demon spoke with his eyes closed as he rested against the wall. His skin was beginning to pale and grow ashy in hue. Daylight must be approaching.

"Of course you would know," Jen said coyly, "you've been working with Z.E.R.O since it was created." Demon laughed, smiling back weakly.

"Hammer's Dad is a member of the High Council...so is he like the head cheese of the whole organization?" Jeff was still trying to learn the hierarchy.

"Pretty much," Sentinel replied, "all members of the High Council are like sittin' board members of a corporation. Some have more clout than others. High Commander Hammer is bein' looked at as the next Commander in Chief when High Commander Orden retires this year." He released a large yawn.

"Sheesh..." Jeff muttered. Jennifer checked her watch as she began to pace back and forth in the hall.

"It's already 4:00 A.M…I wonder if we should hold off on interrogating Chaz until tomorrow." She looked to the rest of the group to make a decision. Chaz's screams had died down. They looked at each other's tired faces, and shrugged in silent agreement. Tomorrow might be a better option. Jeff heard a static build in the earpiece he hadn't removed.

"*Don't even think about it. I'm on my way back now.*" Hammer's voice echoed in through the communicator.

"The master has spoken. Shall we?" Demon gestured for everyone to return to the room.

As they entered, Jennifer gestured for Jeff to stand against the wall in the corner, opposite to Chaz. He looked over at her confused, but did as he was told. He was about to ask her why, when the door burst open. Jeff's nostrils were hit with the smell of rot and decay. Like a rabid dog on a leash, George clawed his way in, held back only by a heavy chain leash wielded by Hammer. Hammer grinned a sadistic smile, while Chaz scurried, and attempted to make himself as small as possible in the corner of the room. Jeff noticed Chaz was bleeding from his neck where he had been scratching earlier.

"AH! Jesus!" Chaz screamed.

"Chaz, meet George, the *bad cop*!" Hammer used his body weight as a tether against George's pulls, as he clawed in Chaz's direction. His face held no emotions and he was missing a cheek. The muscle and sinew flexed as George chomped in their hostage's direction. George was strong, but Hammer was able to keep him just out of reach of causing harm.

"We know you weren't locked in a bathroom the whole time. What were you doing there?" Jennifer began the interrogation.

"I told you the truth!" Chaz pleaded. Hammer let the chain loosen a bit. George leapt a few inches closer. "Jesus!"

"I'll ask again. What-Were-You-Doing-There?"

"Just delivering a keg, I swear!" Chaz sweated profusely, and his blood-shot eyes kept shifting as he answered. Hammer began to gesture that he was losing grip of George, and Chaz screamed.

"The truth!" Jennifer bellowed.

"Okay! Okay!" Chaz started to cry, his voice grown hoarse from his pleads. "Some asshole paid me fifty bucks to lace the keg I dropped off with some fucked-up drug."

"What was it?" Hammer asked through gritted teeth.

"I don't know, okay? All I know was that I was supposed to lace the keg and then leave."

"Why didn't you?" Jennifer continued being the lead in questioning.

Chaz groaned. "There was this bitch that had an enormous rack, and she was already drunk as hell! Thought I could hook up tonight. But when all hell started to break loose, the bitch tried to bite me. Then the others started to clamber into the room. But they weren't right. I pushed my way through them, and as quick as I could, I slammed the door shut. There was blood all over the place. The security guard came in, and began questioning me. He heard a thump in the back bedroom. I told him not to go in there, but he didn't listen. He opened the door, and those...those THINGS grabbed him. I tried to pull him, but it was no use. I slammed the door shut again, and I contemplated escaping through the bathroom window down that tree. But I'm not exactly in the greatest shape. Then you guys were shooting up the place, so I waited. I figured the military had come or something."

Jennifer clenched her fists until her knuckles were white. "The guy who paid you to lace the keg, who was he?"

"I told you he didn't tell me anything. He was a young guy like you all. Thirties maybe. He had a shaved head. I mean everything, no eyebrows or hair on his face at all. Had uh...blue eyes I think. It was dark, hard to see. Tattoo on his right arm. Really weird lookin', like a symbol or emblem with some kind of sun thing." Jeff gaped as Chaz rambled. He remembered the tattoo in the photos of the undead girl they had just identified. It sounded the same.

Jennifer glared at Hammer with an "*I told you so*" look in her eyes. She crossed her arms, and dug her nails into them. She was angry, and trying to retain her emotions in front of their suspect.

"If that shit could be placed in the beer, then you were right. Someone's managed to weaponize a virus of zombification." Hammer's color went a few shades paler as he processed the information.

"At this point," Jennifer said, turning to Sentinel and Jeff to give orders, "all we have to go on is a very vague physical description of the perpetrator. Knight, you and Sentinel are gonna have to do some detective work. Try to do some research on cults with members that have a similar symbol. Kelsey, the girl from Nebraska. She obviously crossed paths with them. Start there." Sentinel was already writing down the description Chaz provided in the little notebook he kept in his vest.

"So, can I go home?" Chaz asked sheepishly. Jeff never expected the rage and darkness that Jennifer had in her. She whipped her body around, reaching her arm back as she prepared to attack Chaz. Jeff felt air run past him as he extended his hand to stop her. It took him a moment to realize that air was Demon, who had leapt across the room, grabbing her. He pulled her back before George even realized she was within reach. He was still mesmerized by the smell of blood running down Chaz's neck from his insistent scratching, his dirty fingers reaching and pulling against Hammer's hold.

"There were twenty-five kids at that party! All of them died so you could score fifty bucks and take advantage of a girl!" Jennifer screamed and struggled against Demon's hold. "Since you value life at no more than two dollars per person, I could care less if you make it home or not tonight."

Holy shit...

Jeff was scared of Jennifer. Her eyes were cold, and he believed every word she said. If Demon hadn't held her back, she would have killed him. The guy was a creep, but he was still a human.

"Fuck you, bitch! Call it my need to eat!" Chaz spat back, completely forgetting about George. "Keg delivery don't pay shit!"

Jennifer relaxed a bit in Demon's grasp. She regained her composure, but her eyes were still mad with rage. Demon let her go, but stayed close to her side.

"Can you remember anything else?" she asked coldly as she crossed her arms again. The points on her arm turned white where her nails dug into her skin, burrowing deeper than before.

"Yeah, something else weird...the guy said his God of their holy church thanks me for my efforts. I asked him which church he went to, and he said '*The Sons of Judgement.*' That's all I got."

"Fine. Sentinel, Knight add that to your search." Jennifer rubbed her temple like she had a headache, and ushered everyone besides Hammer out of the room, "We're not getting anything else outta him. Hammer, feel like letting him go?"

"Why not." Hammer's sadistic grin appeared again.

"Oh my God! Thank you!" Chaz praised and then his eyes widened when he saw who they were talking about. Hammer let go of the chain that held back George. The revenant leaped onto Chaz with a fury, ripping his flesh from his body. Chaz screamed in agony as his insides were torn apart.

The group turned to see what had transpired as Hammer stepped out of the room, shutting the door behind him. Chaz's screams died into a gurgle. Hammer stared blankly at their disappointed faces.

"Oh, you were referring to Chaz? My bad." Hammer laughed it off like he'd made an innocent mistake and hadn't just sentenced a man to a slow painful death.

Jeff glanced at Jennifer, and for a brief moment thought he caught a look of satisfaction on her face as she gazed at Chaz's corpse, before she shook her head disgruntled and marched off toward the elevators. Demon laughed as he headed in the same direction, with Sentinel following silently behind. Jeff was left standing alone with Hammer. He gazed in horror through the glass window. Hammer pulled out his gun as he opened the door, and shot Chaz in the head. He locked the door again, and patted Jeff on the cheek.

"We'll grab George later. He's more docile after a meal. Unless you wanna stay and watch?" Hammer looked at him, slightly amused.

"Fuck...."

"Come on, Kid. We've got somewhere to be." Hammer grabbed Jeff by the sleeve of his shirt and dragged him down the hall.

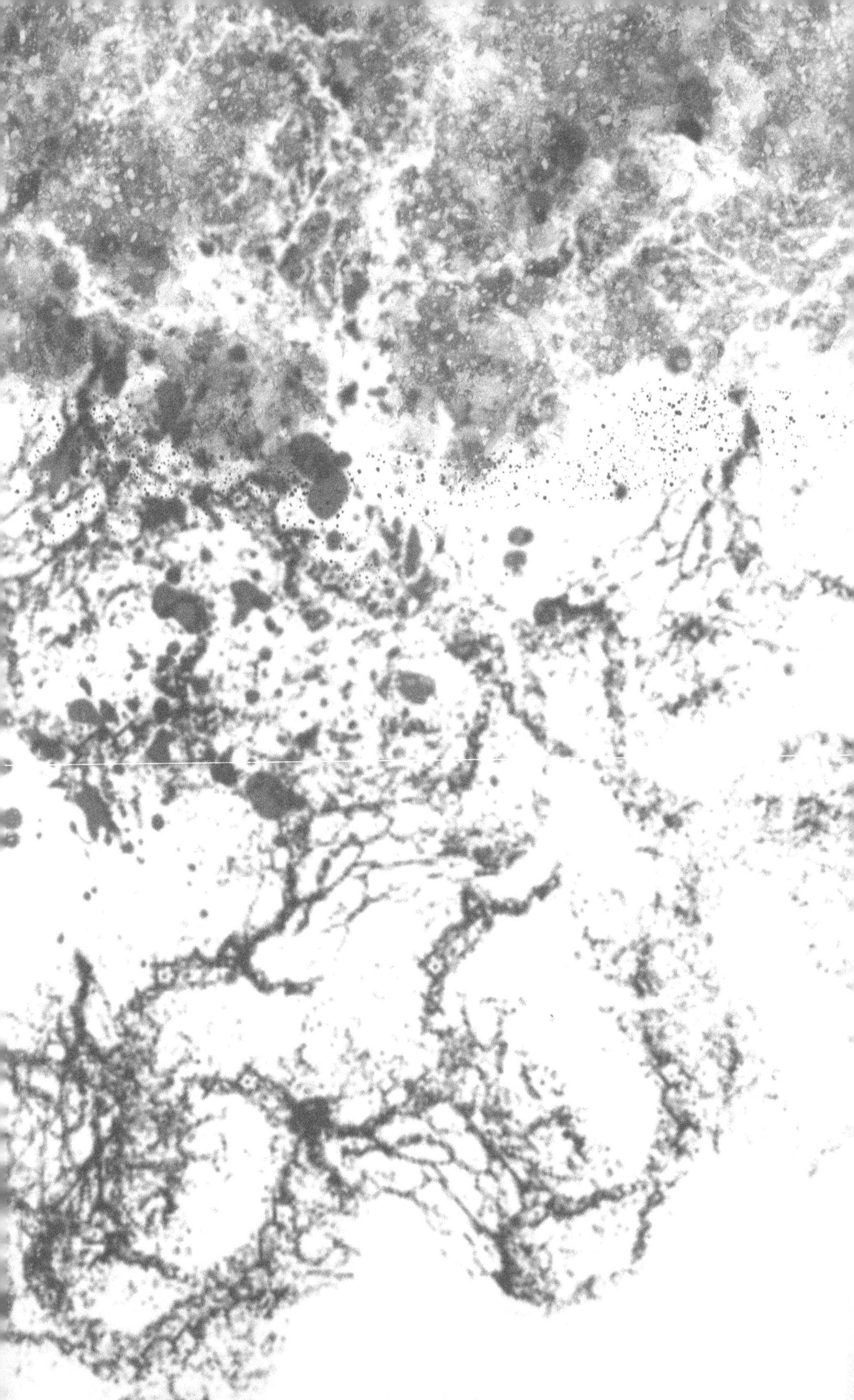

CHAPTER 14

Jeff felt sick. How many of the recent missing person's cases were actually a result of poor management practices by a secret organization that hunted monsters? Chaz was a douchebag, but he didn't deserve the horrible death Hammer had given him. He still couldn't understand how Hammer was their leader, outside of nepotism.

"How big of a prick do you think I am?" Hammer asked as they turned the corner toward the elevators.

"The guy was defenseless! He was a witness and you fed him to a zombie for Christ's—"

"He was infected. We wouldn't have been able to let him go. He was going to die tonight anyway." Jennifer's voice caught Jeff off guard; he thought she had left for the evening. Her words were cold and hateful. She entered the elevator and held the door for them. Her eyes still held a dark rage in them that made Jeff uneasy. She pressed for the bottom floor of the base. Her arms had deep red nail marks where she had been applying pressure earlier in the interrogation room. "The High Commander is still waiting in your office. Go talk to him. I'm going home." The elevator opened and she walked off toward the locker rooms without making eye contact with either of them.

Hammer glared at her back as she huffed down the hall toward the lockers. He had a mix of anger and confusion on his face, like internally he was asking *"The fuck I do to you?"* Hammer let out a frustrated breath and mashed the button to close the elevator doors again. Jeff caught one last glance as Jennifer disappeared around the corner. She'd wanted to talk earlier tonight, but with everything that happened, it probably wasn't a good idea.

"God dammit, can a man get a break?" Hammer grumbled as he punched the button on the elevator to go back to floor B1, where all the offices and day to day items were handled. The doors opened and they walked down a long hall, past the security area.

The back offices had heavy black reinforced doors with the names of different departments and officers in charge on them. When they neared the end of the hall, Jeff noticed a door with Jennifer's name on it, and next to that was one labeled "*T. Hammer, Commander.*"

"Kid, this will only take a minute and then we'll finish our conversation from earlier." Hammer walked in the office, swinging the door behind him. It slammed against the frame, but did not catch the lock. The door bounced back, leaving it slightly ajar. Jeff couldn't help his curiosity and peered through the opening.

The desk in the office was covered in papers. On the file cabinet behind it were an assortment of blades. Jeff adjusted himself so he could see just a little more of the room, curious as to what a man like Hammer valued. Near the desk was what looked like a mini bar adorned with bottles of scotch, bourbon, and tequila. There were various expensive crystal glasses on top of the bar. Standing next to it, holding a glass, was High Commander Tobias.

"Yeah, just go ahead and help yourself, Dad." Hammer grumbled as he walked toward his desk.

"I paid for it, so why not? You don't really need the extra alcohol Jr." Tobia's voice had a tone of sarcasm. Hammer ignored it. He sat down and put his dirty boots up on his desk, wet sand speckled onto the papers beneath them. He pulled out his flask and took a long slow drink to his father's dismay.

"I don't know what you're talking about." Hammer's mouth curled into a devilish grin. Tobias let out a disappointed sigh and walked over to the desk. He picked up what Jeff made out as a video game sitting on top of one of the piles of papers. Jeff squinted to make out the title, "*Dead Survival.*" Jeff had an internal chuckle. He'd played that game a million times with Adam. It was an online multiplayer zombie first person shooter, where the goal is to make it from the spawn point to the destination while surviving hordes of randomly generated zombies. He found it ironic that Hammer would enjoy that, considering what they dealt with on a day to day basis.

"Really? Don't get enough kicks killing the real things?" Tobias frowned, dropping it back onto the desk.

"Call it my outlet to the regular world. And hey, it's entertaining." Tobias let out a "*hmph*" before he took another sip from his glass.

Jeff felt a yawn building up inside him. He tried to suppress it. It must have been nearly 5:00 A.M. His body felt heavy from the lack of sleep; he slouched forward and he touched the door, just enough, causing it to creak. Full of renewed energy, Jeff shot off the door, moving hastily to the wall opposite it. He tried to cross his arms like he had been leaning against the wall the whole time. He felt stupid, because he was sure Tobias and Hammer had looked right at him through the crack in the door.

God, I hope they didn't see me...StupidStupidStupid...

"Seems like we have a rat," Tobias mused.

"I don't hire any rats. It's just my F-N-G." Jeff heard Hammer get up from his desk as papers were shuffled and heavy steps approached. The door swung open, and Hammer's large body filled the frame as he dug in his pockets. Tobias smiled and raised his glass with a nod, acknowledging Jeff. Jeff smiled sheepishly back.

Again, Tobias' smile seemed off, discomforting like before. He couldn't tell if it was his eyes, or the over brightness and wideness of his grin when he parted his lips. Like he was overcompensating for appearances. Though on the other hand, Jeff was so tired he probably wasn't seeing straight. Hammer finally pulled his car keys out of his pocket and placed them into Jeff's hand.

"Go to my car, bring it out front. I'll be there in a few." Hammer turned to leave, but faced Jeff again, "Take a shower, you don't need all that crap on you in my car."

"Yes, sir. Sorry sir," Jeff stammered.

"Enough of this sir crap. Just go do it." Hammer walked back into his office, slamming the door shut behind him this time. Jeff waited by the door and heard the muffled voices of Hammer and Tobias quickly rising in level. He jogged down the hall to do as he was told.

***

Jennifer slammed her fists relentlessly into the two hundred pound punching bag of the training room. Every time she closed her eyes she kept seeing the smug look on Chaz's face when he thought he was saved. Chaz had shown no remorse when he'd looked at the pile of bodies he had caused. All for fifty fucking dollars. Each time she ran the images through her mind, she punched into the bag harder and fiercer.

Assholes keep surviving and good people are dying.

Then there was the issue of the man that supplied the pathogen. Her theory was right; there were humans out there helping to create monsters. They were probably the same group making those strange holes in the cemeteries. They were pumping whatever they created into the ground. Probably testing the potency to bring back already dead humans. Then there was the girl, Kelsey. If it is a cult, she was probably a member. Was she infected on purpose?

She punched again in successive hits. Always in sets of three. Right, left, right. She breathed in, shifted her weight, and there was Chaz's self assured face again. She was glad George was released. In fact, she had enjoyed the delivery man's terror.

No...it's wrong. He deserved to die...but not like that. What's wrong with you Jen?

She let out an exasperated sigh, and began punching again. Left, Right, Left. She wasn't really mad at what Hammer did. She would have to apologize for being cold with him later. She didn't like how glad she'd felt when George had torn into Chaz's flesh. His death wouldn't solve their issues. They needed to find the supplier of the bioweapon.

She changed her position again and moved around the bag. She glanced up, noticing Jeff on his way out of the locker room. She grabbed the heavy bag to stop it sway, and watched as the door to the hallway shut behind him. Another problem for her today. She had told him she wanted to talk. She wasn't even sure what she wanted to talk about. She remembered the scared look in his eyes when he'd seen her rage.

There would be no way he would feel comfortable around her now. He saw the shadow she tried to keep hidden. Jennifer began to beat into the bag again. Infuriated with herself. The darkness in her heart had started when she'd lost her family. It had only grown after she'd joined Z.E.R.O and witnessed more horrors in the world. When she had lost Conor, that had been the hardest, and the last bastion of light to keep the rage in her heart at bay. She enjoyed the hunt and the kills she got from it. It gave her power over her pain, revenge for those who'd lost their lives. That's why Chaz's death made her feel happy. It was just another monster the Earth was saved from.

Good riddance too.

Jennifer let out a frustrated scream and put her full body weight into her next swing. That's when she felt her mistake. A sharp pain radiated throughout her knuckles.

"Ah, shit!" She waved her hand up and down, trying to cool off the burning sensation that ran through her split knuckles. She knew she hadn't wrapped it correctly in her haste to start punching out her rage. She looked annoyed at her hand as the blood began to seep through the tape.

Dammit...

In her rush out of the training room to deal with her injury, she noticed Sentinel on his way out. She couldn't imagine anyone still here at this hour. She rushed into the shower room to put some cold water on her injury. She slammed through the swinging door, using her back to open it as she cradled her right hand. After she was sure it was open, she spun to walk through, but hit a cold, hard, wet mass. She looked up to see Demon smiling down at her, still wet from his recent shower. The smell of his soap and cologne was intoxicating.

"Mmmm, smells fresh. Bringing me a snack?" He was teasing her, like he always did. Depending on her mood it either cheered her up, or just pissed her off more. It took Jennifer some effort to not take in his perfectly sculpted form, covered only by his boxer shorts and towel around his neck.

"Very funny." Jennifer grumbled past him to the sink. She unwrapped her hand, and winced from the sharp pain that radiated through it. Demon came over, grabbing her hand gently. He slowly unwrapped it from the last of the fitness tape.

"You really did a number this time," Demon commented. A drop of blood fell on his finger and he put it in his mouth. "Still sweet though."

"I wish you would stop."

"Sorry, I couldn't help myself. I haven't eaten yet, and your blood was always a favorite..." Demon trailed off as he averted his eyes from her gaze.

"No, I'm sorry. I'm just still upset about today."

"Understandable. I thought you were going to rip him apart worse than George for a minute there." She couldn't look Demon in the eye either. She watched her blood, bright red, drip against the white porcelain of the sink.

"Yeah. Thanks for the save."

"I'll always look out for you." Demon let the tape fall to the floor and turned on the tap water. She had split the skin in between the knuckles. He held her hand under the sink. She winced from the burning pain as the cold water touched her exposed wound. He made it so hard to move on when he acted so sweet toward her.

"Thank you," she muttered.

"How does it feel now?" Demon let go of her hand, turning off the water. Small diluted droplets of her blood ran down.

"Just sore. I should probably put an ice pack on it, so it doesn't swell." Jennifer examined her knuckles, which began to feel stiff when she flexed her fingers into a fist. The skin swelled from the blood collecting underneath. She walked over to the bench and sat down, examining her hand. Demon sat next to her, and wrapped her hand in the towel he removed from his neck.

"I could help you with that." He nodded at her swollen tissue. Jennifer instinctively held her hand closer to her, knowing full well what he meant. "Otherwise it could take longer to heal and you could be out for a while. Just saying."

He was right. If her hand hadn't healed by tomorrow, Hammer would put her on desk duty. If they got a lead on their bioweapon terrorists, they would be sure to keep her off of it. She removed the towel and shoved her hand in his face.

"Do it." Demon's eyes widened in surprise. She shook her hand in his face. "Before I change my mind, please."

"Okay, now for the record, anything happens, not my fault...entirely." Demon popped out his long white vampire fangs and pulled her hand up to his soft cool lips.

"I know. We're both adults here, just start already." Jennifer rolled her eyes.

Vampire bites secreted saliva with super antibodies. It would keep her from getting an infection better than any human antibiotics. It also prevented swelling. The only problem? It also had a pleasurable euphoric effect on the human to keep them docile during the feeding. However, if the vampire already had a relationship with the human, it could have a sexual-inducing effect on the human and the vampire. Jennifer still had conflicted emotions for Demon. She just hoped her physical will would keep her head clear enough until he finished. She licked her lips in anticipation.

Demon kissed her hand and winked at her. She felt the sharp pain as his teeth sank into her flesh. He sucked on her hand, softly, his tongue lightly brushing her skin as her blood gushed out into his lips. She felt the familiar tingling sensation that always followed the bite as his saliva mixed into her bloodstream. It spread from her hand, snaking its way up through her arm as her vessels carried it toward her heart. When it hit her chest, an explosion ripped across her body, spreading the tingling sensation back out across her and waking every nerve receptor that prompted pleasure. She turned away, and tried to conceal her growing lust toward Demon. She wanted him closer, to feel his lips on hers. Memories of previous occasions when their bodies formed as one filled her mind and excited her more. She felt Demon's lips quiver on her skin.

She turned back toward him as he tugged more on her hand. His eyes were focused on her. Intense and hungry. She moved in closer. He must have felt the same way as he pulled her in the rest of the distance and began to kiss her neck. She leaned into him, accepting every touch on her skin. She reached her arms around him, feeling her way down his smooth back. She gasped when he bit into her neck, sending another surge of pleasure through her body as she dug her nails into his skin. He slid his hand under her shirt, groping her breast. She caressed his cheek with her hand, prompting him to unlatch from her neck, directing his gaze toward her. He wanted more of her. She wanted to give more.

Her blood dripped from his mouth as she drew him in and pressed her lips to his. She could taste the iron on his lips. She had grown used to tasting her blood when they kissed over the years, however tonight it felt wrong again. She had the same feeling of regret she had a couple months ago when she wanted to sleep with him.

He picked her up off the bench, carrying her into the shower stall at the end. He held her against the wall of the shower, kissing her, making her feel all the pleasure she had wanted and had been missing. She rejected the negative feelings that briefly fluttered her mind, and pulled off her shirt, tossing it to the ground. When she tried to kiss him back, again, it felt wrong. Her mind screamed at her, like from a deep fog, telling her to stop, but her body urged her on. She couldn't understand what was happening. This was Demon. She wanted to be with him, like so many times before. However, she couldn't stop the feelings of guilt. She closed her eyes as she tried to get her brain to become attuned with what her body wanted.

Her thoughts wandered to memories of the park star gazing with Jeff. His smile when he laughed. His willingness to open up to her, and his attentiveness when she spoke of her past. Her fear for him when she thought he was going to die at the hands of the zombie in the cemetery tonight. The guilt she felt when she saw the fear in his eyes at her anger toward their suspect.

Jeff...

She was shocked out of her thoughts and carnal urges when a spray of cold water rained down from above. She looked up into the shower head, surprised. Demon put her down, breathless from the recent excitement. She noticed his hand on the controls for the water.

"Whoo! Let's stop before we do something we regret," Demon laughed, his smiling teeth covered with her blood. He looked down at Jennifer, caressing her cheek in his hand.

"No...but I—" Her heart raced in her chest. Her mind felt clouded and hazed thanks to the vampire saliva still pumping through her system.

"Like I said earlier. I'll always be here for you, but I respect if you don't feel the same for me anymore. This right here was artificial and I could tell." He pulled her in close, kissing her on the head gently. "My Fire, you don't owe me anything."

Jennifer's cheeks flared up again, but this time in embarrassment. She closed her eyes and let the water run down her body. Demon turned off the shower. He poked his finger with one of his fangs then rubbed his blood on her neck and hand. She felt the strange sensation that signified her cuts were closing in her skin, but it left no scars as long as Demon stayed fed on fresh human blood, so she was thankful.

"There, you're all set." He walked out of the shower stall and picked up his towel from earlier. He tossed it to Jennifer. "Go home Jen, get some sleep. And for the love of God, talk to the boy tomorrow."

He walked out, leaving her breathless, wet, and confused. She smacked her cheeks a few times to get her head out of the blood lure, and used the towel Demon had tossed at her to dry off. She reached for her shirt she had thrown to the ground. It was soaking wet and covered in her blood. When she pulled the shirt near, she noted her hand was already looking normal again. She let out a long slow breath as she walked back into the locker room to get changed to go home. Demon was nowhere to be seen.

She tossed her bloody shirt in the laundry bin, glancing across at the other row of lockers, and noticed that Jeff's gym bag strap was still hanging out of his locker. He hadn't gone home yet. She sighed and opened her locker, noting the small puppy calendar she had hanging on the door. Today was the three month anniversary of when she'd met him. She bit her lip, her conversation with Demon lingering.

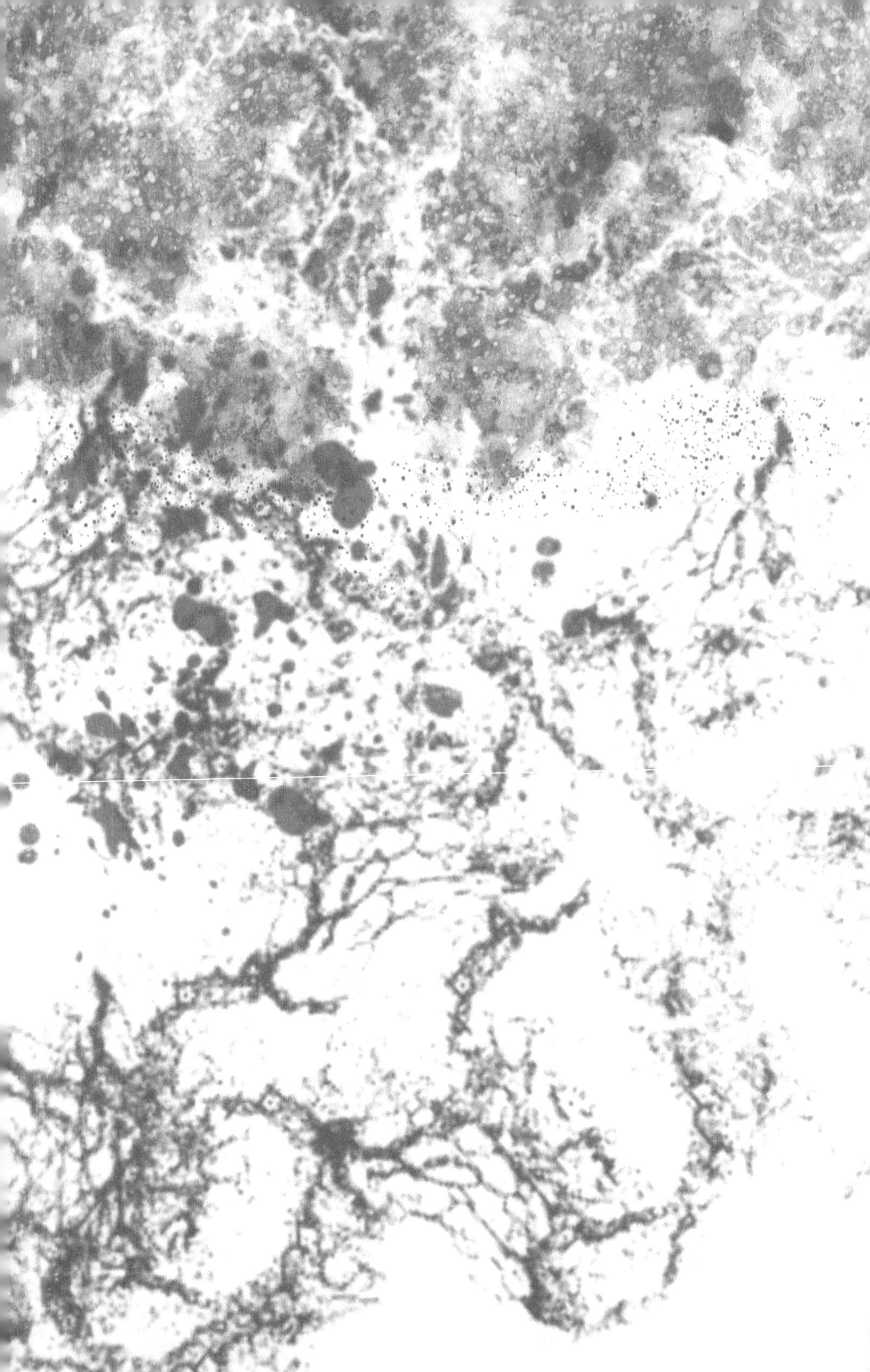

Jeff waited in the passenger seat with the window down so he could see the sun rise. The sky was developing a golden hue with streaks of orange and pink across the clouds. The air was cooler and he liked how it felt as it hit his skin. He was still dirty from their evening activities, and was looking forward to a full shower later. He had stopped by the locker room and noticed Jennifer beating the crap out of a bag in the training room. She seemed to still be upset, so he decided to avoid her completely and go to the showers. Demon and Sentinel occupied the two shower stalls, and he wasn't sure how long they would be, so he decided to give himself a five-minute sink scrub down instead. Leaving Hammer waiting would not have been a good idea. He put on some clean clothes and ran out. He took the time while he waited for Hammer to call his manager and quit his retail job. No reason to keep up the double life now that he was out of probation. He closed his eyes, and was beginning to drift off into sleep.

The faces of the people...no monsters, he killed last night filled his vision. Their pupils dilated and mouths covered in blood. Their skin pale, and lips changing colors to a dark blue hue. Their outward appearances were still close to who they once were. He watched, frozen, as each bullet he fired met its mark, causing the flesh and skull fragments to erupt onto the next victim. There was a loud explosion as each bullet left the barrel of his gun. It wasn't muted by a silencer this time. His mouth became dry, and his heart rate increased. He looked around him. His teammates were gone. It was only him. The zombie horde came closer. He couldn't move. Their noxious breath filled his nostrils. He didn't want to die, become a monster. Out of the horde lunged a man with brown hair and crystal blue eyes. It was him. But no longer human. It grabbed him, and knocked him back. Jeff tried to fight with his zombie doppelganger. He was too weak. Its rotten maw opened wide over him—

"BOO!" A loud voice awoke Jeff from his nightmare. His heart pounded and for a moment he forgot where he was. Jeff's eyes focused on Hammer, sporting a devilish grin. He was out of his uniform, wearing a black SlipKnot t-shirt with some dark blue jeans.

"Hah! Should have seen your face!" Hammer smacked the side of the door and walked around to the driver's side.

"You're an ass." Jeff yawned. He wasn't about to tell Hammer about his nightmare.

"Maybe." Hammer turned on the engine and it roared loudly. They drove in silence. Jeff tried to make out the area they were driving to. The cookie-cutter suburban homes disappeared as they hopped on the highway, heading south toward St. Petersburg. Highway I-275 was a mad man's design of entry ramps and exit ramps merging into one lane. The speed limit may have been posted at 65 mph, but Hammer was doing a steady 80 mph along with a majority of the other drivers. Jeff hated driving on this highway. The lack of blinkers and high speeds made you want to pray everytime you had to jump on it. As he gazed out the window, corporate office structures of the clustered city areas whipped by, with the occasional iconic palm tree sprung up between them. The rising sun glared in through the windshield with a bright orange light, prompting Jeff to flip down the visor. The smell of salt-water hit his nostrils as they drove on a man-made slip of land within the Gulf of Mexico. The mildew aroma of algae grew stronger as they rode closer to the coastline. A pelican sat undisturbed by the racing vehicles on some of the never-ending construction of this highway.

"Where are we going?" Jeff asked as more palm trees appeared in decorative clusters, and the bright facades of the beachside hotels came into focus.

"Shut up and enjoy the ride. We'll be there soon." Hammer opened his window, pulling out a cigar. He offered it to Jeff, who shook his head in decline. Hammer shrugged his shoulders, lighting it for himself.

"Whatever..." Jeff watched the lines of the road as they passed on the highway.

"What we do here ain't always pretty, but it's necessary." Hammer talked while Jeff continued to gaze out the window. "I understand being an idealist. I do. Believe it or not, I used to be one myself. The world isn't black and white, though. If you're going to hang with us, you gotta ask yourself at the end of the day, '*Did I do more good than bad today?*' If that answer is yes, then that's all you need. If it's not, then maybe Jen was wrong about ya, and you find yourself another gig."

Hammer continued to gaze at the traffic ahead of him as he navigated the highway. The hum of the engine and the wheels hitting the asphalt was the only sound between them. Jeff knew what Hammer said wasn't completely wrong. It was just a hard notion to get around. Before Z.E.R.O his biggest worry had been meeting the right girl and finding the right job. The fate of humanity didn't weigh on him or his decisions. However, it didn't forgive Hammer's actions of feeding Chaz, dying or not, to a monster like that.

"Yeah, but I wasn't the only one who had a problem with what you did today. I know Jen was pissed."

At least I think she was...there was that brief moment after George was released...

"I know. But she knows it was the dumbshit's fault all those kids died that way. If this was a regular terrorist attack, the guy would have been an accessory. Besides, he did get scratched on his back. I saw it when I cuffed him. He was going to turn into one of them. I just expedited the process."

Jeff scoffed at Hammer, who didn't notice or care.

He was dying anyway, so why not just torture him to death? Divine justice?

"So I'm just supposed to follow you blindly like everyone else? How come everyone is such a robot with you?" He turned his gaze from Hammer and instead watched the road as they pulled off an exit. An old concrete road replaced the finer asphalt of the highway. There were small sea shells mixed into the gravel, and their crunch could be heard as the wheels ground against them. They continued to drive west toward the white beaches of the Gulf Coast past a few brightly colored single story homes with lawns that looked too immaculate to be natural-grown Florida weed. The roads became more and more broken as they got closer, with more and more sand.

"They aren't robots. If you want to know about anyone's past, and how they got here, you gotta ask them. Everyone's story is different, but we've all been here long enough that we understand what needs to be done." Hammer pulled into the parking lot of another bar, relatively close to the beach. Jeff looked over at the rusty sign that hung above the entrance and read, '*The Drift in Seagull.*' Hammer turned off the engine. "We're here."

Another bar? A team of alcoholics saving the world, one shot at a time...

The *Silver Bullet* was high class compared to the dump that Hammer took them to. The exterior of this building looked old. The siding was never re-finished to protect it from the salt water, sand, and sun it was exposed to on a daily basis. Some of the boards were rotted, and broken against the bottom trim. The paint on the boards was peeled and faded. Its color was reminiscent of a seafoam green at one point in its history. Considering the early hour, Jeff wasn't surprised there were no cars in the surrounding parking lot.

"What's with you guys and bars?"

Hammer stopped in his tracks, dumbfounded by the question. "What the hell is wrong with you? There is always time for beer!" Hammer exclaimed as he approached and opened the door for them. "But that's not why we're here. Meeting a friend of mine. Retired FBI agent."

Jeff could tell the air conditioning system was not working well. The air was heavy and humid inside the bar. He scanned the room. The interior furniture was mis-matched. The stools didn't match the decor of the booths or the bartop. Many of the cushions on the stool seats were burst open, their interior foam spilling out of the vinyl that once covered them. Hanging on the bar, Jeff saw three left over drunks from the evening before, and a group of rowdy people dressed in scrubs; probably off a late night shift at the hospital. The bartender, a gruff older looking woman, noticed Hammer and nodded, granting him access to a back room.

The back room was filled with extra furniture and a thick layer of dust covered everything. Among the junk, Jeff made out a scruffy old man, probably in his late sixties, sitting at a small table. He was wearing a pair of khaki shorts and a Hawaiian bowling shirt. His happy-looking clothes were the opposite of his rough features. His eyes were old and hardened, he had a thick scruff around his face and neck, and his white hair was oily and yellow. The table in front of him was covered in miscellaneous folders and documents. There was a cigar tray full of old cigars buds and various mugs that Jeff assumed didn't have coffee in them, strewn over the table.

When the old man glanced up at Hammer, his roughness subsided. He jumped up with open arms.

"Terry! It's been a while!" His voice was gruff, probably due to years of heavy cigar smoking. He gave Hammer a hug, with a heavy pat on the back. He didn't seem to notice Jeff as he sat back down in his chair.

"Yeah, sorry, work's been a bitch." Hammer pulled over a chair and sat on it backwards across from the man. "Knight, this is Frank Maero. Maero, new guy, Jeff Knight."

Maero gave Jeff a quick look over and extended his hand. "Pleased to meet ya. Sorry about your luck running with this guy."

"Fuck you, you old cunt!" Hammer joined in with Maero's laughter. It was a side of the Commander that made him seem more human, and normal.

"Charming as ever." Maero rose up from his chair again and shuffled over to a mini fridge tucked away in the corner behind more unused furniture and boxes. He pulled out three bottles of beer. He handed one to Jeff and another to Hammer. "So what brings you to my humble abode?"

"We need some information. We busted up a kegger last night. Someone laced the keg with some kind of pathogen. Needless to say, they all fell down and got back up. The only clue we got is some cult guy connected with that runaway you helped us ID. Says he worships with the '*Sons of Judgement.*' You ever heard of them?" Hammer gulped down his beer. There was a spark in Maero's eyes when Hammer mentioned the name of the cult.

"Ah, shit..." Maero rubbed his forehead as he got up again. He walked to the door leading to the main bar area and closed it.

"So I'm taking you've heard of them?" Jeff asked as Maero searched the stacks of files lying around.

"What do you know?" Hammer asked, placing his beer on the table in front of him.

"Not much. It's a doomsday cult." Maero walked back over to the table with a green file he flopped down in front of them. "They believe mankind has done a thorough job of fucking up the planet, and that those things you guys go after are a calling from some vengeful deity, to rid the planet of the human filth. I think they call it Greyven."

"Lovely." Hammer began to flip through the file.

"Anyway, the group's extremely well funded. So I'm not surprised they could be experimenting with different toxins and bio-chemical agents."

"These people are all a bunch of hypocrites," growled Jeff. "To get rid of humanity means they would have to die too. Why create something that can't be controlled?" He slumped into an empty chair.

"Smoke and mirrors kid. They came into the picture as I was heading out of the department. I heard that Hitler sent SS Occultists over to the US to experiment with different mystic arts and sciences. Wanted to bring about an unstoppable army to usher in the Fourth Reich. The occultists never stopped the research. They want a global genocide of anyone not associated with the cult, and it looks like they're willing to cross you guys to do it. They got a lot of influential people buying into it. That's the scary part."

Jeff glanced at Hammer. His eyes were blank as his mind processed the potential apocalypse. Jeff's fingers tapped his beer bottle nervously. Yesterday he was worried about balancing a double life. Today, the end of the world could happen at any moment.

"And the bureau, CIA, or whatever group, hasn't taken them down because?" Hammer reached for his beer again. Maero sighed at the question.

"I've got my reasons to speculate. But like I told you two, lots of influential people. How'd y'all find out about these guys anyways?"

"The keg delivery guy was the sole survivor," Hammer stated.

"Might like to question that guy."

Jeff and Hammer looked at each other. "Uh...you may need to wait for George to pass him." Hammer chuckled.

Maero rolled his eyes and slammed his beer down on the table. "Jesus! Don't tell me you still keep that fucking thing like it's a goddamn dog! Why didn't you put him down like I told you to?" Hammer put up his arms and shrugged at Maero.

"Jen's attached to it. It'd break her heart..."

"Un-fucking-believable." Maero held his face in his hands. When he looked back up at them, there was a new earnestness. "If you're into it with the 'Sons of Judgement,' tread carefully. They have a big bank and can hit you in places it hurts like hell. Watch your backs."

Hammer chugged the rest of his beer, placing the empty bottle on the table. Jeff did the same as he stood up to leave. He was over tired and very hungry. The one beer gave him a slight buzzed haze. The combination of no sleep and no food in his stomach for the last twelve hours. Hammer gave Maero a hug and slapped fifty dollars on the table. Maero looked at the money and back at Hammer, puzzled.

"Go buy some ammo and shoot the idiot that sold you that shirt."

"Well that's a problem, because that would be you. Trying to buy a suicide?" Maero laughed in unison with Hammer. Jeff felt like an awkward third wheel in their bromance, chuckling along half heartedly. When the laughter died down, Hammer grabbed the file from the table.

"Just a sec guys." Maero shuffled over to another tower of folders, pulling out a single folded piece of paper. He handed it to Hammer, who opened it, revealing a photocopy of a crime scene photograph. Jeff leered over Hammer's arm at the image. "That's the last of it. Pretty much everything I just told you will be in that folder, and that image—"

"Their shitty logo. Not too original." Hammer looked at the symbol on the back wall of the crime scene Maero pointed to in the photograph. The same image as the tattoo they found on the young girl Kelsey's back.

"If I hear anything, I'll let you know."

"Thanks for this." Hammer lifted the folder, nodding goodbye to Maero. Jeff followed close behind.

"So what's the next move?" Jeff asked after they were back in the parking lot.

"Well, you heard the old man, we need to exercise caution when dealing with these pricks right?"

"Yeah. So I guess we gotta—"

"Hit them in the fucking mouth! That's exactly what I was thinking!" Hammer looked ecstatic at the thought of destroying this cult. Jeff wasn't so sure. They walked back toward his car when Hammer stopped suddenly. Jeff noticed him looking at the intersection on the corner.

There was a woman leaning against a lamp post smoking a cigarette. She had short black hair and a black beach dress that hugged her small curves. A large black dog was at her side. There was something familiar about the woman. He couldn't place where he might have seen her before. When Jeff tried to remember, his thoughts became fogged and hazy. It was probably the buzz from the beer he drank, jumbling his memory.

"One sec kid." Hammer handed the file over to him, walking over to the woman. Jeff waited by the car, and observed their interaction. The woman smiled at Hammer, though it didn't seem welcomed by him. She glanced over in Jeff's direction and waved enthusiastically. Jeff lifted his arm hesitantly, waving back. She pulled something out of her pocket book and handed it to Hammer while she got intimately close with him. Hammer kissed the woman briefly, pulling away. He bent down and petted the large black dog before returning. "Alright let's go."

"Who was that?"

"It's none of your business. Get in the car."

Hammer turned on the engine, which roared to life. Jeff looked at the dash, and noted the time. It would be another hour in good traffic to make it back. He glanced at the intersection where the woman and dog were, but she was gone. It seemed strange. It was a pretty open space, and unless she had gone in the bar and passed them without either of them noticing, she should have been visible. His thoughts were hazy again as he thought about it. He was tired and needed sleep. The thought of his new night terrors when he fell asleep, however, was not inviting.

"Tomorrow we are getting the team together at the diner early. I'm gonna send Demon out tonight to get more information on this cult. If it involved Nazis, the vampires probably know something about it." Hammer began driving back to the highway, speeding the whole way.

"Diner?"

"Yeah, it's Sunday, we always do the pancake special. Fuel up for the week. Since you're officially part of the team, you're invited. So when I get you back, go straight home and get some rest."

Jeff yawned while he nodded. He had completely forgotten that it was Saturday. His days blended into each other with these late nights. The small buzz he got from the beer was starting to wear off, but he was tired as hell. He closed his eyes, letting the wind from the window hit his face. Maybe the little bit of alcohol would dull his brain enough that he wouldn't be plagued with new undead nightmares.

He let his mind wander as he reviewed the new information they acquired. There was something about the symbol that seemed familiar, just like when he'd seen it in Kelsey's autopsy photos. He knew he had seen it recently, but where?

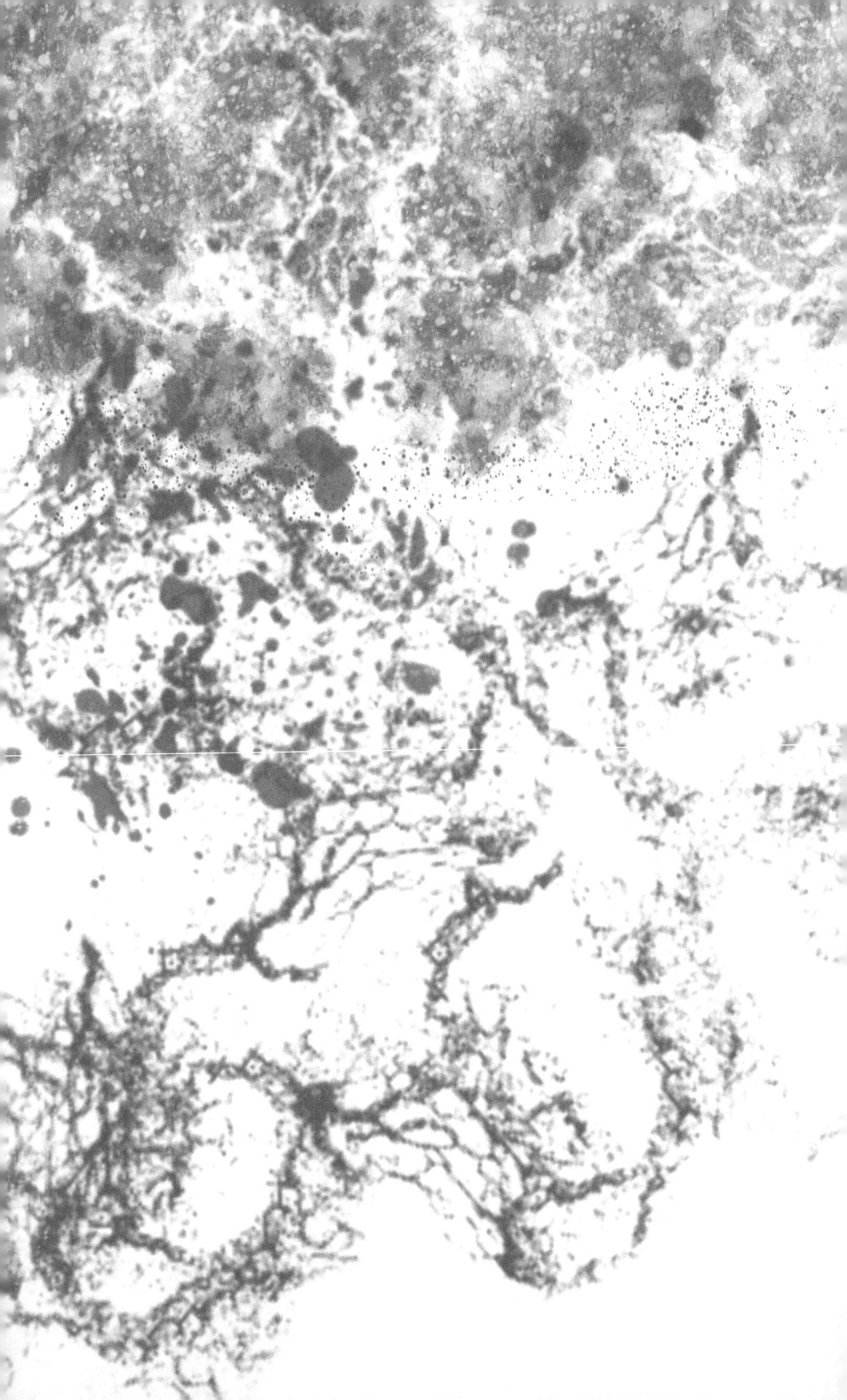

CHaPTer 16

Jennifer pulled into the parking lot of *The Silver Bullet*. It was already past noon and she hadn't slept well due to her shower room close encounter with Demon. If one of the other guys had come back and seen them...

If Jeff—

She shook away the thoughts. Since her time with Demon in the showers, her dreams had been flooded with images of Demon and her together. Though as the night went on, and Demon's influence began to cease, it wasn't Demon's sweaty body leaning over her in her dreams, but Jeff. She would wake up with her heart racing in anticipation of what might have occurred if she'd continued to dream. Demon's vampire saliva was really doing a number on her. Thankfully, the effects were finally wearing off in her system.

A country song began to blare out of her cell phone sitting in the cupholder. A welcomed distraction from her internal dilemma.

"Rick? What's up?"

"Oh...I uh...didn't think you were gonna answer. Was gonna leave a message." There was a pause, and Jennifer could hear the small tick of his tongue, followed by a small inhale. Was Sentinel smoking? *"I...uh...wanted to apologize for last night. Hammer might have took things too far."*

"He did...but you don't have to apologize for that."

"I know—but—I was there. I should have been a little more—"

"You're thinking about George..."

There was another pause. Jennifer heard the same tick and inhale as before. He had to be smoking...but his words seemed slurred. Was he drinking too? What changed?

"*Yeah.*"

"That wasn't your fault either. It was—"

"*Yeah, I know. I need to stop self analyzin'.*" Sentinel chuckled softly, "*Anyway, you really sure about this guy being a good fit? He was askin' a lot of questions last night. 'Bout you and boss man. Sure he's not...well...you know. I mean kind of convenient you found him when—*"

"I don't like what you're implying." Jennifer tucked a loose strand behind her ear, and messed with the A/C control in the cabin. She was feeling hot, but the blasting cool air did nothing. "He doesn't know anyone in the group. Maybe you should try to get to know him more, so he won't find the need to ask so many questions."

"*I'm sorry.*"

"No...it's okay. You're just looking out. Remember what I told you when you joined our group?" Sentinel didn't respond, but she knew he was still listening. "We're a family. If you need to talk, we can."

There was a slight shuffling coming through the speaker, then a small sniffle. "Yeah... Just be careful around him. His background check came out super clean, and that just sent my warnin' bells off. I'd be less suspicious if he had a juvie record. Alright, I'll see ya tomorrow at the meeting. I'm gonna get some shut eye. Bye Jen."

The line went dead, "What was that about?" Jennifer stared at the dash.

Rick must be feeling overcautious after the cult discovery last night. Jeff isn't—

She stepped out of her truck and looked up at the sky. Another hot day, despite it being the second week of September. To battle the hot weather, she'd chosen to wear her black tank top with a built-in bra, ripped blue jeans skirt, and flip-flops. Not having to wear her bra helped her feel cooler. It wasn't fair, when she thought about it, that guys can walk around topless in hot weather, while girls just gotta wear a little less clothing than usual.

Jennifer caught her reflection in the side view mirror. She took some time to put some makeup on today. Nothing too special. A little nude and brown-colored eye shadow to bring out the small flicks of amber in her dark brown eyes. She drew more attention to her pupils by lining her eyelids with black liner that came to the end like a cat tail, and black mascara to darken her long, dark brown lashes. A small amount of highlighting powder to accentuate her cheekbones, and contouring too. She didn't do it for anyone, just for herself. One of her few girly attributes she enjoyed on her time off. If they didn't have to hide from the public so much, she probably would have been an Instagram makeup guru by now.

She walked into the bar. The usual "drunks" were scattered around nursing their drinks while keeping a watchful eye. She waved at Tina, who was bartending this morning.

"Looking nice there, Jenny, date tonight?" Tina smiled while she walked down the bar with a beer.

"Nope, just doing work. I'll see you later, Tina," Jennifer continued down to the base.

It was quiet. This was the best time of day to get some research done. She figured she would go through the records and see if their organization had ever encountered this cult in the past. The name was not familiar, but she could at least start pulling all the files with cults involved. She rode the elevator to the second level, which was almost entirely empty. To conserve power during the slow days, the base had installed motion lights in the halls that flickered on as people walked down the hallways.

When she approached the records room, she was surprised to see a light reflecting out of it. She peered into the window. Someone had hooked up the projector screen to one of the computers. It was running a search of the archives and was only twenty-five percent complete.

I wonder who is here besides me?

She walked into the room and scanned the rows of computers. At the corner of the back row was Jeff, sleeping at the desk. There were piles of papers stacked around him in a form of organized mess. Curious if he was the source, she crept up and peeked at his screen. It was his computer running the search. She smiled, looking at his innocent face as he snored quietly. She bit her lip as she watched him sleep soundly among the mess. Her recent dreams flashed into her mind as she pictured his shirtless body leaning over her.

Ugh, get your head together Jennifer. You still have all those hormones surging through your system from Demon.

She needed to stop looking at his buttoned nose and his parted full lips. She gave his chair a kick, startling him awake.

"You know, we don't pay overtime. Were you here all night?"

"Huh?" Jeff looked at her, his groggy eyes barely open. "Uh, yeah...um no...what time is it?"

He got up and stretched. He wasn't in his uniform and looked like he'd had time to shower. His gray t-shirt had a sign that read *"Nope, not today,"* and he was wearing a pair of dark blue jeans bottomed off with a pair of brown flip-flops. It was strange seeing him out of his uniform or normal gym wear. She had grown so accustomed to it over the past few months. He rubbed the tiredness out of his eyes. She looked down at her watch to get him the time he'd asked for.

"It's 1:15. Terrence sent me a message saying there was new information he wanted to go over tomorrow. I figured I would do some homework before the meeting."

"Yeah, I know." Jeff yawned briefly, but looked at her concerned once his vision focused. "You okay?"

"What?"

"It's just I saw your shirt covered in blood in the laundry basket, and there was blood in the showers..." He rubbed the back of his head while he asked. She quickly realized what he was asking about and instinctively held her hand on her neck where Demon had bitten her a few hours ago. There was no scar to give away her transgression, but that didn't stop her cheeks from burning.

"Oh...uh...Demon was helping me with something..."

"Oh...OH!" His eyes widened as his brain processed what that might be. "I didn't know you guys were uh...together."

He looked down away from her. The way he said "together" sounded like he was disappointed. Jeff slumped back down in his chair.

"We're not!" Jennifer blurted out louder than she intended, startling him. Her face was definitely glowing brighter and her cheeks became warmer. "He really was just helping me...I hurt myself in the training room...vampire saliva has a bit of a healing effect. It was completely platonic!"

She couldn't read Jeff's expression. He gazed blankly back at her with his crystal blue eyes that made her heart skip. She could see circles under them though due to his lack of sleep.

Why should he care if Demon and I did something together? Why do I care if he cares?

She rushed to change the subject. "What are you doing anyway?"

"Well after the Chaz incident, Hammer took me to some dive in St. Pete. We met someone."

"Maero?" That's the only person Hammer would have taken him to. Which means Hammer liked her rookie. He doesn't introduce Maero to anyone.

"Yeah, you know him?"

"We all do. You went to ask about the cult?"

"Yep. He gave us this." Jeff dug through one of the piles of folders and pulled a ratty green-looking one out. He handed it to her. It was filled with copies of old investigations into the Sons of Judgement cult. Jennifer scanned the details of the file, focusing on what the bureau was looking into on the cult: arms dealing, drug production, and bio-chemical terrorism.

"They sound like tons of fun...I see why they were on Maero's radar, but we never heard about them before, so why are you looking in our archives?" She glanced over the dates on the stack of files around him, noticing some of them went back to the 1940s. "Why have you pulled all these?"

Jeff's eyes brightened at her question, like he'd been waiting all morning to tell someone what he'd found. It was cute. He grabbed the file from her and walked over to a cleared table. He pulled out a photocopy of a crime scene photo from the folder, slamming it down. Then he marched back over to one of the stacks, taking out more crime scene photos from all the files there. He placed them together on the table in front of her, pointing to a symbol on the first sheet, and waved her in closer.

"This is the symbol for the Sons of Judgement that Maero gave us. It's the same as the tattoo on Kelsey's back. I thought something looked familiar with it when I saw it on her too. When Hammer dropped me off here, it clicked. I remembered seeing it in some of the case files you had me study of past D-Day events." Jeff looked at her to make sure she was following. She was still inquisitive but nodded in response, "So I pulled out these photos. And if you look carefully at the graffiti in the back there..."

He ran back to the computer desk where she found him and pulled out a magnifying glass from a stack of papers. He raced back over and held it over one of the photos. Jennifer looked at it, then back at the first photo that he pointed to and gasped when she finally saw the symbol in the Z.E.R.O archive photographs.

"They were there...it's like a calling card." She saw now why he was so excited.

"Exactly! And to be sure I wasn't jumping to conclusions, I started pulling older files. In all of them, somewhere, that symbol is branded, to blend in. It's almost like a message for someone specifically."

"Nice work, Knight! But why are you running that search?" Jennifer pointed to the screen projection in front of them. He looked up at it confused, a blank stare on his face. After a few moments, his eyes flickered brightly, like a bulb turning on.

"Oh well, I figured it would be faster to have the computer search through each picture and incident that's more recent than I could. I was getting tired." He laughed. "I looked in the files that weren't on the server and this would look at anything past 1960. I hoped we could see a pattern."

"So far all these files you found it in have only been D-Day events?" Jennifer recognized the black folders strewn about that they used to distinguish D-Day case files from their normal everyday reports. She picked up one of the photos, leaning in a little closer to Jeff.

"Pretty much. Which makes me think—" They looked at each other, just about a nose width apart.

"They have been behind it all along!" Jennifer finished excitedly. "If we can stop this group—" Jennifer felt her heart begin to race in anticipation as she gazed into Jeff's eyes.

"We can save the world from a Zombie Apocalypse!" They smiled at each other. Jennifer's nightmare of the never-ending undead was almost over. Maybe she could have some sort of normalcy in her life. She looked at Jeff's contagious smile.

A normal life...

They leaned in toward each other. Her heart began to race again with a different type of excitement. She closed her eyes. She was going to kiss him, or he was going to kiss her, she felt it. She was willing to see where this went.

A loud alarm blared out of nowhere in the room.

She jumped back, embarrassed. Jeff's face was bright red as he turned his head away from her toward the obnoxious sound.

What the heck are you thinking?

He ran back to the computer, digging through the papers for the source of the array of sirens and car horns that were sounding off. It grew louder as he shoved the papers out of the way. Finally, he found the source, his cell phone. He turned around with his phone in hand. His face and ears were bright red. Jennifer had to stifle a laugh.

"Sorry, I put an alarm to wake me up. I was hoping this thing would have been done by now. You all need to upgrade." He chuckled nervously as he shoved his phone in his pocket.

"I'll keep that in mind at the next shareholder meeting," Jennifer laughed. She crossed her arms and gazed at the status of the search; it was only at twenty-five percent.

This is going to take hours...

She heard a low grumble come from the direction of Jeff. He sheepishly rubbed his stomach.

"Heh, didn't eat today." He looked at the clock on the wall and frowned. Jennifer couldn't imagine going so long without anything. Food was something she could never skip.

"Hey, you did a lot today. As your commanding officer, I'm telling you to take a break." She smiled at him as a tempting idea began to form. "I can get someone to tell us when this is done. Why don't I cook us a late lunch? Maybe stream a movie? We never hang out outside of work-related things. It could be fun."

"Uh...sure." He looked surprised by her offer. His ears reached a new pigment of red and again she had to suppress a giggle. She turned around, heading out of the room, waving for him to follow her.

Okay Demon...I'll give this a try...

***

Jeff was surprised by Jennifer's offer. He couldn't tell if she was just trying to be a nice friend, or if there was something else there. It did seem like she wanted to kiss him a minute ago...if his stupid alarm hadn't gone off he wouldn't be wondering about this right now. On the other hand, he was a bit jealous. It wasn't hard for him to put two and two together about her and Demon. Maybe he'd got it wrong. He wasn't familiar with vampire lore and practices except how to kill them...

Why am I jealous...we're friends...that should be enough. Ugh, Who am I kidding?

He'd had a hard crush on Jennifer since the first day they'd met. Aside from being smoking hot, as he'd gotten to know her more he realized her personality was just as attractive. Her passions and dreams, as well as her regrets. He wanted to know it all. Maybe she was right, this could be fun.

He followed her back to the elevator, standing slightly behind her as she hit the button to return to the ground level. He couldn't help but notice her outfit. In the few months he had gotten to know her, this was the first time she'd been in something other than gym clothes or their uniform. She looked good. Her outfit accentuated her natural assets. When he'd spoken with her in the records room, he was having a hard time not looking at her breasts, which looked round and plump in her tight top. It was even harder in the elevator. He caught her staring back in the reflection of the elevator doors and rubbed his eyes like he was still tired. He tried to focus on something else.

She stepped back next to him after selecting the floor and crossed her arms. Jeff looked down at her again, but had to quickly look away. She was all boob today. He couldn't help but look down at her chest when he glanced at her due to their difference in height. He decided the safest option was to look ahead at the elevator doors until they opened.

"So how are you doing?" Jennifer's soft voice broke the silence as they exited the elevator and walked through the quiet hallways toward the lobby.

"Um...okay I guess." Jeff wasn't sure if he should tell her about his recent night terrors.

"Good. You seem to be handling things a little better than the first time you came across a fresh one. I know they're harder because...they still look human." She didn't look back at Jeff as she walked, but he didn't need to see her face to know she understood what was bothering him.

"Yeah. I'll admit, I may have some issues sleeping for a while. I keep seeing their faces when I close my eyes." Jeff rubbed his eyes as his recent night terrors flooded his vision again. Jennifer stopped.

"I wish I could say that it gets easier..." She crossed her arms, her back still toward him, "I've killed a lot of things over the years. Some harder to deal with than others...some that I'm not proud of."

Jeff stared at Jennifer's back. She seemed rigid and her voice was flat. He couldn't tell if she was sincere in her words, even as uncomfortable as she appeared talking about it. She turned around, taking his hand softly in hers as she looked up at him with her dark eyes. Jeff felt his heart skip. Her gaze was piercing, yet also comforting.

"As your mentor, I want you to feel okay to talk to me about any of that stuff. I've been where you are. Just let me know what I can do to help."

Her hands were warm in his as she squeezed his fingers between hers. Jeff squeezed back, rubbing his thumb gently over her hands. Now that they were in the bright hallway, he noticed her makeup. A neutral light brown that drew out the small amber light in her eyes, brightened by the contrast of her dark bangs. Her hair was down across her shoulders. Her long layers framed her face, accentuating her eyes and cheekbones more. She looked more beautiful than ever…he wasn't sure if the butterflies in his stomach were just hunger pains anymore.

Who are you kidding Jeff?

"Thanks." Jeff hated how his voice cracked as he gave his small gratitude to her. Jennifer's cheeks blushed at his one word. She snatched her hands away from his touch.

"No problem!" She turned and hastily walked to the lobby. Jeff followed. After a few more moments of silence, they finally arrived at the parking lot. Jeff stopped as he stared at their two vehicles.

"So do I just follow you to your place?" Stupid question but it seemed like she hadn't thought about it either as she gazed back blankly at him. He watched as she bit her lip.

"How about you drive?" She smiled up at him, "But we gotta stop by a store first. I gotta pick up some things."

"Uh, okay."

She didn't mention a specific store, but he knew a grocery nearby. She was quiet on the short drive as she gazed out the window. Jeff couldn't help but peek at her as the sunlight hit her face, and shifted in his seat uncomfortably. Staying friends might not be as easy as he'd hoped.

"You look nice today," he blurted out. Jennifer looked at him confused for a moment, glancing briefly at her outfit. He caught the roseyness in her cheeks as it grew into a darker shade.

"Uh…thanks. I try to wear more than sweats and combat boots." She smiled, glancing back out the window.

When they arrived at the store, he followed her as she walked through the aisles. She knew what she wanted. He watched as she grabbed some wine bottles and rice, before she led them to the Spanish foods section. She picked up a jar full of something green, as well as some small pigeon beans, chorizos, and extra virgin olive oil. When she was satisfied, he followed her to the freezers, where she grabbed some dough discs and ground turkey from the meat section across the way. He remained quiet as she marched purposefully aisle to aisle. He was starting to feel this was more than a friendly meal.

His hand brushed hers briefly as they walked, and she didn't pull away. Jeff licked his lips, wanting to test his ground, and purposely brushed his hand with hers this time.

Jennifer loosely linked her fingers around his. They felt soft and delicate. As they walked further, she intertwined them into a stronger hold. Jeff's heartbeat raced at the firmer grasp.

"Yo, Jeff!" A familiar voice yelled his name. Jennifer yanked her hand out of his as she hurried away. He turned to see Adam holding a box of donuts. He had horrible timing as usual.

"Uh, Adam, hey…"

"Was that Jen? Are you guys—?" Adam winked very hard and looked in the direction that Jennifer had ran off. Jeff grabbed his friend in a headlock, turning him around.

"Dude…seriously?"

"What? You guys were holding hands. Honestly, I thought you were already dating with the amount of time you've been spending together."

"That's because she was my trainer for work…I told you this yesterday." Jeff sighed, letting go of his friend, "I don't know. She asked me to go to her place to eat, maybe watch a movie. We were working just a little while ago…I think she wanted to kiss me, her eyes closed, we were very close… I don't know. I'm probably just searching for something that's not there—"

Adam grinned like a devil. "Duuuuude, she's totally asking you out here! Come on, Netflix and chill? You can't be that dense. Besides, you said she tried to kiss you?" Adam was his usual obnoxious self and if it was true what he was saying, he was killing any mood they might have been creating.

"Yeah, like I said, I don't know! My stupid alarm on my phone went off, so we bolted apart…then we had a moment near the elevator too. At least I think we did…I'm getting so many mixed signals."

"I think she wants you." Adam was overly giddy about this situation.

"Hi, Creed." Jennifer's voice was a specter behind them. The two of them turned abruptly to face her. Jeff's heart pounded in his ears. How much did she hear? "I was gonna cook a nice meal at my place for us. Wanted to celebrate Jeff's official hiring after being with my company for three months. Do you want to come?"

Celebrating my graduation onto Alpha Team? Well, maybe she wasn't planning a date…she did take my hand earlier…god she's so confusing!

"Uh nah, that's alright. I got plans with my new lady. I gotta get back. We're making some donut sundaes!" Adam held up the donuts, winking hard at Jeff. He wished Adam hadn't. "You two kids have fun. I'll see y'all later."

Adam waved goodbye, leaving Jeff alone with Jennifer again. They stood awkwardly. The space between them felt bigger than ever. Jennifer looked in the basket she was carrying.

"I think I have everything I need. We can head out now."

"Oh okay." Jeff was relieved she hadn't made any comments about his conversation with Adam. She had to have heard them talking.

She kept her distance from him as they went to the register, a pregnant silence forming as they waited to check out which continued awkwardly to his car.

She's close to me, she's not close to me...Are we friends, does she want something more? This back and forth is driving me crazy! Keep it together Jeff...

"You okay? You don't have to do this, I can just get a burger." He didn't want to make her feel like she was obligated, but she looked at him surprised, and was she blushing? Or was she getting rosey from the hot air?

"No! It's no problem. I don't live far from here. You'll just go down that road and make a right at the light. My townhome is around the corner." Jennifer pointed to the nearby road.

They drove in more awkward silence to her place. She gave more directions as they got closer. Her community was a quiet neighborhood that consisted of a collection of townhome condominiums, all attached in long lines. Each home was distinguished only by their different exterior paint jobs. Her place was on a corner and she had him park out front.

It wasn't much of a walk up from the parking space to the front white door. Just a simple grey sidewalk, with no decorations, and a simple welcome mat. Jennifer unlocked the entrance and Jeff grabbed the bags of groceries from the back of the car. The interior of her home was simplistic in design. The walls were an off-white eggshell color, with brighter white trims running along the edges. The hard tiles on the ground were an almost white beige with a marbled design. The lightness of the walls and tiles reflected the natural light evenly from her windows and back French doors throughout the small space. There was a short hall leading from the entrance where they stepped into an open design concept, connecting her kitchen, dining, and living room areas. Considering how much Z.E.R.O members were paid, this was not what Jeff expected her place to be like. It was simple and homey.

He followed her into the kitchen area, placing all her groceries on the ceramic stove top. The cupboards were white, and the counters were a dark pewter gray marble.

"I might need your help after I cook the meat. In the meantime, you can make yourself comfortable in there." Jennifer pointed to the living room, "Pick something for us to watch."

The living room area featured a large burgundy red couch flanked by a matching love seat to its right, and a black coffee table nestled in between. On the wall rested a large fifty inch TV above a black entertainment stand covered in ornaments of Phoenix figurines, roses, and misplaced DVDs. There was a set of carpeted stairs to the right of the living room leading upstairs.

"Uh, okay." Jeff was drawn toward the white French doors in the back. There was a small garden, with a red brick patio space. A white park bench sat against the left side of the fence with plots of roses growing nearby. There was a small baby cherub statue in the middle of the flowers, holding a plaque with an inscription, blocked by the flowers around it. Jeff squinted as a small breeze rustled the flowers. He made out only "*In Loving M–*" from the plaque. Jennifer banged pots as she pulled them out of the cupboards. Jeff walked back to the coffee table where the TV remote rested, and picked it up, turning on her TV while he looked up at the high ceiling with three light chandeliers dangling just out of his reach.

"You got a nice place here."

"Yeah, it's quiet. My little escape from our busy city." Jennifer climbed up on her counter, pulling down wine glasses from the top cabinets. He stifled a laugh. She was short, and it was funny watching her navigate her kitchen that was clearly designed for taller denizens.

"You need any help?"

"No I got it." Jennifer clambered down and rinsed the glasses in the sink. She filled them with the pink rosé she bought. She brought him a glass, and smiled warmly. "Actually, there is one thing. Could you go upstairs, and grab my cardigan sweater? I left it on the bed, I'm a bit chilly."

"Uh sure." Jeff put his glass on a gray stone coaster on the coffee table, and headed up her carpeted stairwell.

There were three rooms up there. The first he opened was a small office space, with a single desk and computer. A bookshelf in the back was loaded with miscellaneous thrillers, sci-fi, and romance books. Jeff recognized a couple of zombie literature series he had enjoyed, and chuckled. The next door was a bathroom with a standing shower and a toilet cramped near a single sink. He opened the last door, and found her bedroom. Bingo! She had a large king size bed, the sheets were white, and the comforter had a design of water-colored sakura flowers in a black ink. On top of the bed was a gray knitted cardigan that seemed more like a jacket than a sweater. Probably what she wanted, there was nothing else on the bed.

As he turned to leave, his eye caught a series of photographs framed on the dresser. The first was of a family. A woman that looked a lot like Jennifer, just darker brown skin tones, smiling next to her husband, a Caucasian man with salt pepper black hair and blue eyes; standing behind two little girls. One Jeff recognized as a very young Jennifer, maybe around five years old. The other had to be the sister she had mentioned to him as they got to know each other. She looked like she could be Jennifer's twin, but she had the mother's darker complexion. This was the family she had lost. He had never lost anyone, not like that. He and his mother had walked out on his abusive father when he was young. As much as he wished the man was dead, it never occurred to him how he would feel if he really had died back then.

Another, smaller picture frame, showed Jennifer as a teenager, standing with a younger and leaner Hammer. They were smiling together, holding some fish they had caught, in front of a small pond. He couldn't believe how different Hammer looked. He seemed happy. There were no dark circles under his eyes. His hair was a mess, but more of the mess expected with a teenager, and not someone who is stressed with every aspect of their life.

Jeff's eyes wandered to the last picture that was in a metal embellished frame, a series of roses and vines formed in the design. The background of the photograph caught his eye first as it contained the Eiffel Tower. In the center under the tower he saw Jennifer, kissing a man. The man had dark black hair with small curls. Jeff couldn't make out his face, but from the bulk of his muscles under his shirt, he must have had a more-than-average build. Jeff gazed at their embrace. Their hands were both holding Jennifer's swollen stomach. She didn't look much different today than she did in that photo. It must not have been taken that long ago. From the size of her stomach, she must have been about five or six months along.

Wait? She was pregnant?

He looked around the room. There were no signs that a man lived in this home with her. Or a child either. Jeff wondered what could have happened between the time the photograph was taken and now. A dry lump formed in his throat as he remembered the cherub angel statue nestled in the roses of her garden, and his heart sank into his gut. The plaque must have read, "*In Loving Memory of...*" Whether it was for the man or this unborn child in the picture, he wasn't sure. She had lost one of them, or maybe both? He shouldn't have been up here looking at her pictures. He gazed at Jennifer in the portrait again. Her expression happy, a smile fixed for eternity a moment before she returned the kiss of the man who held her.

"Did you get lost?" Jennifer yelled from the bottom floor.

"Uh, yeah, sorry! I found it." He grabbed the cardigan and ran back down the stairs. She took it from him and put it on quickly. He wanted to ask about the photograph he saw upstairs, but didn't want her to feel he was snooping...though he definitely was. He wasn't sure where he was standing right now with Jennifer. She opened a door for him today, allowed him into her home. He didn't want to overstep his welcome.

"Thank you. I got the meat and rice cooking on the stove. Should be ready in about twenty minutes. Then I might need your help making the patties." Jennifer walked back to the couch and grabbed her glass of wine.

"Why don't you raise the temperature if you're cold?" Jeff asked as he followed her.

"It'll warm up here with the cooking. It's just because we came in from the heat outside. Besides, it's easier to bundle when it's cold than cool off when it's hot," Jennifer mused, as she drank a few gulps from her glass. She patted the cushion next to her for him to come and sit.

"I guess." He grabbed his glass and took a drink of the cool beverage. It was a little sweet. Not something he usually drank, but nice. He sat next to her as she pulled up Netflix on the TV.

"Anything you're interested in?" she said as she scrolled through her watch list. Jeff noticed she had *Dagger,* the vampire daywalker, saved on her wishlist.

"You like *Dagger*?" he asked her. She looked at him and laughed.

"Yeah, we can watch that if you want. It was based a little off Demon you know? He saved the original comic creator from some unruly vampires." Jeff laughed at this revelation, that made sense now.

"I can see that, though he's not a daywalker." He chuckled, and took another couple of gulps from his wine glass, leaving it almost empty. It didn't take long for the alcohol to move from his empty stomach to his bloodstream. He felt his face begin to warm.

"Yeah well, we know that! The poor guy didn't. Makes for good fiction though." She laughed, and took a few more large sips of wine from her glass. Promptly she grabbed the wine bottle and refilled both their glasses.

"We could watch something else if you want." Jeff playfully reached for the remote. Honestly, he didn't want to watch a movie with her that made him think of Demon...or what might have transpired in the shower last night.

"No it's alright." Jennifer snagged the control back, "It's more of a comedy now that you know the truth. It could be fun to watch."

Jennifer started the film and sat an even cushion space apart from him on the couch. Jeff's muscles were tense. He glanced at her: she sat very stiff and straight, clutching her wine glass between her hands tightly. About five minutes into the film, she got up and walked into the kitchen. Jeff tried to relax, kicking off his flip flops, and leaning more into the couch. He guzzled down more wine to calm his nerves.

The smell of the cooking food was really good. It definitely wasn't something he'd smelled often. It reminded him of the Cuban restaurants and bakeries he'd visited in the Ybor district. There was a mixture of spices and vegetables in the air. Garlic? Oregano? Green Peppers? He glanced over at the kitchen. Jennifer was checking on everything for the third time. Every time she came back to the couch, she refilled their glasses and sat a little closer to him. He was beginning to feel the heaviness in his cheeks after they polished off the first bottle, signifying he had drunk enough to be officially buzzed. His only sustenance today had been beer for breakfast and so far wine for lunch. Jeff tried not to laugh when he noticed Jennifer was also a little tipsy. Her cheeks were as red as her red-tinted lipstick, and her eyes had a soft gloss over them. She stumbled a little when she went to remove the meat from the heat, but insisted she was fine. She pulled down some plates and called Jeff over.

"Pause the movie, you're gonna help me make the meat patties."

"Uh, sure." Jeff got up, and felt the room spin. He definitely needed to hold back on the alcohol. He walked into the kitchen and saw that Jennifer had a small bowl filled with some of the cooked meat.

"Here, try it." She grabbed a spoonful and held it to his lips. Jeff opened his mouth as she scooped it in. He was immediately shocked by the rich flavor. It was a mix of cilantro and garlic, with tomato sauce. Probably the best thing he'd ever tasted.

"Wow. What is that?"

"I don't really have a name for it, but it's the filling for these." She pointed to the dough discs she had on the plates in front of them. She grabbed a new spoon, and lifted a helping onto one end of the disc. She then grabbed some shredded cheese, and sprinkled it on top. "So I want you to do this, and then you're going to fold the dough over, and seal it with the fork, like this." She pressed on the ends of the dough, and it made little marks along the edges. When she was done, she picked it up, and put it on a longer plate near the stove top.

"Okay, I can do that. These are empanadas right?"

"Empanadillas." Jennifer mused. "It's what my mother called them."

Jennifer knocked her hip into Jeff, but due to their alcohol levels, it was rougher than she intended. Jeff grabbed the counter to refrain from falling over while he laughed.

"Right. I forget sometimes you're Puerto Rican. So, do you speak Spanish?"

"A little. I had to teach myself, so my accent is horrible." Jennifer continued to work on some discs. They quickly got into a groove, taking turns filling the discs with the contents, and closing them.

"I'd love to hear it." Jeff knew his ears were on fire. Jennifer's rosy cheeks were a darker shade. She bit her lip.

"Okay. Um.." Jennifer kept her head down as she worked, "*Yo se creo que tú me gustas.*" Jeff had no idea what she'd said, but he felt an electric thrill pulse through his body at the sound of her accent. Jennifer looked up and smiled bashfully at him. "Let me start frying. Finish those for me."

Jennifer went to the pan she had heating oil and began placing each set they made into the bubbling liquid. It wasn't long before she was flipping the small fried meat bundles onto a plate covered in paper towels to drain. She put in the last set that Jeff had made and mixed the rice she was cooking. The smell was beginning to drive him insane with hunger.

Jeff took a peek over her shoulder at the orange-colored rice that contained the green pigeon beans and chorizo he saw her buy. "So what do you call that?"

Jennifer smiled, "*Arroz con gandules.*" She grabbed a fork and picked up a small morsel, "Here."

Jeff leaned forward and let her deposit the sample into his mouth. The meat before was good, but this was amazing! Jennifer smiled as she watched him enjoy it.

"You should have been a chef."

"Thank you. I don't get to cook much for others. We all usually do our own thing when we're off. Demon is the only one I've cooked around in the last five years, but he doesn't eat." Jennifer grabbed plates from the dishwasher, and began to pile the food on it.

"You and Demon are pretty close huh?" Jeff didn't need to hear an answer. Jennifer froze with her serving spoon above the pot. When she moved again, it was slow.

"We were, for awhile...he's a good friend." Jennifer handed Jeff a plate, "Let's finish the movie."

Jeff walked with her back to the living room. She refilled their glasses with a new bottle of wine. Jeff dug into the plate, and they ate quietly as the movie played.

When they finished, they placed their plates on the coffee table, and Jennifer relaxed more around him. She pulled her legs up onto the couch, holding her wine glass in one hand while her other arm rested on his lap. He reached his arm around her, and she didn't shy away. He took another drink as his heart raced. He briefly glanced at the depictions of the vampires and their weaknesses as they were depicted in the film to distract himself, she was right, it was comical.

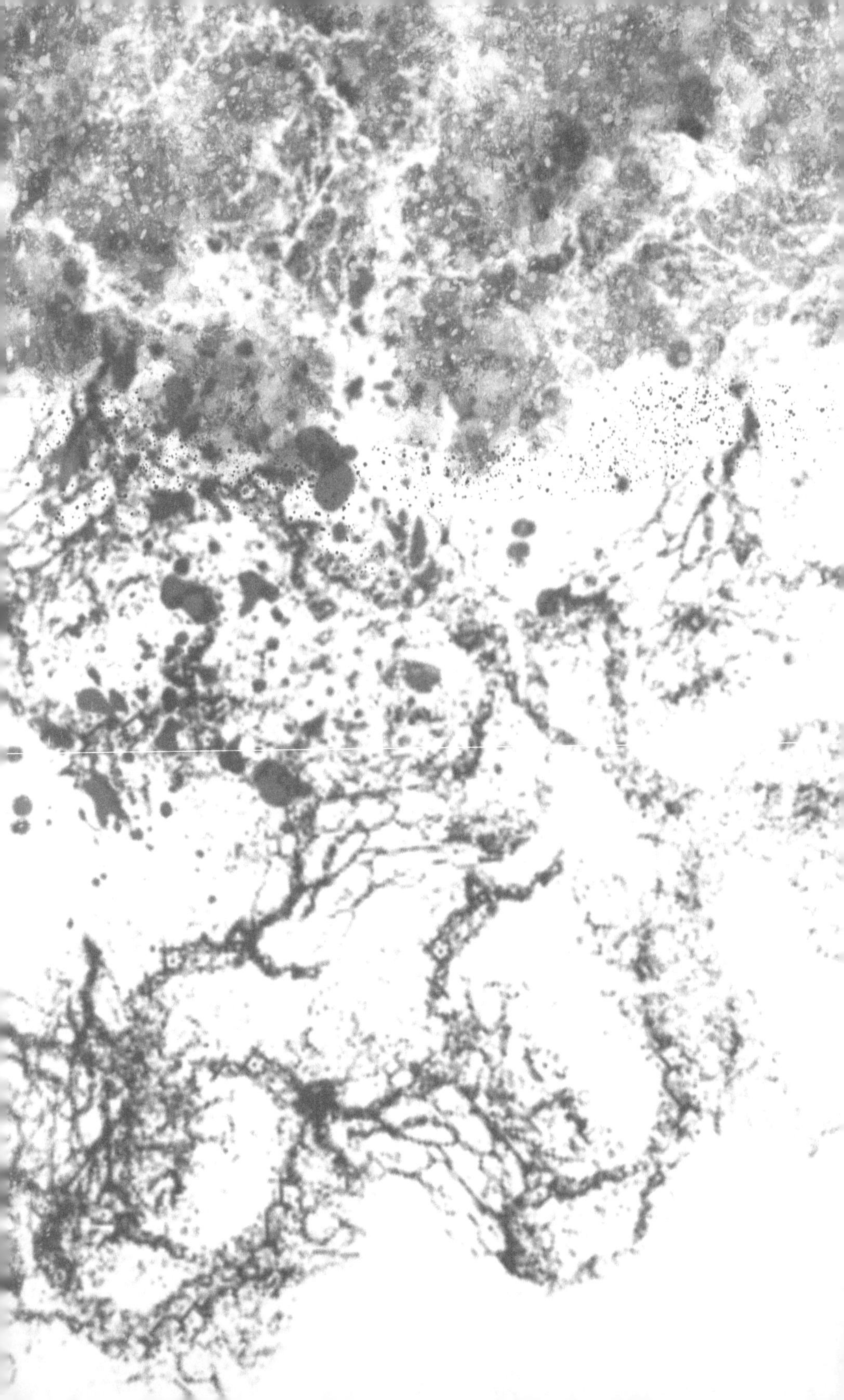

"You know, I don't understand why they always make it a pleasurable thing when your life is getting drained out of you," Jeff commented on the movie. Jennifer couldn't stop herself from spitting out the wine she was drinking in laughter.

"Well it is..." she mumbled behind her glass.

"What?"

"Think of it as that moment in sex right before you orgasm, when you are at the peak of pleasure...that's what it feels like," she mumbled in her glass again. Her cheeks felt hot.

Why am I telling him this?!

"Oh...so that's why they always make vamps so sexual?"

"Well, when you get your blood sucked, and if you're uh...having sex, it's like multiple orgasms radiating through your body. You really can't help it if you are drawn to the vampire more."

Shut up shut up shut up!

"Wait, so you and Demon?" He looked at her in shock and it just embarrassed her more. Maybe the wine was a bad idea.

"Well not yesterday, but in the past..." She filled up her glass again as she tried to avoid Jeff's curious gaze.

Well Jennifer you're already going down this hill, might as well keep rolling with it.

"Oh…" He sat quietly for a moment. "So you're telling me that if I was a vampire and drank your blood, you would find me irresistible?" Jeff grinned widely at her, showing off his small canines. His cheeks were bright and warm.

"Uh…maybe?" She wasn't sure where this was going.

"I don't know, being a vampire is starting to sound really good. Might have to get Demon to turn me." He laughed. She grabbed one of the pillows from the couch and threw it at his face giggling together with him. "Shh, you're ruining the movie," he mused.

They stayed quiet a bit longer. Jennifer's nervous energy began to build. When he wrapped his arm around her again, she felt her entire body charged with exciting electric energies that made her heart pound. How much of this excitement was due to the alcohol pumping through her veins, she wasn't sure. The wine was definitely a bad idea.

What are you doing here Jennifer?

"So uh." Jeff spoke again, "Demon seems like a great guy. Why aren't you two together?"

She looked up, surprised. Not something she expected to talk about with him, especially within his warm arms.

"I had no future with him." Jennifer looked down at the floor, remembering the first time she had met Conor in Ireland. Her and Demon were separated at the time. "I wanted a family. That's not possible between a human and a vampire."

"Oh…" She watched as he processed the information, his eyes glued to the movie, which was almost over. She tugged on her cardigan and felt like an idiot for sending him up to her bedroom to retrieve it. He must have seen her pictures on her dresser. She used to look at the picture with her and Conor celebrating their engagement and pregnancy everyday since she'd come back from Europe five years ago. Over the past year and a half, it had slowly faded to become just another ornament on her dresser. She hadn't thought of it when she had sent him up there.

He had to have seen me with Conor…and our baby…why isn't he asking me about it?

"So no *Twilight* weird half vamp, half human pregnancies huh?" Jeff grinned at her jokingly, breaking the awkward silence. The anxiety in her throat, that felt like a lodged ping pong ball, was gone.

"No! That would be horrifying!" Jennifer laughed as she playfully slapped him.

"Well if it means anything, I think you'll make a great mom someday." Her cheeks reached a new level of warmth. She could have sworn that his did too as he looked away from her again.

She smiled, resting her head on his chest. She heard his heartbeat pick up. He felt warm…comfortable. Jeff squeezed his arm around her shoulders and they stayed like that together, only half watching the film.

"Hey, Jen?" He spoke so softly, she almost didn't hear it over the sound effects and music. She looked up at him just as his face came in and kissed her.

***

Jeff drank more than he planned. Together they downed the two bottles of wine. He knew when he'd passed the point from buzzed to drunk as his face went from warm to numb. He drank past his normal limits partly to relax his anxious nerves. The other reason? Jennifer was a welcome distraction from thinking about the bodies he'd killed last night.

She had an aura around her today that was there long before the wine. Her soft olive skin glowed in the sunlight filtering in from her garden French doors. Every time Jeff glanced at her today, he felt his heart race in anticipation, more than it had in the last three months he had spent with her. It wasn't because she'd taken extra care today. She'd opened herself up to him. Showed her more vulnerable side. Her real self.

He loved when she smiled and laughed with him. Her real laugh and smile, not the false facade she used to please others. He wanted to make her feel like it was okay for her to feel happy again.

When she placed her head on his chest, it was nerve wracking. His whole body vibed from the softness of her head as it laid against him. He looked down at her as she watched the film, her breathing soft.

Fuck it, just go for it…

"Hey, Jen?" he whispered to her. She looked up at him, her mouth rosy and plush. His lips shook as his heart pounded furiously. He bent toward her, connecting their lips before he could change his mind. To his surprise, she didn't pull away, but instead kissed him back. She tasted sweet and tart with the flavor of strawberries and citrus wrapped in the faint scent of sweet flowers from the wine. He kissed her again and she returned it.

He felt more fervent with each time they pressed together. She pulled herself up from her awkward position and they started exploring each other's bodies.

His hand moved and felt up her smooth thigh. When she didn't reject it, he moved it up her skirt. He felt her vibrate from his touch. He repositioned himself and moved her onto her back. Her hands were under his shirt quickly, squeezing his back muscles as he leaned over her, and moved shortly into the back of his jeans. It excited him more. He pulled back, and took his shirt off, tossing it to the floor, and commenced kissing her again. Her face grew red from his unshaved skin. She wrapped her legs around his hips, and they started to move their bodies together. She moaned with pleasure when he slipped his hand down her top and squeezed her soft breast. Jeff pulled himself away immediately from Jennifer when his body's excitement prompted him to take this to a new level.

"Is this okay?" he asked her. She gazed back at him surprised by the sudden halt of passion. He didn't want to move too fast. The sexual tension for him had been there since the beginning, but if she didn't want to continue, he would stop. She said nothing to him as she sat up. Her eyes showed a previously unseen hunger.

She took her cardigan off and reached down for the bottom of her tank-top. She pulled it off, tossing it to the ground. She wasn't wearing a bra and her pale breasts were exposed in the warm sunlight that filtered through her curtains.

She pushed him back into the couch, mounting herself onto his lap, leaning into his neck kissing him again. Jeff put his hands on her hips, and suckled her bare breasts. She moved her hips back and forth over his waist, exciting him more. Her fingers unlocked his jeans, and she reached in. Jeff hadn't been with anyone since Kylie. Every time she touched him, it sent static electricity through his body. Jeff moaned as Jennifer touched him again, continuing to arouse him. She pulled away as she leaned into his ear. Her warm soft breath tickled as she whispered.

"Let's go upstairs..." He looked into her deep brown eyes and nodded. He wrapped his arms around her waist, and tucked his hands under her. It took some effort, but he lifted them both off the soft piece of furniture. She wrapped her legs around his waist, while he carried her up the stairs to her room.

He placed her on the bed, and she removed the rest of her clothing. Jeff kicked off his pants and crawled on top of her.

***

Her body quivered every time he touched her. His hands were warm and calloused, yet gentle with every touch. A touch she longed for. Her face was flushed, but it wasn't due to the wine anymore.

This arousal was different than last night with Demon in the shower. She understood now what Demon had meant when he'd said their lust was artificial. Every ounce of Jennifer's body and mind urged her to continue. Her body's pleasure nerves vibrated, like a current was turned on, when they finally became one.

Their bodies intertwined easily, like they had done this already a million times in the past. They tousled back and forth for power in her sheets.

They took turns in control, exploring each other's bodies, then joining again in a new position to start again.

***

Jeff collapsed next to Jennifer as he tried to catch his breath. His body was still tingling all over. Her sheets felt cool on his hot, sweating skin. He felt invigorated, and kind of like a teenager again.

Was this a one time thing?

He gazed into her deep brown eyes. Her cheeks were red, and despite her hair and makeup being a mess now, she looked like an angel. He really hoped this wasn't a one-time affair.

Jennifer lay on her stomach, and Jeff gazed at her full tattoo, admiring its details up close. They lay quietly together, enjoying each other's company. They were both physically pleased and exhausted. She grabbed his hand in hers and played with his fingers. Jeff took his free hand and followed the design of her tattoo with his finger across her skin. Her skin shivered excitedly against his touch. He was exhausted, but happy for the first time in a while.

"So...uh..." Jeff tried to catch his breath.

"That was good..." Jennifer laughed through her own tired breaths. She pulled herself up, onto her side, and kissed him. "Good thing we don't have an HR department."

"Heh. Yeah, I guess you would call this conflict of interest. Really glad we figured this out here, and not in the locker room or someplace where someone might walk in," he chuckled.

"Oh God! I would never hear the end of it," Jennifer laughed heartily. He had never heard her full honest laugh before. It sent vibrations through him. He wanted her again. He began kissing her shoulder softly. The sunlight began to dip from the window.

"What time is it?" Jennifer rolled away from him, looking at the clock on her bedside table. Her phone rang loudly from downstairs. She slid hurriedly out of the bed, draping one of her sheets around her.

She stopped to lean over and kiss him again before she left the room to catch the incoming caller. Jeff sat up, ruffling his hair, his mind wandering through the recent events. A few minutes later Jennifer came back and tossed her phone on the bed. She dropped her sheet, walking right into the master bathroom. He heard the shower turn on as she poked her head back out.

"The computer's done with the search. I have a shower in the middle bathroom there. Let's get dressed so we can go over everything before the meeting tomorrow." She shut the door before he could respond. He sighed while he sat alone. It would have been nice to have been able to shower together...though they had just had sex for over an hour. He wasn't in a position to complain.

Jeff slid out of the bed and found his boxers on the floor, with his jeans proceeding to the middle bathroom as instructed. It had clean towels on the rack and small travel bottles of shampoo and soap inside. He washed up quickly, eager to return to Jennifer's company. He dressed himself with the clothes he had and walked downstairs to see Jennifer was already cleaning up dishes, placing them in her dishwasher.

She was in a different outfit than earlier, wearing a set of dark blue jeans now, and a teal shirt with a V-neck cut. Her hair was still wet, pinned back with what looked like a rose hair clip. She looked gorgeous.

He began to hunt for his shirt in the living room area, which he finally found next to the TV stand where he had tossed it. He put it on and grabbed the empty wine bottles and glasses as he walked into the kitchen.

"Just put them on the counter, I'll take care of it later. You ready to go?" She beamed up at him.

"Yeah in a minute." He grabbed her around the waist and pulled her in, kissing her again. He waited for what seemed like ages; he wanted to enjoy their special bubble a little longer before they went back to their regular world. She kissed him back, and pulled out of his grasp.

"Don't go getting cheesy on me. Work comes first. If this is gonna be a problem we can stop." She winked at him as she walked toward the door.

"Yes, ma'am!"

They were quiet on the drive back to the base. But it wasn't that awkward nervous silence like before. Jeff had the radio on and Jennifer placed her hand on his thigh. He picked it up in his, kissing the back of it. She smiled and went back to gazing out the window.

When they arrived at the base, Tina was at the bar wiping down the counter. She eyed them as they entered with a coy smile like she was aware of their recent transgression. It was a Saturday evening, and the usual college-aged crowds were beginning to filter in to *pre-game* before they decided to hit the clubs. Jennifer lifted the small counter top piece that allowed people to travel between the front and back of the bar. Jeff followed quietly behind her as they entered the back kitchen. The cooks were bustling as the orders out front began to spill in. Jennifer kept some distance from him as they moved through the base below, and Jeff figured she wanted to be professional around her staff, though Jeff wanted to hold her again in his arms. When they stepped in the elevator, Jennifer stuck her hand in his back pocket while she leaned over and nibbled on his ear, teasing him. He tried to hide his recent excitement, but of course she noticed and giggled. She removed her hand right before the door opened. As they walked down the hall, Jennifer stopped at the break room.

"Hey, how about I make us some coffee to clear our heads. We drank a lot of wine and I think we need to rehydrate with some caffeine." She laughed. "I'll meet you in the lab."

"Okay, sure."

She went into the break room, and Jeff continued down the hall. When he arrived at the records room, he noticed the projector was still connected to the computer, displaying "*Search Complete.*" He walked over to the computer, plopping his body down in the chair. He put his face in his palms and breathed out heavily, then ruffled his hair as he tried to get his brain to focus properly. He looked up at the screen, to start seeing what had come up in the results. At the top of the list was "*Z.E.R.O Personnel Files.*"

"Why did that come up?" Jeff clicked it. It was only Alpha Team's files in the results. He looked at the door, feeling like a guilty child with their hand in the cookie jar, and then closed the link.

"Nah, that'll open a can of worms I'm not ready for." Jeff read the next file down, a "*1992 Zombie Attack—North Carolina,*" and clicked it open.

***

Jennifer pulled two paper cups out of the cabinet in the break room and placed them next to the coffee machine as it finished dispensing the rich black nectar. She leaned against the counter, holding her finger to her lips, her cheeks blushing a warm red. She couldn't help but think about what had just happened. Sleeping with Jeff wasn't something she was planning to do today. She trembled with excitement just thinking about his touch. She shook her head. She had to focus and stop thinking with her hormones.

Probably could have handled that better. Need to remember to take my pill when I get home tonight...

She pulled the coffee pot off the machine and poured its contents into the two cups. Her cheeks were beginning to hurt from her constant smile.

"Then again, maybe later we could do that some more...it could be fun." She giggled and finished putting in the sugar and cream for both cups. She might tease him again like she did in the elevator. She loved how easy he was to excite. She walked down the hall with a small skip in her step, back to the computer room with a cup in each hand.

Using her elbow, she pressed down on the handle of the door, and used the weight of her body with her back pressed against it to open it.

"I don't know how you like your coffee, so I just put two sugars in and some—" She finished turning and finally noticed the image on the projector. A newspaper article from her private personnel file. The headline read, "*Family Slaughtered in Grizzly Bear Attack, 6 Year Old Girl Sole Survivor.*" She dropped the coffees from her hands, numb to the hot liquid as it splashed onto her feet. She looked over at Jeff as panic set in. She wasn't ready for him to know her dark past.

How could he? What else did he see about me? About Conor? Europe? Maybe Rick had a point about—no!

***

"Jen, I didn't know." Jeff really hadn't meant to look in her file. Why the computer put this in the zombie attack file as opposed to being locked in the personal files he couldn't figure out. He never would have willingly betrayed her trust.

"What gives you the right to look into my personal files? You think you have that right just because I let you sleep with me? I thought you were better than that Knight!" Her eyes were red from her oncoming tears.

"Jen, it's not what it looks like. I could have clicked on your file, but I swear I didn't. I just clicked on this zombie attack from 1992! I swear! You gotta believe me!"

"You think I'm stupid? Don't lie to me! Not after what happened today." Tears streamed down her face, he wanted to hold her and make her listen so she would understand. "I would have told you about my past in my time. Ugh! I was so stupid to think you were different. You had no right!"

"Jen, I said I was sorry, I swear. I know how important your past is to you. Just look here." Jeff ran to the computer and hastily tried to zoom in on the picture in the newspaper clipping. He selected the cabin in the background, and the image loaded in with a slight blur, still pixelated in low resolution. There was nothing but what looked like normal wood showing.

Piece of shit computer don't do this to me! Not now!

Jen's features crumpled in disgust. "Nice try. There's nothing there! I need some space. If you need something, ask somebody else. You'll stay on the team *for now*, but you will work with anyone but me."

Jennifer bolted out the door, just as the computer finished rendering the higher resolution image, revealing the Sons of Judgment's symbol carved on the cabin's exterior. Jeff slammed his fist on the table, cracking the top finish.

"GOD DAMMIT!" He collapsed in the chair, and pulled at his hair.

How the hell am I gonna fix this?

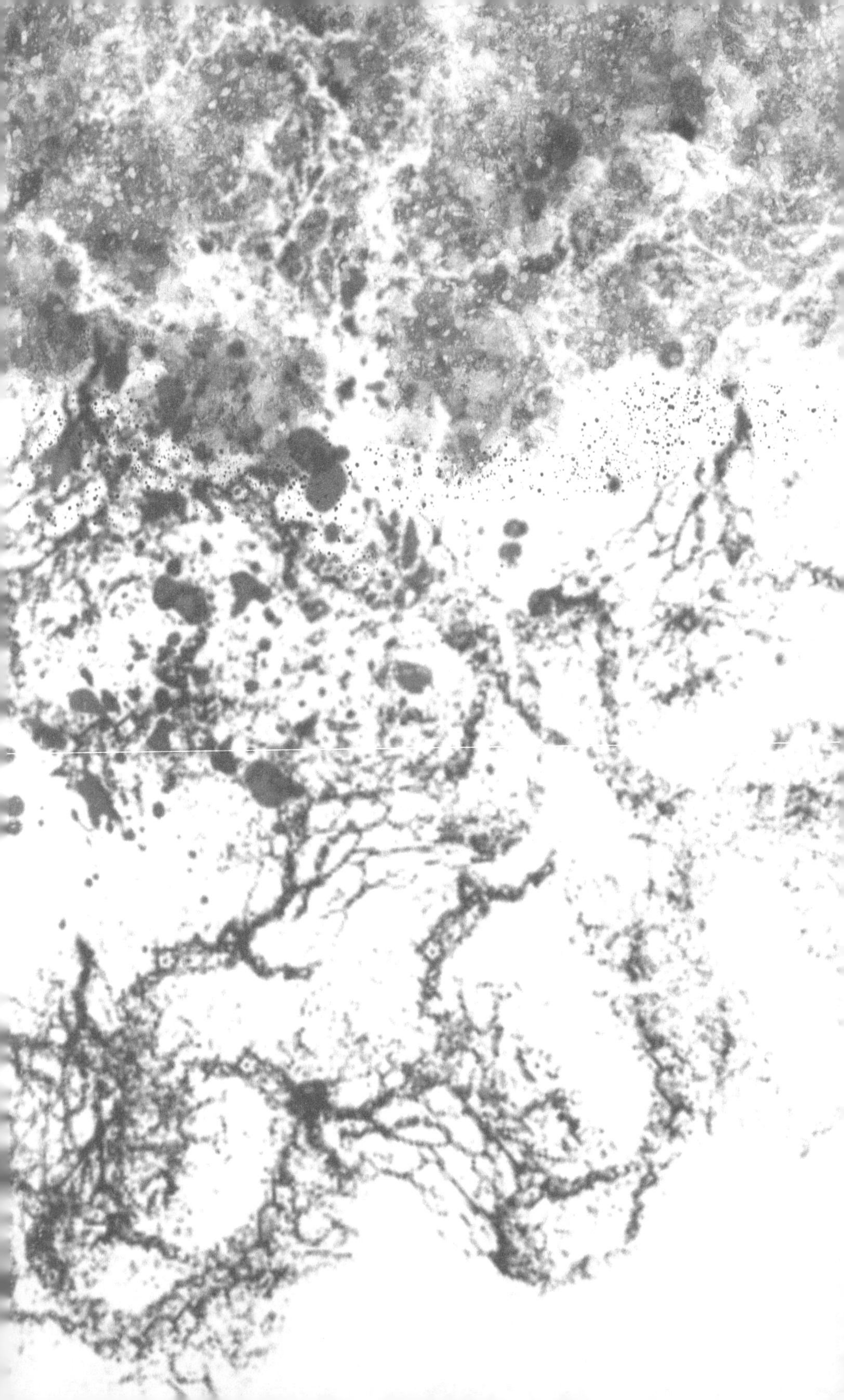

CHAPTER 18

Jeff again couldn't sleep. It wasn't the night terrors that plagued his mind this time, it was Jennifer. He thought of how they had lain in bed together, gazing into each other's eyes, enjoying each other's company. The image was immediately followed by his memory of her heartbroken face as she ran out the door of the records room. He hadn't betrayed her trust, not on purpose. He contemplated calling Adam for advice, but decided that would be a bad idea. He would want to know details of the *"booty call"* first, and Jeff didn't feel like sharing it as a conquest. He felt a mix of rage and frustration at himself, her for not believing him, and at that goddamn computer. She wanted space though... Jeff didn't try texting her to explain. She was too angry to listen. Hopefully he could talk to her at the team meet up and explain.

The next morning he went to the diner for the meeting. It was a small restaurant in the Brandon city area, but it seemed to get a lot of business. He was surprised by the decor when he walked in, a call back to a 1950s burger joint. The floor was a bright red and white tile design, and the booths matched the red hue of the floor tiles. The walls were white with golden records of the era mounted on them. Jeff spied a few Elvis popular singles and an assortment of Motown hits. Against the back wall was a giant jukebox blaring off old pop tunes. Jeff scanned the room for his teammates. He recognized Sentinel's face in one of the back booths. Sitting across from him were the backs of Demon's and Jennifer's heads. Jeff grimaced. He'd never been a jealous person before. Besides, he had no right to be. He had slept with Jennifer, but it didn't mean they were exclusive. He didn't know what they were at this point.

He approached the table. It was a little jarring to see everyone wearing regular civilian clothes. Demon was in a black t-shirt with a matching leather jacket. Jennifer, to his right, was in a white T-shirt with the faded logo of an emo band Jeff had been obsessed with in college. Sentinel looked like a cowboy wearing a signature rancher's hat and a plaid button-down shirt that hung open at the collar with the sleeves rolled up. Jeff smelt a small whiff of cannabis from someone at the table, and he noticed that Sentinel's eyes were red and dilated.

Jennifer did say everyone had their vices...

Jeff grabbed a chair from an adjoining table, and placed it at the end, rather than sliding into the booth with Sentinel. He looked over at Jennifer; her eyes were puffy. She glared back at him when their eyes met, quickly looking away out the window of the restaurant. Jeff crossed his arms, slouching in the chair. He caught Sentinel mouthing to Demon, *"What the heck happened with those two?"* Demon shrugged.

"Everything okay kiddies?" Sentinel asked with a heightened pitch in his voice.

"It's fine," Jeff and Jennifer responded simultaneously. They looked at each other, and then away again.

"I usually like to stay out of these things," said Demon, as his eyes moved back and forth between them, "but this is strange. You two were so chummy before...and...you smell kind of different." Demon grinned with his last comment.

Jeff's ears burned, and he noticed Jennifer was also bright red. He didn't know Demon could smell...*that*!

"If you two know what's good for you, you'll drop it." Jennifer stated icily.

"Is this you or our superior officer talkin'?" Sentinel grinned at her, but she just glared coldly back at him. He quickly frowned, "Both, got it. Shut up, check."

Demon laughed, and Jennifer elbowed him in the rib cage, causing him to cough. Jeff was ready to change the subject.

"Soooo, anyone else learn anything new?" He made sure to only look at Sentinel and Demon as he spoke. He couldn't handle Jennifer's accusatory gaze.

"I did some research with my former coven. The image of the cult—it looked...you'll know soon enough." Demon tapped his fingers on the table with added aggression.

"Waitin' for Hammer." Sentinel responded to Jeff's questioning look.

They sat in an awkward silence. A waitress came over with cups of coffee for everyone but Demon, who politely declined. Jennifer began to play with the napkin on her silverware, actively avoiding Jeff's gaze. It was starting to embroil him.

Really? Are we in high school?

He remembered the picture of Jennifer and Hammer in her room when they were younger. He was getting fed up with her. He didn't do anything wrong. He wanted to push her buttons.

"Does it not bother you guys that our boss is a rampaging drunk? I mean seriously, the guy's got a bottle of whiskey in every room he walks in." He got a small chuckle from Demon and Sentinel, while Jennifer turned into a ball of fire.

"If you had any idea of some of the shit he's seen or had to deal with..." she hissed through gritted teeth.

"No, I mean...it's just..." Jeff realized he might have pushed too far. He knew how hard it was to live with an alcoholic. "I just think he goes a little overboard with it. I mean he's a good guy and all but...I just worry about him, that's all. I told you about my dad, Jen."

Jeff caught a brief look of guilt flash across Jennifer's face at the mention of his father. She opened her mouth to say something—

"What the fuck? Why is Bullet-Sponge getting all menstrual on me?" Hammer's voice boomed behind Jeff, startling him out of his chair. He wasn't planning on Hammer hearing any of that.

"It appears that young Jeffrey is concerned with your drinking."

"D, what the hell man?" Jeff exclaimed as he got back up. Sentinel slid over in the booth, and Hammer shoved Jeff into it, taking the seat that Jeff had previously occupied.

"He also feels that it's appropriate to refer to people by one letter," Demon mused.

"Goddammit, Meat-Shield, I already had a mother and she ain't at this table. Any who, I've called all of you already individually, and filled you in on what me and Jeff learned from Maero about the Sons of Judgement. Anybody got anything else to add?"

Jeff didn't tell anyone but Jennifer about what he'd found in the old files. He looked at her for approval. Her body language was still rigid, but she knew what he was thinking. She nodded for him to go ahead and share his findings.

"I've got something."

"When did you get something new?"

"Yesterday, when you dropped me off. I thought that symbol for the cult looked familiar. So I went through the archives."

"Okay. Go on." Hammer actually gave him his full attention, turning his body in Jeff's direction as he crossed his arms.

"If you were to look at all the photos from the different crime scenes, you'd see that somewhere on a close-by building, tree, garbage can, or wall that their insignia was there."

"Which crime scene photos?" Sentinel asked.

"All of the D-Day events in the US at least," Jennifer answered coolly. "Or any of our other 'freak' outbreaks." The rest of the group was silent as they absorbed the new information.

"How far back did you look?" Demon asked Jeff.

"Since the end of World War Two. I couldn't really find anything before that." Jeff watched their faces as he answered. A small amount of color drained from all of them.

"That can't be right. I know for a fact that there have been undead around before that. I've seen them." Demon frowned and his eyebrows furrowed. "That symbol...I've seen it before the forties."

"Yeah, but it wasn't till after World War Two that we started having such large quantities of undead like the D-Day events." Hammer tapped his finger on the table while he was thinking.

"And this goes with what we learned about the cult being formed around that same time." Jeff continued.

"If we can stop this group, we've pretty much stopped one of the biggest paranormal plagues on the human race," Jennifer said with restrained excitement. Jeff contemplated what this news really meant to all of them. He was still new to all of this, but they had been at this hidden war for much longer. Z.E.R.O hunted zombies mostly; no zombie hordes meant they could have somewhat normal lives.

"Fuck. I'm gonna need to find another job. Never thought I would see the day that would happen," Hammer said as he leaned back in his chair. The rest of the team stared blankly at the table in front of them. "Well boys and girls," Hammer continued, "we got some work to do. So does anybody else got something new? I don't know what tops what we just heard."

"I got some news that may be related to this too," Demon chimed in.

"From the vampire community?" Jennifer asked.

"Yes. As all of you are aware, except for Jeff here, the vampires that still find themselves above humans made their own type of hunting group that much of Z.E.R.O's tactics are based on. Of course, most of the members think of themselves more as cattlemen protecting their flock, rather than helping another race," Demon explained. "I used to be the leader of one of those teams before I was excommunicated."

Okay, that's disturbing...vampires only keeping humans around as food...

"Well, it turns out quite a few members have gone missing recently, with no clues or warning, and others have shown up, but not normal." Demon waited patiently for everyone around him to contemplate what he was trying to tell them.

"No offense, Demon, but what's *not* normal for a vampire?" Sentinel chuckled.

"You have a point," Demon smiled at his friend briefly. "But the ones the coven were able to locate were different, mutated. No sense of their former selves, just rabid. Feeding on the flesh of others instead of just blood. Like they were infected with zombism."

"Wait," cut in Hammer, shocked, "you had vamp-zombies? What the hell is going on? The only species that can get infected by any of these mutation diseases are humans. The strains don't cross between the creatures." Hammer tapped his finger on the table rapidly, a slight loss of color to his skin.

"Which is why there is concern. If vampires can be turned into zombies now, we have a problem. Can you imagine what could happen if a lycan were to be infected?"

"Undead, giant zombie dogs...sounds like tons of fun," Jennifer muttered disgustedly.

"It's as horrible as you are imagining. They came across one. It took two teams to take it down. They are much stronger than their vampire brethren. So, coming to my original point." Demon sat up straight and placed his arms on the table, cupping his hands. He took a long look at everyone around the table. "My coven has reached out for our help. In exchange they promised to give us information they have on the Sons of Judgement."

Everyone was quiet again. Hammer stopped tapping his finger. Sentinel's joking face grew dark. Jennifer stared at Demon with utter shock. Jeff didn't quite understand why Demon's coven asking for help was such a big deal. He was still trying to wrap his head around zombie-werewolves and zombie-vampires. Sentinel leaned on the table, his face the most serious Jeff had seen him yet.

"What are the *Tenebre Orbis's* thoughts on this?" asked Sentinel. "Your covens like to be hidden from humans. Even humans like us, that know about you, for fear of war or unsanctioned attacks." Sentinel clasped his hands in fists in front of him, almost mirroring Demon, his knuckles turning white.

Jeff had researched some of the vampire culture and practices during his training, but the names of all the different groups and factions were still garbled in his memory. He remembered seeing the name *Tenebre Orbis*, but couldn't remember where they stood on the hierarchy.

"Excellent question," replied Demon, winking at Sentinel. "The covens are traditionally hidden. Meaning they wish to stay out of the public eye and conduct all their business with humanity from the shadows, including us at Z.E.R.O. When I was poised to take control of the one in this city, however, I based a lot of my campaign on new ideals. I wanted us to come out into the public eye, at least to our partnership in Z.E.R.O, and coexist with the human race as much as possible. No more blood orgies and forced donors. It's part of why I was excommunicated. But it seems this will be an under-the-table matter. The *Tenebre Orbis* will not be directly involved. Neither will the smaller council. We are only meeting with one coven...my old one."

"How?" asked Jennifer, one confused eyebrow raised. "The *Tenebre Orbis* are very clear on their rules, and they keep a close eye on all the covens. You told me they denied you a meeting when I sent you a few months back. What's changed?" Jennifer's skin was pale, and small goosebumps formed on her arms. Whoever this group was, Jeff wasn't so sure that he wanted to meet them.

"My old protege...Orcus. He has reached out to me personally." Demon growled while saying the coven leader's name.

"Orcus? He chose that name, or was he named after a whale?" Jeff couldn't help his slip of the tongue when he was nervous. Jennifer glared at him for interrupting.

"You may not be up on your lore," Sentinel said smugly, "but Orcus is a Roman demon of death that has been heavily associated with Hades and other gods of death." The Texan leaned back in the booth and stroked his beard as he thought.

"I dislike his methods, but Orcus has ways of doing things without the *Tenebre Orbis* finding out. The number of missing vampires is rising too much out of his control now, and this could be to our advantage later. If he owes us a favor, it will be very lucrative down the line." Demon's disgust for Orcus was very apparent. His eyes flashed briefly as he spoke, from his deep dark brown to the bright yellow of his vampire nature.

"I still don't like this. I feel like we're being set up here." Hammer rubbed his temple like he was getting the onset of a migraine.

"I agree." Jennifer looked up at Demon, growing concern in her eyes.

"Look," said Demon, his face deathly serious. "I understand your apprehension, and I'll accept it if you don't want to help. I won't bear any ill will, but I'm going. I may not like or agree with Orcus or his plans, but my community is suffering. And—I need to know...never mind." Demon stood up to leave.

"Hey brother, now we might not be comfortable, but we never said we weren't goin'. I'm in," Sentinel said, his wide white smile back.

"I can't believe you even had to say that. Of course I'm in." Jennifer grabbed Demon's hand in hers and squeezed it tightly. Jeff felt a knot in his throat.

What is wrong with me? You joined this group because you wanted to make a difference. Not for her. Say something!

"Me too!" Jeff announced louder than he liked. Jennifer released Demon's hand at his outburst. Mixed emotions flashed across her face. He couldn't tell if she was annoyed by his loud acceptance.

The group turned to Hammer, who had not responded to Demon's request for help yet. "Do I get to shoot something?"

"If the situation requires it," Demon chuckled.

"Alright, fuck it. When do we meet 'em?"

"It has to be today, unfortunately. At noon. I told him I wanted us on an even playing field, and this was the only way he would do it. The midpoint of the day would be the safest for you all."

"Works for me. Demon, you take Matthews and Knight to get some silver bullets. I don't want to walk in naked. Looks like no one's getting pancakes today." Hammer frowned as he looked at the time on his watch. Everyone began to slide out of the booth and leave. Hammer grabbed Jennifer's arm before she could slide out.

"Hey Jen, hang back a minute." She looked at him questionably. Jeff hurried out of the diner. Seeing Jennifer today infuriated him more than he was expecting. He'd never felt like this before. It bothered him how quickly she seemed to run back to Demon's arms after one fight. One fight that never should have happened. If she wasn't so stubborn, and actually listened to what he was trying to show her, she would know the truth. He'd never planned on betraying her trust. The fact she was unwilling to listen to him infuriated him more. He didn't like this person he was becoming. He jumped in his car and sped off. He needed to cool his head before he sat alone with Sentinel and Demon.

***

Hammer grabbed Jennifer's arm when she attempted to slide out of the booth. His expression had her worried. Since Hammer had taken over as Commander of their base, he had been distant. She had always equated it with the burden of leadership. It was rare that he ever showed her any emotions, other than the asshole persona he put on to keep everyone away.

"Hey Jen, hang back a minute." Jennifer nodded to him. She watched as everyone left. Especially Jeff. As soon as they were dismissed, he sped out of the diner. She couldn't understand why he was acting like he was the one that was hurt. It was her trust that *he* broke. She was up most of the night crying because of his betrayal. She'd finally let someone in and they'd betrayed her right away. Her eyes were sore from her tears, but remembering the events from yesterday evening filled her with burning rage again.

"How big of an asshole do I seem right now?" Hammer asked her.

He's probably thinking about Chaz from the other night.

"Remember when you got shitfaced on that mission in the titty-bar, and vomited on that stripper in the VIP room? Then you walked out on the eighty dollar lap dance tab?"

"Vaguely," Hammer chuckled.

"Not quite that big." She kept her expression serious as she gazed at him, but began to laugh when he looked dumbfounded back at her. "What's on your mind Terrence? Does this have to do with Uncle Tobias?"

"You could always see right through me," Hammer sighed.

Jennifer and Hammer weren't super close as siblings, but they balanced each other out. He was always more outgoing and boisterous, eager to poke the wasp nest. She on the other hand was more reserved, carefully analyzing a situation before stepping in. Emotionally, they had tried to keep their individual problems to themselves, as the stress of their day to day was already enough without the extra burdens. This meant they'd become proficient at silently reading each other for support. The fact he was taking an effort to open up to her now meant that this was really important, and that worried her more.

"The High Council wants me to stop going out into the field and start gearing up for a spot on their little group."

"Oh my god! That's fantastic!" She was thrilled by the news but he didn't share her feelings on the matter. "What are you going to do?"

"What do you think?"

Jennifer grinned. "You're going to tell them to go to hell, and that you're a fighter not a politician, aren't you?" His stubbornness and hatred of policy was going to be the end of him one of these days.

"You really do know me too well."

"Terrence, this is an amazing opportunity! No one has ever made it onto the Council this young." Jennifer grabbed his hands on the table as she tried to reassure him, "We used to worship these guys when we were rookies remember?"

"Used to." Hammer took his hands away from her. "When they actually helped people instead of getting into a dick-measuring contest every five seconds. They don't pass anything that is helpful to the teams that doesn't line their own bank accounts. They're not heroes anymore Jen. They're politicians. What have I always said about politicians?"

"That the saddest thing about fifteen dead politicians is that someone ran out of ammo?" Jennifer rolled her eyes, this was stupid. "I cannot believe you're going to piss this opportunity away! You know how many Z.E.R.O operatives would kill for a shot like this?"

"So one of them can have it. I'm not interested!" Hammer's hand pounded the table hard. Other people in the diner turned to look, but went back to their meals eyeing them suspiciously.

"You can't say no to these guys." Jennifer lowered her voice, hissing the warning. There were consequences for going against the council, no matter how good an asset you were to them.

"I'm not doing it, Jen. End of story. Really only leaves them two options." Hammer held up his fingers as he counted them out. "One, they keep me with this unit, where I continue to develop good soldiers to be transferred to other areas of the organization. Or two, I'm relieved of command and sent off somewhere that no one will ever hear of me again."

"And what happens to us? What happens to our base?" Jennifer was worried now. Since Hammer had taken over, they'd remodeled their district into an efficient machine. A new bureaucrat in charge would ruin everything they created.

"The next in command will take over." Hammer looked right into Jen's eyes. "Last time I checked, that was you."

"What? Terry I can't!" Jennifer didn't want to lead as much as Hammer didn't want to go to the council. Leading a single team was easy. She didn't want to be responsible for the two hundred soldiers in their division. She didn't feel she was ready yet. She fell apart when losing just one soldier a year ago. It triggered memories with Conor. Her father was a leader, not her. Hammer grabbed her by the shoulders, and looked directly in her eyes.

"You can! There's no one else I'd feel comfortable with taking over the crew, Jen. And no corporate asshole is gonna get appointed and take over *our* family. I won't have that. I'll shoot the prick myself."

"What about Demon and Rick? They have way more experience than me."

Hammer shook his head. "Nah. They look up to you, but still need direction. Demon may be old, but you saw him today. He needs someone to keep him focused. And Rick hasn't been right since he lost his sister and niece."

"And who would be my right hand then? They don't know me as well as you do. They can't keep me grounded from going too far."

Hammer leaned back and shrugged. "Your call. If I was you though, the new kid is willing to follow you into the mouth of Hell. And he's got a good head on his shoulders in regards to morals." Jennifer scoffed at him. If he only knew what was going on he would probably say differently. He held up his finger, preventing her from saying what she wanted, noting her scowl. "*Regardless* of the reason why you are so pissed off at him right now. I don't know what he did, but I think it might be more you than him in this situation."

What the hell? You're supposed to be on my side. Jeff took advantage of my trust, he intentionally looked at my personal files without permission...he knows about my time in Europe with Omega, and Conor...maybe Rick's right and he's a plant from the cult but—

Jennifer re-processed what had happened the night before. He couldn't have accessed her personnel file. He didn't have the security clearance. He only had access for all logged attacks. They had never tried to cover up what happened to her family. She did have them lock up the file on Conor, and her time in Europe. He could have asked her about Conor when he was at her home, in her bedroom. She knows he must have seen her picture. But he didn't. A sickening weight formed in her stomach as realization hit. She'd let her rashness get the better of her and possibly ruined something that could have been special. How could she have been so quick to judge?

"Face it Sis, this is in your blood." Hammer was still going on about her leading the division. She had fazed out his speech while contemplating her recent faults, "Even if your parents were still alive, you'd have found your way here. I mean Christ-sake, you were dead-on about Jeff! I never would've called that! You see the potential in everyone, and you have a natural ability to elevate their game to another level."

Jennifer shook her head, refusing to budge. "All the skills I learned from you. You trained me, remember?"

Hammer shook his head, and got up from his chair, He gestured for her to move over in the booth. She slid over and was surprised when he gave her a hug. He hadn't been this close with her since they were children. "Nah, I just make sure I'm the first one in, and the last one out. I don't know much about boosting potential in others. Besides, Connor trained you better than me. When you got back from Europe, you practically re-organized the base when I took over by yourself. You don't need to do what I do to get respect. Just promise me you'll think about it okay?"

"Okay, I promise. I'll think about it." Hammer gave her shoulders a tight squeeze and called over a waitress. "Well I'm gonna have my mother-fucking pancakes today, you want anything?"

"Uh, no, I gotta go actually. There's something I gotta fix." Hammer moved so she could leave. She had to talk to Jeff, she had to apologize. She jumped in her truck and headed to the base. Hopefully she could catch him before they had to leave.

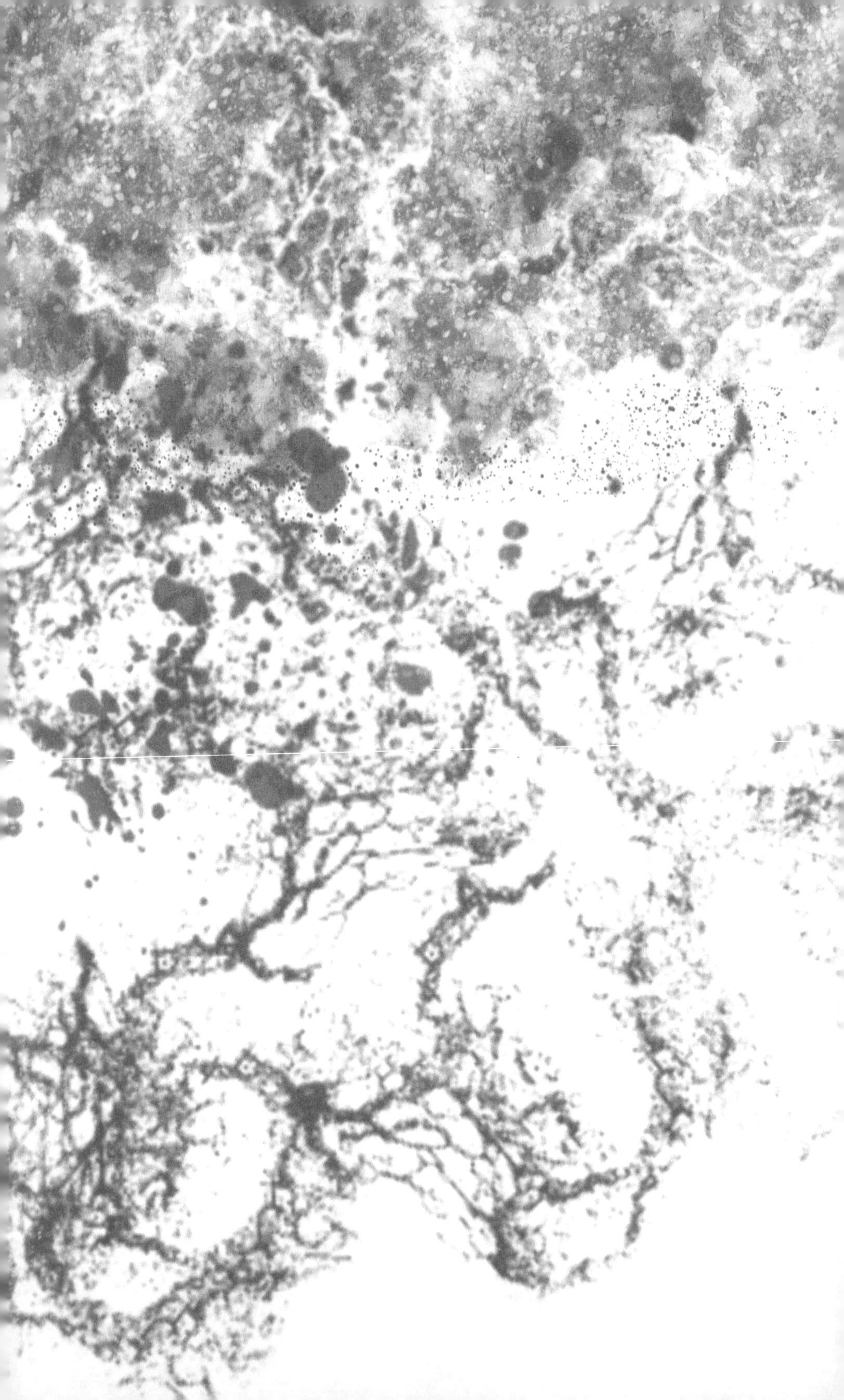

CHAPTER 19

Jeff, Demon, and Sentinel sat in the locker room, loading silver bullets into magazines. Demon wore gloves as he worked with the silver, to protect his skin. The three of them had already changed out of their civilian clothes and were in their combat gear. Demon explained he was unsure how full the coven was, so in case the meeting went sour, he suggested they bring the extra ammo. Between the three of them, that meant loading twenty magazines, with about two hundred rounds of silver bullets. Jeff checked his watch. They had two hours to finish loading everything, and head to the location. Demon wouldn't tell them where they were going exactly, only offering to direct them while they drove. He didn't want the directions plugged into a GPS that could be pulled up later by a higher up of Z.E.R.O and he knew that his team wouldn't betray his trust if they happened to remember the directions. Even if he was excommunicated from the coven, he still had a duty to protect his kind from the curious eyes in Z.E.R.O.

They worked in silence, the only sound in the room the small clicks as the metal of the bullets clicked against the metal of the magazines. Sentinel's phone vibrated loud on the bench next to him. He picked it up, and frowned when he looked at the screen. Jeff recognized the number as an international number.

"Hey guys, I gotta check on a few things, will you be alright without me for a few? Should just take a minute." Sentinel looked to Jeff and Demon for approval.

"You talk with China?" Jeff's curiosity slipped out again. Sentinel clutched his phone in his hand a little tighter, surprised by the question.

"Yeah. We're international. How did you know it's a Chinese number?" Sentinel's brow furrowed, and the light that Jeff was used to seeing in his eyes was overcast. It made him feel unsettled.

Jeff shrugged. "I used to order rare anime items from Japan. They used to get stuck in Chinese customs all the time. I had a friend that spoke Mandarin, used to have to call them all the time just to get my stuff to ship."

Sentinel's rigid body relaxed. Demon continued to work on the bullets. There was an awkward silence as Sentinel's phone began to vibrate in his hand again. He looked down at it, and then back at Jeff, his big bright smile back on his face.

"Cool! You'll have to tell me what anime you're into. I've got quite the collection," Sentinel nodded, then answered the ringing phone as he walked out of the room. "*Duìyú nàgè hěn bàoqiàn. Wǒmen zhèngzài kāihuì. Zhǔnbèi hǎo biāoběn.*"

"Sorry about that. We're taking the meeting"... Something about preparing something? God I wish I'd paid more attention to Mike when he was trying to teach me the language. Who is he telling about the meeting? I thought this was top secret to Alpha Team only...

"Yeah sure," Jeff responded emotionlessly as Sentinel walked out. He was still unsure if he'd translated what Sentinel said correctly. Demon heard his tone and gazed at him curiously as he went back to work.

Demon's color had grown pale and sick as the day moved on. If the vampires they were meeting would be this way too, it made Jeff feel more comfortable for what they were about to walk into. They continued with their labor. Jeff's thumb was sore with every bullet he pushed in. He still had two boxes left to load. The room was quiet again, except for the soft click, click, click as they worked.

He glanced up briefly at Demon, remembering how Jennifer had grasped his hand in the diner. The look in her eyes when she'd spoken with him. The same look he gave back to her. They were close. Very close. He knew they were together the night before in the shower room, even though she'd said nothing had happened. Maybe something did happen between them, and she'd lied about it. He felt like she'd used him as a rebound while she worked something out with Demon.

He tried to rush the bullets into the magazine to put some space between him and Demon. A stubborn shell flew out of his grasp, hitting Demon in the arm. There was a sizzling sound, and it left a small burn mark. As Jeff looked over at him, fear set in. Demon seemed pretty laid back, but Jeff had never caused him bodily harm before. Demon bent down and picked up the bullet, wordlessly. He walked over to Jeff and placed it in his palm. Jeff's eyes glanced at Demon's arm, the skin already boiled like a second degree burn.

"I'm so sorry!"

"Don't worry about it. It doesn't really hurt. After I eat, I'll heal up." Demon checked out his arm like he'd only been bitten by a mosquito, and went back to working in silence. Jeff found himself eyeing Demon, reviewing all of his attributes. He was attractive, in body and mind. Of course Jennifer was into him, maybe still in love with him. He was a vampire, with eons of knowledge and life experiences. Jeff was a nobody, just a stupid human that had never accomplished anything in his life.

Demon put down the magazine he was working on. "You have something you want to ask me?"

Do I have something to ask? What am I really looking for here?

"You and Jen used to be together?" Jeff kept his focus on the magazine in front of him, afraid to look Demon in the eye.

"Yes," Demon answered calmly. He didn't seem upset by the question.

"How long?" Jeff finally met Demon's gaze. He needed to know what they were, where he stood in all this.

"I've known her since she was a child." Demon held up his hands in defense when he noted Jeff's face of disgust. "Hey now. Time moves differently for me. I have known her for a long time, let's put it that way. I was never romantic with her until she was an adult. We have been off and on for a few years. I think the question you're looking for though is: is it over? It is."

Jeff returned to work. Click, click, click.

"What about what happened in the shower Friday night?" He stared carefully at Demon to judge his reaction again. He was briefly surprised, but returned to his cool demeanor.

"So she told you about that. Good." Demon chuckled at Jeff's confusion, "Nothing happened. She hurt her hand, I fixed it. Did she tell you how it works when a host is giving us blood willingly?"

Jeff remembered the conversation with Jennifer during the movie. She explained about the sexual sensation that was almost uncontrollable for the host when the vampire feeds.

"Yeah...but—"

"I'm a little hungry right now. I can give you a taste of how it feels if you want. I got no preference in gender. I'm free loving." Demon smiled and popped out his teeth, while his eyes changed to a lion's predator yellow. Jeff dropped the magazine from his hand. It clattered to the floor, loudly, echoing in the small space.

"No, that's alright. I'm sorry. I don't know what I'm thinking." He picked up the magazine, and tried to get back to work.

"So I was right, you and Jennifer." Demon laughed heartily. Jeff's ears burned. "Nothing to be ashamed of. I don't know what happened in the small timeframe any of this could have occurred in, but Jennifer can be...difficult. I call her my Fire, because that's what she is. A wild flame that will keep you warm, but burn you if you are not careful. She can't be tamed. She does mean well. It's been a while since I've seen her connect with another human the way I see her interact with you frankly." Demon finished his stack of magazines and put them in a duffel bag.

So I should just excuse her for accusing me of prying into her life? She treated me like an enemy. Yes, I read the file. Her poor family was slaughtered by a horde of zombies. They never found her sister. Still, was it worth the reaction she gave me? What else is she hiding that she was afraid I would see? The man from the photo? The baby?

"I don't know how I feel right now."

"You have time to find out. Besides," Demon closed his eyes and inhaled like he'd smelt something sweet and familiar, "talking might help. I'll let Sentinel know we're about done here."

Demon went to exit the room and was met by Jennifer standing in the doorway. He brushed past her wordlessly as she came in quietly, her gaze flashing at Jeff and then at the ground as she walked by. Jeff returned to his work. He opened the last box of ammo, and began to load the last magazine. There was no sound in the room except the squeaky hinge of her locker when she opened it, followed by the sound of the bullets as Jeff pressed them into the head of the magazine. Click, click, click.

"I'm almost done here if you want me to leave," he muttered as he noticed her standing quietly with her gear laid out on the bench.

"No, you can stay." Her voice was small. She always sounded so confident that it caught him off guard. She seemed like she wanted to say something more, but she turned away and began to change her clothes instead. She kicked off her shoes and took off her ankle socks. She moved slowly with every movement, like she was unsure what she should be doing. Jeff went back to work. He finished the magazine, and glanced over at her again as she undressed. His heart raced with excitement as his body remembered their time together, but the memory of their fight put a knot in his throat.

"About yesterday," he muttered. She put her jeans in her locker and turned back to him. Jeff tried not to look at her exposed body.

"I'm sorry," Jennifer said quietly. He glanced back at her again as she nervously pulled at her fingers. "It has come to my attention that I may have overreacted. I've been hurt in the past, and I keep a wall up." She waited for him to say something. He didn't know how to respond without sounding like an ass with an *"I told you so"* attitude. "You wouldn't understand." She turned around and grabbed her pants off the bench. She slid them on hastily.

I wouldn't understand?

"So you're the only one that's been hurt by someone? You're the only one with a wall up?" He felt his veins bulge with anger, and his head felt hot. He understood betrayal of trust. It was a pain that would never go away and he didn't want to do that to anyone else. He threw the magazine in his hand to the ground. "Did you forget what I told you about Kylie already?"

"Okay, so maybe that was the wrong choice of words. But I keep my past hidden for a reason. I don't like people looking at me like a victim of circumstance!" Jennifer screamed back at him. Any sadness or remorse she had in her eyes was gone now, there was only fire.

"God you're so infuriating!" Jeff slammed the locker next to him with his fist. A thunderous clap radiated through the room. "You think you're special because you had a tough childhood? Everyone walks on eggshells around you, because they're afraid of how you'll react. You're making yourself a victim. Own up to it! My childhood wasn't easy either. I had an abusive father that almost killed me in one of his drunken hazes! The last straw to get my mother to leave the bastard."

Jennifer was screaming now. "I saw my family murdered, torn apart by those things! I lost my fiancé to other monsters! And I lost my—" Jennifer stopped herself from speaking more as her eyes swelled with the approaching tears. "I relive those moments everyday. I'm a survivor, and I go out there every night just to kill them, but it won't bring my family back! It won't bring any of them back!"

Jennifer's eyes erupted with the warm tears she was trying to hold back. Jeff grabbed her and held her tightly in his arms. He felt as the rigidness in her body collapsed and she pressed harder into his chest, finally releasing her wails of pain she had been bottling up for years.

Her fiancé huh? So he died, and left her alone with a baby...no wait...that's not what she said...she lost the baby too?

A hollow emptiness opened in his chest as he put the clues together of the man and the missing baby. Jennifer had lost her fiancé, and her child. He couldn't imagine what he would have done in her situation. To have had all that loss in his life. His childhood was rough, but he still had his mother, his family. All his anger dissipated. He squeezed her tighter in his arms. His eyes began to burn. He wanted to cry with her. There was a lot they still had to learn about each other. She was a human being, like him, and not the super soldier she had made herself appear.

"You gotta believe me. I didn't intentionally look at your file. I really didn't want to betray your trust."

"I know that now," her muffled voice responded, her face still buried in his chest. "I realized today that you didn't have the security clearance to actually open the official file. That you still don't know everything. I promise I will tell you, when I'm ready."

Jennifer pulled back and wiped the tears from her eyes, but they were still streaming. He placed his hands on her cheeks and tentatively wiped away the falling streams with his thumbs. Her soft rose lips started to spread in a small smile. He reached his head down toward her, kissing her gently. She didn't fight or pull away, kissing him back. The knot in his throat lifted, despite the hollow pain he felt for her still remaining in his chest. He wrapped his arms around her waist and kissed her again, holding her tight. He wanted her to feel how much he cared for her. She squeezed her arms around his body as she returned the kiss.

There was a loud knock on the door. The two of them scattered back to opposite sides of the room like two teenagers about to get caught by their parents.

"If you kids are done in there, we would like to get going." Demon's voice was muffled on the other side, with an air of amusement.

"Yeah, be there in a minute!" Jennifer screamed back as she hastily wiped her red face.

She scrambled to get her gear on while Jeff loaded up the remaining ammo in the bag that Demon had left in the room next to her locker.

"Hey, Jen." He grabbed her hand and pulled her to sit down at his side. "I want to tell you what I really found when the article came up on the computer."

She looked at him confused. "Okay." She seemed hesitant, but he placed his other hand on top gently. She sat down next to him on the bench.

"I saw the Sons of Judgment symbol on the cabin." Jeff looked her in the eyes, so she could see he wasn't lying. Her body became rigid again, her hand tightened in his. "If we take these guys out, maybe you'll get some peace about your family."

She sat silent, her lips pursed shut. A new expression of rage was etched onto her face. She stood up, and took her gun out of her locker, clearing it briefly before she placed it in her holster.

"We need to get going." Her voice was flat, with resigned emotion. She had that same look in her eye as the night they interrogated Chaz.

***

Jennifer's brain switched to autopilot the moment Jeff had told her what he found. The Sons of Judgment were responsible for the death of her family. They were there. They used her family as guinea pigs in their schemes.

She didn't remember walking out of the base with Jeff, or getting into Hammer's vehicle, as they rode together. She was angry. She thought of all the ways she would kill their leader, Greyven he called himself. He was the one who probably gave them the order.

But why? Why my family? Did they know my family was Z.E.R.O? My father was in a high position. He was picked to join the High Council before Uncle Tobias. Did they not want him in that position? Who is Greyven?

"Phoenix, you alright?" Hammer was holding the door open for her to get out. Jennifer didn't realize they had arrived.

"Yeah I'm fine." She hopped out of the vehicle. She had to get her head in the game. She didn't know what type of situation they were going into. No human, not even Z.E.R.O humans, were invited to meet directly at a coven's home. All meetings were held at pre-approved locations by both parties, to ensure the safety of both species. They didn't trust Z.E.R.O not to exterminate their nest, and Z.E.R.O didn't trust they wouldn't try to eat their soldiers. She looked up to see Jeff's concerned face as he jumped out of the large vehicle behind her.

"You sure you're okay?" he asked her as he handed her ammo from one of the duffle bags at the back of the vehicle.

"Yeah, I'm fine. Don't worry about it. Just been thinking about what you told me." He frowned and continued with equipping himself. He was trying to make her feel better when he told her about the cabin. She hoped her short response didn't make him think she was mad at him for telling her.

Jennifer finally took in her surroundings. They were in a more affluent section of the city. Before them was a two-story plantation style mansion. The exterior was white stone with beige accents, and large white columns adorned the front deck. A relic of the South's dark history. The large windows were covered on the inside by crimson red black-out curtains, hiding any threats they may be walking into from their vision. How far back the property went in scale, she could not make out from their position. At the heavy oak double doors of the entrance were two pale skinned guards in matching black suits wearing sunglasses.

She looked at her team, gathering near the front of the hummer. Someone was missing from the group. She heard the sounds of a man retching on the side of the vehicle, hidden from view. She walked around to find Demon, throwing up blood-filled bile. The daylight was doing a number on him. She wondered how the vampires inside would be if he was this bad.

"Are you going to be okay, Demon?" She placed her hand on his back as he upchucked again another pool of blood. To a normal human, they would probably think he was dying.

"You know me and my morning sickness. Hammer's driving didn't help." He tried to smile.

"Did you eat today?"

"Not really." Demon looked like he was going to barf again, but held it down, "I figured this might be worse if I did."

"You idiot." Jennifer sat him down where the vampires standing guard could not see them. "You need to drink something, or this day is going to be very long for you."

She held her arm out to him, but he pushed it away.

"No. I'm not gonna ruin anything for you and him." Jennifer scowled at him.

"Ever the gentleman. Stay here." She walked around to the rest of the guys.

"What's up?" Hammer looked at her questionably.

"It's Demon. He thought he would be better off if he didn't eat before leaving today. He's puking his guts out over there. We need him to be more Demon, and less of a sick vamp."

Hammer grimaced. "For fuck's sake. We gotta start heading in, or those guys are gonna think we're up to something," Hammer said as he watched the guards.

"I just need to borrow Knight. We're gonna take Demon into your car, we promise not to make a mess." She smiled and winked at Hammer as she grabbed Jeff's hand and dragged him back to Demon. "Help me get him in."

She opened the door and the two of them lifted Demon inside. He was very pale, his skin an ashy gray, like it was becoming dry. She let Jeff in first, closing the door behind all of them.

"What do you need me for?" Jeff's puzzled face looked between Demon and her.

"Mr. Romantic here won't drink from me because he's worried about you."

"Oh..."

"We're gonna get really friendly here in a minute." She grabbed Jeff's hand. And turned to Demon. "I got it solved, you're gonna eat from both of us, okay?"

***

"Wait, WHAT?" Jeff's eyes widened.

"If it's from both of us, none of us can feel guilty about anything." Jennifer sighed, pulling her combat knife out of its shoulder holster and cutting Jeff's forearm before he could protest. The cut she made burned and oozed blood. Demon's eyes changed to that same predatory yellow he had seen in the locker room and his fangs popped out. Jennifer shoved Jeff's arm in front of Demon, who grabbed it, and immediately started to suck on his wound.

What he felt next was almost indescribable. The burning pain stopped, replaced with a burning pleasure, like when a hot pad is placed on a sore muscle. He looked at Jennifer as she waited, amused and overly eager with what was happening.

"Give it a minute," she laughed.

That's when he felt a tingling, pleasurable sensation travel from his arm toward the rest of his body. His blood carried this feeling to his heart. It wasn't long before his whole body was pulsing.

"Holy Hell...." Every nerve became excited, sending more pleasure vibes throughout his body. This was what Jennifer was telling him about. He grabbed her hand and squeezed it. She laughed and kissed him on the cheek.

That's not helping... But holy shit. I can see now why people volunteer for this crap.

"Alright, Demon, time to switch up," Jennifer said after a few minutes. She reached over Jeff, holding her arm up. Demon released Jeff's arm, but every electrical soothing vibration Jeff experienced continued to pulsate through his system. Demon took Jennifer's arm, immediately drinking from her. Jeff held his hand over his cut in an effort to slow the bleeding. His head was spinning as he tried to get focused.

Jennifer grabbed his leg with her free hand and immediately started to squeeze it. Her cheeks were full on red. This time however, as Demon drank, Jeff noticed something a little different. Demon seemed to enjoy the flavor of Jeff's blood, but when he drank from Jennifer, it was like watching someone eating their favorite rare treat. It didn't last long, as he made a face, like something was off.

There was a loud bang from the door outside. Hammer's voice came through, startling them all.

"Ya'll better be getting nothing but Demon's lunch on my seats or I swear to God!"

Demon released Jennifer's arm, and poked his thumb with his fang. He rubbed his blood across Jennifer's wounds, and motioned for Jeff to give him his as well. Demon rubbed his bleeding thumb over Jeff's cut. The wound closed immediately. There was no scar, or scab when he wiped the blood away.

"Thank you. Both of you," Demon said as he wiped his mouth. Most of his color had returned. He turned to Jennifer. "You taste different."

Jennifer looked at him, confused at his question. "What do you mean?"

"It's weird, kind of hard to describe, but...you taste a little like him." Demon nodded in Jeff's direction.

What does he mean she "tastes" like me? Maybe we got the same blood type?

Jennifer continued to gaze at Demon confused. Her brows furrowed. A look of shock spread over her face as she came to an internal realization. Like she understood something the others didn't.

"Jen, what's wrong?"

"It's not important right now. We gotta get going. Get out, both of you." Jennifer gestured for them to exit the vehicle; Jeff hopped out but noticed Jennifer was still sitting in the seat, looking at her arm.

"Jen?" Her sudden change in behavior concerned him.

"I'm fine, I'm coming."

Everyone gathered around Hammer near the entrance of the mansion. They formed a tight group to make sure their hosts did not overhear them.

"Okay people, listen up. We are headed into unfriendly territory. I don't care what they say, we don't surrender our weapons. Yes, it's their house, but they asked for our help. Demon's got the most experience with these guys, so he's taking the lead."

The group nodded in agreement and marched up to the large wooden doors of the mansion. The closer they were to the entrance, the more nervous Jeff felt, like they were about to walk into the den of a lion pride. He felt Jennifer's hand go into his. She squeezed it and smiled up at him.

"You're gonna be okay. Just remember your training in case anything happens. Besides, it's daytime. I promise you, they're all feeling like Demon right now if they are awake."

She let go of his hand as they walked in. The doors were closed promptly behind them, making a loud echo when they entered. Inside the foyer there was a grand staircase leading up to the second floor of the mansion. To their left and right were sitting rooms filled with posh Victorian-style furniture, oil paintings in gaudy gold frames, and antique oak furniture. They were also filled with a large number of highly attractive people, all vampires, recognizable by their yellow glowing eyes. They were dressed in a mixture of high fashion evening attire that glowed with rich exuberance. He felt uneasy as their predatory gaze fell on them, curious of the new human guests that entered their den. Jeff examined his teammates as they scanned the area vigilantly. Their eyes never settled on one spot for too long as they searched for threats. Demon, however, looked more concerned than frightened as he gazed at the masses.

"Either something is very wrong," Demon growled, "or Orcus is truly up to something. We're supposed to keep our numbers low, so we don't attract attention. This is the largest gathering I've seen since the ordinance was set in place two hundred years ago." Demon walked the group forward through the mansion until they were stopped by a rather large bouncer blocking their path. Demon was a tall six foot three inches at least, but this guy towered over him, another six to seven inches.

"Welcome, humans." The large vampire's voice was deep and gruff. He turned to Demon directly. "Hello, Demon. Lord Orcus has been expecting you. I'm afraid I must ask all of you to surrender your weapons before you proceed any further."

"I'm afraid that won't be possible. My friends were instructed that under no circumstances were they to surrender their weapons." Demon's face remained stoic as he stared back at the guard before them.

"Lord Orcus requires that any, and *all guests,* surrender their weapons upon entry—" The guard stopped speaking as Hammer removed his gun from its holster and pointed it straight at the large vampire's head. His eyes glowed a brighter yellow as the vein bulged on the side of his bald head.

"My policy is to keep our weapons." Hammer flicked off the safety of his gun. "You didn't think we'd work without a safety net, did you?"

The guard snarled at Hammer's defiance, looking over to Demon for aid, who stayed quiet.

"Fine. This way," the guard grumbled as he led them further into the building.

"Much obliged," Jennifer quipped as she followed behind him with Sentinel. Jeff held back. Hammer wasn't phased by the interaction, but Demon was silent, his hands in tight fists by his sides. The mood was heavy in the air.

Jeff walked close to Hammer's side. "That went well boss."

Hammer scowled at Jeff and hit him in the back of the head. It was hard enough to make Jeff's head sting. Probably a better idea if he kept his smart-ass comments to himself for the time being, but he wanted to relieve some of the tension.

"Shut up," Hammer continued, but was stopped by Demon blocking his path. His eyes had already been glowing in the dim light, but there was a bright fury in them now, similar to the guard that Hammer had just threatened.

"You said you'd let me handle this. There are too many vampires here, sunlight or not, don't piss them off," Demon growled at him. This was a side of his vampire companion that Jeff hadn't seen yet. A reminder that Demon was a predator, and not human. Hammer remained unphased by Demon's anger.

"So handle it. Nobody takes my guns." He pushed past Demon into the back. Demon flexed his fists, his eyes still bright yellow orbs in his pupils. He marched into the back room after the group, and Jeff followed quietly behind.

When they stepped into the back room, it was like the vampire residents had tried to make a small throne room out of the original decor. The room was originally designed as a ballroom with a wide hardwood floor, high ceilings, large windows, and chandeliers casting soft light down on them. The dark, heavy curtains on the windows kept the area dimly lit. Around the room Jeff witnessed about a dozen different vampires sucking on the bodies of five humans. They were all moaning with pleasure. He thought about his recent experience just moments ago and shivered. This was like a drug house for nymphomaniacs. There was a platform on the floor toward the back, probably originally designed as a stage for visiting musicians and performers who would have been invited to the space. Alone in that area was a single large throne-like chair.

On the throne was a man of Asian descent. He was lean, but fit, dressed in a silk-lined pewter gray suit. He sat relaxed in the chair, his legs kicked up over one armrest, his back leaning against the other. There were six women doting on him. One was pouring him a new glass of a dark red liquid that was too thick to be wine. Another was brushing his short jet black hair with her fingers, creating a feathering swoop across his brow.

This guy must be Orcus...

Jeff and the others formed a straight line parallel to the small stage. The man didn't seem to notice they had entered as he laughed with the women around him. Jennifer stayed close to Jeff; Sentinel was to her right, followed by Hammer and Demon at the far end of their line.

Standing off to the side of the throne, behind the women, was another man. He seemed squirrely in nature as he nervously turned his attention to the group in front of him. His suit seemed too large for him, and ill-fitting. He eyed Demon just as they'd finished entering, his eyes glowing bright yellow.

"Demon!" The scrawny male yelled, sounding as squirrely as he looked. Unpleased with their presence, he added, "how dare you bring these scum into our coven! This meeting was supposed to be closed."

"Silence!" Orcus's voice boomed through the room as he lifted up in his chair. "These are my guests." He smiled, and it made Jeff's stomach uneasy. It had that same strange eagerness as Tobias. A false sense of security from the pearly white teeth. The weasely man immediately returned to his spot off to the side of the stage.

Orcus pushed the women off of him one by one, and stood up. They were all attractive, like his own personal posse of supermodels who would dote on him whenever he was so inclined. Jeff couldn't help but note that one of the women looked a lot like Jennifer. Her skin was slightly darker, and her eyes were shaped differently. Her features were more Indian than Hispanic in some places, but otherwise they could have almost been twins. The woman caught his gaze as he looked at her, and smiled at him. A succubus eyeing their next meal. It made him uncomfortable. He glanced over to Jennifer by his side, who also caught the woman's lustful stare. She looked more annoyed than when they had first entered the building. The sooner they got out of here the better. Jeff focused his attention on their host, Orcus, who buttoned his suit jacket as he stepped down off the landing toward the group. He kept his unsettling smile fixed on all of them as he approached.

"Soo, these are the legendary Zombie Elimination and Rescue Operatives? The protectors of humanity, and killers of all creatures of darkness." He stopped in front of them, and opened his arms in a welcoming manner, "Welcome to my home. Your reputations precedes you all."

Orcus began to stroll by each member, examining them up and down. He approached Jeff and stopped, slightly confused.

"All but you it seems. Who are you?"

"Knight," Jeff answered, trying to sound not as scared as he was. He felt a hole in his throat, and his nerves were on edge. Orcus moved in closer, and he could smell the iron in his breath from the blood he had consumed.

"Well Knight, you look barely old enough to shave. Let alone stain your hands with blood. Either recruitment is suffering or—" Orcus sniffed the air around Jeff's neck. "You must have some other reason to be here."

Orcus continued his march down the line again. He stopped at Jennifer. He sniffed the air around her and then chuckled as he raised a questioning glance back at Jeff.

"Ah, Jennifer Mayer. Your beauty is surpassed only by the story of your hatred for the undead and lycans. I would *love* to make you one of my concubines. My third wife Selena, she kind of looks like you." Orcus brushed a bang off Jennifer's face with his finger. She glared back at him coldly, her body more rigid than before.

"Go fuck yourself!" Jennifer spat in his face. Orcus only looked mildly annoyed as he wiped it away from his cheek, but his smile quickly returned.

"You have a lot of hate. I like that. Probably stems from your family issues...frankly, I think you're lucky to have lost them at such a young age. You dodged another bullet five years ago I hear when your *mate* died...what was his name again? I guess it doesn't matter, he was obviously weak."

The light in her eyes dimmed as her muscles tensed, and her veins throbbed as her pigment went a deep red. Her knuckles whitened on her fists she held tight at her sides. The weight of all the eyes in the group was on her. Orcus smiled, amused he had successfully gotten under her skin, and continued to walk down the line.

"Rounding out the pack are Sentinel and Commander Hammer, legendary leader of Tampa Z.E.R.O. You needn't worry about being fed upon. We offer Z.E.R.O the respect due our most dangerous enemies."

Hammer scowled. "Let's get one thing straight right now. You want to pull this B-movie bullshit, and act like some sucker trying to mystify the shit out of us, you're barking up the wrong tree." Hammer's anger only seemed to amuse Orcus more.

"Ever defiant! Just remember, a man without fear of death is a man without hope of a life."

"Spoken like it's on the back of a mother fuckin' fortune cookie," Hammer responded, his annoyance with Orcus still clear on his face.

"That mouth of yours might get you into a great deal of trouble one day," Orcus frowned.

"I'm standing right here, chickenshit. Take your best shot." Orcus smiled at Hammer, as if he was considering the request. Instead he chuckled and moved on to Demon.

"Demon, it's been said you can judge a man by the company he keeps. If that's the case, I'm disappointed in this...regression. You used to have higher standards."

"And I can see that you've all but abandoned the old ways. How many vampires exactly do you have assembled here right now?"

"The old ways are obsolete, as are you Demon. This is precisely why I was the one to take control of the coven." Demon's eyes, which had calmed to soft glowing sunset embers behind his natural brown, flashed bright again as he became enraged. He bared his fangs at Orcus as he answered.

"You and I both know you took control only because Nobu believes that I murdered his daughter."

"As well he should." Orcus seemed bored with the conversation.

"I didn't! I was innocent and you know it!" Demon growled.

"You have been many things, my brother, but innocent has never been one of them."

"I am no longer your brother! I have killed other vampires before you rose to power, but I did not kill Lillith!" Demon's rage deflated upon mentioning the woman named Lillith. "Why would I? I was in love with her..."

Orcus laughed, and turned back to his throne, more giddy in his step.

***

Jennifer's anger reached a new level when Orcus brought up Lillith. Demon had told her about his vampire love many years ago when she was in mourning over Conor. They had helped each other through their grief, though he shouldered his for almost seventy-five years before he even met Jennifer.

Orcus smiled with pure hate and disdain toward Demon. A silver bullet right between his eyes sounded like a good idea. Orcus thought he was untouchable. She wanted to show him how wrong he was. It took every fiber of her being not to act on her thoughts. His laughter was like nails on a chalkboard to her ears. They were here for information. She let her anger go when she spat on him. She had to make sure she didn't act too rashly again, at least until they got what they came for.

"Love?" laughed Orcus. "To hang onto that pathetic human emotion. Look at what's become of you. How pathetic you are. Why are vampires so damn monogamous? We live so long, we can have more than one being for pleasure. You're too much of the old ways Demon." Orcus walked back onto his stage and lounged back on his throne. The other vampires in the room began to leer at them. Jennifer glanced over at Hammer and noted the pigment in his face grow steadily to a red hue. She knew that he was near the end of his boiling point, too.

"Listen Shitbag. You called us here! Tell us what you know about the Sons of Judgment. Get to the point, so you, and the rest of your orgy, can go back to jerking each other off."

Orcus slammed his fist on the arm of his chair. The thunderclap of the impact echoed throughout the room. All the soft sighs and moans of the other vampires and humans ceased, creating a pregnant silence.

"Does your profanity know no bounds?" Orcus growled at him. Hammer, now satisfied, smiled wide back at him.

That's my brother.

Jennifer stifled her smile for her adoptive sibling. This is why he was good at what he did. He didn't let any *beings* walk over him. She glanced over at Orcus, who seemed to have regained his composure.

"Very well." Orcus motioned with his hand for the room to be cleared. Without a word, everyone left, except for his dutiful assistant and the two guards that Jennifer had observed at either exit of the room. "What I'm telling you is of great importance to myself, this coven, and the future of the *Tenebre Orbis*. It also states who I believe is truly behind leading this Sons of Judgment group. Are you aware of our ongoing conflict with the lycans?" Orcus seemed to aim his question at everyone but Demon.

"Why do y'all always like to fight with the werewolves?" Sentinel asked his question with as much southern angst he could muster. Orcus sipped his blood from the glass in his hand, ignoring Sentinel's inquiry and sarcasm.

"We were fighting for who gets to rule your race," Demon responded to everyone's surprise. It was true no one really knew the original reason that war started, just that they have been fighting for years. "We vampires don't think highly of the wolves."

"Yes," Orcus frowned, "and like a pack of rabid dogs, they would charge headfirst into any trap the vampires set, so long as the bait was human meat. They were a disorganized pack of savage beasts." Orcus rose up again, pacing in front of his throne. "However, all that changed in 1839, before my time as a vampire. A new pack leader emerged. He taught his wolfen brethren strategies for attacking the vampires, and he knew how to get through our weaknesses. The Covens had been dispersed for safety. We were no match for them. Their packs continued to decimate our forces greatly through the years."

Demon continued the story. "They started attacking us during the daylight hours, when we were vulnerable." While he spoke, Orcus walked over to a door off the stage, and knocked softly on it.

When it opened, there was a woman in rags with a tear-stained face, dragged out by the vermin assistant. He slit the woman's wrist and held her bleeding arm over the glass. She cried, looking to them for help. Jennifer clenched her fist...they couldn't help her. When the glass was full, Orcus took it in his hand. Just as quickly as she appeared, the woman was whisked away again, while Orcus swirled her blood around the glass.

"In an effort to strengthen our defensive capabilities in the daylight hours, we turned to a scientist, Helmut Rommel. He was making radical breakthroughs in the science of genetic manipulation and viral augmentation." Orcus took a long, slow sip of his drink and smiled, satisfied with the flavor. "Most likely due to his time working for the Third Reich on chemical and biological weapons for those human camps."

"Wait, Third Reich? He was a Nazi?" Jeff's question wasn't directed to anyone in particular. Orcus grinned, amused by his inquiry.

"Ah, so you have heard of this! Yes, after World War Two ended, his theories were seen as a bit too...radical. Hence why he was so welcomed by us, despite being of the human condition. He claimed he could mutate a virus he discovered elsewhere with our DNA, allowing us to retain our abilities in the daylight hours. We were also able to take one other advantage that the lycans had over us too..." Orcus loved to pause for dramatic effect "...their fast regeneration without the need to consume blood."

"If this truly worked, we would have been stronger and more than able to defend ourselves, without the aid of Z.E.R.O." Demon spoke like he also couldn't believe what he was hearing.

What kind of virus could do that to a vampire?

"And where exactly did this base virus come from?" Demon asked.

"Three guesses," Sentinel frowned.

"I only need one," Hammer grimaced, and spat on the floor.

"Yes, the virus came from a reanimated corpse. A mutation that occurred in humanity." Orcus gazed back at them, giddy with his theatrical reveal as he gauged their responses.

"Fuck me..." Jeff muttered under his breath.

"Whatever keeps those corpse-fuckers moving is cluster-fuck given form, and you guys started downing it by the gallon?" Hammer yelled angrily at Orcus. Jennifer was more concerned with what Demon might do. Demon's primal hunter eyes glowed brighter in the darkly lit room.

"The Elders would have never allowed this!" Demon screamed at Orcus, who continued to smile in return as he walked back up to his pulpit.

"I commissioned the doctor only after you ran like a coward. There were grumblings among the Elders that I wasn't fit to lead. I would prove to them that I was, by giving our people an advantage over all other races."

Demon was furious. "What you've done is nothing short of abomination! Mixing the genetics of the lycans with us and the undead is sacrilege!"

"I did it for the benefit of our race!" Orcus's eyes glowed for the first time since they'd arrived. Demon had angered him. Good.

"The only thing you were benefiting was your damned ambition!" Orcus didn't deny Demon's claims as his eyes returned to dark brown. He simply took a drink of his blood-filled glass and prattled on.

"One vampire, a lone *volunteer* that we procured. He had mutated when administered the pathogen. Became more monstrous like legends of old. Most vampires only need to feed every two to three days if they don't move around in the daytime, once a day if they do. This one needed to feed every few hours despite the time of day."

How have we not heard of this?

"He is immune to sunlight, and silver. His metabolism burns at such an increased rate that his hunger is nearly insatiable. When the hunger gets to a breaking point, he becomes ravenous, and animalistic. Needless to say we quickly lost control of him."

"Why am I not surprised? You're saying in the seventy years since you created this guy, you haven't once been able to find him?" Jennifer was disgusted by the incompetence, yet also frightened that it had gone on for so long with no one in Z.E.R.O ever hearing about it.

"Of course I've tried!" Orcus bellowed back, "I sent my best hunters after him and they just became his minions! When he feeds on vampires, they become like a zombie, only much faster, with our inherited speed and more carnal in their savagery. He can also infect lycans. They lose their ability to shift back to their human state, and become undead giant beasts."

Orcus snapped his fingers and the two guards stepped out of a door on the opposite end. They returned shortly, a large cage with thick steel bars, reminiscent of a tiger cage you might see at the circus, dragging behind them with what appeared to be a zombie inside. Jennifer watched the monster as it moved around the cage, trying to reach whatever it could, squeezing its arms through the small bars. When it was brought closer, they could make it out more clearly. Jennifer gasped at the sight of the creature. It was indeed a zombie-vampire hybrid, a mutant. Its skin was pale and decayed like that of a regular zombie. However, its mouth was what scared her the most. When it snarled in their direction, it opened to reveal not the normal fangs associated with a vampire, but a large row of shark-like teeth. Its skin cut at its cheeks to allow the further opening of its razor-filled maw. Instead of the pale white eyes of a dead corpse, the sclera around the pupils were bloodshot with a deep red as all the blood vessels had burst. The pupils retained their bright yellow glow of its former vampire brethren.

She was not the only one pale with fear at the sight of this new abomination. She looked at her comrades. Jeff's and Sentinel's bodies shook with fear next to her. She hadn't felt carnal terror like this before. She couldn't see Hammer or Demon's expressions from where she was standing, but she didn't have to. They were the same as the rest of her teammates. Terrified and angry.

If these things got out, it would be the death of us all...

"This is what he does to my men. I've spent the majority of my manpower to keep these mutations away from the human populous." Orcus snapped his fingers again. His assistant came over with a gilded box. Orcus pulled out a gold-finished M1911 with a handle grip made of ivory. He loaded the gun and aimed it at the monster. "Like their zombie brethren, they can only be killed with a bullet to the head. Since they are of a vampire base, however, silver bullets are all you can use. This is why I require your assistance."

Orcus racked back the gun and shot the mutant in the head; the blood sprayed out from its cranium and landed like a Jackson Pollock painting before their feet. It crumbled to the floor with a loud thud. He placed the gun back in the box, and his assistant walked off with it. The guards rolled the large cage back out of the room. Orcus was a bit dramatic, but he made his point.

"Your 'D-day,' as you call it, happens once every twenty to thirty years, correct? This is because the monster we created must hibernate for that long. His followers create panic, releasing the pathogen derived from his saliva, to throw you people off. He feeds in a frenzy, and then goes into his hibernative state. Now is again a time of his rise, and my soldiers have discovered he is in the area. You will have only one chance to find him before he disappears again anywhere in the world."

Orcus sat back down on his gilded gold throne, swirling the remaining blood in his glass and drumming his well manicured fingers on the velvet-red covered armrest of his chair. Jennifer felt her blood boil as she stared back at him. All the events in their families' lives were because of this man right here. All the lives that were lost due to zombie outbreaks over the years. It was all him.

Hammer stepped forward and glared furiously at this team. "Don't anyone on my team say they will lift a fucking finger to help this prick, cuz if you do, that finger is getting shot off!" Orcus didn't waiver from his pompous smile. He obviously had another card up his devilish sleeve.

"You really don't have a choice. Lycans and vampire numbers are dwindling as a result of this monstrosity. Once those food reserves run dry, who will be left?" His gaze met each of them as his smile widened. "Only the humans."

Every muscle in Jennifer's body tensed. Her blood pumped hot through her veins. Before her brain could tell her otherwise, Jennifer's body was moving—barely making two steps before Jeff and Sentinel grabbed her arms.

"You son of a bitch! You're responsible for everything!" She struggled against their hold. Jeff leaned into her ear.

"Jen, calm down. Please." She didn't care about peace talks, or orders. He didn't deserve to live. He'd put his own species at risk for his ambitions, as well as hers. Jeff continued to plead with her, as did Sentinel. They wouldn't release her until she relented. She let out a deep breath, and released her hands from their balled up fists. She felt the grip of Sentinel and Jeff ease on her arms. She would try to control her anger. She glanced up at Orcus, who continued his cruel smile at their pain.

Orcus' attendant returned from the room behind the staging area, wielding a black file in his hand. He passed it off to Orcus, and took his spot behind the throne. Orcus placed his glass on the nearby small table, and walked the file over to Hammer, who snatched it out of his claw.

"This has the information about your target. As well as his last sighting. I do wish you all the best with your hunt." Orcus turned to walk back to his throne, but stopped, twisting toward Demon instead. "Demon, I really think you'll be interested in helping me procure this target. Why do you think I really went to your group for assistance, and not another unit of Z.E.R.O?"

"What are you talking about?"

"You have an advantage my other hunters didn't. Look at the name of the *volunteer* of the project." Hammer handed the file over to Demon, who scanned the contents quickly. He was quiet as he read each page. Everyone in the room remained silent as he coursed through the document. Jennifer realized something was wrong as soon as she heard the paper crinkle and tear.

"This can't be...I didn't want to believe it..." Demon's voice cracked in shock. The group gathered around him to look at the photo still clutched in his hand. The image black and white, old and faded from age. A single subject's portrait gazed back at them, a young man, only in his thirties or forties. His hair appeared to be a light sandy blonde or brown. He had an angular jawline, like that of an Eastern European genealogy, and light colored eyes.

"Demon buddy, what's goin' on man?" Sentinel asked as he laid a hand on his friend's shoulder.

Demon said nothing as he handed the file over to Jennifer. He pushed everyone aside. His eyes glowed yellow with a previously unseen brightness. Demon lunged for Orcus, but didn't make it far. He was quickly pinned down by the guards in the room. Demon struggled fervently to get out of their grasp to continue his attack.

"You fucking BASTARD! Taking Lillith from me wasn't enough for you! I wish I'd never asked Nobu to turn you! You turned Beaumont into a monster!" This was the first time Jennifer had seen Demon with so much pain and anguish. Orcus remained unphased by Demon's outburst. He watched calmly from his seat, that same awful smile on his face. Jennifer made her mind up.

When this is over, I'm sending in a black squad to kill him…I don't care if the High Council agrees with me or not. Orcus needs to go before he can do any more damage. We can fix things with the Tenebre Orbis later.

"You forget, Demon, he volunteered," Orcus mused. Demon became more infuriated by Orcus' baiting. He managed to release himself out of the grasp of one of the guards and advanced several feet forward before he was pinned down again.

"Beaumont would never have volunteered for this! I was told he died in battle during the war!"

Orcus didn't answer. Jennifer put her hand on her gun, releasing the strap restraining it in her holster. If they didn't let Demon go, she was going to put a bullet in both the guards' heads, and Orcus, if she could get the shot in. Her team was armed to fight their way out of here if they had too.

Orcus, satisfied with the entertainment, motioned for the guards to release Demon. They did as commanded and allowed him to stand. They held his arms behind his back, keeping him restrained. She moved her hand away from her side arm, as the situation had seemed to have de-escalate, for now.

"All the more reason," sneered their vampire host, "for you to find him and find out for yourself what has happened. Now it would be in your best interests to leave now. It's near meal time, and I presume that you don't want to be part of it." Orcus gestured for them to go. Sentinel and Hammer went to Demon's side. She couldn't hear what they whispered in his ear. Whatever it was, worked. His eyes returned back to his dark brown, retaining a slight yellow glow due to the dark light in the room. The guards finally released their grip on him. Demon rubbed his arms as he turned to leave; there were dark bruises on it where the guards had held him. They all followed behind him. The sooner they were all out of here, the better. Orcus snapped his fingers again.

I'm going to cut those annoying fingers off first…

"Oh! One more thing before you leave." Orcus nodded to his assistant. They jogged up to Hammer and handed him a small syringe with a vial full of a weird royal blue liquid.

"What the fuck is this shit?" Hammer held up the vial to the little light in the room as he tried to observe its contents.

"The only thing that can stop him and end his misery Demon. It's the last of the antivirus that we created. We've tried stabbing him with it, which just caused him to become more deformed. It must be ingested, through human blood. A blood bag won't work either. Must be from a *living* volunteer."

Hammer glared at Orcus suspiciously, and placed the syringe with the anti-virus cocktail in his side pack. They began to leave again, but heard Orcus yell after them.

"Maybe you can use your new rookie the same way you lost your last one, George!"

Jennifer caught Jeff's expression as he looked back at Orcus, confused. When he turned back to the group, she felt like he eyed them more suspiciously. She didn't say anything. They were ashamed about what had happened to George. He was her trainee, much like Jeff was now. Her last one before she'd handed off the responsibility completely.

"Young Knight, why don't you ask your mentor Phoenix for some answers!" Orcus cried after them again, his mocking voice following them out into the light.

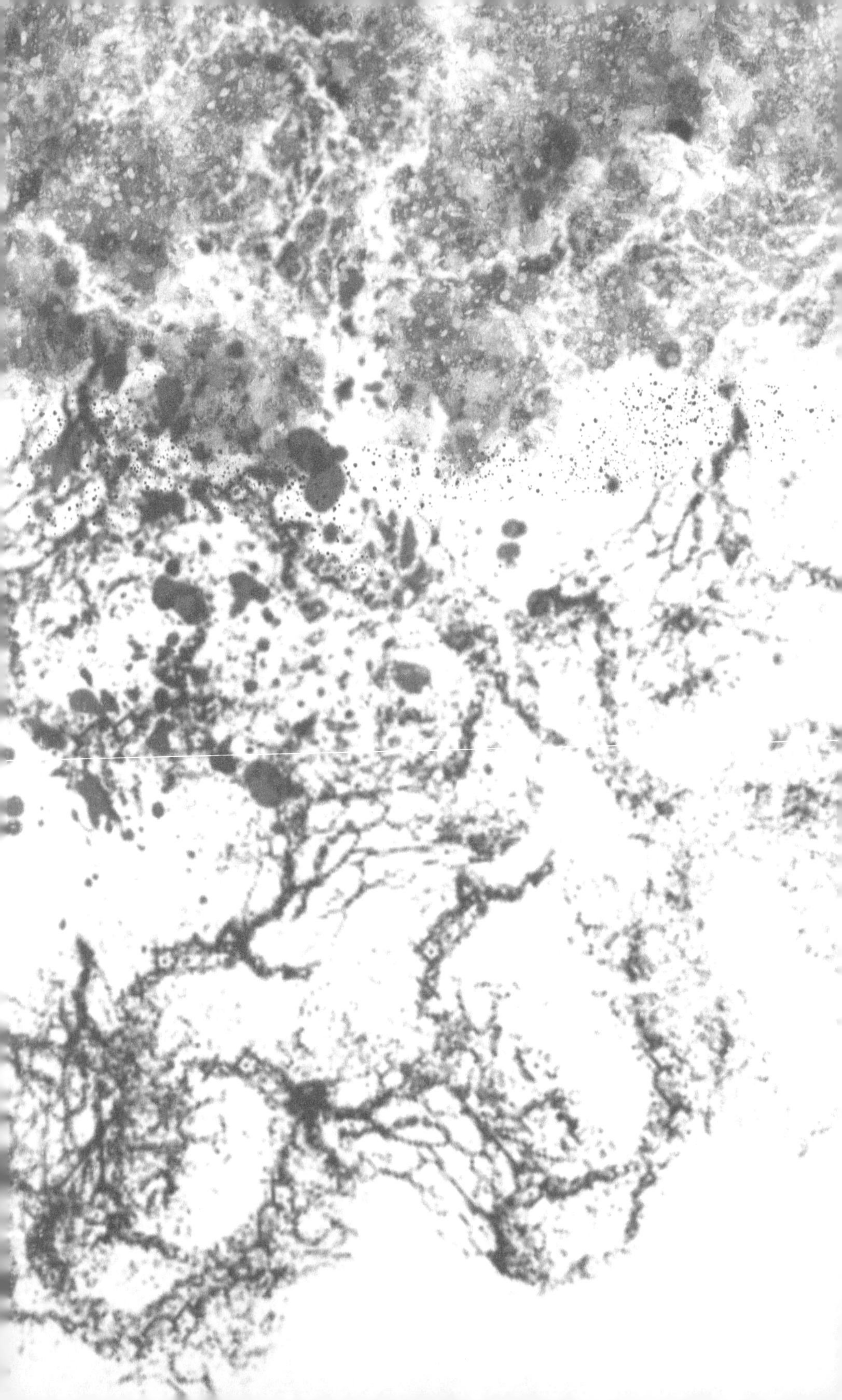

CHAPTER 20

Jeff felt uneasy about Orcus' words. George's current state must have been the result of an accident in the field. Memories of Jeff's struggle with the zombies on his *graduation* night flooded his head. He glanced at Jennifer to see if her face would show any reaction to Orcus' claims.

What's he talking about?

The group remained quiet as they headed out of the mansion. When they were finally out of earshot of the vampires, they began to speak again.

"Boss, you think this test subject is the Greyven that's leading the Sons of Judgment?" Sentinel asked as they piled into their vehicle.

Sentinel sat in the front with Hammer. Demon and Jennifer climbed in next to each other in the back. Jeff went in last, slamming the door shut behind him. He felt uncomfortable, like an outsider again. There are always secrets in this group. They claim to be a family, but they kept hiding things from him and excluding him from information.

What did Orcus mean about George? Did they do something on purpose to make him a zombie?

"Too many similarities between the two for it not to be," Hammer said as he began to drive. "Demon, who is Beaumont? You have never mentioned him before."

"Beaumont was my brother. Not by blood. We had the same maker and the same morals in our new life as well. I still can't believe that he would have volunteered for this...he was a man of honor...unlike Orcus."

"Okay. What are the odds Orcus is leading us into a trap?" Hammer picked up speed as he navigated the roads.

"Very likely," Demon responded.

"So they're gonna fuck us the first chance they get," Sentinel commented.

"What are we going to do about this anti-virus?" Jennifer asked, her eyes flashing to him nervously.

Why is she looking at me like that?

"Not now, we'll discuss it back at the base." Hammer turned another corner. Jeff peered out the window. They were back in their district of the city, as the old Spanish style structures were replaced with modern business landscapes of cookie cutter strip malls and chain restaurants.

The conversation on Greyven, the anti-virus, and the Sons of Judgment had ended. Hammer took the back streets to return, in case they were being followed. Jeff felt uncomfortable, still. They were packed tight in the vehicle, but he couldn't help but feel distant. The silence was heavy in the air around them. Jennifer recoiled away from his touch when he placed his hand on hers.

Is she upset with me again, or is this because of what Orcus said about George?

"What happened to George?" Jeff asked, breaking the tense silence.

"What?" Jennifer snapped her head back, surprised by his question.

"What did Orcus mean by *I* should be asking what happened to him?" She fidgeted in her seat, and bit her lip. He had been around her long enough to know she was hiding something and was thinking about how to spin her truth.

"Well, you know he's a zombie. What more is there to tell?" Hammer, as usual, had a blunt, unhelpful answer.

"You know what the fuck I mean. What are you guys not telling me?" Jeff's anger was building toward the group. It was getting harder for him to keep his rage at bay the more they lied to him. He was tired of all the secrets. If he was a part of this team, they needed to let him in on what they knew. He glared at Jennifer, who was avoiding his gaze. She had a guilty look in her eyes when she glanced his way. "Jen please, I gotta know."

"Fine." Jennifer looked ahead, and Jeff caught Hammer's eyes in the rearview mirror eyeing her back. "He's right, he deserves to know."

"Ugh, go ahead," Hammer sighed as he focused on the road again.

"I recruited George while investigating another case out west," Jennifer began, "He was with Bravo Team for a year, but then I tagged him for Alpha. I was in charge of his training."

"A few months after his transfer, we heard there were some attacks happening at the port. Could have been because someone was trying to ship zombies as bioweapons. It happens sometimes. Only problem was, we were a team of four, and when we got there, the horde was already large. The other problem was the area had a lot of ground to cover. So we decided it would be easier to draw them to one area and kill them all at once."

In other words, they had used George as bait for the horde, and it obviously hadn't gone well.

"We told him we were nearby and plotted where he had to run when he had their attention," Jennifer continued. "We didn't tell him he was essentially alone out there. I wanted him to feel safe. He was a friend...I was worried that if he knew how far we were from his location, he could panic, and make a mistake." As Jennifer spoke, Hammer pulled into the parking lot of their base, killing the engine.

"You used him as bait and didn't tell him?" Jeff remembered how they had handled him his first night with the group. Hammer had refused to let anyone help him when he'd fought the fresh zombies that had tackled him in the cemetery.

"It wasn't meant to go down the way it did. Our comms didn't work right for some reason. One of the storage containers was in the wrong location, blocking our short cut. He got overrun. I care about all my trainees—" Jeff gaped at her. She cared about all her trainees, yet was willing to let one become bait? George shouldn't have been put in that situation in the first place. Jeff shouldn't have had to wrestle with a zombie alone a few nights ago. He could have died.

"So I get it now, what Orcus was saying." His rage was building toward everyone in the car, who were showing a distinct lack of remorse for what had happened. They all knew they were complacent with his death. On top of that, they kept George as a pet! He was a human being!

***

Jennifer was remorseful for what had happened with George, but it really was a freak accident. They had done drills for that type of operation a hundred times with new recruits and veterans. Jeff's rising anger toward her and the rest of the team confirmed her concern that he wasn't understanding how it was unintentional. He himself could be involved with a mission like that if he stayed around long enough. The funnel method was always the best way to handle a horde. That night was different. Too many unknown variables.

"Alright I get it. Kill the F-N-G. Wouldn't want to ruin your fucked up family," Jeff said through gritted teeth. Her anger was dark, but this seemed to be on a different level. His rage boiled off of him in waves. He didn't understand. She needed to make him understand.

"It wasn't like that," Jennifer protested. "He volunteered for it."

"How'd you get him to do that? You give him false assurances, like every other chump in this place? Seduce them with your pleasantries until they aren't useful anymore?" It felt like she was sitting next to a different person. His words were so cold.

Where the hell is this coming from?

"The fuck you just say?" Hammer turned around in the front seat. Jennifer could tell he was ready to strangle Jeff for how he'd spoken to her. Everyone was already on edge thanks to Orcus, and this was just the last straw

"Fuck you, Terry! You've hated me since I got here!" Jeff yelled back at him. Jennifer noted that the only thing keeping Hammer from whaling on Jeff was the fact he couldn't get over his seat.

"Okay, I think y'all a bit on the wrong foot here." Sentinel tried to calm everyone down.

"I didn't join this group to be wasted away as a guinea pig the moment you needed a body *for the cause*," Jeff yelled. "I have heard it from everyone since I got here. Only family, *bloodline,* join Alpha. I'm not bloodline, making me expendable, just like George."

"It's not—" Jennifer wanted to tell him how wrong he was. It was true. Only blood lines had been recruited onto the Alpha Teams before, but that was an archaic tradition. George was the first civilian she had promoted to Alpha prior to Jeff. It was because of their skill and knowledge. They were never cattle fodder.

"Forget it, I'm out." Jeff opened the door and marched away to his car. Demon held her back.

"Let him go. It's for the best until this shit blows over," Hammer said as he stepped out. Jeff sped off immediately. She knew Hammer was right, but she wanted to make him understand. He was as rash with anger like she tended to be, but she knew his anger was in the right place.

They began walking back to the base. She gazed at the road Jeff had sped off into. She wanted to follow him. She didn't like leaving their conversation where they did. She felt numb as an empty hole filled in her chest.

"Jen, you coming?" Hammer held the door open to the back entrance of the bar.

"Yeah." She took a deep breath as she walked through the door leading to the kitchen. They continued together as a group through the pantry and down the quiet stairwell. Their heavy boots echoed with each step. It wasn't until they took the elevator to the labs on the second floor that someone finally spoke. Hammer pulled the anti-virus out of his side pack, holding it up to the fluorescent lights above them.

"I'm hoping that our scientists can make something of this. I don't want to sacrifice anyone." Hammer looked to Demon for an opinion.

"Nothing against the Z.E.R.O scientists, but ours are immortal and have had about seventy years to work on this. Despite the source, I trust their work."

"Damn, so who's it gonna be?" Sentinel looked at Hammer and Jennifer, the only other humans in their group. It was a death sentence for whoever took the concoction.

It was an impossible situation. Whoever they choose, this would be their end.

"It should be me." Hammer brought down the vial, looking right at Jennifer as he spoke, "I'm practically on my way out anyway. If the kid comes back, we can't let him do it. He has a big heart, and a long future with us."

Hammer's gaze never left her as he spoke. He may have been talking to the group, but she knew he was talking to her specifically. He was right. They had spoken about it just this morning. He had no plans on retiring from the High Council. If he could go out guns blazing like he always wanted, he was going to take it. Jennifer still wasn't ready to accept that as their only choice. She began to shake her head in protest but Hammer glared at her sternly. He had made his decision, and she had to follow it, whether she agreed with it or not. Hammer placed the syringe and vial back in his pack.

"Alright. We have a location," Sentinel explained. "We are gonna send Bravo Team to do some reconnaissance. We need time to prep for this. I think we should attack in two days." He pulled out his tablet to work out a plan.

Jennifer nodded in agreement with her comrades. This was it. The end of a lot of their problems. Now she had to work on some personal ones.

She followed Demon back to the locker rooms, taking the elevator down together. She could tell he was still upset, but she had to ask him. She had gotten so distracted when she thought Jeff had betrayed her that she hadn't taken her normal precautions.

"Are you okay, Ayo?" He was caught off guard being called by his real name. She only used it when she felt like it was important. With his current rage level, it was the only way she could get through to him.

"I'm fine. I just want to find my brother and bring him the peace he deserves. I can't imagine how he suffered all these years as that abomination." Jennifer couldn't imagine how she would feel if she found out any one of her family members were alive but living as monsters.

"Yeah, you're right. Do you think he's still in there? In Greyven's psyche?" The doors of the elevator opened.

Demon sighed as his head slumped down into his palms and he wiped exhaustion from his face. "Some part of me hopes there isn't. I would like to think he has no memory of his past self to have done what he has for so many years."

She continued to walk by his side. She worried about him, but she had other thoughts fluttering through her head she needed answered. She struggled with how she could ask him her question.

"What's wrong?" He could always tell if something was bothering her. Whether it was because of their link, or because he could hear her anxious heartbeat, she was never sure.

"I've been thinking about earlier, when you had my blood, and said it tasted different. Like Knight's...you sure it wasn't because you just drank from him before me? Maybe it got mixed a little?"

Demon let out a hearty laugh that removed all the tension from his body. "That's what's bothering you?" Jennifer continued to stare at him, concerned. She wanted to show him it wasn't a joke to her. He sighed and continued. "Yeah, I'm sure it's different. Think of it this way. Could you tell the difference in flavor between a steak and mashed potatoes that are on the same fork?"

"I guess you have a point. But I was wondering if you could check, just one more time?"

"If it bothers you that badly, then yes. Come on." Demon grabbed her hand and walked with her into the break room. He grabbed one of the paper cups from the cupboard. He turned to her and picked her up, sitting her on the counter. "Alright, cut yourself and drip it into here. I'll drink it." He pulled one of his sharp silver tipped blades from his vest and handed it to her.

She grasped the blade as she nervously cut her arm length wise. The cut burned as her blood trickled out into the cup Demon placed underneath. She watched as the cup's bottom quickly filled with a thin layer. He grabbed a piece of paper towel and placed it on her wound when she had released enough. She pressed down on her wrist hard to slow her blood loss while Demon examined her blood in the cup. He stuck his finger in, coating it in the thick red substance, and tasted it.

"Well?"

"Still sweet. Maybe it was, as you say, a fluke." Jennifer felt a weight come off her chest. Demon looked at her, confused. "Is this about you and Knight?"

"Uh, yeah." She looked at him, embarrassed by her internal panic attack. She had been through this anxiety before and she hoped she would have handled this better if it had ever happened again. She thought she would have noticed something different. Then again, it was still way too early to notice if something had changed.

"Okay..." Demon grabbed her arm again and squeezed out more blood into the cup. He drained enough that it filled the whole bottom quarter of the cup this time. Demon popped out his fangs when he drew the large swig of blood into his mouth. He made a face. The same face he had made earlier in the car. He looked at the cup and then back at her, concerned. Her heart sank into her stomach.

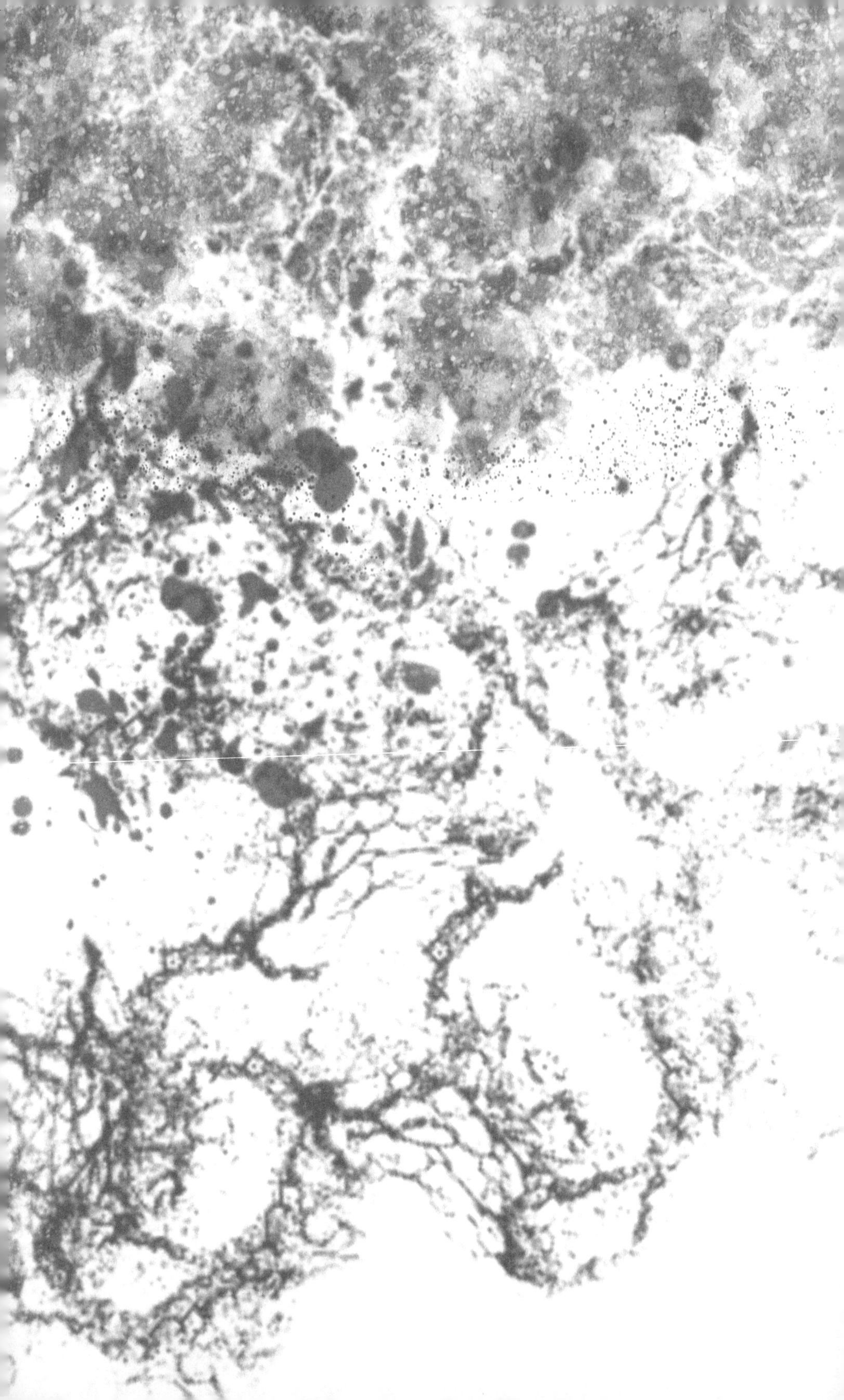

CHAPTER 21

Loud sirens, bells, and other miscellaneous noises blared out of Jeff's phone all at once on the nightstand. He reached for it, his eyes blurry from sleep. After a few haphazard attempts, he finally silenced the ear-bleeding noises. When his vision finally cleared, he noted the ten missed calls from Jennifer. He threw his phone back on his nightstand and rolled over in his bed with a loud groan. He didn't want to talk to her right now. Maybe he'd overreacted yesterday, maybe he hadn't. He was angry. Jennifer had used him...just like Kylie...earned his trust until they'd got what they needed out of him and she would have pushed him aside. Could he blame them? He was a nobody and he would always be a nobody. Replaceable.

He had driven around for about an hour yesterday before returning to the base in an effort to avoid his team. Everyone was gone by the time he returned, allowing him to leave his uniform in his locker with a note that read *"I quit"* in large, unmissable letters. Before he left, he gazed at the training room he had spent so many hours in with Jennifer. It made his chest hurt, followed by the sick feeling in his gut that none of it had been real. How much did she care about him and how much was it just to gain his trust? To be honest, he really didn't know anyone here. They could have all been manipulating him. The F-N-G.

Jeff sat up, staring blankly at the wall across from his bed. A movie poster for *The Evil Dead* was placed prominently in the center of the wall space, flanked on each side by a poster from *Night of the Living Dead*, and the horror movie festival he had attended three years ago with his independent film. A different time in his life, when this was all just fantasy. The whole situation was shit. The fate of the world literally could be resting now on their shoulders, and he had walked away, like he always did when things got too difficult. He fell back into his bed, screaming into his pillow. He needed to find a job if he was really done, but then again, it wouldn't matter if the whole world was flooded with the undead. Who was he kidding? Z.E.R.O had been dealing with this crap for years, they could probably handle this too.

It's not your problem anymore...

Then there was Jennifer. Did she really care about him, or was she using him like everyone else seemed to be? He needed to clear his head before he tried to speak with her. He was angry with her involvement. She wasn't as removed from it as she might think. Maybe he had already ruined everything with her. With everyone for that matter...

He let out a long sigh. He was back where he started three months ago. Miserable and alone. He grabbed his phone to text Adam to hang out. He needed to speak with someone *normal* today. Adam responded back within minutes, arranging to pick him up.

Jeff dragged himself out of bed and into the shower. He closed his eyes as the water hit his face, thinking of Jennifer. So many things had changed in their relationship in the last seventy-two hours. Images of them together at her home in bed, followed by their meeting with Orcus, and his explosion of rage on the ride back, filled his thoughts, like a bad movie on repeat. He hurried out of the shower. He didn't want to be in his head, opting to hurry up outside. By the time he ran downstairs, Adam had already pulled up.

"Hey! What's happening?" Adam was full of energy as usual, his signature backwards ballcap on his head and one of his graphic tees. This one was red with a small baby chick holding a shovel, sporting the phrase *"Chicks dig me..."* His smile seemed wide, and annoying. Jeff was grumpy, which was turning into his standard mood.

"Hey." He stepped into the car, crossing his arms tightly around him. "Can we go to the mall?"

"Uh, yeah sure. You sure you're okay, man? Something happen between you and Jen?" Adam pulled out of the parking lot.

"I'd rather not talk about it right now. I don't think it's gonna work out between us."

"Ah man, I'm sorry to hear that. You guys seemed great a couple days ago."

"We were..." Jeff avoided eye contact with him. He didn't want to talk about it, but of course Adam wasn't gonna let him off easy.

"So what happened after I left you guys at the store?"

"We went back to her place, we cooked dinner..."

Adam raised an eyebrow. "That's it?"

"Yeah."

"I mean you guys were *really* tight when I last saw you. I mean—"

"I banged her! Is that what you wanted to hear?" Jeff didn't mean to yell. Who was he turning into? He never used to be so temperamental. The stress was beginning to weigh on him. He took a deep breath and responded calmly to Adam, "I slept with her...it was great, but then I found out she wasn't being honest with me..."

"Oh..." Adam became quiet. He was there when Jeff had fallen apart last time because of Kylie betraying his trust. He wondered if he felt guilty about how things ended with Jennifer, as Adam was the only reason Jeff had met her in the first place. Adam fidgeted with the radio dials on the dash, immediately blaring the heavy rock music he loved. Jeff turned his gaze out the window as Adam drove on.

When they arrived at the mall, Jeff stepped out, still upset and huffy. Just as he closed the door, a car pulled into the space next to him, a little too close for his comfort. When the driver opened the door, Jeff wanted to release all his built-up frustrations on him.

"Hey watch it!" The man was easily six foot five and towered over them.

"Sorry, I didn't see ya. You okay?" The driver of the adjacent vehicle was oblivious to Jeff's anger.

How the hell didn't he see us?

Jeff had had it; even a stranger wasn't taking him seriously. He really wanted to punch someone today, and this guy seemed like a good option. He geared himself up, when Adam put himself between them.

"Yeah, we're cool. Don't worry about it." The guy locked his car, and walked into the mall. Adam turned around, leaning into Jeff's face. "Dude what the hell is wrong with you? That guy was twice your size! What's wrong? I have never seen you like this before."

"Nothing, let's go." Jeff pushed past Adam toward the mall entrance.

Adam grabbed Jeff by the arm as he waltzed off. "You sure you're okay man? What are we even doing here? You know it's just a bunch of Halloween sales starting."

Jeff took a deep breath, and removed Adam's grip from his arm. "Exactly. I gotta beg for my old job back. Busy season right now just before the holidays, best time to ask."

"What happened to the security job Jen got you in?" Adam eyed him suspiciously as they stepped through the doors to the food court area. There was a series of chain restaurants around the area like Sbarro, McDonalds, and Charlies, as well as small independent sellers of boba tea and Asian food choices. The seating area was full of white metal chairs and metal tables, with the paint chipping from years of use. Jeff stopped, gapping back at him, while he thought of how to answer.

Should I tell him there's an undead zombie hoard being controlled by a zombie-were-wolf-vampire hybrid monster? That the only way to kill it is to sacrifice my life, hoping that some serum given to us by the bad guys who created the monster works? That it seems the relationships I was building since June was nothing, and they probably just had me as a backup scapegoat this whole time like their previous rookie?

"Didn't pan out. They were going to screw me," Jeff carried on.

"Okay..." Adam was clearly still confused, but that wasn't his problem. Adam stopped him again, "Hey, let's get some food and talk. I won't let you squeal out of this either."

"You paying?" Jeff looked at the surrounding venues, contemplating Adam's request. He hadn't eaten right for days. He was hungry.

"I guess I should, considering you currently have no income." Adam directed him toward the mall's resident Japanese fast food cuisine. Behind the food glass were two Japanese men dressed in a white chef's jacket and tall white chef hat. They were in front of a large skillet full of chicken, shrimp, and vegetables, filling orders into styrofoam take out containers with rice, and whatever meat the customer chose.

They didn't discuss the matter as they got their food and seated themselves at a table. Jeff ate quietly. A food-filled mouth meant he didn't have to speak. Unfortunately, when he looked up from his plate, Adam's face said otherwise.

"Alright, lay it on me. Jen broke your heart, so now you're quitting. I told you when you started, the only reason you were working that stupid job was because of her."

"It's not that simple." Jeff popped two large pieces of teriyaki chicken in his mouth so he wouldn't have to say more. Adam continued to look at him skeptically as he pawed at his food with his plastic fork.

"Jeff, I've been your friend since we were kids. There's nothing you could say that I wouldn't get. Just lay it on me. What happened?" Jeff gulped down his soda while he took a moment to think how he would explain this all to his friend. He didn't like keeping secrets from him. At the same time, he knew how critical it was to not tell him the whole truth.

"Alright, how about I give you a hypothetical situation?"

"Hypothetical?" Adam already looked confused, but this was the best way he could tell him.

"Yeah. Let's just say a guy, not too different from myself, was to join a secret mercenary group that got hired to kill uh…" He swallowed a gulp of air "…zombies."

"Hah!" Adam slapped his leg like Jeff had just given him the punchline to a good joke. "Okay, I'm listening."

"Okay, let's say when this guy first started, he was a bit interested in this chick, who was basically like a mentor to him. And that was the only reason he joined at first. But after he started working, he found he actually enjoyed the job. Aaaaand found there could be a higher goal for his life than he thought previously…with said girl, and also said secret group."

"But I still don't get where this is going," Adam responded, his mouth full of chicken and rice. Jeff didn't really know himself. He tried to think.

"Well, so the guy and his group discovered there is this real bad dude, who can basically cause an undead apocalypse any minute." He watched as Adam's eyes glossed over with excitement. He probably doesn't believe him, but that doesn't matter. "The only way to stop him, cause he's some mutated vamp-zombie-wolf-thing, is to have someone inject themselves full of an anti-virus to get their blood drained by the monster. With the very likely chance they will also die, and become a part of the undead."

"Sounds like an awesome movie plot. So what's the conflict of our hero? Is he gonna take the bullet for the betterment of mankind?" Yep, Adam didn't believe him, but talking about it helped.

"Well…he would have. It seemed like the girl, and the rest of his team decided that already without asking him, though. It made him feel expendable…" Jeff trailed off.

"Did they actually say that?" Adam scrutinized him carefully.

"Not really. But from what he heard about a previous rookie, it was *implied*." Jeff consumed his soda and food again. Adam put down his fork, and Jeff knew he was going to lay down his *wisdom*.

"If this *guy* is anything like you, Jeff, then I'm gonna figure he got hot-headed and acted before really looking at the whole situation. Adam's stupid grin spread across his face, "There's really one question for this conflicted guy. After he joined, did he stick around only for the girl, or because he actually liked the work he was doing? Even if it meant a shorter life?"

Adam was right in his weird way. Jeff had let Orcus's words get in his head. He did like working for Z.E.R.O; actually, he loved it. He felt like he was really doing something with his life. It may have started as an interest in Jennifer, but he had worked a long time there already, without being in an actual relationship with her. A new dark cloud hovered over him as he remembered yesterday. He had said some pretty shitty things. It would be surprising if Jennifer took him back at all.

"But of course this is all hypothetical," Adam continued. "I would love to join a team that goes monster hunting. And get paid for it? Shit I'm in! We should do that for our next film project!" Jeff choked on the food in his mouth as the irony set in. Adam began to stuff his face again. He was right. Jeff had it pretty good, and here he was acting like a spoiled child.

When did Adam become the mature person in our dynamic duo?

They continued to eat. Jeff's earlier tension and aggression subsided. He would finish here with Adam and try giving Jennifer a call first. He owed her an apology. A BIG one.

He watched the people as they ambled between stores and around the food court, conversing excitedly between themselves, satisfied with their recent purchases. Children ran between adults and tugged on parent's arms as they pointed to the lastest "it" item displayed in the store windows. It was peaceful. Something was bothering him, though. Like an odd feeling in his gut, and it wasn't the food. He began to notice more people approaching from the western wing. First, it was just a few walking fast away from the area. Then, slowly, more and more patrons appeared in a more hurried and panicked state. It wasn't long before he heard a loud blood-curdling scream of a woman coming from the same direction. Jeff and Adam rose to their feet as another scream followed shortly after. Then more screams, as a swelling tide of shoppers began to pelt full speed in the direction of the exit.

"What the hell?" Jeff began to run in the direction of the commotion. He didn't have to encourage Adam to follow behind him. They pushed through the oncoming crowd, trying to escape the unknown danger. One of the escaping civilians slammed right into Adam, knocking them both to the ground.

Jeff looked down at the man who had run into Adam. He had a tattoo on his shaved head; an eye of Ra above people praying encased in a triangle, the Sons of Judgment logo. Adam helped the guy up, but Jeff was frozen as he stared in horror at the tattoo.

This isn't good. Is this it? Are they starting their D-Day attack? Why here?

The man noticed Jeff staring at his tattoo. He quickly turned and ran off before Jeff could question him. Adam stared off at the man, insulted.

"Rude much?" Adam was oblivious to what was going on. Jeff had to make sure Adam made it out of here, but he also had to see what the Sons of Judgment cult member had been doing in the west wing.

"Shit. Adam, stay close to me, okay?" Jeff didn't have time to explain things to him. He bolted down the hall toward the source of the screams, weaving in and out of the people running away in terror. Jeff stopped when he found the source of the commotion. There was a woman standing near the wall screaming uncontrollably. Some employees of the local shops gazed in horror through the shop windows, peaking past faceless clothed mannequins wearing the latest trends, at the gruesome scene in front of them. Nearby there was a man being mauled by two male zombies. They held him face down onto the tiled white floors; his body twitched as their teeth tore through his clothes and shirt, pulling them from the man's back with a sickening snap. There was the sounds of squishing sinews in their jaws as they bit and tore away at their victim.

"They filming a movie? Looks so realistic!" Adam had caught up to Jeff.

"This isn't a movie." Jeff jogged over to check the girl, who was crying hysterically. He tried to decipher what she was saying to him. It was a dribble of tears and mumbles.

"Are you okay? Were you bitten? Scratched?"

"No...I...we...were walking, and that guy...thing...he just...he just attacked him! What the hell is going on?" She started to cry again.

"Dude...this shit isn't real, right?" Jeff followed Adam's sight as it focused further down the hall. There was an approaching horde of undead shambling toward them. Jeff scanned their faces; they were blank of expression and pale. Their clean clothes were ripped and torn with blood-soaked patches. Some shoppers still had their shopping bags wrapped around their wrists as they reached forward, grasping for anything to sink their teeth into and spread their plague. He didn't have time to explain things to him. There was a clothing store nearby. Jeff grabbed the girl and Adam, dragging them in the direction of it.

"Hey get in here! Follow me!" Jeff screamed to the people nearby. About ten listened and ran inside the store. Jeff scanned the store in front of him as he counted the amount of people inside. The walls were covered in accessories such as earrings, sunglasses, purses, and hairclips. Nothing he could really use. The clothes were woman's fashion hung on metal bars, with grey faceless mannequins in striking poses nearby sporting the outfits. Jeff finished scanning the space; there were at least seven more people he was responsible for near the glass register counter in the back.

Stay focused Jeff, this is what Jennifer trained you for...

He checked the security gate of the store and was glad to see it wasn't automated, requiring a key to release it. He and Adam could reach up to pull it down, securing it with the locks in the corner.

"Adam, grab the gate on that side. We can't let them get in." Adam was pale as a ghost, but he kept his composure as he nodded, doing as he was asked. Together they jumped up, grabbing the gate. Their combined weight brought the gate crashing down.

If it can keep out burglars, hopefully it can keep out zombies.

Jeff scanned the store again. The clothing rack in front of him was similar to the one he'd used in his old store, so he knew how to disassemble it quickly. He rushed over and removed all the clothes, letting them fall to the floor. He disconnected the main bar from its base and the arms that held the clothes from the top. He could use it like the staff he had in training with Jennifer. He tossed the shorter metal rod to Adam. He used to be on the baseball team, so he would have a good swing with it.

"You're not seriously thinking of going out there are you? These look like the real deal!" Adam's color was starting to come back.

Jeff grimaced, his face gravely serious. "They are the real deal. I would very much not like them to get into the rest of the mall. I know from all the events I've seen at this end of the wing that this section can be closed off from the rest. There's a huge gate like this one that comes down with a button control, and we can use the tables and chairs in the food court to create a barricade too." Jeff began to pace as he looked at the frightened faces around him. He could do everything easier with fewer civilians. The people in the store could probably be let out through the fire exit corridors in the back of the mall, and he could send Adam with them. He turned to one of the employees.

"Hey, you have a fire exit in the back?"

They all shook their heads.

A frightened employee with teary eyes stepped forward. "Our manager has it locked, and they left on their lunch break right before this started. We can't open the door without their key."

Okay Jeff, rethink. You have to get all these people back to the food court, before that horde gets too big. You're running out of time...

Jeff pulled his phone out of his pocket and dialed. He noticed Adam's questionable gaze on him.

"Who are you calling? The cops? Can they even handle this shit?" Adam's eyes kept shifting between Jeff and the approaching monsters outside. Jeff hadn't seen him this scared since they were children.

"No, someone better."

"*Thank you for calling ZERO Security Firm, what's your emergency?*" A male dispatcher answered the call.

"This is Corporal Jeffrey Knight of Alpha Team. ID number 07121987, Tango, Bravo. I'm at the mall off Fowler, we have a shituation." Jeff watched as Adam's eyes widened when he figured out what really was going on.

"*You aren't the only place experiencing this, we have—*" The male dispatcher was cut off and Jeff heard the familiar voice of Hammer barking in the background.

"*Is that Knight? Give me the fuckin' headset and go make yourself useful.*" There was some static before he heard Hammer's voice clearly. "*Hey kid, this is Hammer. We got zombie sightings all over the place. Where are you?*"

Jeff wanted to apologize for yesterday, but knew that time was of the essence.

"The mall off Fowler. I'm going to try and contain them in the western wing. I don't know how many might have gotten out. I could really use some back up. I saw a *Sons of Judgement* cultist when this started."

"*Hey, don't sweat it. Me and Rick are on our way over with Bravo Team, hang tight.*" The line went dead. Jeff put his phone back in his pocket. The sounds of the moans grew closer outside. He peered through the gate. The woman's dead friend was beginning to twitch and reanimate. He remembered how strong the fresh zombies were that he had fought in the cemetery a few nights ago. If a whole horde of fresh monsters surrounded them right now, they would be finished. They needed automatic weapons.

"Adam, we gotta go. Get everyone together."

"You! You're the Guy! Hypothetical my ass! This is so awesome!" Adam was taking everything better than Jeff thought he would. His color was back and the sparkle of excitement was back in his eyes.

"Adam, I really need you to focus now."

"Yeah, of course." Adam used his loud voice to call the attention of everyone, instructing them to gather around Jeff.

"Alright, listen up! My name is Corporal Knight. I'm a soldier with a special task force that deals with these situations." Jeff was surprised how everyone listened intently. Fear was a great motivator. "I need to know were any of you bitten, scratched, or were exposed to any blood from the things outside?"

Three people who had ran into the store with them raised their hands. They were probably infected, and being trapped with them in the store was not a good idea. He didn't know how fast this virus amplified in the body. They were ticking time bombs. He bit his lip, he didn't want to show concern, but he didn't have a good poker face either. Adam noticed it, and sidled close to him, whispering in his ear.

"Jeff? What's up?"

"They could be infected. There's no cure," Jeff whispered back to Adam. The group continued to stare at him intently.

"So what are we going to do? We can't just leave them here."

"I know. But I can't risk them infecting the rest of the populace either. Damn it!" Jeff turned and kicked the wall, startling everyone.

"Make a decision, dude. They're getting closer. As is, we are gonna have a problem." Adam pointed to the woman's dead friend from earlier. It had gotten up, along with the two that had eaten his face off. His clothes were matted with his own blood now, and he struggled to pull his legs forward. The other two were more limber, aware of their new undead state, and shambled quicker in the direction of the group. The noise of the customers' screams of horror were a beacon for the monsters.

Jeff cleared his throat. "Alright people, we're gonna get back to the food court. Stay close together, and whatever you do, don't let them touch you at all. There's no guarantee that me or my boy Adam here will get them off you." The group nodded in panicked silence. "Those of you that are hurt, I'm going to ask that you see one of my team members that will be waiting for us there."

He turned to Adam, and motioned they should move the gate back up. They both took a position at either end of it, unlatching the locks.

"On three?" Adam asked. For once there was no jokey expression on Adam's face, only determination.

"Yeah. One thing though. Use the skills you learned in Jen's class if you lose your billy club there." Adam was skeptical but nodded. The two of them began their count in unison.

"One..." The people huddled closer together in anticipation.

"Two..." The three zombies in the hall were almost at the gate.

"Three!" They tossed the gate up as high as they could in one throw, and bulleted out, with the other survivors close behind them.

Adam swung his metal club at the head of the zombie that used to be the crying girl's friend, knocking it to the ground. Jeff sped past him and knocked down the other two zombies that had been eating the man earlier, their heads caving in with a sickening crunch from the hard swing of his makeshift bat. The group ran past them back toward the food court. There were about three more zombies shuffling sporadically down the hall. Jeff and Adam went straight for them, allowing the civilians to run past them to safety.

When they turned the corner to the food court, he froze. There were small piles of dead bodies everywhere. He gulped back as he saw the maimed and mutilated bodies. Some were missing arms and legs. Faces had missing eyes, noses, and skin. The corpses were contorted, thrown haphazardly into the piles. He glanced up from the bodies and noticed two Z.E.R.O officers dragging them onto another pile. He recognized the forest green uniforms of Bravo Team. He'd made it; they were going to be safe. He looked around some more and spotted Hammer and Sentinel talking with yet another member near the entrance of the food court.

Jeff began to jog over to them, however the two Bravo members who were moving bodies nearby noticed him and his party of survivors, immediately drawing their weapons on them.

"Drop your weapons! Down on the ground now!"

"I'm one of you!" Jeff yelled at them, dropping his bloody and bent metal bar with a heavy clang that echoed in the space.

"Shit! Calm the fuck down! Figures I get killed by people." Adam threw his bloodied bar down too. The Bravo members continued to act like they hadn't heard them.

"Get down now!" they continued to yell, almost on top of them with their rifles. Jeff signaled to Adam and everyone to cooperate, dropping to his knees. Hammer and Sentinel finally looked in their direction, curious about the commotion. Hammer let out an inaudible curse and rushed over.

"You fucking idiots, he's your superior! Put your fucking guns down and continue with clean up!" He smacked them both in the head. He reached his hand out to Jeff, who accepted it, pulling him up onto his feet. "This is why I don't like taking them to active scenes. Bunch of idiots. It's bad enough outside that I had to let them use live ammo today."

"Hey man, you just can't seem to git away from us," Sentinel smiled.

"Apparently. Where's Jen?" He needed to apologize to her the most. Jeff searched the faces of all the soldiers buzzing around for her.

"Left her at the base organizing another team for clean up," Hammer said while he looked over the survivors. "Any of them infected?"

"Yeah, I think at least three are. What are you going to do with them?" He felt he knew the answer to this already.

"Standard protocol. We quarantine them from the rest. Explain to them the situation, and do a mercy kill to all those that want it." Jeff glanced over at the three people who had told him they were injured. One of them was just a teenager.

"It's not fair."

Hammer grimaced. "Never is, but we don't have a cure. We fight to prevent these things from happening. Some are lucky and last a couple of days before the virus takes over. Others, just hours."

"Sucks that you can't do anything for them," Adam said as he joined the conversation. Jeff forgot he was there for a second, not used to his two worlds colliding. Hammer looked at Adam with an expression of, '*Who the fuck are you?*'

"Oh, this is my friend Adam."

"Pleasure." Sentinel nodded in Adam's direction. If he was wearing his cowboy hat from yesterday, Jeff was sure he would have dipped the brim with the greeting.

"Yeah, whatever. We got work to do." Hammer turned to the group of survivors. "Hi. I would like to ask all of you to talk to that man over there so we can inform your families that you are okay. Thank you for your cooperation." Hammer pointed to a Bravo member talking to a group of people in the corner with a medical team. This was the most polite Jeff had ever seen Hammer. He changed his attention over to Sentinel. "Sentinel, call headquarters, get our next location."

Sentinel nodded, whipping out his tablet from his gear.

"HQ come in. This is Sentinel. Do you read me?" Sentinel furrowed his brow, and spoke a little louder, "HQ come in. Are you there? Please respond."

"What's up?" Hammer's eyes were piercing when he questioned Sentinel. From the little that Jeff knew of him, he was definitely annoyed.

"No one is answering," Sentinel responded, his voice shaking as he checked his tablet to confirm he was connected.

"Did you try Demon or Phoenix? Your lines ever get congested with calls?" Jeff was starting to worry. He didn't know how many soldiers were with Jennifer at the base, but if they were like the Bravo Team members he had just met here, she could use the help.

"Our lines are wireless through a satellite system. We have emergency channels open on D-Day events so we can stay organized." Sentinel tapped a few more times on his tablet as he tried another line.

"Do what the kid said, try calling one of them on our private channels." Hammer took out his flask and took a gulp, not caring about the offended glances some of the civilians flashed at him. Sentinel nodded and changed the active channel on his tablet, tapping away again at his screen. Adam stared with curious eyes between Sentinel, Hammer, and Jeff.

"Demon, Phoenix. Come in. This is Sentinel." Everyone watched Sentinel as he continued to pace around them, waiting anxiously for a response. The Texan finally looked up as he realized someone was replying. "Where are you?...so Phoenix is at the base?"

Jeff felt his heart drop into his gut as an anxious lump formed in his throat. It sounded like Demon wasn't with her.

"When was your last transmission from HQ? Alright, hang on." Sentinel stepped back over to Hammer. "I got Demon on the line. He left on a call about ten minutes ago. Phoenix was still at HQ. He can't get in touch either. What do you want us to do?"

"This stinks like a skunk's ass. Alright, we're going back to HQ, have Demon meet us there." Hammer headed out toward the parking lot. Jeff ran after him.

"What about me?"

Hammer shrugged. "What about you?" Hammer glared as he waited for Jeff to answer. Sentinel continued to run outside, talking to Demon on his communicator. Jeff couldn't blame Hammer for being upset after the way he'd acted yesterday.

"I'm coming."

"Fine. We'll leave Bravo team here with this guy." Hammer pointed to Adam. "He's a buddy of yours so I guess we can trust him."

"Sweet!" Adam was definitely living out one of his fantasies.

"Don't get too excited, you just help Dumb and Dumber over there with blocking this section off and help survivors. Have them give you a weapon in case any break through." Hammer pointed to the Bravo members picking up tables and dragging them over to where Jeff and Adam emerged with their group of survivors. The soldiers had managed to bring the gate down to close off the wing, so Jeff felt a little better about leaving Adam behind. Adam nodded and ran over to the Bravo Team with a huge grin on his face. Hammer gave them a thumbs up. One of them took out their side arm, handing it to Adam.

Good thing he knows how to shoot. Stay safe Adam.

"Alright, let's go."

Jeff followed Hammer out into the parking lot, which was now crowded with large black vans. He had seen them parked behind the bar, but prior to today, they'd had fake decals on them, hiding them as other commercial vehicles.

How the hell are they going to cover all this up? People have cellphone videos of these monsters, and it sounds like this is happening all over the city...

They walked down a few aisles of cars, until Jeff saw Hammer's large hummer, twice the size of the other vehicles around it. Sentinel had the back open, and he pulled out a duffel bag. He tossed it at Jeff, who caught it, gazing back at Sentinel curiously.

"I had a feelin' we'd run into each other again. So I took the liberty of gathering up your gear for ya." Sentinel smiled and jumped in the passenger side. Jeff couldn't help but grin. There was no way he could really quit this job.

"Hurry up. You can change in the back. We gotta go!" Hammer said as he jumped behind the wheel and slammed his door shut.

***

Jennifer was in the main armory by the locker room in the third sub-basement when she felt the facility shake. She had two Charlie company soldiers with her, a man a little older than her she didn't really know beyond his name, Sean, and Ally, a woman that used to be a university security guard. They were helping her load up gear for another zombie attack report they had received from dispatch five minutes ago. She was supposed to have gone with Demon on his call, but he felt it would be better for her if she stayed behind to prep another team. Besides, it sounded like something he could handle on his own.

The lights were barely working and flickered between the red emergency and standard white fluorescents, but Jennifer felt in her gut something was very wrong. The alarms blared throughout the facility. They rarely had earthquakes in Florida. Especially any of a magnitude that would actually affect their facility. The base was made with a combination of reinforced steel walls and cinder blocks to prevent the shifting sands outside from penetrating or causing the base to buckle from pressure.

"Grab a rifle and follow me. Something's not right," she commanded her soldiers. She opened the door to the hall, checking either end. Most of the personnel were on the upper levels. A couple of trainees came out of the shooting range. She motioned for them to return inside. She ran with her two Charlie Team soldiers down the series of halls toward the elevator shafts. She stopped short around the corner before the elevator, motioning for the two soldiers with her to wait. She could hear screams coming from the upper levels, muffled but clear enough through the shaft.

Are we under attack?

The elevator dinged as it reached their level. The doors opened and ice ran down her spine. She heard the moan of the undead. Eight bodies piled out of the elevator. Five of them were people Jennifer recognized as Z.E.R.O Charlie members and scientists, and three of them were people she didn't know. They had bald shaven heads, and appeared to have matching tattoos on their bodies.

Sons of Judgment? How the hell did they find our location?

She braced herself on one side of the hall, directing the two soldiers with her to follow on the opposite, and gave them non-verbal queues to shoot the approaching zombies. They looked scared, but she didn't have time to build their confidence. Charlie Team handled base security, and dealt more with people than monsters, so she understood their hesitation. They were all trained on how to handle zombies, however, in case there was ever a breakout from quarantine in the labs. She aimed, shooting two of her former comrades in the head. Their bodies collapsed at the front of the elevator. Blood that used to be in their bodies sprayed the walls, and pooled around them. The automatic closure of the elevator doors failed as the bodies held them into an open position. The soldiers with her began to fire as well. Their aim was not as accurate, but they managed to take down the rest of the group with her.

"How the hell did they get in here?" Jennifer asked it more out loud to herself, and wasn't really expecting an answer.

"I don't know, but we seem to have lost communication with upstairs." She looked over at Sean, who had pulled out their phone, and was not getting a signal. This could only mean that whoever was attacking must have knocked out their Wi-Fi network. It was usually protected in their security office. They were cut off from all outside communication unless they could get that fixed.

"Considering the alarms, they must have blown the doors to get in. That explains the seeming earthquake." The other soldier, Ally, looked up in a panic as the screams grew louder on the second level, echoing down through the open elevator shaft.

There was another loud explosion and the facility shook again. Smoke poured in through the elevator shaft and filled the hall. Jennifer ripped the bottom of her shirt and tied it around her face to filter out some of the smoke. Their oxygen filtration system might have received damage. She had to find a way for them to get upstairs.

"What the hell? That was just up one level." Ally's voice betrayed her terror as she tied a handkerchief around her face.

"Why are they blowing the upstairs out? They've already made it inside the base," Sean commented as he messed with the communicator and tried to reach someone. "Unit 2 come in. What's going on?"

Jennifer leaned against the wall. The A/C system was failing. Her sweat began to run down her brow. She closed her eyes to focus. What was their plan? She ran her brain through all the information they contained in their offices that might be of value on the second level, the artifacts they had housed in the security sector of that floor, and the specimens they contained in the labs. She opened her eyes when she realized why they had set off a second explosion.

"They let George out. Our labs are on that floor!" Jennifer ran to the wall and opened the panel near the elevator shaft. There was a keypad, and a switch that unlocked with her code. "I have to quarantine the facility. We can't let any of them out. There is a chance everyone is already dead or infected upstairs."

The two soldiers turned pale. They just needed to survive long enough for the field teams to get back. They could do this. She punched in her administration code and placed her hand on the switch.

"If you do that. We'll be trapped." Sean tried to reason with her, his voice shaking and eyes frantic, but this needed to be done.

"It's better if we die down here, than everyone out there. We fight till they're all dead." She turned the switch, and the hallway went dark as the lights died. She could hear the main power drain in the building, as everything went on reserve energy. In the far distance she could hear the heavy metal shutters coming down over all the essential areas that were barred off in the event of an outbreak to prevent any biohazards from leaving. After a brief moment, the red glow of the emergency lights flickered on.

I'm sorry...

She heard heavy thuds crash into the ceiling of the elevator shaft. She peered into the elevator. The pounding continued. She walked quickly back to her soldiers. The thuds grew in intensity as a choir of moans filled the hall. The zombies were falling down the shaft. They were trapped.

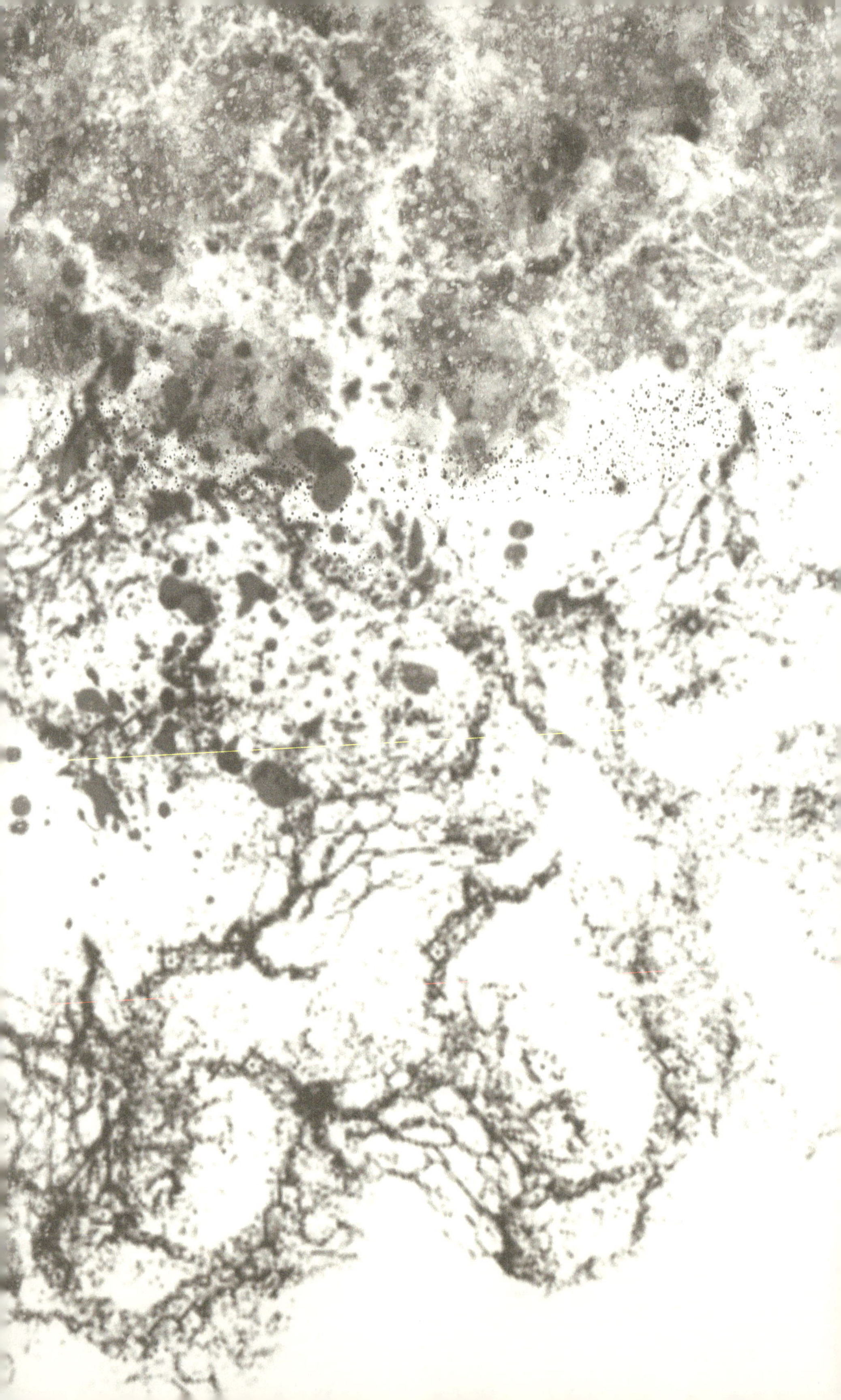

CHAPTER 22

Hammer swung the vehicle into the parking lot of the bar they called home. Jeff held onto the door as he was tossed with the G-force of the turn around the interior cabin. There were a bunch of vehicles he didn't recognize around the parking lot. Hammer popped the back open, and jogged around to meet Sentinel, who had already jumped out. He pulled out a combat shotgun out of the back and handed Sentinel the twin magnum .50-Caliber longslides that sat there as well. Jeff struggled to clip his vest on; changing in the back of a moving vehicle was not easy, especially with Hammer's driving. Hammer handed him an AR-15 and an M1911 side arm that he noticed was modified to fire .45's.

"Finally getting to use the big guns." Jeff examined everyone's weapons.

"We don't know what's inside. Vamp, zombie, people, or some combination. Either way, this would do the trick," Hammer commented as he grabbed boxes of ammo and magazines.

Hammer loaded his shotgun and belt with buck shots from a box labeled silver. He handed Jeff two magazines for his rifle as well as two magazines for the handgun, and Sentinel four magazines for his magnums.

"Silver, the universal monster killer." Sentinel's voice had a flair like he was trying to do an infomercial ad.

Jeff taped the two magazines for his rifle together in opposite directions so it would be faster for him to reload if he needed. He put the extra ammo for his handgun on the vacant slots on his vest and grabbed one of the hunting knives. It was silver, like all their other weapons. He slid it into the holster on his vest and handed the other two blades to Hammer and Sentinel.

"Enough chit-chat. I got a bad feeling." Hammer slammed the back of the car shut and marched toward the bar entrance. It was eerily quiet for the busy center of the city. It was the unnatural silence before a major hurricane. There were no sounds of cars driving by, no people, no animals. The palm trees by the road barely moved. A heavy weight was in the air. Jeff gripped his rifle tightly as they approached the door.

They stepped inside, immediately walking on broken glass. There were thick clouds of dust in the air. They always had people in the bar as lookouts, so the base should be safe. At least that's what he kept telling himself until he noticed bullet holes on the wall, near the door as he walked by. A lump formed in his throat.

There was an attack...

They walked behind the bar and stopped dead in their tracks. The bartender, Ralph, had a large bowgun bolt in his head. His handgun was on the floor near his body. Jeff reached over to Ralph's frozen gaze and closed his eyes.

"Shit," Hammer muttered, walking back into the kitchen area.

"Aside from the broken glass, everything almost looks normal," Jeff commented as he moved on.

"Not really. There's no power," Sentinel noted as he tried to flick on the lights to the kitchen.

Hammer frowned. "I wonder if someone activated the quarantine down there. It would stop power to all non-essential systems." They turned the corner and stopped.

The kitchen was covered in dust and debris. Cooking utensils were strewn across the floor. The door to the pantry was off its hinges. The "cooks" bodies were dead on the ground with bow gun wounds, and charred skin from the blast.

Hammer pulled a light out of his pocket, shining it into the pantry. The shelves were warped from the heat of whatever bomb had been set off. The shelf that hid the entrance to their base had fallen on its side, with all of the contents destroyed and splattered on the ground in front of it. The secret door was barely hanging on its hinges.

They continued through, down the dark stairwell, Hammer lighting the path. There was an eerie quiet as they descended the dark chasm. Jeff had never noticed the soft buzzing the electricity made every time he ran down these steps before, now gone. The group's urgency increased as they took the steps two at a time.

When they finally approached the bottom set of stairs, they slowed down. The large metal door that sealed the main base had a hole blasted through the center of it. The attackers weren't amateurs, only C4 or thermite would do that.

Jeff and the others gathered around the opening in a breach formation. Hammer was on the left side of the entrance, and Sentinel and Jeff were on the other. They nodded to each other and ran in. When they stepped into the open area, there was no one around, just blood smeared on the floor being reflected as a black ink due to the blinking red lights that filled the room. The hall to the right with the elevators was blocked by a heavy metal shutter. The security hall and offices to the left were littered with papers and bullet holes. There was no sound in the facility.

Jen...please be okay!

Hammer lowered his gun as he walked over to the shutter. He tapped on it with his knuckles. The sound of the metal vibrating radiated through the hall. Jeff swallowed but his mouth was dry.

"Yep, quarantine. This is gonna be harder to get through," Hammer muttered as he turned around. "Jen probably did it." Jeff saw a brief look of pain on his commander's face at the thought of what might have happened to his sister.

"We can go to the security office. I might be able to override it from there." Sentinel pulled out his tablet as he tried to connect to the base's systems.

They cautiously advanced down the security wing. Hammer took point, and Jeff held up the rear. When they turned the corner toward the office, Jeff heard footsteps approaching behind them. He signaled to the others, who gestured to him to huddle against the wall. Sentinel waited against the corner of the hallway. He slowly pulled the magnum from his holster. When the sounds of the steps were close he whipped around the corner and held his weapon to the head of the stranger. However, Sentinel soon realized he had a long onyx black blade placed against his neck. It was still too dark to see who it was wielding the weapon.

"Sentinel?" Demon asked, his voice sounded tired.

"Man, this daylight is really killing your mojo. We all heard you coming," Sentinel laughed as he held back his gun.

"Well I've been running around in it all morning. I could use a drink." Demon laughed and dropped his blade.

"Demon, you look like shit." Hammer exclaimed as he came around the corner. Demon's skin was extra ashy and pale in tone. He was even perspiring.

"My powers are drained. I haven't eaten since what Jeff and Jennifer gave me yesterday. The longer I stay up, the worse it's going to get. I need to feed..." Demon's steps seemed shaky as he moved, holding the wall for balance.

"So let's get going before your battery runs out." Hammer put his arm under Demon's shoulder to help him walk.

"What happened here?" Demon asked.

"Don't know yet. Headin' to security to assess our situation." Sentinel pointed at the door they were searching for, the security room in which Jeff had met Chris, Hallie, and Gary on his first day.

Jeff cautiously opened the door. There were three Z.E.R.O operative bodies around the room. Chris was on the floor with a crossbow bolt lodged in his shoulder. Hallie was limp in one of the chairs. Gary's body was next to her, unmoving. Hammer and Sentinel checked them and shook their heads.

Jeff remembered his first day when he had met Hallie. She was so cheerful, with a warm smile. Now her skin was pale and cold. There were tears smeared down her face, mixed with the blood that seeped from the bullet hole in her forehead. Her once bright blonde hair was dark red and matted to the gaping hole in the back.

Demon checked Chris on the floor and he moaned. Instinctively, all three humans in the room drew their weapons on him. Demon waved them all to stand down.

"He's alive. Barely." Demon's fangs popped out. "I gotta wait outside, the blood..."

Demon stepped out of the room, covering his mouth like he wanted to hurl. Hammer went to Chris' side, pulling out first aid supplies from his side pack. He pulled out gauze, along with the anti-virus Orcus had handed him yesterday. He hastily shoved the vial back in his side pack after catching Jeff's curious glance.

Sentinel tapped Jeff on the arm and motioned him to help move the bodies from the chairs. They lifted Hallie first and placed her in the hallway. They picked up Gary next. When they stepped back in the office, Sentinel noticed the computer and camera system still had power. He connected his tablet to it, and began to work.

"Hey buddy, talk to me. What happened here?" Hammer was speaking with Chris as he dressed his wounds. Chris had opened his eyes, but his vision seemed unfocused.

"He...he called himself Greyven." Chris muttered through pained breaths.

"Greyven? But how did he know where to find our base?"

"He...he...mentioned Orcus..." Chris wheezed.

"I knew he would betray us! He used me as bait to draw out Greyven!" Demon yelled as he slammed his fist against the wall. He may be weak, but it still left a hole. Chris nodded, confirming Demon's response.

"Alright buddy. Just hang in there. Demon's a little out of it so he can't heal you just yet." Hammer turned to Sentinel, "You have anything?"

Sentinel pounded furiously on the keyboard in front of him. Jeff watched the screens as some cameras became operational again.

"Some of the cameras were busted from the explosions. But I noticed someone did a recent search through our system." Sentinel pulled up the recently searched files on the screen. It was Demon's personnel file.

"It was him. He was looking for Demon," Chris answered.

"Yeah, but why his personnel files?" Sentinel glanced at Jeff after he noted another file. "He pulled up Jen's too. He knows they were an item."

Jeff didn't care about that stuff right now. He cared that Jennifer was targeted by this monster, and he needed to get to her. It seemed Demon was on the same page as he burst back in the room full of a new rage, his eyes glowing brightly in the dark light.

"Where is she? She's in danger. He's going to use her as bait for me. He doesn't know that she's with—" Demon stopped talking abruptly and looked at Jeff, his eyes wide and panicked.

"She's with what?" Jeff asked.

"She's with you." His more calm demeanor returned, but his eyes continued to dodge Jeff's gaze. "Humans don't mate like vampires, you are more fluid in your relationships. They change," Demon said as he tried to balance himself on the wall.

Sentinel turned to them. "I'm running what's left of the computer and camera network to locate her on facial recognition. I know she was in the third sub-basement. That's the last time her personal codes were read."

Hammer helped Chris lie down and get more comfortable. Then he turned to inspect the computer. Sentinel pressed play on a loop of footage, showing when Jennifer activated the quarantine.

"Why would she lock herself down there?" Jeff knew it would have been a death sentence if they hadn't arrived to help. There was no way through any of the floors of the facility without using the elevator. It was a bottleneck.

"It's standard procedure, better her than everyone else outside." Hammer answered.

"Can we kill the quarantine?" Jeff looked at a camera that was on the metal shutter for the main hall.

"I need access to another computer further in. The only thing I can do from here is open that first shutter in the lobby." Sentinel pointed to the screen Jeff was staring at, "Only problem, look what's on the other side."

Sentinel pulled a new camera feed up on another screen. There was a horde of zombies wandering near the other side of the shutter door. They were fresh; the faces of the people they used to be gazed blankly at the walls around them. Due to the red lights of the facility, their bloody clothes looked splattered in black ink, with matching black smeared hand prints on the once white walls. If they could manage to open it, they would have to deal with them very fast.

"If we all work together we can take care of them," Demon said, as he wobbled on his feet.

"And what are we going to do about him?" Sentinel tapped on another screen. They could see George wandering with his chain, followed by two other former Z.E.R.O members as zombies.

"Capture him if you can. Not a priority right now," Hammer answered.

"Let's hurry, the longer we take the more likely Jennifer will be in danger. Maybe I can reason with Beaumont. He was my brother." Demon slid down to one knee.

Hammer shook his head. "I can't let you do that Demon. You are too valuable of an asset. Besides, there's no guarantee that Beaumont is still in that thing. To be sure we stop him, it has to be one of us." The commander tapped his side pack. Jeff bit his lip.

"No. You don't know if that anti-virus will really work. It hasn't been tested." Demon coughed up blood while he tried to regain his composure.

Hammer opened his mouth to respond, but was distracted when a camera feed suddenly came alive. Everyone huddled around the small screen. Standing in the center of view was a monster they had never seen before.

There was no color on the screen, but Jeff could see he was pale. His eyes were dark, and probably the same red bloodshot color as the hybrid vampire-zombie they had seen at the coven. His face had cuts at the edges of his lips, like it was ripped apart. His ears and fingers were reminiscent of depictions of Nosferatu from the old black and white films Jeff had watched with his nana; sharp pointed lobes and long sinister talons. This must be Greyven. The creature smiled into the camera, but it felt like he knew exactly who he was looking at. It sent chills up Jeff's spine. Greyven stepped aside to reveal two Sons of

Judgement cultists holding a bound and beaten Jennifer on the floor. A lump formed in Jeff's neck.

Jennifer! She's alive, but he's got her!

Greyven pointed to the communication microphone for the room. Sentinel flicked a switch, activating it. The sound of static filled the office.

"*Hello Ayo.*" Greyven's voice was raspy but deep. "*I know you are here. I can smell you miles away.*"

Ayo? Who the fuck is Ayo?

Demon pushed through everyone to the front of the microphone.

"Beaumont, why are you doing this? We can help you. Just let her go." Greyven's smile faded upon hearing Demon say his old name.

"How dare you call me that name!" Greyven snarled, "And you, help? I heard you picked up the research that made me and were going to continue it. Creating an army for your Z.E.R.O human masters! I have a witness claiming Orcus handed you the research file and your humans took the pathogen they developed."

Demon's face contorted into a grimace. "That's a lie! Orcus can't be trusted. He handed us information about you. He wanted us to kill you."

"Kill me?" Greyven started to laugh, "I'm immortal, a God!"

Jeff looked past Greyven at Jennifer. She was breathing heavily and glaring into the camera. He noticed her eyes moved constantly to the left hand side of the screen, like she was trying to point to something. Jeff leaned in, noticing the end of one of the racks they kept their staves on. She was in the training room! He would have to find another way there without the elevators. Jeff slid out of the group to one of the other computers. He pulled up the blueprints of the facility.

I'm coming Jen, hang on.

"Beaumont, you're sick. Let us help you please. Let the girl go." Demon was still attempting to plead to Greyven's former self. Greyven briefly winced when Demon said his old name again. He regained his composure as he looked over at Jennifer.

"Oh yes, your woman. Because of you, a woman that I cared greatly about was lost. You couldn't save her in time, and you claimed you loved her too!"

"That was—"

"An accident? Hmph, don't mock me Ayo." Greyven waved his hand, and two Z.E.R.O soldiers shambled into view of the camera next to him. They didn't attack him, or seem interested in Jennifer. "Aside from being able to make zombies, I also have the ability to control them. A gift extended from our vampire nature. I'll give you five minutes to get down here before I change her too." Greyven's threat released a new panic in Jeff. He rushed to get the pages that came out of the printer. "And to make it more interesting," he continued, "I have a horde of monsters heading to your base. Some are my special children made from our vampire brothers. Ayo, you will decide who is more important to you. The humans, or your woman."

Greyven turned from the camera and waved his hand. The two Z.E.R.O zombies were shot in the head with crossbow bolts. The camera went dead as they slumped to the ground. Everyone turned to Sentinel to see if he could bring it back.

"The mic is out too," he informed them. Demon found a new strength as he picked up his onyx black sword, the little light in the room illuminating the silver lining, and turned for the door.

"Where are you going?" Hammer yelled after him.

"I can get down there in five minutes, even with the lockdown. I'll dispatch Beaumont, and with his death the undead army he's controlling should fall if it really is related to our fledgling control," Demon responded.

Hammer shook his head fervently. "Or they will just go wild. We need all hands topside. There are more innocent people out there than here." Jeff couldn't believe it. Their commander was ordering them to abandon Jennifer. Jeff marched over with all the printouts he needed in hand. He wasn't going topside.

"And what about Jen? Are you going to just let her die down there? I thought you said she was like a sister to you?" Jeff couldn't contain his rage. Hammer didn't respond right away, but he could see there was some conflict in his eyes.

"I have no choice. We are located in a very populated area of town. We need to kill those undead he's sending for us." Hammer's hands turned into fists as he looked away from Jeff. "Besides, she knows what the job means. Sacrifice one for the many."

"You son of a bitch! You can't do that to her!" Jeff yelled. He couldn't let her die.

"You quit us, remember? You don't get a say in the matter. For the time being you're just another meatshield with a gun!"

Jeff lunged at Hammer, punching him across the face. Hammer's eyes filled with rage. The two traded blows, and Jeff reached for Hammer's waist. He slammed him into the wall, using Hammer's height and weight against him. Hammer struggled to remove his grip. Sentinel grabbed Jeff from behind. He was stronger than Jeff expected. He pulled Jeff off just as Demon grabbed and restrained Hammer.

"Whoa! Y'all need to calm the fuck down!" Sentinel yelled at them. It didn't matter. Jeff needed to do that, he had to save Jennifer.

Demon struggled against Hammer's strength. "As much as I do understand your feelings Jeff, I have to agree with Hammer. The people above are more important. She would not want us to waste resources on saving her if it meant innocent people getting killed."

Demon may have been right, but that didn't matter. Jeff relaxed in Sentinel's grip and was released. He picked up the blueprints from the floor and glared straight at Hammer before he spoke again.

"Sentinel. Do me a favor. Unlock the gate for me to get through. You can relock it once I'm on the other side." Jeff was going down there no matter what they said.

"Sure." Sentinel walked back to the computer, and began hitting some keys. "I'll wait until I see you by the door." Sentinel tapped the screen displaying the entrance.

"Thanks man."

"Good luck." Sentinel saluted him.

"Fine, if you want to get yourself killed, go right ahead!" Hammer growled, then mumbled. "Jen will never forgive me if you die."

Jeff walked out, taking one last look at Hammer's twisted expression of anger and remorse, and marched back down the hall to the shutter. When he arrived, he looked at the diagrams he'd printed of the base. If he could go straight down this hall, and get to the elevator shaft, he could slide down the ropes to the bottom floor. Then, if he cut through the break room, he could be near the lockers and the training room in three minutes. Granted there weren't too many obstacles between here and there.

Jeff made sure his weapons were loaded and looked at the camera pointed at the door. He nodded at it. He heard the static as the speaker turned on under the camera.

"*Alright, I'm opening it up.*" Sentinel's voice cracked through. The door began to rise, and Jeff crouched down so he could see under it. He immediately sighted the first zombies he would have to kill, and took aim. He fired at the first three within view, black residue splattering onto the ones stumbling behind them. Another five started to shamble quickly in his direction. The door continued to rise. Jeff raised to his knees as he fired at them, their bodies making hard thuds onto the others before them. When it was high enough to pass through, he ran in. The remaining walking corpses snapped in his direction, rigor mortis already setting in as they struggled to move toward him. Jeff quickly fired off eight more shots, the muzzle flare blinding his eyes in the quick succession he pulled the trigger. He strained his eyes to make sure he hit every target. The door immediately began to slide down behind him as he heard Hammer's voice radiating through the speaker.

"Godspeed kiddo. Alright, let's go kick some zombie tail while he saves Jen. Demon don't say I never do anything for you. Drink up, mother fucker." There was a brief moment of silence before Hammer's voice boomed through again, *"Fuck!"*

Jeff shook his head and began making his way down the hall. He glanced at his watch. He had to get to the elevator shaft. He had four minutes left to reach Jennifer.

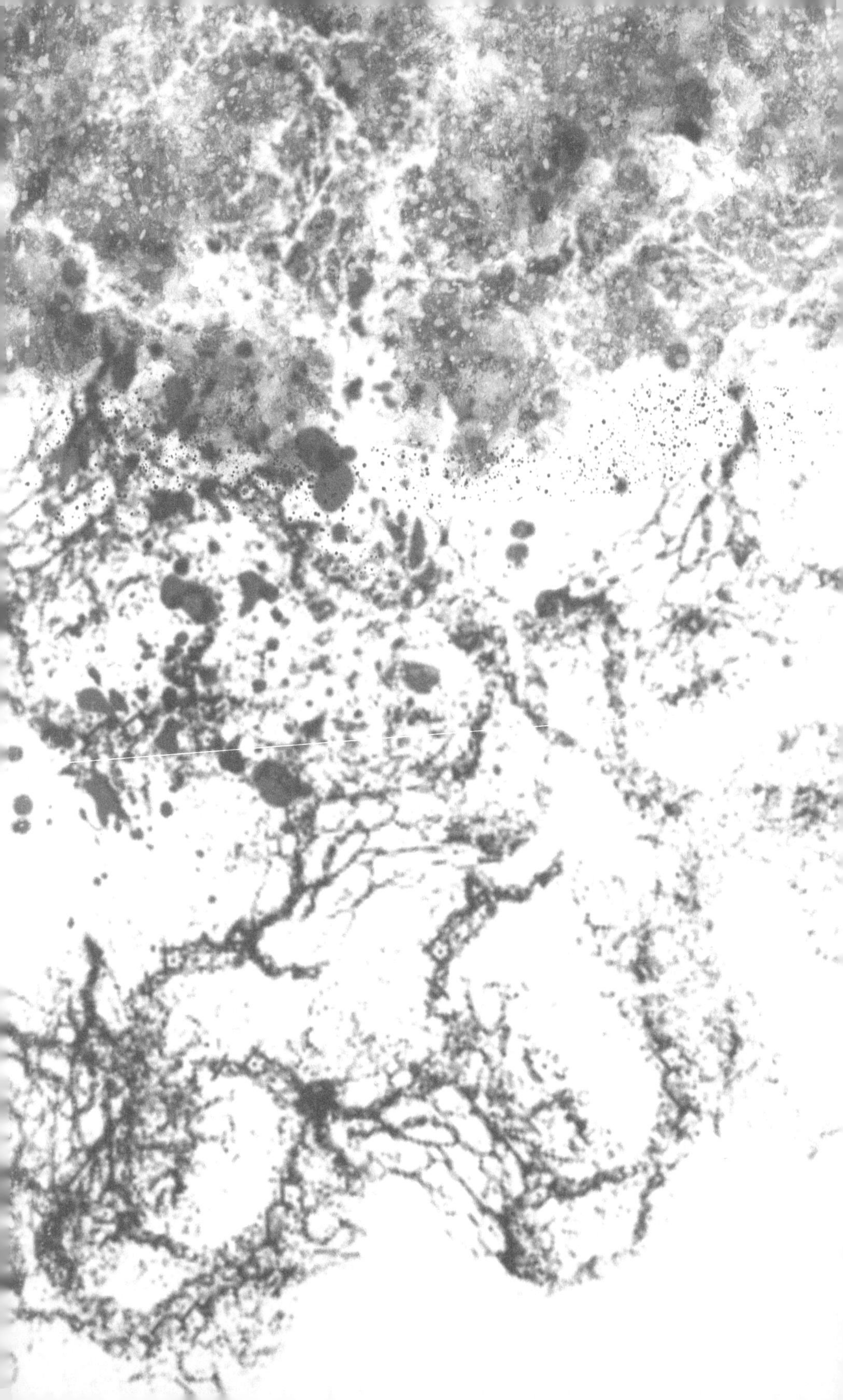

CHAPTER 23

Jennifer's face was sore. Her cheekbone had swollen where they had hit her and knocked her out. Her team had run out of ammo killing the zombies that had continued to crash through the elevator shaft. She and her soldiers were so distracted by the horde overrunning them that she didn't see the humans coming through the elevator shaft too, somehow unharmed by the zombies around them. *He* killed her soldiers in front of her, opening his mouth into a wide maw. Instead of a normal set of teeth, Greyven had two rows of sharp bladed fangs like a shark. He ripped into each one of them, tearing huge chunks of wet flesh away with his razor shark-like teeth, and drained their lives. She had failed them.

She tried to clue in Demon into what room she was being held in while Greyven dribbled on. She wasn't sure if he would come. She didn't know if any of her other teammates were there as well. All she could hear was Demon's voice coming through the room's speaker. Any doubts she had about Greyven being Beaumont were gone as soon as he used Demon's real name.

I don't care if you were Demon's brother. You're dead after what you did to my men...my family!

She tried to note the number of people there were in the room. And they were *people*, easier to handle than zombies or vampires. She had to figure out how she would get out of here.

"Aside from being able to make zombies, I also have the ability to control them. A gift extended from our vampire nature. I'll give you five minutes to get down here before I change her." Greyven was still taunting him, but Jennifer's heart sank.

No one is coming for me...

When Greyven threatened the civilians outside, she knew her team was not coming. The people outside were more important. She wanted to live. She wanted to find Jeff. She had to tell him...

There were seven Sons of Judgment members in the room with them. All equipped with crossbow guns. That's why they were able to get so far into their base. The bow guns were silent. The soldiers were probably killed upstairs before they could react. Jennifer knew she could get out of her bonds. That wasn't the issue. The issue was, how would she kill Greyven?

She didn't have the anti-virus on her. It was still in Hammer's possession. She had to get away from him. That was her only option. She had to survive. They could worry about killing Greyven later. If she could get out, they could keep him trapped inside the base with the quarantine at least.

The cultists had tied her hands with rope. First thing she needed to do was get out of these knots, and then she could figure out how to do the rest.

***

Jeff managed to make it to the elevator shaft. There were less zombies than he was expecting. He looked down the dark shaft, and saw a faint red light flashing at the bottom.

The doors must be open for the hall lights to be seeping through. I just gotta get down there...

He flipped his rifle behind his back and grabbed the terry cloth he had in his pack. Jeff examined the gap separating him from the main elevator cable in the shaft. It was about six feet. He took a few steps back; a running jump should give him all the momentum he needed.

"Please God, don't let me fuck this up..." He took a deep breath, sprinting full speed at the shaft. Right before the edge, he put all the effort he could into his legs and launched himself into the dark void. He reached out his free hand and grabbed the cable. "Holy Shit!"

He swung with one arm over the dark abyss, taking in a gulp of air. He didn't have much time left to rest and marvel at his feat. He grabbed the cable with the terry cloth and wrapped his legs around it. He covered both hands under the cloth the best he could and released his grip just enough so he would slide down. Even with the towel protecting his skin, he was starting to feel the heat from the friction on the steel rope. He would never make it in time if he didn't do this. He gritted his teeth as the friction began to hurt his palms.

Just a few more feet.

When Jeff was five feet from the bottom, he tightened his grip to slow down and felt a pull on his shoulders as his muscles tried to fight with inertia. He peered down to see the top of the elevator was covered in bodies. Some appeared to be hanging through the maintenance hatch on the top. Jeff wrapped his arm around the cable to hold him while he reached for his sidearm. He shot the heads of everything he could see and dropped down. He peered into the maintenance hatch. A mangled mess of bullet-ridden corpses were holding the elevator doors open. The bullet holes were probably from Jennifer and her soldiers trying to survive.

He lowered himself down and walked out of the elevator toward the small corridor. It was quiet. He approached the corner, stopping as a bullet nearly grazed his face. He immediately pinned his back against the wall as more bullets riddled past him. He wasn't expecting *living* people to be shooting at him. He checked the timer he had put on his watch. He had a little less than three minutes left. He grabbed his assault rifle and popped out the magazine. He didn't have many shots left and had already expended his spare. He popped it back in and banged his head against the wall.

Okay think...they got the hall covered...you gotta do your own cover fire somehow with half a magazine of ammo...a cardboard box wouldn't get you out of this situation...you gotta stop thinking about video games when you're nervous Jeff...

He pulled out his sidearm, putting in his last magazine of eight shots. He needed to see how many attackers he was facing before he could figure out a plan. He pulled out his phone, placing the camera in selfie mode. He slid down the wall, pointing the phone around the corner on the floor. He took a picture and slid back up to examine it. There were only four of them. Two on each end of the hall.

He would have to sprint. He put his sidearm back in its holster and took a deep shaking breath...his hands shook as he tightened his grip on the rifle. He could do this...he *needed* to do this. Jeff released the held breath in his lungs as he pointed the rifle around the corner and pressed the trigger. He sprayed the hall with bullets as he willed his body to run down the hall. Just as he hoped, they stayed in cover, not attempting to return fire. When his rifle clicked empty he released it, letting it drop against his body, swinging on the strap by his side. He let his body drop to the floor as he noted his attackers begin to peek their heads around the corner.

His body went into a full slide the rest of the distance of the hallway. He reached and pulled out his sidearm. Taking quick aim at their heads, he somehow managed to hit all four targets, only to see a fifth as he began to get up. He ran full speed in the direction he had to go, and dove into the break room inlet that connected the two halls he needed to get through. He stuck his head back out and fired two shots, killing the last cultist. Jeff took in a gulp of air. He had just killed people, not monsters. It had all happened faster than he was able to make his mind process.

You had no choice. You need to help Jennifer. Now move!

He ran full speed toward the locker room. He turned the corner and froze. Just outside of the entrance was the one thing he had hoped would not be there.

Fuckfuckfuckfuckfuck FUCK!

As if the creature heard his internal screams, it cracked its decaying pale neck in his direction. Its red, bloodshot eyes widened as if Jeff had surprised the creature, and its wide shark-filled teeth maw opened as an ear piercing scream escaped its lungs.

"Nope."

Jeff did a quick turn, his boots slipping against the smooth tile underneath him as he began running full speed in the opposite direction of the vampire-zombie hybrid. Every nerve in his body sparked as his brain screamed danger. He needed to put distance between them. He only had two silver bullets left in his magazine.

Jeff slid down the first hall on his right, taking a quick turn into a storage room he remembered had an additional exit back into the previous hall. He didn't have time for this. The red glow of the security lights barely reflected off the covered shelves. He moved fast, as the creature was already banging on the door behind him. He pushed the shelf on the wall against the door.

If it works for Leon versus the Gandos, hopefully it should work for me! Okay Jeff, a Resident Evil reference now? Not that it's not accurate...cut it out with the games talk and FOCUS!

Jeff knocked over another shelf, making a wall to hopefully slow down the monster once the door burst open. He only had two shots to kill this thing. He hid behind the last standing shelf in the room and slid over the boxes, making a window. His palms were sweaty and getting worse as he gripped the handle of his sidearm. He felt his blood pulsing through every vein of his body as the banging began on the door in front of him.

"Come on...come on..."

Jeff needed to hurry back to the locker rooms. He glanced down at his watch as the seconds flashed away. Jennifer was running out of time.

A burst of dust and debris filled the air as the monster finally bashed down the door, its grinning tooth-filled maw salivating at the sight of him. The dust stung his eyes as he tried to focus. Jeff held his breath, using the shelf in front of him to assist his aim and fired.

"Shiiiiiiiiiiiiitttttttttt."

He missed and the monster knew where he stood now. Jeff put his full body weight into the door behind him and ran down the hall. He could cut back through the shooting range and be in the same hall again as the locker room.

Dumb ass, should have went there first. There might be more bullets.

Jeff felt for the key he was always instructed to keep around his neck and sighed. That's right. He had turned it in yesterday. Stupid stupid stupid. He had one shot left. It was now or never.

Jeff slammed into the shooting range. The place was eerily quiet. Since his first day, this room had always been full of soldiers training. He ran over to the small supply area. The bullets were gone. He had only what was left in his magazine.

Jeff looked at the wall and cracked a smile. There was a round button, normally green, but it looked black in hue due to the red lights that bathed the room. Sentinel had installed what he called "the party button," claiming it would help soldiers train for situations with a lot of noise and distraction. Jennifer had never used it with Jeff, claiming it was just an excuse for Sentinel to make a party area.

The door slammed open as the creature busted through. Jeff raised his hand to the button.

"Okay, let's party."

He slammed his palm down hard as the creature rushed toward him. A chorus of lights began to circle the room, like in a club, reflecting off an obscenely large disco ball that lowered into the middle of the room. EDM music blared from unseen speakers, pulsing hard off every surface. The creature stopped, as if it was disoriented from the lights and sound.

Demon said vampires have increased senses. Thank you Jesus this worked!

Jeff raised his gun swiftly and squinted his eyes to see better in the fractured lights. He aimed for the creature's head and fired. With the strobing lights, the head of the creature flipped backward in slow flickering motion as its brain splatter shot out the backend, spraying the wall behind it. The body collapsed to the floor.

"Yeeesssss!!! That's what you get!" Jeff slammed his palm on the button again, stopping the noise and lights. He peaked at his watch, "Shit, no time!"

He ran back into the hallway, now only a few paces from the locker room. The hall was thankfully empty of any new threats.

Jeff stopped in front of the locker room door. Not knowing if there would be more assailants inside, he crept down low as he edged the door slowly wider. After a quick scan of the round room, he hurried inside.

The locker room was dark, with only the red emergency lights illuminating the benches and dark lockers. He could barely make out the figures on the other side of the training room glass. He approached the door cautiously, keeping his body low to the ground. When he reached the window on the door, he peeked in. He could see Greyven speaking to Jennifer. Seven more *human* Sons of Judgment cultists were inside the room. They had their hands tightly on their weapons, on edge from his recent gunfire.

He slid down the door and leaned his back against the nearby wall. He took off his rifle and placed it on the floor; it was useless now. He looked at his side arm. It was spent. He didn't have any more ammo on him.

"Out of bullets...some rescue..." He chuckled quietly as he closed his eyes. He rested his head against the wall taking in a deep breath while he tried to figure out his next move.

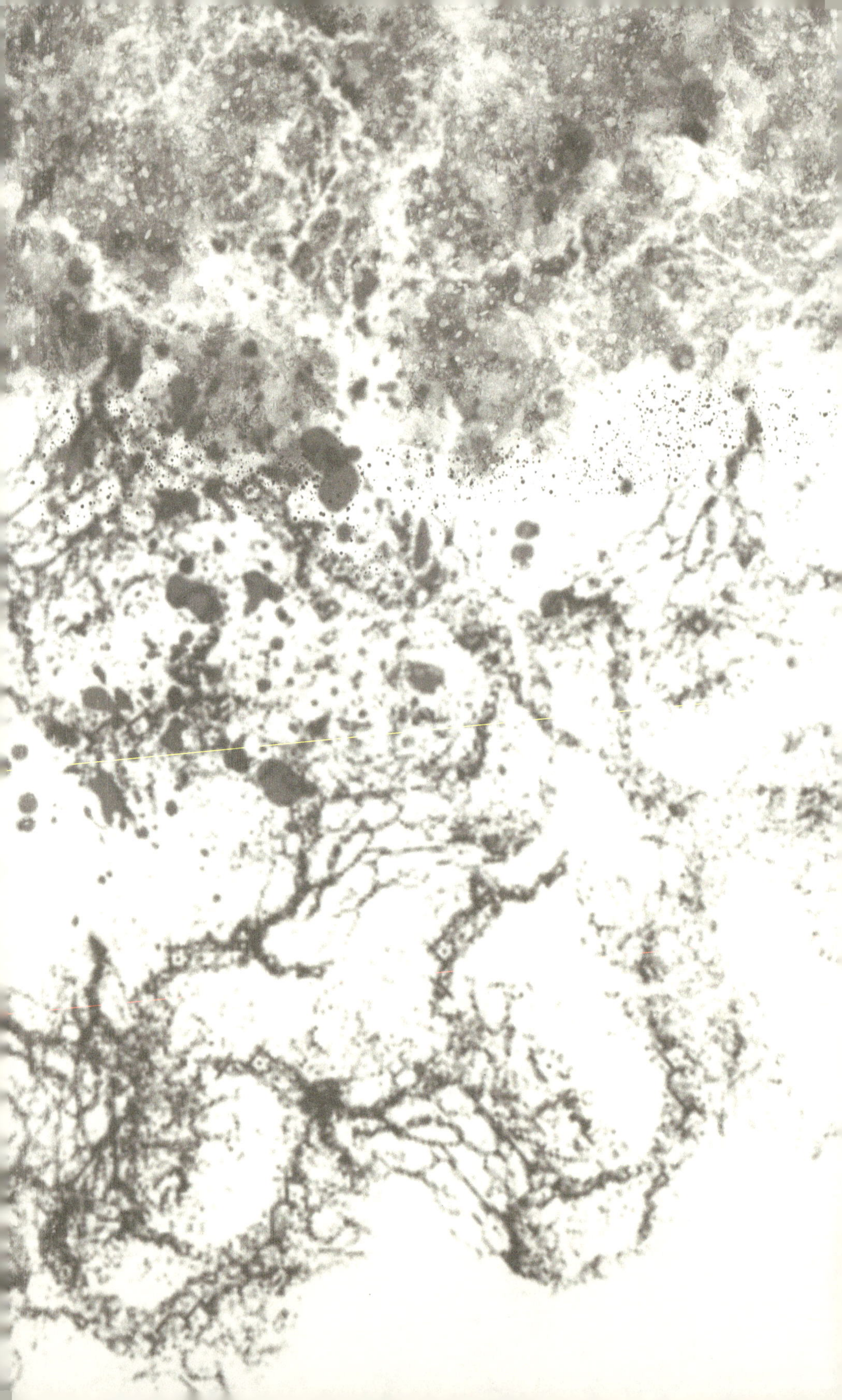

CHAPTER 24

Greyven's pacing was beginning to aggravate Jennifer. Every time he glanced at the clock in the room, he ticked his tongue, annoyed. She continued to work on the ropes that bound her while he was distracted. The knot was shoddy, it was starting to loosen. She just needed another minute—countdown be damned.

"You know he's not going to come for me. Demon and I ended a long time ago." Jennifer had caught his attention, good.

"Once a vampire loves, that bond is eternal, no matter how small. Besides, I smell him on you." Greyven bent down in front of her and deeply inhaled the surrounding air, making her skin crawl. Demon had drank her blood just yesterday and used his to close her wounds again.

There was the sound of gunshots outside getting closer. Greyven looked up and smiled. Someone else was down here fighting back. Jennifer didn't know how far away they were, but the shots sounded relatively close. The other cultists in the room tightened their grips on their weapons.

"Well well well. Seems I was right." Greyven chuckled softly. He came over to her again, close enough to her face that she could smell the rot on his breath. His talon-shaped finger rested cold under her chin. "I know I said five minutes, but if I bite you now, you should just be finished changing by the time he comes through that door."

"It's not Demon. Those were gunshots. He doesn't use a gun. It's probably some Charlie Team officers that your men failed to kill." She gazed into his blood-shot yellow glowing eyes cooly. They flickered with anger. She didn't know who it was outside, but she wanted to give them time to get to her. "You change me now, you'll miss your opportunity for your revenge."

Good, keep him distracted.

Greyven struggled to suppress his annoyance with her, as he ticked his tongue again. It was only for a brief moment. His cruel, deformed smile returned to his rotten lips.

"As long as you die by my hands, it doesn't matter. If he survives my hybrid children I have coming outside, he will come down here eventually. If you happen to be a zombie, oh well."

Greyven opened his mouth wide, revealing his shark-like rows of fangs again. Before she could react, the door from the locker room burst open. Jennifer turned to view her savior. Standing in the doorway, with his handgun aimed at Greyven's face, was Jeff. She couldn't believe it was really him standing there. After yesterday, she was convinced he would never step foot inside Z.E.R.O again.

Jeff had managed to gain the attention of all the cultists around her. This was her chance. She rolled her body and pressed on her elbow to push herself upright, and began to slide her legs under her to get herself off the ground. She was almost on her feet when one of the cultists near her noticed her escape attempt. Her hands were still bound so she couldn't prevent him from grabbing her arms. He pulled her up quickly, pulling a knife out. She felt the cold metal touch the skin on her neck.

This fucker is gonna cut my neck on accident. His hand is shaking like an idiot.

She scanned the rest of the room, and noticed that another one of the assailants had their bowgun aimed at her. The remaining members in the room had their weapons pointed in the direction of Jeff. He shouldn't have come here, but she was so glad he did. The heavy weight and knot that was sitting in her chest since their fight yesterday lifted. Her heart pounded with anxious energy.

"Who are you?" Greyven stared at Jeff in complete confusion.

"My lady, your knight in shining armor has arrived!" Jeff smiled his stupid cocky smile that sent exciting electric waves pulsing through her body.

Why is he such a dork?

"Really? You couldn't come up with anything else?" she laughed, despite the imminent threats to her well-being.

"Hey, I'm working with what I got." He shrugged his shoulders, but kept his weapon aimed at Greyven.

Greyven looked back and forth between them. He gazed blankly. His plan for revenge was crumbling in front of his eyes, and by someone he didn't even know. Watching him as he tried to figure out the situation was gold to her eyes. Every second that went by, his face began to contort more in rage. She didn't care that she had a knife to her throat. She was getting out of this.

"Enough! Who are you, and where is Ayo?" Greyven growled at Jeff.

"The name is Knight, and Demon's not coming." Jeff flexed his grip on his gun, but didn't lower it from Greyven's face. Greyven growled with anger. Jeff glanced right at her, slightly moving his chin, signaling her to prepare to move. She nodded back just enough for him to see she understood. Jeff would create a distraction again, and she would get herself out. They weren't as subtle as she hoped. Greyven looked between them both again, and laughed, a dry deep raspy laugh that echoed throughout the room.

"You and her? She sure does get around! I wanted Ayo, but I might as well take my anger out on you first."

Jeff tossed his gun at the cultist that was holding Jennifer, causing him to duck away from her. When he moved, he lost his grip on Jennifer. She took that opportunity to get out of his hold. She spun around and kicked him in the head. With her first captor out of the way, she rolled aside just as the other cultist with the bowgun took a shot in her direction. She managed to bend her arms under her, and slide her legs through to pull her bound hands in front of her. She got to her feet again, just as Greyven lunged at Jeff. He managed to dodge and pull his knife out. She had to regain her attention on her opponents. One of the cultists took one of the swords off the wall, and ran at her. He thrust it down at her. She caught the blade, using his motion to cut the ropes that bound her.

The man wielding the sword was an amateur. He didn't know how to fight, at least not with that type of weapon. She had years of experience on him. As long as she focused, this would be a breeze. She dodged the next swing of the sword, and twisted around to get a grip on the blade. She pulled it from his hands, and used it against him. She plunged the blade into his chest with a sickening rip and squelching of his flesh. She had twisted it while she pushed, disrupting as many organs as possible. She released her bloody hands from the grip and let his body fall with the sword propping his torso up from the ground.

She felt no remorse at the death of a fellow human. These people were all monsters to her. She focused on her next target, the one who had tried to shoot at her before.

He had reloaded his crossbow and was taking aim at her again. Sweat ran down his face as Jennifer made eye contact with him, and his eyes widened in fear. She moved in quickly, knocking the bow gun out of his grasp. She spun around, smacking him hard with his own weapon, knocking him out cold. She turned immediately, aiming at the approaching attacker, and fired.

That's four down...three left.

***

Jeff had to keep his distance from Greyven. He had no plans on what he was actually going to do. He just wanted to get Jennifer out of there. He jabbed at Greyven with his knife, but the beast quickly avoided it. Each time Jeff jabbed at him, the hybrid monster would move away and chuckle in amusement. Like a cat playing with a mouse desperately trying to scare the large creature away to survive. He was taunting Jeff. As they circled each other in the room, Jeff caught glimpses of Jennifer making quick work of all the Sons of Judgment members around them. She was a living action hero.

She will be okay. You need to focus on how you two are going to get out of here.

"You plan to beat me? A God, with a knife?" Greyven mused, as he continued to move around Jeff. Greyven's movements were slower than Jeff expected as he laughed and mocked him. Jeff tried to keep his frustration in check. Jennifer only had three adversaries left to deal with and then they could try to run.

A bolt flung past their heads, hitting one of the nearby members in the chest. The body collapsed to the floor by their feet. Jeff glanced over in the direction the arrow came from and found Jennifer wielding the weapon. Greyven seemed curious as well to know who had fired near his head. As he turned to look, Jeff found his opening. He lunged, stabbing his knife into Greyven's skull with the most strength he could muster.

"It's not just any knife. It's made of silver!" Jeff screamed as steam sizzled off the knife from contact with Greyven's flesh. Greyven was still a vampire, and Jeff wasn't sure if he could trust Orcus' words, so he had to try something. Greyven staggered back, away from him, as if he was about to collapse. Jeff began to smile. His stupid idea might actually work.

Yes! Silver bullets work for his hybrids, so a silver knife should be just as effective on the master.

Jeff's sense of accomplishment was short-lived as Greyven regained his composure. His dark maniacal laughter sent chills down Jeff's spine. Greyven pulled the knife out of his head and tossed it to the ground away from Jeff's reach. His flesh sizzled as it closed immediately over the wound.

"I said I was a God! Immortal! My mutation negates all my prior weaknesses! You can't kill me." Jeff's heart pounded furiously in his ears as the nagging hole in his chest screamed at him to run. He was going to die if he didn't figure out something else to do, and fast.

"Shit."

Greyven was clearly done playing games. Jeff tried to focus on avoiding Greyven's claw-like fingers as he swung them. While he dodged Greyven's attacks, he tried to keep one eye on Jennifer. She was dealing with a lot more foes than him.

Jeff ducked out of the way of another of Greyven's lethal swings. He glanced behind him as Jennifer took a knife from yet another member, and stabbed them with their own weapon. She had cleared most of the room. There were two more remaining foes. She approached her next opponent. They attempted to swing at her, but she was too fast for them. She jumped on their body, and using her own momentum, she swung herself around him. She wrapped her thighs around his neck, using her force to grapple the man to the ground.

Jeff dodged another attack from Greyven. As they danced around, he noticed that Jennifer hadn't seen the last cultist approaching her from behind, taking aim with their bowgun, as she still struggled with the foe she grappled.

"Jen, LOOK OUT!" Jeff yelled.

Without hesitation, Jennifer grabbed a small knife off the cultist still pinned between her thighs, choking. She looked behind her, throwing the blade into the head of her last attacker. Their lifeless body fell to the ground.

***

"Jen, LOOK OUT!" Jennifer heard Jeff scream in her direction. She miscounted and forgot about one. She looked down, seeing the knife on the belt of the member she had pinned. She grabbed it, throwing it at the foe behind her, successfully landing the blade in their eye. Their body folded under its dead weight, crumpling to the floor. She turned to thank Jeff for the cover. That's when she saw it. Greyven had taken advantage of Jeff's distraction with her. Time moved slowly in her vision as Greyven moved behind Jeff, his arms reaching for him.

"Jeff!" She was too late with her warning. Greyven grabbed him, pinning his arms behind his back. Jennifer knocked out her last opponent with a hard punch to their face. She rose to her feet, frozen.

"You humans are so weak with your emotions." Greyven turned his attention to Jennifer, "And you, why couldn't you behave? This boy didn't have to die for you today."

Greyven pulled Jeff toward him as he struggled to get out of the tight grip the monster had around his arms. All of the training Jennifer gave him to break out of holds was useless against the raw strength of Greyven.

Jennifer scanned the room frantically. There had to be something she could do to save him. She couldn't lose him...not *now*! She looked down at the Sons of Judgment member lying beneath her to see if they had any more blades she could throw at Greyven. No such luck. The dark red light in the room made it hard to see; even if she could throw something, they were so close she could hit Jeff on accident. She searched desperately around her. All the other bodies in the room with weapons that were more accurate were too far and out of reach. The seconds flew by as she struggled to find something, anything!

Oh God no!!!!

She was too late. Greyven's mouth opened wide to reveal his two rows of fangs, and he plunged them into Jeff's shoulder. She was helpless to do anything as she witnessed the life and color drain from Jeff's body. His screams of agony echoed in her ears.

She felt nauseous. Her legs were lead and could no longer support her. She collapsed to her knees. Her hot tears rained down her face. When Jeff was devoid of his pigment, Greyven tossed his limp body aside, satisfied. She crawled over to Jeff's body. He wasn't moving. He felt cold to her touch. His breathing was hard and shallow. He would probably turn soon, but she didn't care. She wanted to be with him in his last moments. She laid his head gently onto her lap, and caressed him. He blinked in the dark red light of the room, he was barely conscious.

"I guess that was pretty stupid of me," he spoke weakly as he gave her the dorky grin she fell in love with. She wiped tears from her cloudy vision.

"Yeah, it was. Try not to talk." She needed him to save his strength for as long as possible.

"You know, Adam thinks that I do things only because of the girls I like." Jeff choked out a laugh; he had blood in his mouth that was probably getting in his airway. She slid him up higher on her lap to help him breathe. "I have to say," he continued weakly, "this is one of the first times it started like that, because I wanted to know you. But I really found a calling, for once in my life." Greyven sat back, laughing at their misery. "I got to protect you, and everybody else that I care about. Too bad I figured it out so late." Jeff coughed up more blood. She smiled down at him.

"Please, save your strength." Jennifer leaned down and kissed his forehead. He felt cold and clammy. She could hear Greyven's dark laughter behind them continue. He would probably kill her after he got bored watching them.

That's when she heard it. A cough. It was small at first. Like someone who was laughing too hard and having an issue catching their breath. The cough quickly outgrew the laughter, followed by the sound of choking. She looked over at Greyven. He scratched at his throat, struggling with an intense burn inside it that he wanted to get out. She heard a faint laugh come from Jeff.

He grinned a blood-filled grin at her, and struggled to hold something up. She reached for his hand and opened it. In his palm was the small empty vial Orcus had given them with the antivirus and the used syringe.

"Jeff! You didn't..."

He chuckled weakly.

***

Jeff's wound burned. His skin felt on fire. It felt exactly like being attacked by a hill of fire ants. He could feel their itchy feet as they crawled all over him, spreading the burn with their bites. He wanted to scratch at his skin, stop the itch, but he was too weak to do so. He would probably change into a zombie soon, but it didn't matter. As long as he killed Greyven and knew Jennifer would be safe he would be okay with dying. His mind flashed back to the moment he had come up with the plan.

Back in the security office, Jeff wrapped his arms around Hammer's waist, and slammed him into the wall. He slid his hand into Hammer's side pouch, pulling the vial and syringe from it, tightly in his hand. Concealing it from everyone. When he left the security office, he slid it into his side pack, before going to the main shutter door. Whether Hammer knew he took the serum wouldn't matter once he was past the shutter. Jeff knew he didn't have enough ammunition to do a full rescue and possibly kill Greyven. As he sat in the locker room with his empty pistol in his hand, he pulled out the small vial, full of the royal blue liquid, dark and murky in the red light. He knew what he had to do.

Jeff took a deep breath, filling the syringe with the entire contents of the anti-virus serum. He wasn't sure how much he needed for it to work, so using the entire vial was his logical conclusion to avoid screwing up their only chance of killing Greyven.

"Well, I got nothing left to lose if she dies. Besides, she doesn't need me," Jeff muttered as he looked at the full syringe in his fingers. He remembered his conversation with Jennifer during that wild evening of passion which he wished he could be transported back to now. She had left Demon because she wanted a normal life. "Maybe with Greyven gone she can have what she wants."

He plunged the needle into the aortic artery in his neck and released the serum into his system. Strangely, it didn't make him feel weird at all. He wasn't even sure it would work, but he was out of time. He would make sure Jennifer got out. He picked up his empty handgun and kicked in the door to the training room.

Hearing Greyven as he coughed and convulsed to his death was the confirmation that Jeff needed. The serum had worked. He couldn't help but choke up laughter, even though his own blood was beginning to clog his airway. His body felt cold, despite being so close to Jennifer's warmth. He was dying, or at least going into shock. He looked up at her face, red and stained with tears.

I'm sorry Jen...I hope you find your happiness...

His head felt heavy. His vision foggy and muted. Jennifer's image was fading from his sight. His eyelids were heavy. He closed them to rest.

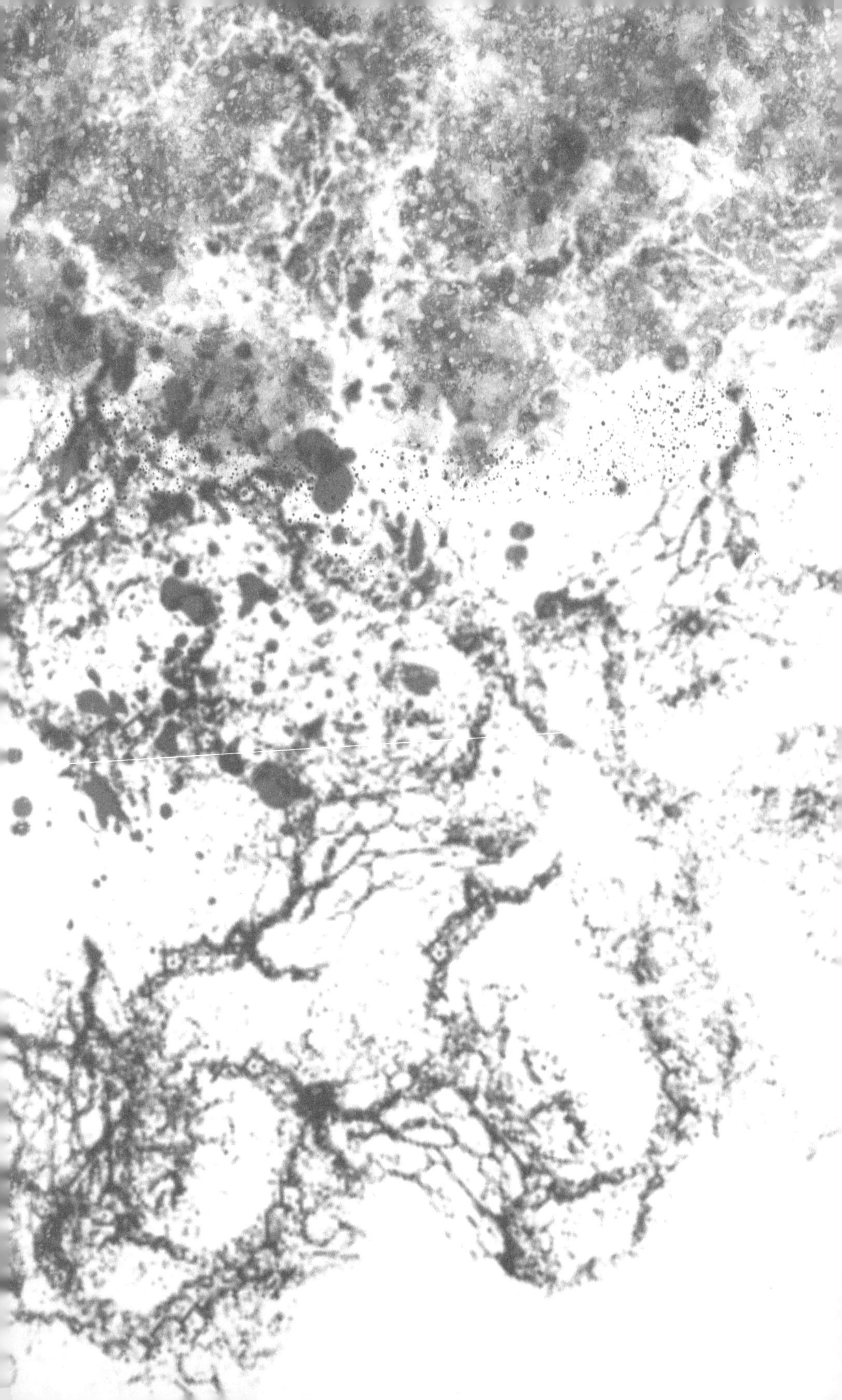

CHAPTER 25

As Jeff closed his eyes, his hands grew heavy and limp in Jennifer's hand.

"Jeff no! Please don't leave me!" She couldn't contain her tears as they streamed down her face. She hugged him tightly, rocking his body back and forth. Her heart felt empty. She hadn't felt this pain since Conor. It was all happening again.

Hammer and Demon burst into the room covered in blood and other bodily fluids that looked like black ooze in the red light. Jennifer turned toward Greyven. He was on the ground, coughing up his own blood. The area around his pupils was no longer dark, but a normal white hue. His eyes still glowed yellow, but different than before. More like a normal vampire. She didn't care to look at Greyven anymore. Not after what he had done. She continued to hug and rock Jeff's limp body. She felt Hammer's hand on her shoulder as she cried desperate tears.

"Ayo?" Greyven spoke weakly.

"Beaumont, I'm here." Demon moved to Greyven's side.

"You were always one to arrive late," Greyven chuckled. His voice sounded different. It was not as raspy, but soft. Almost as if a different person was speaking with Demon.

"Why? Why did you do all of this?"

"I was angry. Our master was killed, then Lillith. As the last straw, Orcus took me against my will. Turned me into this...this monster." Greyven explained weakly.

Red tears brimmed in Demon's eyes, "You could have come to me when you escaped. I could have helped you!"

"I tried...didn't you see the symbol? The mockery we made years ago?" Demon smiled, and nodded. "I couldn't think straight. The virus. It was pure rage. It twisted my thoughts. I went mad. Now…now I'm clearing up. I can feel myself again." Jennifer looked up. Greyven's claw-like hands had reverted back to normal human hands. His ears had retracted from those of an elongated dark elf to those of a human. He grabbed Demon's arm, "Promise me something. Avenge me and Lillith. Orcus must be stopped."

"I promise," Demon told his old friend. "I will do whatever I can." Jennifer wasn't ready to let Greyven die just yet. She needed answers.

"You've taken everything from me!" Jennifer screamed through enraged tears. "Why did you attack my family twenty-six years ago?". Greyven, no Beaumont, looked back at her confused.

"I don't know what you're talking about, I didn't even know who you were before today."

"You're lying! We found your cult symbol on the cabin. North Carolina, twenty-six years ago. You killed my parents and sister!"

"I was in hibernation then. It was not I, nor my group. They only acted out attacks when I was awake, to sustain me." His eyes became unfocused in his gaze. He struggled to breathe when he spoke. "We would not have attacked a small family alone. Unless someone else…took advantage when I was asleep…used my—"

"But why would—"

"Jennifer enough!" Demon growled at her, eyes fully yellow and illuminated in the dark light. This was the first time she had ever seen Demon truly angry at her. She bit her tongue, before she would say something she could not take back. She deserved to know her family's killer, but she didn't want to learn by tarnishing her relationships with the few people she had left. "We will look into this matter later."

"Thank you brother. I'm…I'm sorry…I—" Beaumont struggled to wheeze out air as he tried to speak more. Demon nodded at him, with silent understanding. Beaumont nodded back, barely, as his body gave out to the poison of the anti-virus in his system.

Jennifer turned her attention back to Jeff. She couldn't see his chest moving up and down anymore.

"Jeff?" She shook his body. He needed to wake up.

He can't die…not like this.

There was no response. His body was cold and heavy in her arms.

"Jen, we're gonna have to take care of him. He was bitten. He'll turn soon." Hammer's voice was soft and sweet as he tried to console her.

"No!" She wasn't ready to lose him. She placed her hand on Jeff's face, caressing it. Demon knelt beside them.

"Let me see." Demon leaned in, and listened to Jeff's chest. His heightened hearing could detect if he still had a heart beat. "He's alive...but barely. He needs blood."

Demon dipped his finger in the pool of blood by Jeff's neck and sniffed it. He wrinkled his nose in disgust.

"What is it?" Hammer asked.

"Probably the anti-virus in his blood stream. His blood smells funny."

Sentinel stepped into the room with what was left of their medical team. The white fluorescents flickered on as they ran in. He must have turned off the quarantine.

"I saw it all on the camera when I got it back up. How is he?"

"He's alive," Jen explained. He needs a blood transfusion. Give him mine if our stores are destroyed. I'm O negative." Jennifer let the medical team lift Jeff onto a gurney away from her. They put a gauze to his neck to stop the bleeding.

"We've cleared the bodies out of the shaft, and the elevator is working again," Sentinel informed them, as he surveyed the room's carnage. The bodies of Jennifer's victims were everywhere. Pools of blood surrounded those that she had stabbed and gored. Others heads lay awkwardly from their broken necks. One of the Sons of Judgment members Jennifer hadn't killed moaned as he began to regain consciousness. "I'll secure him. Go!"

Hammer helped her up as they rushed to take Jeff to the infirmary.

The next week was a blur. Jeff needed a lot of blood. There were a few packets that had survived the attacks, and they immediately pumped them into his body. She had donated as much as she could too. They monitored him for signs of change, but he showed no symptoms of becoming a zombie. He had a fever for the first two days, and slipped into a coma. Demon used his blood to close Jeff's wounds from the attack, but he reacted strangely to it. The scar did not heal completely, leaving a shark bite scar near his clavicle and shoulder. Jennifer slept by his side everyday.

Their facility was slowly restored to working order. They would have to move in a couple of months when their back up base was ready. Orcus knew where they were, and they didn't know if he would try to attack them again at their weakest. Z.E.R.O units all over the world were trying to find the remaining cells of the Sons of Judgment, now that their leader was gone. There would be a power vacuum. They needed to stop them while they were still in a panic. She didn't worry about that though. She was only concerned for Jeff.

By the eighth day after the attack, everyone began to wonder if he would ever wake up. They had never dealt with a human surviving a mutation. Their lead scientist, Dr. Zimmerman, was flown in from Washington D.C, and tested Jeff's blood for abnormalities or any sign of the virus or anti-virus still in his system.

It was the middle of October, and the weather was finally beginning to cool as the dew point shifted downward. No longer was the air heavy with water and humidity, insulating the heat of the sun. It felt dry and cold as it blew the small white clouds across the sky. Jennifer was exhausted from worry. She was almost healed from the ordeal. She still had some bruises and aches on her body, but they were something she could deal with.

She laid her head on his bedside, and held his hand, like so many nights previous. She squeezed it lightly, letting him know she was there again, even if he couldn't hear her. To her surprise, she felt pressure as his hand squeezed back.

"Jeff?" She jumped up, examining him. His eyes were still closed. "Jeff, can you hear me?"

He squeezed her hand again. She let him go, running to the back office where Dr. Zimmerman was running some tests under a microscope.

"Doc, I think he's waking up!" Dr. Zimmerman looked up at her from his microscope in his office, matching her excitement. They ran back to Jeff's bedside. The doctor began taking Jeff's vitals just as his eyes fluttered open.

***

Jeff heard voices around him, but he couldn't make them out. All he saw was darkness. He remembered Jennifer crying above him. He wanted to hold her, apologize for causing her so much pain. For acting like a complete ass after meeting Orcus. He felt her hand squeezing his. He squeezed it back. He heard her voice faintly in the distance. He wanted to get back to her. He squeezed her hand again, but then she was gone.

He heard more commotion around him; his head was hurting. He felt cold metal on his chest. He opened his eyes, but had to blink as the light that came in was too bright. Then he saw Jennifer, leaning over him, tears in her eyes but a smile across her face. Her fresh bruises were discolored and faded.

How long have I been out?

"Welcome back." A doctor with curly brown hair and thick glasses was standing over him. When he stepped away, Jennifer pounced on the bed.

"Thank god!" She exclaimed as she began to kiss and hug him.

"I can get used to this." Jeff joked with a sore throat. She stopped and frowned, her almond eyes becoming clouded with new tears.

"I thought I lost you. Don't ever do that to me again." She gave him a light punch in his arm. He felt it in his neck where Greyven had bitten him and winced.

"I promise." He smiled up at her. She leaned down and kissed him again. The doctor walked out of the room, closing the door to his office, giving them some privacy.

CHapter 26

It had been seven weeks since the Greyven attack. Jeff lay awake in Jennifer's bed, staring at the ceiling fan as it spun above them. He looked over at the time as the sunlight was beginning to wane through the windows. They would have to get up soon. It was going to be his first time back with the team since the events of D-Day.

He sighed as he turned over to see Jennifer sleeping soundly next to him. Her rose lips were slightly parted as she breathed softly. His current life felt like a dream. He had almost died over a month ago. He moved his arm to touch his wound from Greyven. It still felt sore. He had a pink scar still in his skin. When he finally saw it in the mirror it resembled a shark bite. That was the story Adam had told Jeff's mother when he disappeared in a coma.

The cover up for the attack was insane too, but people seemed to believe it. It was reported that what had happened was the result of an isolated cell of extremists who had rampaged through the city and attacked people. The zombies? It was the extremists drugged up on bath salts which resulted in the strange zombie-like behavior. Z.E.R.O had ties with the government, so they were quickly able to confiscate and scrub any pictures or videos from the incident. Within a couple of weeks, life was back to normal in Tampa Bay. Of course, there were still message boards with people posting theories about what had actually occurred, but for the most part, the truth was hidden.

A bright spot of this situation was that Jeff didn't have to lie to Adam anymore about his other life. In fact, Adam had been recruited by Hammer after how he had handled things at the mall. Sentinel took the role as his trainer and tonight would be his first time out with the team. Jeff was glad to be getting back to work, and excited to see how Adam was handling his training.

Jennifer rolled over in the bed, pressing her back against him. He reached his arms around her, holding her close. He noted her flat stomach was gone. It had a small hard roundness to it. They had been eating out a lot lately, and she hadn't been training as much as she usually did. Considering what they had been through, he didn't blame her for taking some time for herself.

Jeff remembered Jennifer had been upset earlier today when she had come back from her blood test with Dr. Zimmerman. He was checking her for the virus because of what happened five weeks ago. Dr. Zimmerman was releasing Jeff into Jennifer's home care. All his blood tests leading up to that point had been clean. They didn't think there could still be a danger of the virus if they decided to be intimate. Of course, they hadn't waited to be sure. Dr. Zimmerman had caught them on Jeff's last night in the medical wing in the middle of an impromptu session of naked yoga. It was their first time together since before the Greyven incident. After a brief reprimand, they were told no sex, until he could be sure Jeff was clear. That meant Jennifer would now have regular tests as well. Today was the last blood work she had to do.

Jeff squeezed his arms around Jennifer a little tighter, and breathed in her soft rose scent. He was worried. He really hoped he hadn't infected her with that mutant pathogen. As much as he wanted to have her, he needed her to be okay. She began to stir under his embrace. She looked up, smiling as her tired brown eyes focused on him. Jeff squeezed her tighter. She looked down and noticed his arms around her, and her mood instantly changed. She quickly pulled away from his embrace and yanked her top down over her small stomach. She hastily flipped her hair over her head as she looked at the time.

"We better get up. We have time to get some food before we go in." Her expression changed again. It was the same fake warm smile she had given him when he first met her. Her lips were spread like they should for a smile, but her eyes gave away her discomfort. "How about Chinese?"

"Yeah sure." She had been avoiding his touch a lot lately. If she was conscious about her weight gain, that didn't matter to him.

Jennifer jumped out of bed and went to shower. He grabbed his clothes out of the overnight bag he brought, showering in the other bathroom. He felt good. He wasn't going to let what happened get to him. She would talk with him when she was ready.

When he came down stairs, Jennifer was in a set of sweats with a t-shirt and her hair was in a wet messy bun.

"Do you want to take separate cars?" She looked tired as she grabbed her purse. "You told Adam you would give him a ride, and I have some things that need to get done before we head out on patrol."

"Yeah, no problem. You sure everything is okay? What did Dr. Zimmerman say about your blood results? Are you clear?" Jeff scratched the back of his head uncomfortably.

"Yes, I promise you didn't infect me with the Greyven virus. I just have low iron. It's the move of the base. Lt. Commander is a nice title, but I have a lot of stuff to get in order. Hammer leaves tomorrow to speak with the High Council about what happened. So I'm in charge." She came over and wrapped her arms around his neck, kissing him softly.

"Okay." He pulled her in close and hugged her. When they released their embrace, she rushed toward the door. Jeff felt his phone vibrate in his pocket. It was Adam.

It was crazy to think that just four months ago he was playing zombie paintball with Adam, and now this was their life. He followed Jennifer to dinner before they went their separate ways. She drove to the base and he picked up Adam.

When Jeff arrived at the base with his best friend, you couldn't tell almost seven weeks ago there had been bomb explosions throughout the facility and a mutant vampire siege including zombies, monster hybrids, and crazy humans. The base was operational in a temporary capacity. Things were actively being packed and shipped to a new location.

By the time Jeff and Adam walked into the locker room together, everyone was already dressed in their gear. Everyone but Jennifer, who was missing.

"Welcome back man." Sentinel came over and gave Jeff a pat on the shoulder.

"Thanks. Where's Jen? I thought she would get here first." Simultaneously Hammer, Sentinel, and Demon all pointed to the showers and restrooms. Then he heard it through the door, the sound of her up-chucking her dinner.

"She's been in there since she got here," Hammer muttered. He slapped Jeff on the back and walked out.

"Maybe the food we got was too greasy for her?" Jeff muttered.

"Who knows, she said we can't leave without her though," Sentinel laughed. A flush of the toilet echoed from the shower area, and everyone scattered. Jennifer came out, wiping her face with a paper towel. Despite what he had just heard from the bathroom, she looked normal in color. Hopefully she wasn't getting sick again. She'd had a bug a few weeks ago too.

"You okay?" he asked her as she walked over, rubbing her bloated stomach. She was still in her sweats from earlier.

"Yeah, I'm fine. Sorry, I'll be ready to go in a minute." She turned to Adam, "Sentinel's been telling me you've been working hard. I look forward to seeing you out there."

"Yes ma'am!" Adam saluted and went to get changed. Jeff winked at her and went to his locker next to Adam.

"Hey Adam, you don't look so hot. Kind of tired," he said just loud enough for everyone in the room to hear.

"Man, the way you guys got me running around, I haven't slept well in days!" Adam hurried to get changed. He was eager to get out there.

"I tell you about a guy we had on our team that had a problem of suffering from micro-naps?" Jeff grinned, and caught the side glances of everyone else. It was nice to no longer be the F-N-G.

***

Everyone exited the locker room to head out for the evening except Jennifer, who wasn't sure if she would be throwing up again. It had started to get bad two weeks ago. Demon hung back as he knew what was really wrong with her. She didn't need Dr. Zimmerman's blood test results today to confirm her condition. She had been this way before. The nausea wasn't as bad the first time. This one seemed more aggressive, though they say each time is different.

"So when are you going to tell him?" Demon came up close behind her, startling her.

"I don't know what you're talking about," she muttered as she tied her hair up and shut her locker.

"You can't fool me Jennifer," Demon said assertively, his eyes glowing, "I'm the one that told you about it before Doctor Zimmerman confirmed it for you. If you are keeping it, you need to tell him." With all the events of the last few weeks, after she'd been able to confirm her suspicions, she hadn't had time to think about it.

"I promise, I'll tell him soon." She placed her hand on her hardening stomach and sighed. She would have to. She wasn't sure how much longer she could hide it.

Definitely going to show soon...

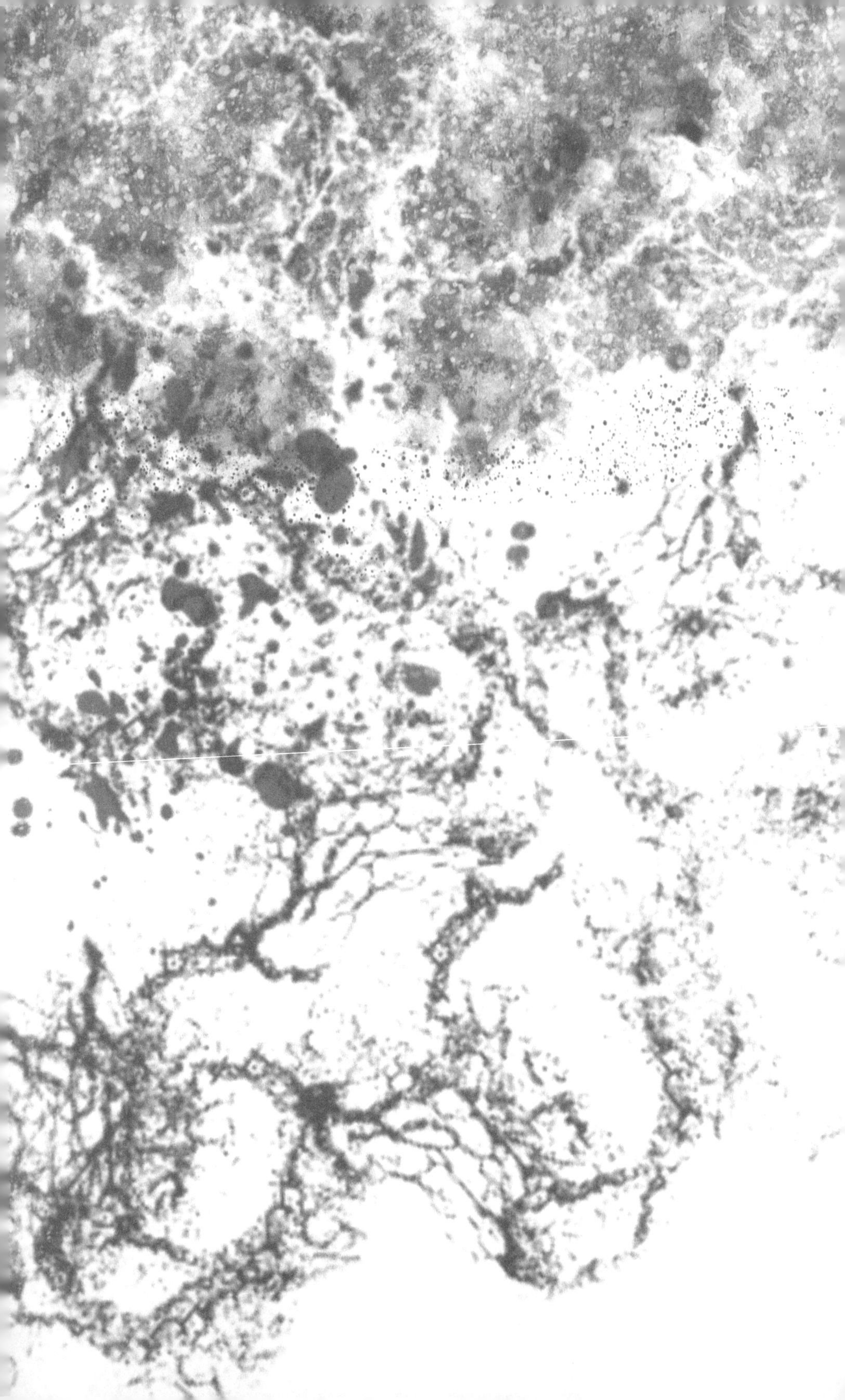

EPILOGUE

Dr. Zimmerman picked up the medical chart for Mr. Knight. He wrote in the new results from the recent tests he had ran on Mr. Knight's cells. He looked over at the blood test results from Lt. Commander Mayer too and smiled. Things were working out better than he hoped.

He reached into his desk, pulling out the phone given to him to provide updates on the test subject's condition and his other research in relation to it. He dialed the only contact listed in it while he re-examined the test results of the Lt. Commander.

"*Yes?*" The voice of High Commander Tobias vibrated in his ear.

"I've done more tests on Mr. Knight's cells. I'll be sending you the new data results shortly." Dr. Zimmerman flipped through the images on his computer he had captured from his microscope.

"*Good.*" Tobias answered, devoid of emotion. He never provided fake platitudes to Dr. Zimmerman. Everything was strictly business.

"Based on the reactions of his cells, I don't want to be too hopeful, but he may be the perfect human." Dr. Zimmerman flipped through his notes. "His blood doesn't show any sign of infection, but recent tests show the reaction we are looking for when administering the zombie pathogen."

"*What about his immunity to vampire and lycan infection?*" Tobias asked, showing no heightened excitement from Dr. Zimmerman's previous information.

"Based on the cells that I had to test with, it seems to be the same thing. He's immune. I would like to run tests on him directly. See the effects on his body during his immune response. What we have here is truly remarkable."

"Yes. I'm interested in your research. Conduct it by whatever means you think necessary. Don't worry about the boy's life if it becomes a problem with the development of the serum." Tobias' voice continued to show no concern or emotion. Dr. Zimmerman liked it that way. It allowed him to perform his research more effectively.

"There was another matter I wanted to bring to your attention." Dr. Zimmerman opened the file with Lt. Commander Mayer's blood work, and attached it to an email.

"What is it?"

"There is a matter regarding a recent change in the Lt. Commander's *condition* that I think will be even more valuable to us." Dr. Zimmerman tapped "send" on the secure email. "I just sent it to you, along with my next project idea. It would require the Lt. Commander's cooperation."

There was a brief moment of silence, followed by a slight, almost undetectable alteration in Tobias' voice when he spoke next. He sounded amused.

"That is interesting. Go ahead. If you have any issues with Mayer, let me know. I'll take care of it."

"Thank you sir." Dr. Zimmerman ended the call, and walked over to the refrigerator in the side of his lab with his samples. He pulled out a vial with a small light blue liquid and smiled. He had already administered one dose to Lt. Commander Mayer when she received her test results earlier today. He was looking forward to the future results of his experiments.

content warnings

Drug and Alcohol Abuse
  Infant/Child Loss Death
  Gore/Dismemberment
  Themes of Depression
  Emotional Abusive Relationships
  Strong Language
  Sexual Content

Acknowledgements

First and foremost, I want to thank my husband, Danilo, who has listened to me on endless days babbling about my characters and the different situations they could get into. You supported me on this journey even when I thought of giving up. I love you, and thank you for sticking it out with me.

My parents, Daisy and Robert. You guys were my first fans. You taught me the joy of reading, and stories from a young age, and encouraged me to seek out my creative endeavors. You have supported me my whole life, and I am truly grateful. I love you both, and look forward to giving you more of my tales to read. (Hopefully lighter ones, hahaha).

My siblings. Melissa, Robert, Denise, and Stacy. Thank you for also supporting me, and dealing with my constant questions on my artwork as I made it for this book. I appreciate all of you...

This book would not have been possible without the support of my friends. TJ, you inspired me to write the original screenplay for Z.E.R.O thirteen years ago with all of our "what ifs" when playing *Left 4 Dead*. You've also inspired one of the most loved characters in the book. Thank you so much for everything you do! I'm glad I was able to make Z.E.R.O a reality. Matthew B, you are a brother to me, and thank you for supporting me and encouraging me everyday to keep going. Lilly and Sam D, thank you so much for being there for me, and helping me when I was stressed beyond belief. I love our crafting days and tea days. You help keep me sane.

My beta readers, Matthew, you really pushed my writing and helped me bring this novel into a new level I didn't think possible. Barry, thank you with adding authenticity to my Irish character. And all my MMCM family. Especially Ann, Emma, and Thea. Thank you for loving my characters, and encouraging me to keep going. Thank you to everyone from Team Tea and Books too! Helen, Laura, Morgan, Lilly, Sarah (both of you!), P, Katrin, and Mel. Your support means the world to me.

My editor, Edward Crocker. Thank you for taking on my book. Your line editing and proof reading has been invaluable, and I would not be here today without you. Thank you for your great sense of humor, that kept me entertained while I edited. I look forward to working with you on future projects.

Finally, I want to thank my cats, Blu and Diana for giving me hours of entertainment when I felt stressed or overwhelmed. I love you little creatures, even if you can never read this. You get extra treats and pets.

ABOUT THE AUTHOR

Portrait of Author Jessica Ungeheuer

Jessica Ungeheuer (she/her) is a writer and artist. While earning her visual arts and digital media degree she studied creative writing and screenwriting. Her favorite genres to read and write are dystopian sci fi and horror. She lives in sunny Bradenton Florida with her husband and two mischievous cats.

You can find her artwork and other stories on her socials through her linktr.ee/JessicaUWriting, or on Twitter and Instagram @phoenixfire110.